William O'Connor Morris

Ireland 1798-1898

William O'Connor Morris

Ireland 1798-1898

ISBN/EAN: 9783337327576

Printed in Europe, USA, Canada, Australia, Japan

Cover: Foto ©Andreas Hilbeck / pixelio.de

More available books at **www.hansebooks.com**

1798—1898

BY

WILLIAM O'CONNOR MORRIS

*County Court Judge and Chairman of Quarter Sessions for the United
Counties of Roscommon and Sligo*

Sometime Scholar of Oriel College, Oxford

αἴλινον αἴλινον εἰπὲ τὸ δ'εὖ νικάτω

ÆSCHYLUS

LONDON

A. D. INNES & COMPANY, Ltd

1898

PREFACE

THE favourable reception accorded to a little book, "Ireland, 1494–1868," written by me some time ago, for the "Historical Series," published by the Cambridge University Press, has induced me to make this sketch of Irish History from 1798 to the present year. The volume comprises part of the period I traversed before ; but it describes events at much greater length, and enters much more into details, than was possible in a very brief epitome ; and it embraces a period not treated in the earlier work, but of supreme importance to the student of Irish History, for it deals with the thirty years which have elapsed since 1868. It may fairly claim, I think, to be, in all respects, an original and independent publication ; I hope it has placed the course of Irish affairs, during the last hundred years, before a reader, in something like their true historical aspect, and in fairly correct perspective.

I have written this book, I trust, in the spirit in which it ought to be written, and ·have taken the point of view which should be taken in considering the subject. I have endeavoured to ascertain the truth and to tell it fearlessly ; to point out the correlation of cause and effect in the evolution of a melancholy, but most instructive history ; to rise, when entering the field of politics, above the blinding dust of party conflicts ; and to be strictly just in the conclusions I have formed as to men and things. But the greatest historical writers, when describing contemporaneous events, or those near their own times, have not been free 'rom the prejudices and prepossessions caused by tradition, education, personal experience, and the circumstances of life; Thucydides and Tacitus, Clarendon and Thiers, are more or less partisans; a humble attendant on a noble procession cannot escape from these subtle but all-powerful influences. I prize candour and frankness; and at the risk of the charge of egotism, shall say a word as to what these associations have been in my own instance. I belong to a family which, on both its sides, has been true to the political faith of Henry Grattan; I am naturally, therefore, what is still called an Irish Liberal. Two, at least, of my kinsfolk voted against the Union in the Irish Parliament; one—Sir John Newport—I remember him when in extreme old age —was one of the last and ablest of the Chancellors of the Irish Exchequer, and resented the financial treatment of Ireland from 1800 onwards. Except when at school, or at Oxford, I was brought up in youth in the class of the Irish landed gentry, especially in that of its old Catholic Houses; I am myself an Irish landlord, who have, for half a century, managed an ancestral estate, the wreck of a great inheritance lost through conquest and confiscation. I have listened to Plunket, Bushe, and Maria Edgeworth, and knew those eminent personages, as a boy can know the old; I have heard O'Connell in what he called The Conciliation Hall, and in the House of Commons; I have often conversed with survivors of the Rebellion of 1798, whether of the victorious or the vanquished party, and with a few aged members of the Irish Parliament. In later life I have been more or less intimate with leading men of the Irish Bar and Bench from 1854 to the present time, and with many Irish politicians of mark, especially with several of the independent gentlemen who opposed Mr. Gladstone's measures of Irish finance; and in a long forensic and judicial career I have become familiar with the ideas, the sentiments, the ways, the tendencies of my fellow country-men of all sorts and conditions. I have been acquainted, but only slightly, with three or four Lords-Lieutenant and Chief Secretaries of Ireland, and with a very few British statesmen; but I have not had the advantage of knowing from a personal side what have been their views on Irish political and social questions. Parnell I never saw, and had no knowledge of chiefs of the Land and the National Leagues; possibly, for that very reason, I have done less justice to the motives of these men than they deserve. For the rest, if I am an Irish landlord, I have not had my rental practically reduced by Mr. Gladstone's Land Act of 1881; and I have censured the administration of that mischievous agrarian law, an administration, for the faults of which its original agents are chiefly responsible, not on personal, but on public grounds only. I may add that, for many years, I have been a student of Irish History, particularly of the history of the Irish Land system; nearly thirty years ago I investigated at length, and on the spot, the subject of Irish land tenure for the *Times;* and the Letters I then wrote, appearing as they did in that great organ of public opinion, attracted much attention at the time, and contributed not a little to the passing of the Irish Land Act of 1870. These various associations have, as a matter of course, affected the statements I have made and the judgments I have pronounced in these pages.

Irish History, unfortunately, is not much read in England; I have thought it right to bring together some of the authorities which form the chief materials for it, from 1798, and the few preceding years, to the present day. The true student of History, like the true lawyer, will always ascend to the fountain and not merely follow the stream. The original sources of Irish History, during the above period, may be classified under five heads. I. The Statutes of the Irish Parliament up to the Union, from, say, 1799; the most striking features perhaps of these are the draconic Coercion Acts; but there is a good deal of valuable domestic legislation; and the great Catholic Relief Act of 1793 should be studied. The Irish Statutes of the Imperial Parliament follow; they also comprise many repressive measures, notably the severe Coercion Acts of 1833 and 1882; the principal remedial Acts are the Reform Acts from 1832 to 1884; the Acts for reforming the Irish

Established Church, and for commuting the Tithe ; the Poor Law Acts ; the Municipal Corporation Act, and the Acts for creating Town Commissioners ; the numerous Education Acts ; the Act for Disestablishing the Protestant Irish Church ; and the series of Land Acts from 1870 to 1896. The Bills, which have not become law, are not very easily procured ; but some are important and very significant. II. The Irish State Trials. The principal of these are the State trials arising out of the Rebellion of 1798 and that of Emmet ; the trial of O'Connell and his associates in 1844 ; the trials of Smith O'Brien and others in 1848 ; and the trials of the Fenian conspirators in 1865-6. But by many degrees the most important of these judicial inquiries are what really was a State trial, the proceedings before the Special Commission of 1888-9. The Evidence and the Report fill four large volumes ; but they form infinitely the best account of the revolutionary and socialistic Irish movement of 1879-85, and they should be diligently perused. III. The next head consists of the Debates of the Irish Parliament, especially the Debates before the Union ; and the Debates on Irish Questions in the British and Imperial Parliaments from 1799 onwards. The speeches of the great statesmen and orators should, of course, be the only ones studied. Collections of many of these speeches have been separately published. IV. The fourth head comprises the numerous Reports of Parliamentary and other Commissions and Committees on Irish affairs ; many of these, with the Evidence, are of extreme importance. The most remarkable of these are the Report and the Evidence on the State of Ireland in 1820-5, an historical document of the greatest value ; the Poor Law and Education Reports ; the Reports, with the Evidence, on Irish Local Government ; the Report of the celebrated Devon Commission and the Digest of the Evidence ; the Mass of Reports, with the Evidence, on the Irish Land Acts from 1872 to 1894 ; and the Reports and the Evidence on Irish Taxation and Finance of 1815 and 1864, ending with the well-known Report of the Childers Commission made in 1896, and the

most important evidence attached to it. V. Under the fifth
and last head we may range the correspondence of statesmen, eminent lawyers, and politicians from about 1790 to
this day. A great deal of this has not seen the light, and
probably never will; but some papers, and even volumes,
are of sterling value. The Correspondence of Castlereagh
and of Cornwallis is of the first importance for the period of
the Union and for some time afterwards. Many of the
letters of Burke on Irish affairs are most interesting and
instructive. Mr. Lecky's "History of England in the
Eighteenth Century" contains a large number of despatches and letters on Ireland that deserve notice. Some
of Pitt's letters on this subject will be found in Lord
Stanhope's biography of that statesman. The Correspondence of Peel when Chief Secretary of Ireland appears at
length in Mr. Parker's volume; and some Irish papers of
Wellington, curious and characteristic, are in the huge mass
of his Supplementary Despatches. Papers by Canning and
by Lord Wellesley on Irish subjects have been published in
biographies of these eminent men; and some letters of
O'Connell and of Plunket in the accounts of their lives.
As we approach more recent times documents of this kind
become rare, but some despatches of Lord Palmerston and
of Lord Clarendon refer to Ireland, and have been published.

As for secondary sources of information, these are ample,
but of very unequal value. For the history of Ireland down
to the Union there is nothing to compare to Mr. Lecky's
"History of England in the Eighteenth Century"; the
volumes on Irish affairs have been published separately.
Froude's "The English in Ireland" contains a spirited
account of the Rebellion of 1798; but this is a bad book,
full of inaccuracies, and written in a spirit offensive to Irishmen. Gordon's "History of the Rebellion" is a fair and
impartial narrative; the reader should be warned against
the passionate partisanship of Musgrave, Maxwell, and other
Orange writers. Plowden's "History of Ireland" is dull
and diffuse, but gives some useful information on events

from 1782 to 1800–1. I may also refer to the Irish chapters of Mr. Massey's " History of England," to Madden's " United Irishmen, " to McNevins' " Precis of Irish History," and to Ingram's " History of the Irish Union," a bit of clever but false paradox. There is no consecutive or complete history of Ireland since the Union ; but a large collection of historical and quasi-historical books of different degrees of merit may be mentioned. Plowden's second work only goes down to 1810 ; it represents the ideas of a loyal Irish Catholic bitterly disappointed by Pitt. The " History of Ireland" from the Treaty of Limerick to 1851, by John Mitchell, expresses the views of a Presbyterian rebel, but is not without value. Wyse's " History of the Catholic Association" is a fair narrative, rather out of sympathy with O'Connell. I pass by O'Connell's " Ireland and the Irish," a book unworthy of such a man ; but the " Reports " of the Repeal Association and the " Essays on the Repeal of the Union" and the " Spirit" and the " Voice" of the " Nation," embodying the views of the Young Ireland party, are instructive, and abound in interest. " Two Centuries of Irish History," from 1691 to 1870, edited by Mr. Bryce, is an able performance from the point of view of English Radicalism since 1886. Mr. Barry O'Brien's " Fifty Years of Concessions to Ireland " and " Irish Wrongs and English Remedies" are elaborate works, full of research from the point of view of a powerful and moderate advocate of Home Rule. The " Young Ireland," the " Four Years of Irish History," and the " League of the North and South," by Sir Gavan Duffy ; the " New Ireland," by A. M. Sullivan ; and " The Parnell Movement," by Mr. T. P. O'Connor, M.P., almost complete an account of Ireland during the last half century, as this is made up by Irish " Nationalists" ; and to these works may be added passages from Mr. McCarthy's " History of Our Own Times" ; Irish chapters from recent histories of England ; Miss Lawless's slight sketch of " Ireland " in the Story of the Nation Series ; and " Ireland since the Union," by Mr. J. H. McCarthy. For the Constitutional History of Ireland

reference may be made to the chapter on Ireland in
Hallam's "Constitutional History"; but more especially
to Ball's "Irish Legislative Systems," an elaborate and
excellent description of the Irish Parliament from the
earliest times to 1800-1, and also of the proceedings relating
to the Union. The admirable treatises of Professor Dicey,
"England's Case against Home Rule," "A Leap in the
Dark," and "The Verdict" are essays that belong to Constitutional History; they should be read, and have never
been answered. As regards the Ecclesiastical History of
Ireland, Mant's work may be consulted; but Ball's
"Reformed Church of Ireland," which carries the narrative
down to the Disestablishment Act of 1869, is a much better
book. Brenan's "Ecclesiastical History" describes the
fortunes of the Catholic Church of Ireland from remote
antiquity to Catholic Emancipation. Reid's and Killen's
works relate to the Irish Presbyterian Church; and on
both these subjects there are other publications of more
or less merit. Books on Irish Education in this century
are abundant. I shall only mention two, written from
opposite points of view, "Education in Ireland," by Mr.
Godkin; and "The Irish University Question," by Archbishop Walsh. In addition to more elaborate works, there
is also a host of essays and tracts, one of great merit by
Butt, and several also very good by the O'Conor Don and
others. The economic and social condition of Ireland
during the last century and a half has been thoroughly
explored and illustrated by a series of careful and intelligent
writers. For the period between the American War and
the Peace of 1815—a period of supreme importance—the
celebrated "Tour" of Arthur Young, and the elaborate
"Account of Ireland," by Edward Wakefield, are by far the
best narratives; these are standard works of great merit;
but many similar publications of the time are valuable; and
special reference may be made to an excellent account of
the old Irish land system by Mr. Lecky in the 27th chapter
of his "History of England in the Eighteenth Century."
Works of this class written in more recent times are less

frequent; but the "Irish Disturbances" of Sir G. Lewis, published in 1836, is a well-informed essay; "The Irish Crisis," by Sir C. Trevelyan contains a good account of the Famine; the "History of the Great Irish Famine," by the Rev. J. O'Rourke, and the "Irish Landlord since the Revolution," by the Rev. P. Lavelle illustrate the ill-will and the passions engendered by that catastrophe; the "Letters on the Condition of Ireland," by Mr. Campbell Foster, republished from the *Times* are well worth reading; and the "Ireland, Industrial, Political, and Social" of Mr. J. N. Murphy is a fair description of the Ireland of 1868-70. The Irish Land Question has, within the last forty years, given birth to a literature of its own; I may refer to the "Emigration and the Tenure of Irish Land," by Lord Dufferin, to the "Irish Land Question" of John Stuart Mill; to the "Irish People and the Irish Land" of Butt; to Judge Longfield's essay on the Irish Land in "Systems of Land Tenure"; to the "Irish Land," an excellent little book by the late Sir George Campbell; and to my own "Letters on the Land Question of Ireland," republished from the *Times*. There have been many attacks; I have never seen a defence of the Irish agrarian legislation of 1881-96. Mr. Lecky's "Democracy and Liberty" (vol. i. chap. 2), criticises it as it deserves. The "Ireland" of Lord Grey is an able, but hostile review of Mr. Gladstone's Irish legislation since 1868; and "Irish Nationalism," by the Duke of Argyll, and "New Views on Ireland," by Lord Russell of Killowen, an Irishman, the present head of the Common Law of England, as the late Lord Cairns, an Irishman, was a head of English Equity, may be studied with advantage. French literature abounds in works and essays on Ireland; the writings of De Beaumont and of M. de Laveleye are of real merit.

This period is fruitful in biographies of Irishmen, and of eminent men connected with Ireland, but these also are of very different degrees of value. The lives of Flood and Grattan are poor performances, but ought to be read; those of Lord Edward Fitzgerald and Sheridan by the poet Moore are

well known ; there is no tolerable biography of Burke and
Lord Clare. The autobiography of Wolfe Tone is a
remarkable work ; it has been unfairly carped at ; Tone was
an enemy of England, but an able, enterprising, and
honourable enemy. Lord Stanhope's "Life of Pitt" is a
eulogy ; but it contains a good deal concerning Irish affairs
and the Union ; Lord Rosebery's short tract is superficial
and misleading ; Macaulay's sketch of Pitt is quite wrong as
respects the Union and the Minister's conduct. There are
biographies of more or less merit of O'Connell, of Lord
Wellesley, of Plunket, of Drummond, of Lord Melbourne,
of Lord Palmerston, which, and especially that of O'Connell,
relate a great deal to Ireland ; the "Peel and O'Connell" of
Mr. Shaw Lefevre, and the "Despatches and Speeches of
Earl Russell" are conversant with Irish subjects, and are
works of a biographical character. There are many accounts
of Mr. Gladstone's political life ; the latest, that written to
contain the illustrations of "Punch," is a dull and undiscern-
ing collection of praise ; but it deals, to some extent, with
Ireland, and there is useful information in it. The Irish
policy, however, of Mr. Gladstone may best be gathered
from his own speeches and writings ; and his character as a
statesman, conspicuously made manifest in his conduct of
Irish affairs, is revealed in numerous reminiscences, and
notably in remarks made by Lord Russell, Lord Palmerston,
and Lord Selborne. Mr. Lecky's "Leaders of Public
Opinion in Ireland," if a youthful, is a very interesting work :
the sketch of O'Connell is particularly good, and should be
studied by Englishmen who have never done that great man
justice. The "Memoirs" relating to this period are not
very numerous ; by far the most important are those of
Greville, the English Saint-Simon ; these often refer to
Ireland from 1829 to 1860, and are very valuable ; Greville's
"Past and Present Policy of England towards Ireland"
bears witness to his fine understanding and impartial mind.
Other books of this class are the Memoirs of Miles Byrne
and of Holt, two rebels of 1798, "The Life and Times of
Lord Cloncurry" ; "Ireland, Past and Present" by J. W.

Croker; "The Memoirs of Lord Hatherton"; "Journals, Conversations, and Essays relating to Ireland," by Nassan Senior; and the Irish chapters in Disraeli's "Life of Lord George Bentinck" are exceedingly good. The novels of Maria Edgeworth, of Maxwell, of Lever, illustrate the life of the upper classes of Ireland as it once was; those of Lover, of Banim, of Carleton, the life of the Irish peasantry. Those of Miss Edgeworth are of peculiar excellence; taken altogether, these works strikingly attest and explain the profound divisions of race, of faith, and of class which form the cardinal feature in the social structure of Ireland. The Home Rule controversy of 1886–93 has also created a literature; this largely consists of essays and articles, in Quarterly and other Reviews and Magazines, some very able indeed; I may refer to the "Parnellite Split," and to two small volumes of great merit republished by the *Times* in 1886; and to "The Truth about Home Rule," "Ireland under Coercion," and many other essays from the Unionist and Home Rule points of view. "England's Wealth Ireland's Poverty," by Mr. T. Lough, M.P., is a one-sided book, but is worth reading.

WILLIAM O'CONNOR MORRIS.

GARTNAMONA, TULLAMORE,
February 9, 1898.

CONTENTS

CONTENTS

CHAPTER VII

CHAPTER VIII

CHAPTER X

CHAPTER I

IRELAND BEFORE 1798

MY purpose in this work is to sketch the history of Ireland during the last hundred years. Recent events must have directed the minds of thinking Englishmen of all conditions to a subject, if distasteful, not the less important. A few months only have passed since the world, it may be said, commemorated, with all but universal acclaim, the sixtieth anniversary of the reign of Queen Victoria; and the loyalty and devotion of a mighty Empire, compared to which that of Rome was but a small possession, were expressed in passionate, touching, and truly heartfelt sympathy. Representatives of kings and peoples from the four continents appeared to do homage to our aged sovereign; princes and leading men of her nations of subjects, from the vast Australian land to the Indian peninsula, and thence to the Great Lakes of Canada, assembled round her throne to give her a duteous greeting. In the immense pageant, gathered within "streaming London's central roar," that seemed drawn from all parts of the earth, the pomp of Christianity, the magnificence of war, and the majesty of a great people, added to the grandeur of a spectacle never witnessed before. The supremacy of Britain at sea was made manifest in an array of warships of unequalled power; and the voices of England and Scotland went forth, in one note of praise, in remembrance of the glories of a splendid era, and of its peaceful and orderly social progress. But a. spectre was not wanting at the great festival; if Ireland made her presence at all felt, it was, for the most part, to show that she had no fellow-feeling with it. Distinguished Irishmen were to be found, no doubt, in the multitudinous throngs of London; hills in Ireland blazed with rejoicing fires; the Jubilee was welcomed by parts of the Irish community. But a large majority of the representatives of the Irish people kept studiously aloof, and even made use of language in Parliament that must be deplored; several of the chief Irish municipal bodies refused to send addresses in honour of the Queen; disgraceful scenes of rioting occurred in Dublin, while London and Edinburgh were alive with rejoicing. Large parts of Ireland are not one in heart with England, are sullen, discontented, and in no sense loyal; and, even as I write, preparations are being made to celebrate the last rising against our rule, which had even the faintest prospects of success.

The causes of these phenomena certainly run up to Irish

history in the remote past; but they appear, also, in the period I shall now briefly survey. I shall glance at the condition of Ireland before it was affected by the influences and the train of events that precipitated the Rebellion of 1798. The country had grown out of the state of misery, of desolation, of often-recurring famines, of which we read in the pages of Swift and Berkeley; settled government, the relaxation of the Penal Code, and the concession of a partial free trade had contributed largely to its material progress. Limerick and Galway had gradually declined, and many of the inland towns were mere squalid villages; but Dublin had expanded into a fine capital, adorned by remarkable public buildings; Cork had greatly advanced since the American War; Belfast, a hamlet in the time of William III., had become a thriving seat of manufacture and trade. Agriculture was still extremely backward; the face of the landscape had little in common with the prosperity and richness of that of England; the southern parts of Munster, and nearly the whole of Connaught, were ill-cultivated and in a state of wretchedness. But fine seats of a resident gentry appeared in many counties; it was, in fact, during the preceding thirty years that most of the large demesnes of Ireland were formed; and the unfenced wastes of pasturage, which once spread everywhere, were widely replaced by breadths of tillage. The rental of the island had doubled, nay, trebled, within living memory; the rate of the interest of money had much fallen; the breeds of farming animals had become better; and the Corn Laws of the Irish Parliament had added to the national wealth, for the present at least. The commerce of Ireland remained small, but it had been augmented since it had acquired freedom; and her manufactures, kept down for more than a century, especially her linen manufacture, were making real progress. The means of locomotion, a sure sign of improvement, had greatly multiplied of late years; and the National Debt of Ireland was not much more than £2,000,000 sterling, a mere trifle compared to that of Great Britain, and was defrayed by a taxation relatively small.[1]

[1] For the condition of Ireland about this period, the reader may consult Arthur Young's "Tour," Crump's Essay, and a number of speeches in the Irish Parliament.

The population of Ireland at this time was between four
and five millions of souls. It comprised three really distinct
peoples, divided from each other in race and faith, and by
long and evil memories of an unhappy past. The Catholic
Irish were more than three millions—the broken remnants of
the old Celtic tribes, held down for more than two centuries
in mere subjection. Only a few of their natural leaders
remained; some of these had carried their swords into
foreign lands; many had sunk into the mass of the serfs
in their midst. This people vegetated on the soil in the
three Southern Provinces, and on more than a half of the
North, under the domination of alien masters, the heirs of
the worst kind of conquest, with confiscation in its train.
The gradual amelioration of the Penal Code had made a
few Catholics owners of land, and many Catholics had
amassed wealth by commerce; but the great body were a
degraded peasantry, and the Irish Catholic was still excluded
from the State, and deprived of political and almost of social
influence. The Presbyterian Irish, the second people, for
the most part of Scottish descent, were settled in the north-
eastern parts of Ulster, and in what are known as the Plantation Counties; they were hardly more than half a million of
souls; they were a population of farmers and traders, strong
in their local association and their hardy natures, but widely
divided from the ruling classes and possessing scarcely any
authority in the State. Presbyterian Ireland had suffered
much from teasing persecution since the day of Strafford; it
had felt the oppressiveness of a harsh land system and of
legislation restricting commerce; it had taken a decided
part against England at the crisis of the American War;
and, while it retained a traditional dislike of the Irish
Catholic, it was discontented with the existing order of
things in Ireland. The Protestants of the Anglican Established Church, mostly of English blood, formed the third
people; they were considerably more numerous than the
Presbyterians, but they were scattered over all parts of the
country, and composed an aristocracy of a peculiar kind
whether in its high or its low gradations, standing apart

from the two other communities and raised to a factitious
superiority by law. They were the owners of nine-tenths of
the land of the country, the grantees of immense and suc-
cessive forfeitures; they had engrossed every seat in the
Irish Parliament; they had a monopoly of privileges in
Church and State; they controlled the administration of
local affairs, and had municipal government wholly in their
hands. From the peer to the artisan and the peasant, they
represented the Protestant Ascendency, as it was called, still
completely dominant in Ireland at this time.

That Ascendency had, in days happily passed, interfered
grievously with Irish commerce, oppressing the Catholic
even in this province. It was now chiefly apparent in the
land system; and though the worst features of this had been,
in part, softened, it had not been essentially changed.
Economically that system was inconsistent with prosperity
and goodwill in landed relations. Enormous tracts of land
were possessed by absentees, and were thus left without the
good influence of ownership on the spot. Millions of acres
had been let to a class called middlemen, who had sub-let
their holdings often three and four deep; the land was thus
kept in a gradation of tenures, oppressive in the extreme to
the occupier of the soil and opposed to security and social
progress. The vices of the system, however, had been made
much worse owing to the position and the relation of the
races and classes seated on the land. Of the Catholics settled
in Leinster, Munster, and Connaught, and, to a considerable
extent, in Ulster, apart from the very few who were owners
of land, a certain number had become large farmers, and
some, since the Penal Code had been weakened, had risen
into the ranks of the middlemen. But the immense majority,
we have said, were a subject peasantry, who held by precarious
tenures and often at rack-rents, and who eked existence out
on the frail potato; as the population had began to multiply,
the poverty of this class had probably increased. This was
the lot, too, in some degree, of the Presbyterian farmer of
the North; he was in many respects a hardly treated peasant,
though he had succeeded, owing to a long established

custom, in securing for himself an improved tenure, which
gave him a better position than his Catholic fellow. Over
these classes stood the class of the owners of the land,
divided, we have seen, from their dependents by deep lines
of distinction. A considerable number of this order of men
formed a body of kindly and improving landlords and a
really valuable landed gentry ; a submissive peasantry had
become attached to them. But hundreds never beheld
their estates; hundreds had practically given them up to
middlemen ; and, as the wealth of Ireland had advanced,
not a few had sought to increase their rentals, and had
become merciless, harsh, and exacting. In fact, in the
position they held, they were formed to habits of oppression,
nay, of extortion, and they yielded to this temptation in too
many instances.

The sentiments, the ideas, the tone of opinion which had
been formed in this order of things were those of a community not in a healthy state, and in many respects were
pregnant with evils. The influences of the eighteenth
century, the almost national movement which had produced the Volunteers, the establishment of the Parliament
of 1782, and the gradual repeal of the Penal Code had
softened away, to some extent, the differences which
divided the Irish peoples, and had been fruitful of the
promise of a better era. A minority of the dominant
Protestants, tending to increase, wished to admit the Irish
Catholic within the pale of the State, and even to give
him some measure of political power. Catholic Ireland,
also, had begun to stir and to seek the rights that belong
to free men ; and though its aristocratic leaders held
weakly back, its growing mercantile and middle class had
made its influence distinctly felt, and had even set a
menacing agitation on foot. The social ostracism, too,
of the Irish Catholics, once complete, had largely disappeared. The Catholic and Protestant upper classes lived
together, for the most part, in harmony, and had even
begun to blend in marriage ; but the great majority of the
Protestant people was still opposed to the Catholic claims

and to raising the Catholics out of subjection; they still looked on their inferiors as a race of pariahs, and resented the concessions which British Ministers had gradually made to their Catholic fellow-subjects. The attitude of the great body of the Irish Catholics was still that of abject servility in nearly all the relations of life, especially in those that belonged to the land. The devotion often shown by the peasant to his lord was largely that of the submissiveness of the slave; and virtuous as the Irish Catholic women were, they too commonly yielded to the lusts of their masters. Occasionally, however, this downtrodden people could show that it was made of sterner stuff. Deprived of the protection of an equal law, the Irish Catholic had recourse to a law of his own; and the peasantry banded themselves into secret societies, controlled usually by unknown leaders, to resist the oppression which was their ordinary lot. These societies, which may be traced back to the confiscations of the past, were known by the general name of Whiteboy—possibly taken from that of the Camisards of the Cevennes; and they occasionally established in whole counties a system of barbarous organised crime, which spread misery and terror far and wide. These agrarian disorders, as they have ever since been called, were general and atrocious as late as 1787, and indeed have never completely ceased in Ireland; it is one of their characteristics that they readily coalesce with revolutionary movements against the State.[1]

Presbyterian Ireland had also, to some extent, combined to condemn the order of things which it felt around it. Societies of "Oakboys" and "Steelboys," as their names were, had been formed to resist excessive rents and the tithes of the alien Established Church; in some districts these had been guilty of outrage. These associations, however, had not been permanent; and the discontent of the Presbyterian Irish had chiefly exhibited itself in large

---

[1] The Irish Statute-Book is perhaps the best commentary on the Whiteboy system. Sir George Lewis's "Irish Disturbances" is an excellent work.

flights of emigrants, who carried into the Far West the
dislike of a stern race to aristocratic rule in Ireland, and
promoted the disloyalty felt at home. The Irish Presbyterians had, to a great extent, forsaken the Calvinism
of their Scotch fathers; they had been widely leavened
by the democratic and socialistic doctrines which, presented by the genius of Rousseau, had become prevalent
in France and even in Europe. As for the Irish Protestants, they possessed the qualities which their ascendency
naturally produced and developed. A tone of offensive
superiority and of self-assertion was very conspicuous in
the lower orders, especially in the corporate bodies of the
towns and in the farmers scattered among the Catholic
peasantry. The middlemen were, for the most part,
Protestants; these formed a grasping and almost an
odious class—exacting and often cruel to their dependent
Helots, addicted to vices and even to crime, and especially
to abductions to secure wealthy marriages. The superior
gentry were a different order of men; elements of a real
aristocracy were to be found in the class, though these
were not perhaps common. They usually lived well with
the Catholic gentry; they were remarkable for the brilliancy of their social life; not a few were eminent for
fine talents. But they were largely demoralised by the
state of things in which they existed; they had the faults
of an exclusive and small ruling class; they looked up
too much to the Government, of which they formed a great
part, and looked down too much on their subject inferiors;
and if their manners and bearing were courtly and high,
they were extravagant, given to excess, and most reckless
duellists. They had much in common with the Seigneurs
of Old France, whose position in the State resembled
their own.

A spirit of lawlessness in all classes—a sure sign of the
absence of a righteous law—was perhaps the most general
and distinctive feature of the social life of Ireland at this
period. We turn to the institutions of the ill-ordered
country—the moulds, so to speak, in which the com-

munity was cast. The Irish Parliament had been all but independent in name, since it had been established on a new basis after the Revolution of 1782. It was in theory coequal with the Houses of Westminster—a sovereign body in Irish affairs, capable of legislation on almost all subjects, not liable to the control of British Ministers. Ireland, under this system, was, in the abstract, united with Great Britain by the tie of the Crown only. The King of England and Scotland was also the King of Ireland; but subject to restrictions little more than nominal —the passing of Irish statutes under the Greal Seal of England and the long-obsolete Royal Veto—the Irish Parliament could do well-nigh what it pleased—could make laws and resolutions almost at will. It had even an inherent right to direct the Executive Power in Ireland, to appoint or to dismiss Ministers, and thus to have the whole Irish Administration in its hands. The Constitutional powers of the Irish Parliament were, however, very different in fact from what they seemed on paper. It was an Assembly composed of a small body of Protestants of the higher orders, depending on British government, it may be said, for everything; its members were British in race and faith; above all, it was kept in subjection by general and profuse corruption, which had greatly increased since it had acquired freedom. As a rule, therefore, it was in harmony with the British Parliament, and followed the leading of the British Ministry; and especially it always accepted the men sent from Downing Street to rule Ireland, and it never attempted to form an Irish Cabinet, or even to make or unmake an Irish Executive. The Irish Parliament, nevertheless, had more than once shown that it had a will of its own; it was especially jealous of its independence, and on three occasions since 1782 it had come in conflict with British policy, and in some degree with the British Parliament, with consequences that might have been unfortunate. Many English statesmen already deemed it a dangerous and eccentric force, difficult to keep within the orbit of the State, and contemplated its abolition by a Union.[1]

The British Parliament at this period represented the people imperfectly at best. It was largely controlled by the House of Lords and by the landed aristocracy in the House of Commons ; property, wealth, and influence were too powerful in it. But it fairly reflected the national will when this was clearly and forcibly expressed ; and it was guided by a public opinion in the main wholesome. The Irish Parliament was a mere caricature of its great original seated at Westminster ; it was in no sense an image of the Irish community as a whole. The House of Lords contained about 200 members, composed of some 24 prelates of the Established Church—submissive instruments of the Government of the day—and of about 180 lay peers, with rare exceptions newly ennobled men, descendants of the old plebeian settlers, and often raised to their high place by the bad corruption, which made them follow the beck of the men at the Castle. The Irish House of Commons had 300 members, and formed one of the strangest assemblies that ever pretended to the name of popular. Each of the 32 counties had two seats ; a shadow of free election existed in these, though here the influence of great landlords was almost supreme. Two hundred and thirty-six seats were engrossed by 118 boroughs, each borough possessing two seats ; and of these only 24 were nominally free, the remainder being really appanages of the Crown, of peers, bishops, and wealthy commoners, and of corporate bodies, usually petty and corrupt. Nine-tenths of the boroughs were small towns and villages with no distinctive influence of their own ; they were so completely under a mere oligarchy that 25 persons, it was alleged, were absolute masters of 126 seats. The Government, as a rule, could count on an overwhelming preponderance of votes ; and of the 300 members more than a third were placemen and

[1] For the constitution and character of the Irish Parliament, see Ball's "Irish Legislative Systems," chap. xiii., and Lecky's "History of Ireland," chap. xxiv. 301–324.

pensioners dependent on it.   The two Houses, it is scarcely
necessary to add, were composed wholly of Irish Protestants, Catholic Ireland being excluded by law, Presbyterian,
it would appear, by established custom ; and the House of
Commons was chosen by an electorate in which not a
single Catholic was to be found, and which was so small
in numbers and essentially weak that even Protestant
Ireland was ill represented in it.

It is remarkable, and a significant proof that institutions
of a representative kind, however faulty, may have good
results, that a Parliament constituted as this was produced,
nevertheless, many eminent men.   Its vices and abuses
were, however, manifest : Flood, a very able and far-seeing
man, had endeavoured to array the Volunteers against it,
and had twice attempted in vain to reform it ; and it was
fiercely denounced by Presbyterian Ireland, the Irish
Catholics, too, lately taking part, as an exclusive, corrupt,
and unjust Assembly—the mere embodiment of evil power
and influence.[1]   Naturally, however, it would not reform
itself, the argument "that things worked well" having
weight, since Ireland had made progress ; and the men in
power at Westminster eagerly concurred ; the instrument
was fashioned to serve their purposes.   The Irish Parliament contained three distinct parties, the first forming an
immense majority, the nominees of the Crown, of corporate
bodies, of great nobles and of powerful commoners, but
distinguished men were found in its ranks.   The master
spirit of this following, though as yet in a subordinate
office only, was John Fitzgibbon, a lawyer of humble birth,
who had forced himself forward by his strong intellect,
and was to play a commanding part in a subsequent
troubled era.   Fitzgibbon was deeply read in his country's
history ; he was a capable and daring man of action ; but
he was a champion of Protestant Ascendency in the

---

[1] A petition from Belfast, presented in 1784, described "the Irish
House of Commons as not the representation of a nation, but of mean
and venal boroughs," with other indignant expressions. Lecky, vol. vi.
p. 366. See also Froude's "English in Ireland," ii. pp. 390-3.

strictest sense ; he believed that concessions to the Irish
Catholics would lead to revolution and complete anarchy ;
and he insisted on keeping things in Ireland without change
or reform.   The second party, small in numbers, but con-
taining very able men, represented the once powerful
school of Flood : it sought to reform the Parliament on a
Protestant basis, but it refused the Catholics political rights;
its ideal was Protestant Ascendency, improved but complete.   The third party was that of the illustrious Grattan :
it comprised the best intellect in both Houses, the flower
of the liberal landed gentry, and many brilliant and profound lawyers.   The aim of Grattan was to combine the
separate peoples of Ireland into a united nation enjoying
just political rights, and to give the Irish Presbyterian and
the Irish Catholic the franchises of citizens equal before
the law.   But Grattan had no notion that Ireland should
break off from Great Britain ; he was jealous indeed of the
Parliamentary rights of Ireland, but he was deeply attached
to the British connection ; he upheld Property, Order, and
Law ; and if he sought to gain for Catholic Ireland liberty,
he maintained Protestant Ascendency in the sense that
its ownership of the land must give it preponderating
power.   Grattan inclined to a reform of the Irish Parliament ; but for the present at least his chief object was to
check its corruption and to remove its abuses.   He was
a real statesman, and one of the most brilliant orators who
have appeared either in England or Ireland.

The Constitution of the Irish Parliament was thus calculated to make Ireland, though indirectly, a subject country,
and to keep the system of Protestant Ascendency intact.
The Lord-Lieutenant and his Chief Secretary had the
administration of the higher offices ; they were, without
exception, at this time Englishmen ; they had practically,
the Executive Government in their hands.   They were
usually capable and well-meaning men, but they were
ignorant of Ireland like most British statesmen ; their policy
was to keep things in their present grooves, to distribute
the patronages of the State among the leading Protestants,

and to rule by corruption and similar methods. The second Pitt, now in power, was no exception; he had refrained from reforming the Irish Parliament, and he maintained Protestant Ascendency as it was. The only healing measure he thought of at this time was a commutation of the tithes of the Established Church; and probably the disciple of Adam Smith, like his master, had a union in view.

We pass on to what was deemed to be another great bulwark of the existing order of things. The Established Church, a scion of the Norman Church of the Pale, had been dominant for more than two centuries; it had grown with the growth of confiscation and conquest; its yoke lay heavily on the Presbyterian Irish, and on Catholic Ireland far more grievously. As a missionary Church it had completely failed, supported as it had been by the whole power of the State; the number of its members had relatively declined, and like all institutions that do not fulfil their purpose, it had become an anomaly injurious to the general welfare. It had had some eminent prelates and divines, but its bishops and leading clergy were for the most part mere servants of the Castle and of the ruling caste, from which they were in a great measure drawn, and they were usually self-seeking and worldly men, chiefly intent on amassing immense wealth. The inferior clergy formed a more worthy class, but they were voices that preached in vain in a wilderness—they had made no impression on the millions that knew them not, and while the revenues of the Church were enormous,[1] they starved in the midst of this ill-divided plenty. The abuses and corruptions in the Establishment almost passed belief, and huge pluralities, parishes without a priest, cathedrals and churches falling into ruins, were the visible signs of this evil state of things. The worst feature, however, of the system, as regards the great body of the people, has yet to be noticed. The Church was the owner of most of the

[1] Arthur Young, vol. ii. p. 112, and Wakefield, "An Account of Ireland," vol. ii. pp. 469–70, dwell on the extravagant wealth of the Irish Establishment.

tithe of Ireland, and it levied this impost from alien and hostile communions, by methods alike cruel and disgraceful. This was a special wrong to Catholic Ireland, for its Church had once possessed nearly all the tithe, and as the vast pastoral lands in the Southern Provinces had been practically exempted from the charge, this fell most oppressively on the Catholic tiller of the soil.

The Church of Catholic Ireland presented a contrast to the Church of the dominant race of a remarkable kind. In remote ages the Church of the Celtic tribes, and almost out of communion with Rome, it had become the devoted ally of the Papacy; and in the fierce and protracted contests of the sixteenth and seventeenth centuries, it had been a principal champion of the Irishry against the Saxon invaders. Its clergy had almost ruled Ireland at one crisis of the Great Civil War; but under the iron hand of Cromwell, and in the events that followed the Revolution of 1688, they had been subjected to the severest proscription. One of the main objects of the Penal Code was, if not to extirpate, to reduce to nothingness the priesthood of the Irish Catholic Church; its higher dignitaries were exiled and banned, attempts were made to break its organisation up; its ritual and ceremonies were jealously watched and discouraged. But the Church lived in the hearts of the people, of which it was the comforter in the night of affliction; and notwithstanding these evil efforts its influence continued, nay, was extended. In the eighteenth century it had done much to improve the morality of the Irish peasant; and though it was still discountenanced and impeded by the law, and its services were performed in wretched places of worship, its ecclesiastical system had not been destroyed : it had been tolerated for many years, nay, confessed to be a power in the land. Its hierarchy and priesthood were at this time recognised and even favoured by British ministers, who had not failed to perceive their influence; and in the absence of their leaders in civil life its authority over its flocks was immense. The Irish Catholic clergy of this age, however, were very different from their

successors in our day, in too many instances mere sacerdotal demagogues. They had been educated for the most
part in France and Spain, and they were, as a rule, a timid
and conservative order of men, devoted to their faith,
taking no part in politics, and attached to the few leading
Catholic families which vegetated among the landed gentry.
Some of the regular clergy, however, were bolder spirits,
and the Church had not forgotten the past.

Other features of the condition of Ireland at this period
deserve attention.   Irish literature had illustrious names,
that of Edmund Burke being easily supreme, and many of
the speeches in the Irish Parliament were remarkable for
eloquence, knowledge, and thought.   Trinity College possessed a school of able and liberal-minded men ; Leland
and Warner were enlightened historians, and as always
she had distinguished masters of science.   But the general
standard of education in Ireland was low.   The leading
gentry sent their sons to be brought up in England ; the
few public schools of Ireland were wretchedly bad, mis-
managed, and usually under worthless heads.   Primary
education hardly existed ; a detestable institution called
the Charter Schools had failed to win the young of the
Catholics from their faith ; and if there were a very few
good Presbyterian schools, Catholic Ireland lay, it may be
said, in darkness, though miserable " hedge schools" in
some degree satisfied the passionate Irish craving for
learning.   Three-fourths of the Catholics probably could
not read or write, and the old Celtic tongue, if dying out
in Leinster, prevailed in Munster and Connaught and in
more than half of Ulster.   The administration of justice
in the Supreme Courts was pure, though still harsh and
severe to the Catholics, but many of the magistracy were
grossly corrupt ; and in the few inferior Courts the Catholic
was often unfairly treated.   There was nothing like a large
and regular police force : this allowed the prevalent lawlessness to run riot, and though the highwayman was beginning
to disappear he was often seen in the neighbourhood of
the greater towns.   Ireland, unlike England, had no Poor

Law. Protestant land was not to be taxed for Catholic
poverty, and the evils of this were beginning to be felt,
though the worst consequences were reserved for the future.
As always happens when government is corrupt, jobbery,
maladministration, and other abuses pervaded every department of the service of the State ; but they were most
conspicuous, perhaps, in the Established Church. It is
hardly necessary to add that there was nothing like a sound,
general, and well-ordered public opinion, there were out-
bursts of vehemence and fitful passion, but there was no
steady and national judgment to direct statesmen. Ireland,
too, on the whole, was centuries behind Great Britain in
civilisation and progress : not the least remarkable cause
of this was that she did not possess a really powerful
middle class.

The influences of the French Revolution, searching the
peccant parts of every community, and disturbing vicious
and corrupt institutions, necessarily affected profoundly an
ill-governed country, separated by wide distinctions of race
and faith and by steep and unnatural differences of class,
in which the mass of the people was kept outside the State,
and a system of injustice and of exclusive privilege, exalting
the few and doing wrong to the many, had produced a state
of society to its very depths diseased. The measures of the
National Assembly and the doctrines it proclaimed made
themselves first felt in Presbyterian Ireland, which we have
seen had various and real grievances, and had been disaffected to the State during many years. Louis XVI. had
been reduced to the position of a covenanted king ; an
aristocracy dominant over the land had been shorn of its
power ; an arrogant Church had lost its possessions, and its
proud hierarchy had been despoiled ; the evangel of the
rights of man had been preached, and the equality of
citizens before the law asserted ; and all this fell in with
the feelings and sentiments of a community of Scottish
descent engaged in farming and trade, which had a
traditional dislike to absolute monarchy, had suffered
many injuries at the hands of landlords, resented the

exactions and the tithe of the Established Church and
the whole system of inequality of class, and had sympathy
with republican and even socialistic ideas. The Revolution
was eagerly hailed in many parts of Ulster; and a movement, spreading from Belfast and other towns, was set on
foot to inaugurate an era of change in Ireland. The fall of
the Bastille was celebrated with loud rejoicings; addresses
were sent to the Assembly at Versailles; a violent Press
began to make wild utterances; emblems of sedition
appeared in the Irish Harp, with a cap of liberty and
without the Crown; and ominous signs were seen in
systematic efforts to enrol again and to arm the old
Volunteers, under the suggestive name of National Guards.
The influence of the Revolution extended also to Catholic
Ireland by slow degrees. The few Catholic nobles and the
small class of the Catholic landed gentry kept indeed aloof,
and so did the dignitaries of the Church and the mass of
the priesthood; these classes were, as always, torpid and
afraid to stir, and their sympathies were on the side of
the falling Monarchy of France. But the trading Catholic
middle class which had grown up in Ireland and had been
active and restless for some years, beheld in the Revolution
the harbinger of hope and liberty; the Catholic Committee,
long established in Dublin, in some measure followed the
example of the North, and Catholic Committees were set
up in different parts of the country to agitate for Catholic
claims and rights. The impulse thus given gradually moved
the inert masses of the Catholic peasantry; nor indeed
could these be utterly indifferent to what they heard had
taken place in France. But the movement as yet was
feeble and not organised; it appeared in a fitful resistance,
in a few counties, to the payment of tithes and even of
rent, accompanied here and there by agrarian disorders.

Presbyterian and Catholic Ireland had been at feud for
ages wherever the populations had been intermixed; at
this very period two large factions, the Presbyterian
Peep of Day Boys and the Catholic Defenders, were
distracting whole counties by furious discord. But the

3

French Revolution had given the two peoples common
aspirations, objects, and aims, in the fall of an aristocracy
and a Church, and an instrument was found to bring them
together. Theobald Wolfe Tone was a young Irish lawyer
of little learning and not conspicuous parts ; but he was an
enthusiast and a very able man of action, the master-spirit of
the rebellious movement that followed. Tone had brooded
from his teens on the wrongs of Ireland ; he had
denounced, in a striking and brilliant essay, the whole
system of Irish government, and especially the abuses
of the Irish Parliament ; but he threw the blame on
British rule and power ; he saw the hand of England
in all that was worst in his country. His purpose
was to liberate Ireland from the Saxon yoke, and
to accomplish this it was necessary, he saw, to combine
all Irishmen against the common enemy, and especially
to make use of the Irish Catholic millions in the general
crusade against British oppression. He founded the
Society of the United Irishmen in Belfast, in the autumn
of 1791 ; and this rapidly spread over large parts of Ulster.
Its leaders were all Ulster Protestants at first ; it was an
organisation on the Jacobin model ; and these preached the
French Revolutionary faith ; their avowed object, however,
being to procure a thorough reform of the Irish Parliament,
to secure for Catholic Ireland admission within the State
and a participation in political rights, and to unite the
whole of Ireland to attain these ends. With the exception
of Tone, a rebel from the first, the chiefs of the movement
thus professed to have only Constitutional measures in
view ; but as they contemplated an Irish National
Assembly, like that of France, but elected by manhood
suffrage, and for equal districts and the absolute emancipation, as it was called, of the Catholic Irish, their
policy was obviously designed to subvert the whole
system of government, order, and law in Ireland, and
was not compatible with the British connection. The
Society, however, and its doctrines, made way in parts of
Catholic Ireland ; it stimulated the hopes of the Catholic

leaders; and it perhaps quickened, in some degree, the agrarian movement which stirred the peasantry. Tone was appointed Secretary of the Central Catholic Committee; it was a significant expression of the alliance that was being formed between Presbyterian and Catholic Ireland.

Before long, probably at the instigation of Tone, the Catholic Committees proposed to assemble a general convention of delegates of their faith, in imitation of the Volunteers of 1782. Some men of high degree concurred in this project; but even the boldest spirits among the Irish Catholics, though they demanded a complete repeal of the remaining Penal Laws, had as yet no thought of violent or extreme courses. They had placed themselves in the hands of Burke; and Richard, the son of the philosophic statesman, had interviews with Pitt and the Irish Government with the object of promoting the Catholic claims. Burke had strong sympathies with the Irish Catholics; he had been their ablest advocate through life. In the struggle with Revolutionary France, which he already foresaw, he wished to engage Catholicism as a great Conservative force on the side of the old order of Europe; and he urged the British Ministry to make an earnest effort to gain Catholic Ireland over by ample concessions. In his counsels to the Catholic leaders he agreed that the Penal Laws should not be allowed to exclude them any longer from the State, and that they ought to possess considerable political rights; but, characteristically, he was opposed to a reform in the constitution of the Irish Parliament and to giving the Irish Catholic a seat in it, though he was willing to admit him to the electoral franchise. Pitt had become by this time a close ally of Burke; but the Minister hesitated for many months to adopt a policy which would disturb in Ireland a convenient established order of things, and which he knew would be vehemently opposed by the men in power at the Castle. Pitt, in fact, we have seen, wished to maintain Protestant Ascendency as it was in Ireland, and the system of Government in existence, until the

time had come for a union ; and at this juncture he
was confirmed in this view, not only by Fitzgibbon,
whom he greatly trusted, but by a loud expression of
Protestant Irish opinion still generally opposed to the
Catholic cause. But when war with the French Republic
had become imminent and the coalition of Irish Presbyterians and Irish Catholics was evidently growing in
strength and giving alarm, the Minister, perhaps reluctantly, made up his mind to yield to a great extent to the
Catholic demands. The Irish Parliament, in the Session of
1792, had passed an insignificant measure of relief which
admitted the Irish Catholic to the Bar and removed some
of the disabilities still imposed on him. In the following
year, just before the outbreak of the war, a much larger
measure was brought in, and supported by the whole power
of the Irish Government. The Bill—here, perhaps, we see
the hand of Burke—gave the Irish Catholic the right to vote
at elections, but kept him, as before, shut out from Parliament and subject to great and vexatious restrictions,
which still left Protestant Ascendency supreme ; it admitted
him to certain offices in the State and to a share of
political power.

This measure, dictated by the British Government, was
probably at heart disliked by the great majority of the men
sitting in the Irish Parliament. It proposed a complete
change of policy in the affairs of Ireland ; and obviously
it should have been made the work of Grattan and of the
Irish Liberal Party, to be carried into effect in the Irish
Houses. This, however, in the existing state of the Irish
Parliament, was not even thought of ; the subservient following, which at all times was at the beck of the Irish Government, assented to the project, opposed as it was to their
traditional views and opinions, and the Bill became law
without difficulty. Fitzgibbon, however, who had received
the Irish Seals, denounced the measure while he gave it
his support. His speech was a diatribe against Catholic
Ireland ; and this attitude of the most powerful man at
the Castle necessarily provoked Catholic resentment and

distrust. The Bill was an imperfect, and even a bad, half measure—a compromise revealing the want of knowledge of Ireland common to British statesmen ;[1] and its defects and vices were very ably exposed. It was justly contended that it gave the Catholic either too much or too little ; if he was to possess political power he should be made the equal of his Protestant fellow, and dangerous agitation would be the result of placing him in his present position. Some speakers even insisted that this policy was an insidious attempt to increase Irish troubles and to set Catholics and Protestants against each other, in order to bring about a union—an object of abhorrence at this time in the Irish Parliament. But the best argument against the Bill was—and this was pressed with great force and insight—that while it gave the Irish Catholic a vote, it did not allow him to enter Parliament ; the electorate, therefore, was to be swamped by an overwhelming mass of ignorant peasants, and the Catholic noble and gentleman was not to have a privilege which he might fairly claim. This reasoning was so obviously just that we can only suppose that Pitt believed that the enfranchisement of the Irish Catholic voter would still leave the substance of power in Protestant hands—as actually happened during many years—and was not alive to the possible dangers.

The Relief Act of 1793, as it was called, was accompanied by measures reducing the Irish Pension List, and lessening the number of placemen in the Irish Parliament, a concession probably to the views of Grattan. Measures of precaution and repression were also passed, a stringent Alien Bill was enacted, the so-named National Guards were disbanded, care was taken to prevent the importation and the use of arms, an attempt was made to enrol a large militia

---

[1] Irish literature and oratory abounds in complaints of the ignorance of Ireland characteristic of English Ministers and Englishmen generally. I quote a single passage from a speech of Fitzgibbon, a staunch supporter of British rule in Ireland—" The people of England know less of this country than of any other nation in Europe." Swift, Burke, Grattan, and O'Connell, repeatedly made the same remark.

force, and all but unanimous support was given to the war. A lull of more than a year in Ireland followed; this may, perhaps, be ascribed in part to the still doubtful results of the struggle abroad, and to the means employed to put sedition down, but the policy of conciliation had also its effects. Emissaries from France, indeed, began to flit to Ireland, two or three United Irish leaders left the country, the United Irish movement made progress in Ulster, and there was a considerable outburst of Whiteboy crime, not wholly, perhaps, without a political object in three or four of the counties of the South. But Ireland was, in the main, quiescent; the Catholic Convention was suppressed without difficulty by a special law; and the failure of a Reform Bill brought in, in 1794, did not arouse Tone and his Society to expressions of wrath, or even cause much apparent resentment. Things in Ireland as yet seemed tolerably secure; the conduct of Grattan and of his party, indeed, had added greatly to the strength of the Irish Government, and had received the deserved praise of the British Ministry. Grattan had, no doubt, been denounced by the United Irishmen, for their revolutionary propaganda was odious to him; but he remained the staunch advocate of the Catholic claims, and his influence in and out of Parliament had certainly increased. He supported the war and the general policy of Pitt; he had broken with Fox and his dwindling party; he had thrown in his lot with Burke, and the Whig secession; and it seemed not impossible at this juncture, that the policy he advocated would ere long triumph—nay, that he might hold a high position in the Irish Government. Should the Irish Catholics, as was his earnest hope, be placed on a level with the Protestants, through the whole range of political rights, a complete reform of the Irish Parliament, the second great object of his followers would obviously be a mere question of a short time. The narrow Parliamentary system of Ireland, it was plain, could not survive the fusion into one community of the separate Catholic and Protestant peoples.

An incident, attended with most untoward results, had ere long darkened the prospect of affairs in Ireland. Lord Fitzwilliam was one of the great seceding Whigs; he had large estates in Ireland, and knew the country well—and he was intimate with Grattan and the chief Irish Liberals. He was an indiscreet and passionate man; but in the events that followed he was essentially right, though accidentally he put himself in the wrong. It was understood that he was to be Lord-Lieutenant of Ireland, and that a change was to be made in Irish affairs in furtherance at least of Grattan's policy; but, before he was appointed, he invited Grattan to assist him in the task of Irish Government, and he appears to have considered that it would be necessary to remove several men at the Castle from their posts, and especially to dismiss Fitzgibbon, the representative of Protestant Ascendency in an extreme sense. This imprudence was deeply resented by Pitt, but the dispute, sincerely regretted by Burke, was patched up, without clear and frank explanation; and Fitzwilliam was sent to Ireland on the understanding that he was not to make the Catholic claims a Government measure, but that, if necessary, he was to give them support, and that Fitzgibbon was to remain in office. He certainly inferred that he might deal with the rest of the Irish Administration as he pleased, and he had scarcely reached Dublin when he dismissed two or three of the Protestant Ascendency chief men in office, and flung himself into the arms of Grattan and the Irish Whigs. This conduct aroused the wrath of the Castle Junto, and gave a sudden and immense impulse to the Catholic movement in the whole of Ireland. The Catholic Committees pressed their demands in determined language; they were supported by the Catholic peers and gentry, who now hoped to succeed by constitutional means. The Irish Parliament met in the first weeks of 1795; Fitzwilliam, as he was directed, did not pledge the Government to a measure of Catholic relief, but in letter after letter he informed the Cabinet that full Catholic emancipation had become a necessity of the times, and that if orders to the contrary were not sent, he "would acquiesce with a good grace." No answer was made to his despatches for weeks; at last he received an intimation from Pitt complaining of the dismissals he had made, and this was followed by injunctions from the Duke of Portland insisting that no countenance was to be given to the Catholic claims, and that the system of government in Ireland was in no sense to be changed. This sudden and strange turn of policy, there is little doubt, was due to the interference of George III., and Fitzgibbon had a considerable part in it. Fitzwilliam was ere long summarily recalled; his indignation is not to be blamed, but he was unwise enough to publish confidential letters, which exasperated his colleagues and did him much harm.[1]

The successor of Fitzwilliam was Lord Camden, a well-meaning but inferior man, and a mere mouthpiece of the British Cabinet. Fitzgibbon, raised to the great earldom of Clare, became the master-spirit of the Irish Government; he ruled the Castle and well-nigh controlled the Parliament. The old system of Protestant Ascendency and oligarchic privilege was defiantly renewed in a changed era when French ideas and arms were overrunning Europe; the proof of this was seen in the decisive rejection—involving, too, the fate of Parliamentary Reform—of a Catholic Relief Bill in the Irish Parliament; the majority which, admittedly, would have made it law a few weeks before, having characteristically turned round at the Government's bidding. Petty measures of conciliation were next tried; the College of Maynooth was founded for the Catholic priest-

---

[1] The affair of Lord Fitzwilliam is a most important episode in this part of the History of Ireland. The account of Mr. Lecky ("History of England in the Eighteenth Century," vii. 32, 97,) is by many degrees the best. See also Froude's "English in Ireland," iii. 122, 137, in which all parties are condemned and George III. extolled. For an attempt to vindicate Pitt and the British Ministry, I may refer to Lord Stanhope's Life of Pitt, ii. 91, 97. Lord Rosebery has pleaded on the same side, but superficially, and with little apparent knowledge, in his "Pitt," pp. 179, 192. The great point made against Fitzwilliam, that his Whig colleagues threw him over, is explained by his indiscretions, but he was in the main right.

hood; Trinity College had, to her honour, opened her
degrees, before this time, to the Irish Catholic. But after
the late vote in the Irish Parliament, the hopes that had
been raised so high were cruelly dashed; a thrill of passion
and despair ran through the country, and trouble and
sorrow fell on Ireland, "creeping," as Grattan said, "like
mist after the heels of the peasant." The United Irish
leaders gave up the prospect of success by any but violent
means, and made preparations to compass their ends by
armed force. Their organisation had hitherto been a civil
one only, associations of a Jacobin type, which disseminated wild and seditious doctrines, and preached the French
revolutionary creed, but were open, and not distinctly rebellious. It was now given a military aspect and form,
arms were collected and bodies of men enrolled; these levies
were assembled in different districts, and placed under
regularly chosen officers; power was concentrated in a
few leaders, and efforts were made to seduce the army,
and especially the newly raised militia. The ramifications of an immense conspiracy, held together by secret
oaths and passwords, extended quickly over whole counties;
and to secure immunity from the penalties of the law,
juries were intimidated and magistrates marked down
for vengeance. Ere long negotiations were opened with
the men in power in Paris, and Lord Edward Fitzgerald,
and Arthur O'Connor, the one a younger brother of
the Duke of Leinster, the other a distinguished member
of the Irish Parliament, were sent over to arrange for a
French descent on Ireland. The heads of the conspiracy
meanwhile laboured hard to drag Catholic Ireland in their
wake, and to make use of its teeming masses; and members
of the Catholic Committees, or their subordinates, in
some districts, lent a too willing ear. They found the
Whiteboy system made to their hands, and agrarian disorder already far spread; hundreds of peasants were in
many places swept into the ranks of the United Irishmen
and sworn "to rise in the cause of Ireland." The movement, however, was still mainly connected with the land,

and exhibited itself in a kind of predial war against middlemen, farmers of the tithes and landlords, accompanied
here and there with atrocious outrages. It was as yet
chiefly confined to northern and midland counties, and
had made little way in Munster and Connaught.

The United Irish movement, as was Tone's object, was
thus combining Irishmen of opposite creeds and races,
and was spreading from Ulster through the provinces of
the South. It was, however, thwarted for a time by another
movement of altogether a different kind, though this ultimately gave it an immense impulse. Recent events had, in
different ways, quickened the savage feuds which we have
seen had made the Peep of Day Boys and Defenders
inveterate foes ; and from 1791 onwards, large parts of
Ulster had been in a very disturbed state. In 1795 the
quarrel became almost a civil war ; the Peep of Day
Boys were merged in the Orange Society composed largely
of Protestants of the lower orders, exasperated at the Relief
Act of 1793 ; and fights, in one instance rising to a battle,
took place between the Orangemen and the Defender
Catholics. Scenes of barbarous disorder and outrage
followed ; Catholic houses and places of worship were
wrecked wholesale ; hundreds, nay thousands, of the
Defenders were driven from their homes, and fled out of
Ulster. Leaders of the gentry in the North condemned these
excesses ; but the Orangemen were backed by the great
majority ; the Government, though not Camden, it is to be
feared, concurred ; and in many districts Catholics were
seized and hurried off to man the fleet by unscrupulous
magistrates. This revival of the discords of race and faith
in Ireland ran counter to the United Irish policy, which
aimed at making a league of all Irishmen ; but the leaders
skilfully made it promote their ends. They announced that
the object of the Government was to effect the destruction
of Catholic Ireland by measures as atrocious as those of
Cromwell ; the hour of massacre and proscription was
at hand ; and the only hope for the Irish Catholic was to
hasten to join the United Irish ranks, and to take part in

the struggle against his tyrants. These appeals, echoed by emissaries sent far and wide—some of them, it is said, were regular priests—made an extraordinary impression on the Catholic masses already terrified by what had occurred in Ulster ; and as the streams of the banished Defenders spread through the southern provinces, the peasantry in many counties were carried away. The Whiteboy move-ment was now, so to speak, swallowed up in the United Irish and rebellious movement ; the military organisation, formed in the North, was transferred to the South ; tens of thousands of men were armed with a rude weapon, the pike, and the conflict which had been, in the main, agrarian, became a conspiracy for an insurrectionary war. Signs, however, of the original movement still often appeared in the burnings of the houses of obnoxious persons, in murders, the slaughter of cattle, and other deeds of blood, and especially in cutting down woodland for the making of pikes.

These scenes were in progress from the close of 1795 through 1796. The state of the country had become very alarming, the power of France was advancing on a flood-tide of victory, and a French invasion had been threatened for months. The Irish Parliament, largely composed of the landed gentry, despoiled and exasperated by the agrarian conflict, was in a revengeful and angry mood ; but it is not to be blamed for adopting measures of repression and against impending danger. The Habeas Corpus Act was rightly suspended, and an Insurrection Act was properly passed to put Whiteboy and rebellious disorder down. But the Government probably deserved censure for refusing to inquire into Orange excesses, and for sanctioning the unjustifiable deportations to the fleet ; and the Parliament as yet, at least, ought not to have granted indemnities to magistrates and others guilty of illegal acts. This policy was condemned by sensible men of all parties in both Houses ; indeed, there is ample proof through these troubled years, that the conduct of the Government was not approved by numbers of independent and enlightened Irishmen. Grattan and his followers made an earnest effort to mitigate the system of coercion the Government had made its own, and to strike a blow at the Protestant Ascendency and the methods of ruling in which they saw the chief causes of existing evils. They exposed the partiality that had been shown to the Orangemen, and the wrongs that had been done to the Defenders. Grattan, especially, in impassioned language, declared that "the poor were stricken out of the protection of the law, and the rich out of its penalties ; " and they brought forward a large measure of Parliamentary Reform and a Catholic Relief Bill that would have made the emancipation of the Irish Catholic complete. These proposals, however, naturally failed in the Irish Parliament in its present temper ; they were derided, in fact, by the men at the Castle. Grattan and his party, thinking further protests hopeless, ere long followed the example of Fox at Westminster, and seceded from an assembly which, for the time, turned a deaf ear to the great patriot of 1782.

The expected descent from France took place in the last days of 1796 ; it was, fortunately, unsuccessful, but through a mere accident. Tone had left Ireland some months before, but he had reached Paris in the beginning of the year ; and he was soon in communication with the French Directory, who had lent an ear to O'Connor and Lord Edward Fitzgerald. His ability and earnestness made an impression on the rulers of France, and even on Hoche, fresh from his triumphs in La Vendée ; a promise was made that a fleet would be sent to Ireland, supported by an expeditionary force. Like all rebels in exile, Tone made extravagant and far-fetched reports ; but his statement that thousands of United Irishmen had been forced into the English fleet—he said, indeed, that they formed the greater part of the seamen—though grossly exaggerated, contained truth ; this had weight especially with the renowned Carnot ; it is a significant commentary on the deportations from Ulster, and on the subsequent mutiny at the Nore. A large French squadron, with 15,000 good troops, set sail from Brest in the second week of December. It reached the coast of Ireland with little difficulty or loss, and it found the south of Munster almost unguarded, and without a single British warship at hand. Cork might probably have been seized and the adjoining counties overrun, and the results must have been very grave ; there would have been an armed rising in Ulster, and even in the South. But Hoche, the Commander-in-chief, had been parted from his ships, and was left isolated in a single frigate ; Grouchy, the second in command, showed the want of enterprise he exhibited on a greater occasion ; and the French armament, after reaching Bantry Bay, was scattered and driven out to sea by a furious tempest. The peasantry in the neighbourhood did not stir and the Protestant corporations of the chief towns of Munster made demonstrations of loyalty doubtless sincere. These incidents, however, though made much of at the time, were not important, and proved little ; the result might have been very different had the French, as Tone proposed, made a landing in a port of Ulster, and even had boldly attacked Dublin.

The failure at Bantry did not daunt the United Irish leaders ; that corner of Munster had not been prepared, and a successful descent had been shown to be possible. The condition of affairs throughout Ireland went from bad to worse in the spring and summer of 1797. England had been left without an ally on the Continent ; she appeared bankrupt, her fleets were mutinous ; and there was every reason to fear that Irish rebellion would be backed by a great French invasion directed perhaps by the warrior who had struck Austria down. The United Irish movement, whether in the North or the South, had also acquired increased strength. A hundred thousand men, it was boasted, were enrolled in Ulster, and two hundred thousand in the three other provinces, and though these numbers were far above the truth, a considerable rebel army partly disciplined and drilled, and under selected officers, no doubt existed. An insurrectionary government composed of five members, like the Directory of France, had been also formed ; this held its seat in Dublin, and had absolute control over the lesser conspiracies wherever they spread ;

its object was to seize the capital, to overpower the Government, and to give the signal for a universal rising, as soon as the French should effect a landing. Meanwhile it had established a far-reaching system of terror; innumerable outrages were committed in the North and the South; the militia, largely composed of Catholics, had thousands of men in the United Irish levies; and justice was paralysed by the violence of a Jacobin Press, and by the intimidation of all concerned in the administration of the law. The Government, led by Lord Clare, stern, calm, and resolute, very properly struck hard, and directed the first strokes on Ulster. The penal legislation of the last year was put in force; whole counties were subjected to martial law; hundreds of suspected persons were thrown into jail; the incendiary newspapers were suppressed, and the leaders of the conspiracy in the North were nearly all arrested. The disturbed districts were then disarmed, thousands of weapons were seized and their owners severely treated, and attempts at resistance were summarily quelled. The rebellion was thus nipped in the bud before it was mature; surprise and boldness effected much; but it was very unfortunate that the Government had few regular soldiers on hand, and had largely to rely on a yeomanry force, composed in the main of Orange and Protestant volunteers; and unquestionably many deeds of blood, of lawless excess, and of cruelty were done. But order was restored in Ulster, and a great peril averted; and whatever of evil was done in the province was a mere trifle compared to that which Ireland unhappily was soon to witness elsewhere.

The pacification of Ulster was complete in the last months of 1797. The heads of the conspiracy in the North had wished to rise as soon as the Government had begun to act; but the Directory in Dublin refused them aid; this was the beginning of divisions that were rapidly to increase. The rebel Government, in fact, had resolved not to strike until the French had successfully made a landing; this was the advice of Lord Edward Fitzgerald, the chosen commander of the levies of the South, a soldier who knew what war meant;

and the great British victory of Camperdown, of which
Tone was almost an unwilling spectator, had made the
leaders in the capital cautious. The insurrectionary forces
having been thus weakened, Clare turned against the conspiracy and its followers in the Southern provinces. With
Camden and the Irish Council he had been made acquainted
by spies and informers from the rebel camps of every step
and design that was being made; he seems to have determined to force rebellion to a head, and to paralyse it before
the foreign enemy could appear. The danger was still
extremely grave; England's overtures for peace had been
rejected; and Napoleon was at this time on the seaboard
of France, meditating a descent at the head of the "army
of England." It must, too, be borne in mind that, as had
been the case in Ulster, the Irish Government did not
possess the means to put disorder down by regular troops,
and had mainly to rely on irregular levies, hostile in
race and faith to the people of the South. The deeds that
were done were, however, atrocious in the extreme; in the
first months of 1798 a Reign of Terror prevailed in many
counties of the South. The passions of a dominant
minority were let loose against the Irish Catholic multitudes; the Orange yeomanry revelled in lawless violence;
the peasantry were hunted down without mercy; towns
were ravaged by armed bands at free quarters; torture was
very generally employed to extract confessions of suspected
persons, imprisoned by hundreds without a shadow of proof.
Parts of the South were thus goaded to rise, and these
cruelties obtained the willing assent of the men at the Castle
and the Parliament, now a mere instrument of Camden
and Clare. Ere long a swoop on the rebel Directory
was made. Most of the leaders were captured, through an
informer's treachery; and Lord Edward Fitzgerald—one
of the famous Geraldine name still held in reverence
wherever the great fallen house had ruled—was arrested
and, happily, died of the wounds he received. A feeble
attempt to make the conspiracy revive was put down by
other arrests; and thus the insurrection was deprived of its

heads; while the masses of its adherents, scattered and ignorant peasants, surprised, disheartened, and already breaking up, were driven, before the time, to take up arms.

If we reflect what the French Revolution was, and what its effects in misruled countries, we may doubt if Ireland could have escaped great or even dangerous disturbance after 1789. The diseased elements in her social condition were such as would certainly be made active by the ideas and principles proclaimed in France; considerable mischief probably must have followed. Yet the policy adopted in 1793, bad and imperfect compromise as it was, did weaken the force of the United Irish movement, and made Catholic Ireland tranquil for a time; and had Grattan's measures of conciliation been boldly carried out the worst evils that were seen afterwards might never have occurred. It is impossible to assert what would have happened had Fitzwilliam not been unjustly recalled; it is evident, however, that from the moment that Protestant Ascendency and the old system of Irish Government was set up again, the prospect for the country became rapidly worse. When rebellious movements were growing to a head, much allowance must be made for the Irish Government; the danger was real and very grave, especially in 1796–8, and in the presence of French invasion at hand; and the Government had instruments either questionable or bad. But it erred greatly in supporting the Orange movement, and in exasperating the whole of discontented Ireland; but for this the Irish Catholics would hardly have turned to rebellion. The resolution and capacity of Clare deserve praise; but the severities of which he approved in the North, and the atrocities to which he gave a free rein in the South, have indisputably thrown a shadow on his name. His policy was for the moment successful, but it led to consequences felt even now; and we must not forget that it was steadily condemned, not only by many distinguished Irishmen, but by Cornwallis and Abercromby, eminent soldiers, who declared that it was unnecessary and could not be justified. The conduct of Pitt and the British Ministry was often feeble, and even tortuous, revealing English ignorance of Irish affairs ; but they were hardly to blame for the deeds of violence that were done. For the rest the period shows how easily led were the weak masses of Catholic Ireland, and how Ireland, as usual, was divided ; its most distinctive feature, perhaps, is that it proves what ill the French Revolution wrought in a distracted and ill-governed country.

CHAPTER II

THE REBELLION—THE UNION

Outbreak of the Rebellion of 1798—It is at once put down in Kildare and the adjoining counties—It assumes formidable proportions in Wexford—Father John Murphy—Oulart and Enniscorthy—The town of Wexford occupied—Battles of New Ross and Arklow—Vinegar Hill stormed—End of the Rebellion in Wexford—Its dregs linger in Wicklow and other counties—Partial rising in Ulster easily put down—Ulster quiescent and why—Munster and Connaught hardly stir—Lord Camden replaced by Lord Cornwallis—Policy of Cornwallis—The descent of Humbert—Death of Wolfe Tone—Complete collapse of the Rebellion—Pitt proposes the Union—His policy and conduct—A proposal for a Union fails in the Irish Parliament in 1799—Means employed to bring the Union about—Provisions of the Act of Union—Pitt resigns office—Review of his conduct—Position of Ireland in the Imperial Parliament.

THE rising in Ulster had been prevented ; things in the South had been brought to a crisis ; the rebel Directory had been arrested ; the rebel army was a flock without shepherds, spread in little knots and bands over parts of the country. An armed rising, nevertheless, took place ; and the Government, though in no sense surprised, had not adequate means to resist a well-combined effort. There were not 15,000 British troops in Ireland ; these were mainly English, Scottish, and Welsh militia, mostly employed as garrisons of the large towns ; the Irish militia were, perhaps, 18,000 strong, but numbers of these were distrusted Catholics ; and the men at the Castle had, as before, to rely chiefly on the irregular yeomanry volunteer levies, nearly all Protestants burning with Orange passions. The insurrection followed,

34

to some extent, the plan that had been arranged by its military heads ; but it was feeble, unorganised, and without direction. The mails were stopped in different parts of the country, on the night of the 23rd of May, 1798 ; fires blazed ominously from the Wicklow and Dublin hills ; and on the morning of the 24th gathering bands of peasants, with arms of all kinds, and in loose masses, rage in the adjoining county of Kildare, the home of the Geraldine House of Leinster. Other bands appeared in the counties of Dublin and Meath ; and the rising spread into Carlow and the Queen's County, the object being to march on the capital, to arouse the armed rebellion lurking within, and to overthrow the Government in its seat. It is unnecessary to dwell on the desultory combats that followed ; they were scarcely worthy of the name of skirmishes. The rebels gained some partial successes ; a small body of militia was destroyed at a place called Prosperous, mainly owing to the treachery of one of the officers ; a few country seats and villages were seized and harried. But the insurrection never approached Dublin ; rude husbandmen could not hold the field against forces with any kind of discipline ; they were scattered or slaughtered in rapid succession ; atrocious deeds were done on both sides ; the massacre at Prosperous had its counterparts in massacres near Carlow, and on the Curragh of Kildare ; and a general officer was loudly condemned, who uttered even a word of clemency. The state of affairs in Dublin was more dangerous. Thousands of men had secretly joined the United Irish ranks, and large stores of fire-arms and pikes had been collected ; there was a well-grounded fear of a treacherous and widespread outbreak, accompanied by excesses of horrible crime. But the city was placed under martial law ; the garrison was in con-siderable force ; and the loyal citizens met the emergency with most praiseworthy courage. They formed themselves into a great and well-armed police force, which effectually kept the cowed rebels down. [1]

[1] A good and tolerably impartial account of the Rebellion of 1798 will be found in Gordon's History. The reader should be warned

The struggle, as had been foreseen, had assumed the character of a religious war from the first, in mockery, as it were, of United Irish dreams, for Protestant Ascendency ranged its adherents on the side of the Government, and the United Irishmen in the South were nearly all Catholics. There were large exceptions, however, to a general rule ; the Catholic militia, led for the most part by Protestant officers, had done well, and Catholic nobles and gentlemen and heads of the Church had given proof of sincere, nay, devoted loyalty. The rising, however, had been so speedily quelled, that order, it was thought for some days, would soon be restored. Rebellion, however, suddenly flamed out wildly in a region where, perhaps, it was not much expected. The counties of Wicklow and Wexford, in the south-east of Leinster, form one of the loveliest parts of Ireland ; the first is largely a tract of hills and defiles, the home in the past of Celtic mountaineers ; the second is a country of fertile plains, peopled by a race of British, Flemish, and Welsh descent ; the gentry, in both, were, for the most part, resident, the peasantry, as a rule, were prosperous. But the evil teaching of the United Irish leaders had been especially active throughout this district ; the notion was spread far and near that an Orange invasion would be made from the not distant capital ; the population became Defenders and took the United Irish oath in thousands, and in this way as in other counties, it was lured into the ranks of rebellion with little knowledge of what was to happen. It should be added that, as in the rest of the South of Ireland, the owners of the land were nearly all Protestants, the occupiers nearly all Catholics ; that a few of the gentry were men of extreme liberal views and some priests disaffected at heart, and that several of the popular leaders had not forgotten the tradi-

against the partisan narratives of Musgrave and Hay. The memoirs of Miles Byrne and Holt are very interesting ; and the Camden, Cornwallis and Castlereagh Correspondence should be studied. Mr. Lecky's chapters are, as usual, excellent. Mr. Froude has described the military events very well, but he has written in the spirit of the mediæval statutes, which declared that the killing of an Irishman was not a crime.

tions of the old tribal life of Wicklow, of the days when the clans called its valleys their own, of the deeds of blood which Cromwell had done at Wexford. Elements of trouble and disturbance, in a word, abounded ; and, especially after the descent of the French at Bantry Bay, these rapidly quickened and became manifest. The look of the peasantry grew dark and sullen, vague rumours of a rising at hand spread, and pikes were secretly fabricated in large quantities. An outbreak, however, would not have, perhaps, occurred had not the methods adopted to make rebellion show itself been employed with extreme and reckless severity. The yeomanry and militia devastated villages and towns, Catholic places of worship were ruthlessly burned, and more than ordinary cruelty was committed, nay, reduced into a regular system, in order to compel the surrender of arms, and in tracking out and capturing suspected persons. Two modes of torture were very generally in use, wretches were half-hanged to enforce confessions, and caps smeared with melting pitch were in numberless cases pressed down on the heads of "croppies," as the sufferers were called.

These excesses maddened the already rebellious peasantry, the insurrection burst forth in Wexford, unfortunately it produced a real leader. Father John Murphy was a disaffected priest, the destruction of his chapel made him vow vengeance ; he summoned the country around his parish to arms by the light of a beacon fired from a neighbouring hill. He was soon joined by tumultuous swarms of pikemen and by bodies of farmers, with long duck guns, practised marksmen from boyhood in shooting wild fowl ; he boldly raised the standard of revolt, the name of the "Irish Republic" revealing his French sympathies. In a skirmish on the side of a hill called Oulart, a loyalist detachment which fell on with imprudent confidence was overpowered and slain almost to a man : this became the signal of a widespread rising, and Father John, drawing other priests in his wake and sweeping in recruits from all sides in hundreds, was soon at the head of a large insurrectionary force. He was a true ruler of men, almost a born general ;

he made for Enniscorthy, a town on the Slaney, and a point
of importance commanding the river, he attacked the
garrison in the place with real military skill, making a
flanking movement with vigour and effect.   A fierce and
well-contested encounter followed, the long fowling-piece
and the pike proved deadly weapons; the assailants covered
themselves with the fire of burning houses, and ultimately
the defenders abandoned the town, which decked itself out
in the rebel colours of green. Father John next placed a
part of his victorious levies in a camp on the adjoining
eminence of Vinegar Hill, and with the rest, swollen to
thousands of men, he marched rapidly to a range called the
Three Rocks overlooking the town of Wexford at a little
distance.   The terror that prevailed in Wexford was intense,
the Protestant townsmen expected a wholesale massacre and
a deputation was sent to the rebel leaguers to treat.   Ere long
a small party of militia, which had approached the Three
Rocks, was annihilated by the rebels on the spot, and a few
hundred armed men who had got into Wexford and had
tried to support the loyalist movement were compelled to
leave the town in precipitate flight.   The insurgents, by this
time fully 16,000 strong, streamed wildly into the defenceless
place—a multitudinous chaos brandishing arms of all kinds,
and accompanied by troops of exulting women bedizened
with the spoils of plundered country seats.

The deeds of blood were not perpetrated that were feared
at Wexford; the town was placed under a kind of government, and a Catholic bishop and his clergy did much to
appease the passions of the armed Catholic masses.   A
strange and half-tragic comedy was ere long witnessed; to
propitiate the victors many Protestants were " made
Christians " by baptisms after the Roman fashion, the rebels
brought by these means to clemency by their priests, rejoiced
with superstitious glee that " the heretics had been saved."
Meanwhile the whole county had risen up in arms, the
insurrection raging from the sea to the Barrow; the Peter
the Hermit of the Irish Crusade found himself at the head
of a wild savage host numbering from 40,000 to 50,000 men.

The rebels, strange to say, elected a Protestant, Bagenal Harvey, a gentlemen with United Irish views, to command "the Army of the People" in chief ; two or three more of the landed gentry threw in their lot with them. Their real trust, however, was in their beloved Father John and in Philip Roche, another remarkable priest, and these leaders had the advice of more than one old soldier who had seen war in the Irish Brigade. An attempt to enforce order and discipline was made, a regular plan of operations was formed that showed considerable insight and skill. The rebel army was divided into three masses, the central column was to advance into the north of the county, and to give aid to an expected rising in Wicklow, the left column was to master the Barrow, and to overrun the counties to the west of the river, which, it was thought, were eager to revolt ; the right column was to march by the sea coast on the capital. The movement of the central column was stopped by a small yeomanry and militia force ; the rebels were driven from the town of Newtown Barry back upon Vinegar Hill. But the effort of the left column was formidable in the extreme, and led to what may really be called a battle fought out, on both sides, with heroic constancy. The rebels, from 16,000 to 18,000 strong, advanced on the morning of the 5th of June against the garrison of the little town of New Ross, composed of about 1,500 men, some of these being regular troops, supported by a battery of field guns. The assailants drove in the first loyalist ranks by forcing against them herds of bullocks ; they then poured into the narrow streets of New Ross, covered, as at Enniscorthy, by the flames of houses they had fired. The fight within the pent-in spaces became desperate, the artillery in vain swept hundreds down, the best horsemen of England recoiled, beaten, before the serried forest of pikes, or fell under the deadly hail of concealed sharpshooters. The weight of overwhelming numbers at last told, part of the loyalist force was driven across the Barrow, and had the rebel army made a combined effort it would have occupied New Ross and seized the great bridge leading into the adjoining County Kilkenny, the object of the insurgent leaders. But the irregular masses broke up, rushing wildly here and there ; Johnston, the able chief of the half-defeated garrison, rallied his men with admirable coolness and skill ; the town, as evening fell, was again in his hands. A party of the baffled insurgents disgraced their cause by a massacre of prisoners at a farmhouse known as Scullabogue, a foul parody, it has been thought, of the September massacres ; it is right to add that Bagenal Harvey severely condemned the crime.

We turn to the fortunes of the right column, under the command of the redoubtable Father John. This was from 20,000 to 25,000 strong, but the men were composed of the latest levies, and were, for the most part, miserably armed, and the bodies of sharpshooters seem to have been at New Ross. An advanced detachment, however, of the rebel army surprised and cut to pieces a loyalist party not far from Gorey, on the 5th of June. The officer in command was slain ; it has been said that if the insurgents had pressed forward and seized Arklow, on the coast road to Dublin, the capital must have fallen into their hands. But Father John had a true military eye ; he probably had good reason to pause, and an eye-witness, afterwards a brilliant soldier of France, has declared that he could not have made the march.[1] Be this as it may, the rebels had reached the outskirts of Arklow by the afternoon of the 9th of June ; they attacked the defenders of the town in three great masses, endeavouring to turn the enemy on both flanks. The loyalists were only 1,600 strong, as usual a militia and yeomanry force, but a skilful officer was fortunately at their head. General Needham had placed them in a strong position behind fences and ditches hastily turned into lines. The attack was intrepid and pressed fiercely home. Needham thought for a moment of falling back, a resolve that might have had the worst results ; but the fire of the assailants was desultory and without aim ; the artillery of the defence

[1] "Memoirs of Miles Byrne," i. p. 114.

told with great effect on the tumultuous masses as they surged forward ; it was impossible to storm the improvised breastworks. The rebels sullenly retreated as night fell ; their ammunition was all but spent ; thousands disbanded in a flight that became precipitate. A curious incident had smitten the superstitious host with panic ; one of their priests had persuaded them that true Catholics need have no fear of heretic guns ; and he had escaped scatheless, hitherto, in the deadliest fights. He rushed into the fray at Arklow raising a green flag, bearing the words, " Death or Liberty," on a white cross ; he was blown to atoms at the cannon's mouth ; the broken spell terrified his disenchanted followers.

The dissolving ranks of the right column drifted partly to Wexford, partly into the County Wicklow. The rebellion by this time had lasted three weeks ; not a soldier had been despatched from England, probably owing to apprehension of a descent from the Channel ; the war had been a murderous strife of Irishmen, marked on both sides by detestable deeds, but giving proof of the inborn bravery of the race. The greatest alarm had prevailed in Dublin, when Father John had drawn near Arklow ; some fine ladies and gentlemen fled ; but at last 14,000 or 15,000 troops were landed ; the issue could then be no longer doubtful. Lake, renowned afterwards for his deeds in India, but not worthy of praise in the Irish rebellion, marched for the great encampment on Vinegar Hill, where scenes of horror had been too common, the spirit of Jacobinism and of religious fury having united as it were to commit atrocious crimes, and scores of Protestants having been done to death after mock trials, like those of Fouquier Tinville. Five armed columns were directed against the insurgent leaguers ; they encountered a stern but hopeless resistance ; but the rebel army would have been utterly destroyed had not one of the columns been backward, and thousands of fugitives escaped through the space it left open, still known as Needham's Gap in the traditions of the place. Lake now made for Wexford, the

only remaining spot where the dying rebellion had even
a show of strength.   The insurgents who had been defeated
at New Ross, had deprived Bagenal Harvey of his command,
and had placed Father Philip Roche in his stead.   Roche
had assembled a considerable force at the Three Rocks,
and he had attacked Moore, the future chief of Corunna,
with no ordinary vigour and skill, a body of rebels from
Wexford giving him aid.   Moore, however, had driven the
assailants back, and in the frenzy of terror and wrath that
ensued, a massacre of Protestants at last took place in the
town which, hitherto, had scarcely been stained with blood.
The rebels now endeavoured to parley with Moore, but
Lake turned a deaf ear to any terms.   Roche was brutally
killed in an attempt to treat ; and the remains of his force,
seeing that they must do or die, effected their escape across
the Barrow with the still indomitable Father John at their
head.   The victorious army occupied Wexford ; Bagenal
Harvey, and the men of his order who had followed his
leading, were rightly condemned ; but we may regret that
the heads of the rebel government who had saved valuable
lives were not spared.   Lake might have learned a lesson
from Hoche in La Vendée.

The rebellion was now almost a thing of the past ; but
Father John made good his way into the plains of
Kilkenny.   He tried to arouse a colliery district ; his
motley force was routed and dispersed ; his own fate is
still, perhaps, a mystery.   The dregs of the rising stirred
for many months in the fastnesses and the glens of
Wicklow, which had been kept down not without trouble.
Holt, a farmer, exasperated by cruel wrongs, successfully
maintained a kind of guerilla war with armed peasants
and part of the levies of Wexford.   This wild region, indeed,
was not completely pacified until a great military road
was made through it, as in the case of the Highlands
after 1745.   Had a French army seconded the rebellion,
or had this been, in any sense, general, the State would
have been in the gravest peril ; Ireland, for a time, might
have been lost to the Empire.   But France did not send

a man at the crisis of events; the rising was confined to
a small part of Leinster; nothing like the universal effort
was made on which the United Irish leaders founded their
hopes. Petty outbreaks, indeed, occurred in Ulster, but
they were put down without the least difficulty; the
province in which rebellion was first hatched and which
had been terribly disturbed for two years before, was all
but quiescent in 1798, and, in a short time, was wholly at
rest. This was partly due to the presence of a powerful
armed force, partly to increasing discord between the
rebel chiefs in Belfast and those in Dublin, partly to
growing distrust of French policy, but principally to the
character which the struggle in the South assumed. It
was at once perceived to be a war of religion, attended
with barbarous deeds of blood; the Presbyterians of the
North, misled as they might be by United Irish ideas and
dreams, had no notion that Protestant Ireland was to be
made the victim of Popish peasants and priests; they were
incensed by tales like those of Prosperous and Scullabogue;
and as the old animosities of faith quickened, they turned
away from rebellion in disgust. As for Munster, there were
garrisons in the large towns; the country districts hardly
made a sign, and insignificant disorders were easily quelled.
The United Irish faith had never made much way in
Connaught, and the province was almost everywhere
tranquil; indeed in this, as has happened in other instances,
it was less in backward and poor regions than in those
which were more rich and prosperous that rebellious
movements had any real power.

Camden meanwhile had given place to Lord Cornwallis,
who had refused to command the army in Ireland the year
before, on account of what was being done by the men at
the Castle, but who became Lord-Lieutenant at the express
request of Pitt. Cornwallis was a good if an unfortunate
soldier, a skilful diplomatist, in some sense a statesman;
but like most Englishmen, he did not know Ireland. He
was ready, also, like many Englishmen, to relieve England
from blame in Irish affairs, and to throw it upon a single

class in Ireland; and he had a fixed idea that a great
measure of Catholic relief would be a panacea for the ills
of centuries. The scenes that met him on his arrival, and
for weeks afterwards, naturally filled a humane disposition
with aversion and horror. The rebellion had been quenched
in ashes and blood; but a white terror reigned in many
parts of the South; the atrocities, which had largely provoked the rising, continued in full swing without scruple
or pity; the whippings, the torturings, the burnings went
on; the yeomanry especially revelled in licence and in
outrages on defenceless women. Cornwallis was justly
incensed, and did much to put these revolting excesses
down; he was earnestly supported, it should be observed,
by Clare; the lordly lion, when it had done what it wanted,
did not care to let the jackals run riot. But Cornwallis was
in error when he charged the Irish landed gentry with guilt
of this kind; in hundreds of instances they denounced and
tried to put a stop to these crimes; these in fact were
chiefly the work of subordinate officers, and of functionaries
of the Castle Junto; and nothing is more certain than
that all that was worst in the loyalist vengeance of 1798
was condemned by the best and the leading men of
Protestant Ireland. Nor is the Irish Parliament to be
visited with unreserved censure, because, at a crisis of grave
peril, it gave its sanction to the severest measures, and even
protected men in office by Acts of Indemnity not to be
justified in other times. Deeds of lawless violence might
be excused when a rebel army was forty miles from Dublin,
and succour from England was not forthcoming—facts
conveniently omitted by English writers—nor can it be
forgotten that there were special reasons to irritate and
offend the Irish Parliament. The United Irish leaders had
caused maps of the old confiscations to be made, and had
offered these lands to the peasantry as a spoil.

It is to the credit of Cornwallis that only four leaders of
the rebel conspiracy suffered death, after regular trials and
convictions; and he extended an amnesty to peasants who
gave up their arms, and pledged themselves to submit to the

Government. Many leaders, however, were still in confinement, and thousands of prisoners had been taken in the
field ; it was being discussed how these were to be treated,
when intelligence arrived of a French landing. Napoleon
had been for months the foremost man in France ; characteristically he kept aloof from Irish rebellion, and instead
of attempting a descent on England, he took an invading
army to Egypt, and the fleet that was destroyed at the Nile.
The Directory, however, fitted little expeditions out ; one
of these successfully reached the Coast of Mayo, but weeks
after the rebellion had collapsed. The prospect of a rising
was hopeless, for this part of Connaught had hardly stirred ;
but the French General, Humbert, a daring and able soldier,
who had disembarked some 1,100 men, veterans of the
armies of Italy and the Rhine, showed what could be done
by real soldiers against armed levies debauched by evil
deeds of licence. He surprised his enemy by a rapid
movement, along a road that had been deemed impassable ;
deceived him by a well-planned feint, and routed Lake
and a militia force twofold at least in numbers, its ignominious flight being still known as the Race of Castlebar.
Finding no support in the country, however, Humbert
made by a forced march for Sligo and the North, but
he was ultimately compelled to lay down his arms, Lake
and Cornwallis having surrounded him in overwhelming
strength. Another expedition was only notable for the
capture of Theobald Wolfe Tone, the brain and soul of
the Rebellion of 1798. Tone had lost hope when he set
sail for Ireland ; but he wished to strike a blow in what
he thought her quarrel, and he fought desperately in a
murderous engagement at sea. The proceedings at his trial
were remarkable for a conflict between a military court and
one of the established tribunals of the State; but he solved
the difficulty, happily perhaps, by suicide. Tone is the
only one of the Irish rebel chiefs entitled to more than the
passing notice of history. He was an enthusiast, but had
insight, energy, and resource; he had real influence over
very able men ; he staked everything in a cause for him

sacred, apparently without a thought of self; he was an enemy of England, but an open and brave enemy. He is not to be judged by passages in a careless diary, selected to hold him up to contempt; his dying words, as they may be called, were manly, pathetic, and full of real dignity.

Danger from the rebellion had now passed away, and Ireland was occupied by more than 100,000 armed men. But agrarian disturbances followed civil war; the struggle in the field was replaced by Whiteboy outrages—one of the worst features of the movements of 1796–8 reappeared in many of the southern counties. Cornwallis, however, went on steadily and honourably with the good work of clemency. Some of the prisoners in his power were transported, others were hired out to serve in the Prussian army, but the immense majority were allowed to return to their homes. The captive United Irish leaders remained; they took a step that helped the Lord-Lieutenant's policy, and promised, that, should their lives be spared, a full disclosure of the conspiracy would be made. Their confession was a skilful, but a misleading document; it told the truth, but far from the whole truth; they incurred the displeasure of the Government, and they were not released until after the Peace of Amiens, when nearly all sought a refuge in France. Arthur O'Connor and Thomas Addis Emmett, a brother of a future ill-fated rebel, were the most distinguished of these men; and some attained eminence in foreign lands, as brilliant adventurers, soldiers, and men of the gown. They had not, however, very remarkable parts, and if it does not wholly refuse them sympathy, history must severely condemn their conduct. They were carried away by the wild illusions the French Revolution spread through Europe; they had, perhaps at first, constitutional ends in view; the wrongs of their country were grievous and many. But they invited a foreign invasion to its shores; they invented the wicked myth of a general Catholic massacre; they made use of Whiteboyism to further rebellion; they are responsible for much that was worst in the rising of 1798. If not wholly, too, it was partly due to them, that the evil divisions of race and faith in the Irish community were deepened and widened, and that class was cruelly set against class; above all, that the noble ideal of Grattan, an Ireland made a real and contented nation, by the union of its peoples, under an equal law, through moderate, gradual, and just reforms, never perhaps probable, was made impossible.

In this condition of Ireland, Pitt began to make arrangements to bring about the Union. We may reject an assertion, plausibly made, and not even without authority, that the Minister let rebellion run its course in Ireland, and purposely delayed in putting it down, in order to exasperate a savage war of class; he was not only incapable of conduct of this kind, but the dates of his correspondence refute the calumny. But Pitt did not hesitate to take advantage of the existing state of the distracted country to promote a measure which he had had long at heart, and which, we have said, had been in the minds of leading English statesmen since 1782. Nor is he in the slightest degree to be blamed; an Irish Union had been one of the great works of Cromwell; it had been advocated by a series of able thinkers, from Petty and Montesquieu, to the author of the "Wealth of Nations"; it would have been joyfully accepted by the Irish Parliament as early as 1707; in the existing state of the world, and of the British Empire, the Constitution of 1782 had become a source of grave danger and trouble : a union, indeed, was perhaps a necessity of State. Pitt, however, had hitherto let things alone; for the Irish Parliament, he knew well, clung to the settlement of 1782, was jealous of its independence and power, and, certainly until the late rebellion would have rejected with scorn the thought of a union, and the Irish community would have concurred. But the opportunity appeared to have come; Ireland was in the hands of a great army; the influence of the Irish Parliament had declined, and its severities had turned thousands against it; the deep divisions of class had greatly weakened the country; Protestant Ireland was alarmed, angry, thinking of change, and this was especially the case with the landed gentry, whose Church and whose lands had been placed in peril. Catholic Ireland was in dread that it would be visited with the consequences of the late rising—perhaps with the revival of the Penal Code; and parts of it looked wistfully to England for relief. In these circumstances, Pitt thought the Union could be accomplished without probably much difficulty, and had he strenuously and boldly carried out the policy which he wished to make an essential part of the measure, without deviating into more than doubtful courses, and lending himself to questionable acts, he would have deserved the almost unqualified praise of history.

The Union, it was the intention of Pitt, was to be accompanied by a large measure of Catholic Emancipation in the fullest sense; by a provision for the Irish Catholic priesthood; and by the commutation of the tithe of the Established Church. This may have been a grand, but was not an original policy, as Macaulay and others have asserted; it had been advocated by Grattan for many years, and by the best men in the Irish Parliament. As for Catholic Emancipation, Pitt, at this time, was aware that the King was strongly opposed to it, and he gave the question up, at least for the present, having learned from Clare that the Irish Parliament would not consent to make it a part of the Union. The Union was to be what was called a Protestant Union; Pitt let this be known to the supposed leaders of Catholic Ireland, great peers and commoners, but with a broad hint that a Union would bring better things, and they assented to a Union on these conditions. Pitt, however, left the commutation of the tithes open; he was thought to be pledged on this subject, and as to an endowment for the Irish Catholic clergy, we find Cornwallis distinctly offering this in the first days of 1799, to the extreme satisfaction of the dignitaries of the Church, though the offer was, perhaps, withheld from the British Government. Pitt took other means to promote his scheme; application was made to the leading boroughmongers, who really all but controlled the Irish Parliament; these

were not reluctant if suitable terms were made ; able
pamphlets appeared in support of a Union, and a Press
was subsidised with the same object. The prospect of the
measure seemed hopeful at the close of 1798 ; but the
Minister, never well informed on Irish affairs, did not
understand the forces being arrayed against him. Protestant Ireland, for the present, rejected the thought of a
Union ; Dublin and the Irish Bar were especially adverse.
And though Catholic Ireland seemed to have been won,
and the great mass of it was quiescent and made no sign,
an active and earnest party among the Irish Catholics, that
which had bestirred itself in 1792–3, unreservedly condemned the intended project. These men perceived that
Catholic Ireland would probably, in course of time, pre-
dominate in the Irish Parliament ; they reasoned, too, as the
event proved, that Catholic Emancipation was not likely to
be easily carried in an Imperial Parliament ; they threw
their whole weight against a Union. They made it a watchword that the Penal Code was preferable with an Irish
Parliament to their existing condition under a Legislature
supreme at Westminster.

This state of opinion was to become manifest in the
Irish Parliament, with marked significance. The Speech
from the Throne as the Session opened in January, 1799,
referred cautiously to a Union ; but an amendment to the
Address—the Government had the support of Castlereagh,
lately made Chief Secretary, because, "though an Irishman he was unlike an Irishman"—was defeated by a
majority of one only, and the Government was beaten by a
majority of five on the Report of the Address. If we bear
in mind that the Irish House of Commons almost always
followed the lead of the Castle—and this had especially
been the case of late—this expression of opinion was
striking in the extreme, and though the Government obtained a majority in the Irish House of Lords, where Clare
ruled a submissive assembly, the project was not pressed
during the rest of the Session. Pitt, however, was almost
the dictator of the British House of Commons ; his pur-

pose was fixed to carry out his policy, and he was supported
by an overwhelming majority of votes.   He moved Resolutions for a Union ; his speech, one of the very few he
revised, is a good specimen of Parliamentary art, but it was
deficient in insight and mature knowledge, and his confident predictions have been largely falsified.   Pitt dexterously soothed the pride of the Irish Parliament, but he
declared that the settlement of 1782 was not meant to be
final ; he pointed out how the British and Irish Parliaments had disagreed on important subjects ; he clearly
showed how two legislatures, all but coequal in rights,
might dangerously clash, and that with the worst results,
especially at the existing time of a great war and trouble.
He abstained from committing himself on the Irish Catholic
claims, but he skilfully dangled out hopes ; were a Union to
take place the Irish Catholic would be in a better position
in an Imperial than he was in an Irish Parliament.   What
might not be expected from impartial British justice ?   The
speaker, however, did not perceive how dangerous it might
be to the State and its interests to trifle with a momentous
question, and though he glanced at "the distracted condition of Ireland," he showed that he in no sense understood
how grave and deep-seated were her political and social ills.
For the rest a Union, he asserted, would increase the prosperity of Ireland in an extraordinary way, would bring
English capital into an impoverished land, and large commercial and financial benefits ; especially it would promote
" tranquillity and heal dissension."   The Minister was
answered in the Irish House of Commons by Foster, the
Speaker, a singularly able man, and who, unlike Pitt,
thoroughly knew Ireland.   He dwelt on the fact that the
British and Irish Parliaments had not once been in dangerous and lasting conflict.   He took his stand on the
Constitution of 1782 ; he indignantly asked if a great
national compact was to be set at naught for the sake of a
plausible theory.   Foster, too, scornfully, and as the event
proved, truly denied that a Union would make Ireland
rapidly flourish ; it would certainly increase her financial

burdens ; it would probably destroy her young manufactures. And what were fictitious or imaginary hopes compared to the loss of independence, the certain increase of absenteeism on an immense scale, and the probable degradation of the Irish landed gentry ? The Speaker, however, was greatly embarrassed on one point : Foster was one of the school of Flood, opposed to the Irish Catholic cause, and he did not countenance the demands of Catholic Ireland.

Warnings such as these, however, fell on deaf ears ; the Union was to be accomplished, whatever the means. A free rein was given to the Irish Government ; Cornwallis, upright and simple-minded, "hated his dirty work ;" Castlereagh cynically acted on his maxim, that "to buy up the fee-simple of Irish corruption," was a small price to pay for a Union. The policy was systematically pursued of securing, at any cost, a majority in the Irish Parliament. Pitt followed a precedent he had made in his proposed reform of the British Parliament ; the Irish close boroughs were treated as private property ; compensation was promised to their patrons when these were extinguished by a Union ; the great boroughmongers were thus gained by a compensation that was so extravagant, that it was little better than a veiled bribe. More questionable expedients were, however, employed ; there was direct bribery, if not very large, peerages were offered with a profusion that must be called scandalous ; reluctant officials were dismissed ; seats were made vacant to procure men who would vote for a Union—"strings going out, and coming in," as was wittily said—the law against placemen being perverted to suit the Castle's purpose. The Irish Parliament was thus dishonestly packed ; but Catholic Ireland, the mass of the community, remained ; it was most important to gain its distinct assent. Pitt saw the opportunity which the well-known divisions between the followers of Flood and those of Grattan, with respect to the Catholic claims presented ; he let it be understood that no measure of Irish Catholic relief would be permitted to become law in the Irish

Parliament; and Castlereagh was informed that though
George III. would not improbably make objections, "the
principle of Catholic Emancipation was approved by the
Cabinet," and that Cornwallis "need not hesitate to call
forth all available Irish Catholic support" on behalf of a
Union. Cornwallis, heart and soul in the Catholic cause,
communicated all this to the Catholic leaders, not improbably giving a distinct pledge; and these, seeing that the
door of hope was closed in an Irish Parliament, and con-
fiding in the words of the British Minister, did all that in
them lay to promote the measure, the Catholic hierarchy
especially using their immense influence with their flocks.
Catholic Ireland was thus induced, for the most part, to
pronounce for a Union, as a condition of relief, though the
active Catholic party still stood aloof. Cornwallis also went
progress through many counties; and the authority of
the Government, always imposing, procured some addresses
for a Union at public meetings. It should be added that
a growing minority of Irish Protestants had begun to
despair of the continuance of their Parliament, and to
think of a Union; and a considerable number of the Irish
gentry were already inclining to Pitt's project, as their
only security after the events they had witnessed. The
Presbyterian North, too, hoped that a Union would improve
its staple linen trade; and the Presbyterian clergy were led
to believe that an increase would be made in the petty
stipend they received from the State.

The Irish Parliament was assembled for the last time in
the memorable Session of 1800. The King's Speech did
not refer to a Union, for the process of packing was not
complete; this was denounced by the Opposition in bitter
words. The Resolutions, however, which had been voted
at Westminster, were placed, in a few days, before the Irish
Houses; and the great measure of Pitt was fairly launched.
A long series of debates followed, marked by eminent
ability on both sides, but also by passionate and wild
invective. The case of the Government was sustained, in
the House of Commons, by Castlereagh, with capacity and

skill; he confronted furious adversaries with the intrepid calmness he exhibited through life, in the gravest crises: if not eloquent he was persuasive and lucid. He reiterated the arguments of Pitt; but dwelt especially on the benefits in commerce and finance that Ireland would attain through a Union; she would grow comparatively rich, and her Debt would diminish, words, that in view of the near future were the sorriest mockery. Clare assumed a different attitude in the House of Lords; he spoke with even more than his wonted arrogance, condemned the Opposition in scornful language; did not spare the bought and overawed nobles he dragged in his wake; and declared that since the unfortunate Relief Act of 1793, and, above all, since the late Rebellion, there was no hope for Ireland save in a Union. His sketch of the position of the landed gentry, though exaggerated, deserves attention; they were "the heirs of confiscation hemmed in by enemies brooding on their wrongs"; Ireland was at the present time on the verge of bankruptcy and general social anarchy. The Opposition arrayed a host of powerful speakers, especially ornaments of the Irish Bar; they maintained their cause by weighty and often brilliant argument. The lawyers dwelt much on the incapacity of the Irish Parliament to extinguish itself; this was urged forcibly by Saurin, Bushe, and Plunket; but the rising powers of Plunket—in after years one of the most sober debaters in the British Parliament, conspicuous for his severe and convincing logic— were most evident in savage and personal attacks on Castlereagh. Foster spoke again with characteristic insight; he laid peculiar stress on the rapid progress which Ireland had made from 1782 to 1789; once more ridiculed the predictions of Pitt; and sternly condemned the evil means that had been adopted to corrupt the Parliament. The most striking passages, however, in his speeches were those in which he reprobated the Union as a bad half measure; it merely destroyed the Irish Parliament; it did not make Great Britain and Ireland, even in theory, one; it left Ireland, in most respects, a separate State, with a shadow

of independence that, in the nature of things, would give
rise to demands to give it substance.

The master spirit, however, of these debates, indisputably
was the illustrious Grattan.   The author of the Constitution
of 1782, when it was too evident that it was in the gravest
peril, returned to the scene of his former triumphs to
defend the settlement, of which he said in after years,
"that I sate at its cradle, I followed its hearse."   Grattan
had been lately dismissed from the Privy Council, an act
of iniquitous and base spite ; he was so ill when he entered
the House of Commons, that he was unable to rise when
he made his great speech ; but genius triumphed over bodily
weakness ; the audience hung on the lips of the great
orator, whose winged words were never more keen and
convincing.   He spoke several times in the Session ; his
speeches, occasionally marked by too fierce invective,
and by mannerism straining at effect, but admirable
specimens of cogent argument, condensed in succinct
and vivid language, often flashing out in most telling
epigram, were far superior to those of any other orator.
Grattan traversed the ground which had been occupied by
the Opposition, at every point, but with a rapidity and
force that were all his own ; he charged Pitt with conspiracy
against the rights of Ireland—"the men he hanged proposed
to substitute a republic for the constitution ; he proposes to
substitute the yoke of the British Parliament"—with an
attempt to subvert a national settlement, by the foulest
and most sinister means, and with the grossest ignorance
of Irish affairs ; and he held up to ridicule and scorn, but
with masterly power, the promises made by a purblind
minister of prosperity and peace to be secured by a Union.
He denounced the corruption that had been employed to
gain the Irish Parliament, but inveighed still more fiercely
against the indirect corruption of holding expectations out
to the Irish community, especially to Presbyterian and
Catholic Ireland ; and in language unfortunately too pro-
phetic, he adjured the Irish Catholics, as their devoted
friend, not to trust Pitt or a British Parliament, but to look

to their countrymen who would yet do them justice. He
dwelt much on Foster's position that the proposed Union
was, in fact, no Union ; "it was not an identification of the
people, for it excludes the Catholics ; it is only a merger of
the Irish Parliament ; it incurs every objection to a Union,
without obtaining one object which a Union proposes ; it
is an extinction of the constitution and an exclusion of the
people." The weightiest, however, of Grattan's arguments,
that which is still of enduring interest, was that the Union by
destroying the Irish Parliament, would destroy an organ of
intelligence, in a sense national, and if far from perfect,
capable of reform, and that this would corrupt, pervert,
and envenom Irish opinion, and lead to faction, agitation,
and evil conspiracies. The peccant humours would be
driven in and would break out in disease.[1]

The Irish Parliament, however, had been made safe ; a
majority was always forthcoming for Pitt's measure. The
Opposition had, perhaps, recourse to the Government's arts
and offered money for votes ; their leaders endeavoured
to obtain addresses against a Union. Twenty Peers, too,
recorded an able protest against the scheme in the Journals
of their House, especially against its financial arrangements ;
the protest, in this respect, was before long verified. The
question was debated in the British Parliament ; the Whig
Opposition made a determined stand ; but the Minister had

---

[1] I quote this striking passage, most remarkable in view of subsequent Irish history :—"When you banish the Parliament, do you
banish the people ? Do you extinguish the sentiment ? Do you extinguish the soul ? Do you put out the spirit of liberty, when you
destroy that organ constitutional and capacious, through which the
spirit may be safely and discreetly conveyed ? What is the excellence of
our constitution ? not that it performs prodigies, and prevents the birth
of vices which are inseparable from human nature, but that it provides
an organ in which those vices may play and evaporate, and through
which the humours of society may pass without preying on the vitals.
Parliament is that body where the whole intellect of the country may
be collected, and where the spirit of patriotism, of liberty, and of
ambition, may all act under the control of that intellect, and under the
check of publicity and observation. But, if once these virtues or defects
were forced to act in secret conclave or in dark divan they would produce not opposition but conspiracy."

an immense majority, and the debates on the subject were
not very important. It deserves notice that, almost at the
last moment, proposals were made in both Parliaments to
ascertain the sense of the Irish Electorate, through a disso-
lution or some other means ; but Pitt rejected these with
haughty contempt ; they were Jacobin appeals to the
sovereign people. His decision, however, is a significant
comment on the assertions loudly made by his followers,
that Ireland, on the whole, approved the Union ; and the
petitions against the measure were more numerous, and
contained ten times more names at least than those obtained
by the Irish Government with all its efforts. The Resolutions, which had passed the Irish Parliament, were voted
again in the Houses at Westminster ; they were afterwards
turned into Bills ; and the Treaty of Union, as it was called,
became law at the close of July 1800. It is difficult to say
what was the real state of opinion in Ireland when the end
had come. Dublin, the Irish Bar, and the earnest Catholic
party apparently were as hostile as ever, as was a large
majority of the landed gentry; as probably was more than
two-thirds of Protestant Ireland. But Catholic Ireland, in
the main, approved, however feebly and under pressure ; so
did many Presbyterians and a great part of Protestant
Ireland ; and there was nothing like a general and indignant protest. Ireland, in fact, was alarmed and largely
passive ; it was felt that the measure must pass, in the
presence of a large army and of an imperious Minister ;
and a strong public opinion could not exist in a country
separated into wide divisions of race and faith which had
been greatly aggravated by late events, and without an
energetic and powerful middle class.

The Union, even as a Protestant Union, was a badly
designed and very imperfect measure. It only merged the
Irish in the Imperial Parliament ; Ireland continued to be a
distinct realm. In Foster's words, the Union left us " every
appendage of a kingdom, except what constitutes the
essence of independence, a resident Parliament ; a separate
state, a separate establishment, a separate exchequer,

separate debt, separate courts, separate laws, the Lord-Lieutenant and the Castle remained." The evil consequences have been made only too manifest ; but this was an insignificant part of the defects of the Treaty. The Union left Catholic Ireland out of its scope, that is more than three-fourths of the Irish community ; it made no provision for the commutation of the tithes, or for the endowment of the Catholic priesthood—the first being the avowed policy of Pitt, the second actually promised a few months before ; and though one of the articles pointed to a change in the oaths that prevented Catholics from entering Parliament, Catholic Emancipation, as was intended, was not referred to. The Irish Catholics, therefore, were directly wronged ; as to the most important branch of their claims, they were left to rely on the hints or promises of Pitt, on the faith of which they had pronounced for the Union, with what consequences was soon to be seen ; and a measure, which ought to have done justice to all Ireland, if it was really to be a great message of peace, was, as to the chief part of Ireland, stamped with injustice. The constitutional arrangements of the Union, apart from the grave error condemned by Foster, do not require to be noticed at length. The Irish House of Lords was, of course, abolished ; but Ireland was to be represented in the Imperial House by 28 Peers elected for life, and by 4 Prelates of the Established Church ; and the Irish Peers were to retain their titles. The Irish House of Commons was also extinguished and 200 of the Irish seats ; but the Irish counties were to return 64 members, and the Irish boroughs and the University 36, in all 100 members to the Imperial Parliament. The perpetual maintenance of the Established Church was made a fundamental part of the Union—time was to prove the value of this security ; the settlement of the land was not changed, the Irish gentry relying readily on this with what results to their successors was to be shown by recent legislation of the Imperial Parliament. It should be added that while the Union left undone what it was essential to do, the corrupt pledges to the boroughmongers were faithfully carried out; "honour," in the poet's words, "rooted in dishonour stood," and the huge sum for compensation was charged to the Irish National Debt, a piece of financial sharp practice which needs no comment.

The commercial provisions of the Union were simple in principle; the trade in raw products between Great Britain and Ireland was made more free than it had been before; the trade in manufactures was still largely restricted, and countervailing duties were retained to keep up equality. The financial arrangements were more important; the subject is one of present and grave interest. Pitt, a disciple of Adam Smith, resolved, in his own words, to "assimilate Great Britain and Ireland ultimately in finance," that is, to place Great Britain and Ireland under the same fiscal system; but he saw that this would be thoroughly unjust, nay, impossible, at the time of the Union. The National Debt of Ireland, in 1800-1, had increased from rather more than £2,000,000 to £28,000,000; but it was even now not a fifteenth of that of England and Scotland; Pitt, besides, knew well that a very poor country could not fairly bear the burdens of a very rich country; it was out of the question, therefore, at this conjuncture to apply the principle of financial unity to the Three Kingdoms. The Union, accordingly, provided that Ireland was to pay a contribution of two-seventeenths of the whole, that is rather more than 12 per cent., to the expenditure of the entire State, England and Scotland contributing about 88 per cent.; and care was taken that this proportion should be subject to revision after twenty years. The Treaty enacted, too, that should the Debts of Great Britain and Ireland be extinguished, or should the contributions, thus adjusted, become to the Debts in the same proportion, Parliament might change the existing order of things and bring Ireland under the British fiscal system; but this was to be expressly subject to the proviso, that Ireland, and, indeed, Scotland,¹ were to have special "exemptions and abate-

---

¹ The proviso was no doubt extended to Scotland because the Union with Scotland was repeatedly referred to in the debates on the Irish Union.

ments " of taxation, should the circumstances of the case
require ; and Pitt and Castlereagh over and over again
announced, that the meaning of these technical words was
that Ireland was not to be unfairly taxed, that is, out of
proportion to her own resources. There is no reason to
doubt that Pitt believed that the contribution of the two-
seventeenths was not more than Ireland ought to make ; but
the charge was declared to be grossly unjust by Foster,
Grattan, and other leading Irishmen ; and this was a chief
part of the protest of the twenty peers referred to. As so
often happened in Irish affairs, Pitt's calculations proved to
be altogether false, while those of his opponents were ere
long verified.

Pitt certainly intended to complete the Union by what he
deemed its required supplements, Catholic Emancipation,
the commutation of the tithe, and a provision for the Irish
Catholic priesthood. This was his policy ; his honour was
practically pledged. He had taken a crooked and unfortunate course ; he doubtless relied on his powerful influence
to overcome the avowed objections of the King, of which he
had been for some years cognisant. But Pitt was betrayed
by his own Chancellor ; George III. was persuaded that his
coronation oath precluded him from assenting to an Act of
Parliament making further concessions to Irish Catholics, a
monstrous idea scouted by his own law-officers ; the Cabinet
became divided in mind ; and the King peremptorily refused
to give his sanction to Catholic Emancipation in any sense,
though he might perhaps have accepted the two other
measures of the first importance even by themselves. Pitt
resigned his office with his leading followers ; he is
entitled to any credit that belongs to this step ; but George
III. had shown, in a number of instances, that he would
not resist the will of a resolute Minister ; and regard being
had to the great interests at stake, and to what must be
considered his own promises, Pitt ought to have insisted on
giving effect to his policy. He did not take the line of duty
which would have led to success ; this is the more censur-
able because Cornwallis soon afterwards informed the

Catholic leaders that Pitt and his party were pledged to further the Catholic claims; and Pitt's resignation only caused the absolute failure of the three great reforms which should have been a part of the Union if it was to be a real harbinger of tranquillity and social progress.

The subsequent conduct of Pitt cannot be justified in the mature judgment of impartial history. He let his master know after a few days that he would not urge the Catholic claims again in the reign; he steadily supported an Anti-Catholic Ministry; he was, perhaps, willing to join it on certain conditions; when he returned to office in 1804 he completely abandoned the Catholic cause. Excuses, no doubt, can be made for him; the King became insane, and Pitt naturally shrank from irritating an aged sovereign by untimely proposals; it was, perhaps, necessary, even after the Peace of Amiens, to add the strength of Pitt to a weak Government; Pitt probably reasoned that, after all, he had accomplished the Union, his main object, and had made a great Imperial interest secure, and that all the rest might be postponed to a more convenient season; and he may easily have deemed his presence at the helm of the State essential when the war broke out again and Napoleon's army was gathering as a mighty tempest near our shores, and that too without too nice a regard to his previous conduct as a man and a statesman. But one cardinal fact stands out from this tortuous maze of inconsistency and intrigues; Catholic Ireland was as certainly betrayed as she was in many passages of her unhappy history; the calamitous results may be traced to this hour, and Pitt is gravely responsible for them. Nor can we forget that Napoleon and his terrors are gone, and that discontented Catholic Ireland remains. [1]

[1] For the history of the Union and its incidents the reader may be referred to the Debates in the British and the Irish Parliaments, and especially to the Cornwallis and Castlereagh Correspondence, the Colchester Diary and the Malmesbury Correspondence. The Treaty should, of course, be studied; its financial arrangements are fully set forth in the late Report of the Childers Commission. Mr. Lecky's narrative is exhaustive and just. The policy and conduct of Pitt may be collected from the same authorities; and see Stanhope's Life of Pitt and

The Union was not only a mutilated piece of work, in which the best of the design was left out, it was effected at a most unfortunate time. Pitt had expressed a hope, in stately Virgilian numbers, that Great Britain and Ireland, "unconquered nations," would be blended together in "perpetual concord"; what was the prospect of this consummation in 1800–1? England was seeking a truce with her ancient enemy, and was soon to be involved in a death struggle in which she was forced to contend for existence. The nation was ruled by the reactionary faith which grew out of hatred of the French Revolution; narrow Toryism prevailed in its councils; it was an unpropitious season to take in hand the government of a backward dependency that required a progressive, a generous, and a sympathetic policy. Ireland, on the other hand, had been half ruined by a barbarous civil war; the animosities of its races and faiths had been fatally quickened; and not only the momentous Catholic Question, but other social questions of the first importance, were requiring consideration and treatment; was it probable, at this conjuncture, that they would be rightly treated? Nor was the Imperial Parliament, in which the voice of Ireland would be feeble, discordant, and very ill understood, an institution adapted to legislate for and to administer a poor and distracted country, especially as Great Britain and Ireland were on levels of civilisation altogether different, as the mass of Englishmen and most English statesmen knew very little about Ireland, and regarded her as almost a foreign land, and as Ireland was in need of measures of reform repugnant to ordinary English ideas. In the interests of the Empire the Union, perhaps, was a necessity of State when the

---

Sir G. Lewis's "Administrations of Great Britain." Lord Rosebery ("Pitt," pp. 224–26), attempts to justify the Minister; but the biographer is as superficial as he is in the case of Lord Fitzwilliam; he ignores three-fourths of the charges that he was bound to answer, and impliedly admits them; and we can only smile at the jaunty statement that George III. would not have yielded on the Catholic Question, when we bear in mind the antecedents and the character of the King.

Treaty was made; in the interests of Ireland it was, perhaps, to be desired that it should alike have been a complete measure, and should have been postponed to a more auspicious era.

CHAPTER III

THE RISE OF O'CONNELL—CATHOLIC EMANCIPATION

Ireland after the Union—Emmett's rebellion—Severe measures of repression—Pitt rejects the Irish Catholic claims—Grattan in the Imperial Parliament—The Catholic Question after 1807—Rise and character of O'Connell—His first exertions in the Catholic cause—The Veto—Schism in Catholic Ireland—Progress of the Catholic Question—Plunket—Peel—Death of Grattan—Ulster becomes attached to the Union—Increase of the Regium Donum—Protestant Ascendency—Orangeism—Ribbonism—Increase of English influences in Ireland and the results—The Irish financial arrangements of 1816-17—Material progress of Ireland during the war—Disastrous change afterwards—Increase of population—The effects on the Land system—Irish rents and wages—Increase of evictions—The resulting evils—The want of a Poor Law—The cheap code of ejectment—Whiteboyism and agrarian disorder—Peel Chief Secretary—Merits and defects of his rule in Ireland—The Irish Constabulary force—George IV. visits Ireland. His welcome—Outburst of agrarian crime and famine in 1822—Progress of the Catholic Question in Parliament—Plunket's speech—Attitude of the House of Lords—O'Connell founds the Catholic Association—His objects and policy—The Irish priesthood—The Catholic Association acquires formidable power—Attempts to suppress it prove vain—The Bill of 1825 and "the wings"—Rejected by the House of Lords—Liberal Protestants returned at the General Election of 1826—The Clare Election—Triumph of O'Connell—Catholic Emancipation reluctantly conceded.

THE Addington Ministry was one after the King's heart; it was formed to resist the claims of Catholic Ireland. Its representative at the Castle was Lord Hardwicke, a plain but upright and sensible country gentleman; Clare retained the Irish Seals for a time. The hills of Wicklow were not

quite at rest, and there was agrarian disorder in parts of the
South ; the first Irish measures of the Imperial Parliament
were to renew, but for some months only, repressive legislation of the Irish Parliament, especially Indemnity Acts to
screen official blunders, a fact left out of sight by English
writers. In a short time Ireland was comparatively at peace,
and remained so for fully two years ; the real causes of this
may be briefly noticed. The Peace of Amiens and the
departure of the United Irish leaders for the moment
extinguished treasonable hopes; the barbarities of 1798 had
long ceased ; a reaction followed the excitement the Union
had caused ; and all this tended to promote tranquillity.
The Government, too, though avowedly anti-Catholic—the
doors of the Castle were closed to the heads of the Irish
Catholics—was, nevertheless, impartial to all classes ; its
equitable administration was highly praised by Grattan ; the
Catholic leaders still put their trust in Pitt ; and Hardwicke
not only continued the policy of his amiable and humane
predecessor, but won golden opinions by devoting funds to
the restoration of Catholic places of worship which had
been destroyed in the late rebellion. Not the least cause,
perhaps, of this season of repose, was the disappearance of
Clare from the scene of events. He had bitterly resented
Pitt's conduct in encouraging Irish Catholic hopes ; he was
indignant that the Minister had condemned the atrocities
which he endeavoured to defend ; he soon discovered that
the House of Lords at Westminster was not to be brow-
beaten like the House of Lords in Dublin ; and he became
a mere cypher in that proud assembly. He was, in a word,
disappointed, angry, and sick at heart ; and an accident
brought on a lingering illness, of which he died when
scarcely past the prime of life. He was certainly one of the
greatest Irishmen of his day ; it is impossible to deny that
he gave proof of great ability, firmness, and courage
during the crisis of 1797–8. But he was a principal agent
in designing and carrying out the evil policy, which
dashed the hopes of Catholic Ireland and helped to drive
it into rebellious courses ; and the deeds of blood and

wickedness to which he at least gave countenance, provoked much that was worst in the rising of 1798.

A conspiracy, however, followed by a sudden armed outbreak, which, though abortive, might have had grave results, disturbed the quiet of Ireland in the summer of 1803. The United Irish leaders, after the late amnesty, had, we have seen, for the most part, repaired to France. In that congenial soil they began to renew the designs they had formed against British rule in Ireland. They were divided, however, by the jealous discords which have so often proved fatal to Irish plotters. Napoleon treated them at first with ill-concealed contempt,[1] though he held them, so to speak, in the leash, should he desire to let them slip on a future occasion ; when troubles with England began to thicken, he lent a willing ear to what they had to say ; and a young enthusiast, Robert Emmett, a brother of one of the ablest of these men, had an interview, it is believed, with the First Consul, and proposed to stir up rebellion in Ireland again, to be assisted by an armed descent from France. Emmett set off for Ireland in the autumn of 1802, but it is tolerably certain that he received no countenance at any time from the ruler of France, or even from the chief United Irish leaders. He was, however, sanguine, reckless, and daring ; he gradually surrounded himself with obscure chiefs of the risings in Wexford and around Dublin ; and he was aided by the counsels of Miles Byrne, a capable subordinate of Father John Murphy, and in after years a brilliant soldier of France. A plan of operations took regular shape ; pikes and other weapons of the late rebellion were collected secretly and in large quantities ; the project of 1798 was revived, as old indeed as that of 1641 ; the Castle was to be seized and the Government destroyed by armed bands

---

[1] Napoleon's estimate of the United Irish leaders, placed on record many years afterwards at St. Helena, deserves notice (Corr. 32, p. 328), "Je n'avais de confiance ni dans l'integrité ni dans les talents des meneurs irlandais qui étaient en France. Ils n'avaient aucun plan à soumettre, étaient divisés d'opinion, et se querellaient continuellement entre eux."

marching in from the neighbouring counties and by the disaffected mob of the capital, barricades being thrown up to paralyse the troops, an idea borrowed, perhaps, from experience in Paris.   The conspirators, however, had traitors in their midst ; the Government was made aware of what was going on, and the "rebellion" ended in an affray in a street of Dublin, unhappily causing the murder of Lord Kilwarden, one of the most eminent of Irish judges, notable for his clemency on the Bench in a dark and evil time.   Emmett was arrested and executed a few weeks afterwards ; he is a hero of rebellious Irish tradition, but history has nothing to say in his praise. ‾

This petty rising caused great alarm in Ireland, and in England provoked indignant wrath, engaged as she was in a death struggle with France.   Strong measures of defence and repression were taken ; the army in Ireland was raised to 15,000 men, though an immense invasion threatened the coast of Kent ; the whole Irish yeomanry force was called out, a grave incentive to evil Orange passions ; the Habeas Corpus Act was suspended in every Irish county ; whole districts were placed under martial law ; military courts were established to try offences that seemed to endanger the State, and even the rights of property.   This system of coercion was to be regretted, no doubt ; it continued with a slight intermission throughout the war, and with partial relaxations for years afterwards ; and, instead of remedies, it was injudiciously applied to social troubles connected with the land and with the exactions of the Established Church, with respect to which it was almost worse than useless.   But a treasonable party with French sympathies existed in Ireland until after Waterloo.   It should be borne in mind that Grattan, through life hostile to the French Revolution and all that pertained to it, gave his high sanction to this very policy ; nor can we forget how great was the national peril when the Grand Army was encamped round Boulogne and the modern Cæsar seemed about to descend on Britain.   The conduct of Napoleon to the United Irish leaders at this critical juncture was characteristic of the man. His opinion of their qualities never changed; but he flattered them as he flattered other "patriots" of peoples of which he desired to make use; he pledged himself, it is said,[1] to Thomas Addis Emmett, that, in the event of a successful descent, Ireland should be treated as France had treated our revolted colonies in the Great War of 1776–83; and an invasion of Ireland has a distinct place in his second great project of invading England.[2] Napoleon dealt, in a word, with Irishmen as he had dealt with Italians and as he was to deal with the Poles in 1807 and 1812; Ireland was to be an instrument to serve his ambitious plans; and meanwhile he turned to excellent account the elements of Irish disaffection to his hands in France. He made Arthur O'Connor a General of the Grand Army; formed an Irish Legion out of the waifs and strays of the rebel levies of 1798; gave it an eagle in homage to Irish pride; and as Hannibal made the Italian Celt his own, he mastered the hearts of a devoted Irish soldiery. The Irish Legion was stationed along the coasts of Brittany as long as a prospect of assailing England remained, but when Trafalgar had closed this page in the Book of Fate the Legion followed the standards of the Grand Army, and sank into its enormous masses. It crossed swords with the hated Saxon in Spain; left hundreds of brave men on the snows of Russia; in a word, proved itself to be a worthy successor of the famous Irish Brigade of another age,[3] "ever and everywhere true" to the Bourbon lilies. As late even as 1840 a few survivors of the Legion offered their swords to France when she seemed about to engage in a quarrel with England.

When Pitt returned to office in 1804, the Irish Catholic leaders—the chief of these was Lord Fingall, the head of one

---

[1] The memorandum of Napoleon appears at length in Mitchell's "History of Ireland," vol. ii. p. 100. It is not to be found in the "Napoleon Correspondence," but much of this has been suppressed.

[2] Napoleon Corr. vol. ix. p. 557.

[3] "Semper et ubique fideles" was the motto on the standards of the Irish Brigade.

of the great houses of the Pale—waited on the Minister to
prefer their claims. They had given proof of admirable
loyalty in the affair of Emmett; they were confident, with
good reason, in the prospects of their cause. Cornwallis,
we have seen, had distinctly let them know that Pitt and his
followers were pledged to do them full justice; he had
placed two remarkable papers in their hands, the import
of which was not doubtful. Cornwallis, it is true, had
explained afterwards that he was in error in announcing
a positive pledge; but affairs of State, and even of ordinary
life, could not be conducted if a colleague, in the position
of Cornwallis, could not bind a superior by the assertions
he had made. It is idle to deny the obligations of Pitt; but
he coolly threw his petitioners over, "though extremely
polite"—are Fingall's words—"he gave us not the most
distant hope," though "he expressed his own opinion as
to the good policy of the measure." The Catholic leaders
now addressed Lord Grenville and Fox; their claims
were urged in the Houses of Lords and Commons in able
debates, the first of a long series; but they were rejected by
large majorities in both Houses. The occasion was remarkable as that on which Grattan appeared for the first time in
the Imperial Parliament; he had been returned by his
friend Fitzwilliam for the borough of Malton. His
mannerism and impassioned gestures were never congenial
to English taste. Pitt regarded the great speaker for a few
moments with contempt. But he soon found that he was
in the presence of a true orator—the Irish Demosthenes
Fox observed—and Grattan's speech, the first of many of the
same kind, if perhaps not one of his very best, was a splendid
piece of eloquence. He trampled down a crazy fanatic
whom he deigned to answer;[1] denounced as monstrous the
doctrine that the Catholic—the tapestry of the Armada
refutes the falsehood—was necessarily, and from his creed,
a traitor to England; contended that the ills of Ireland
were due to the long misgovernment of the past, and not to

---

[1] Dr. Duigenan, a zealot and a buffoon hardly worthy of the bolts of
Grattan, a fit mark for the light shafts of Moore's satire.

Catholicism, as a system of faith; and truly pointed out that, as affairs now stood, the half liberty of the Irish Catholic must either lead to complete liberty or to endless troubles and danger to the State. The orator, however, was perhaps most effective when he urged that the rights of conscience were real rights of man, not after the fantastic ideal of Rousseau; that the principles of the Revolution of 1688 involved the emancipation of the Irish Catholic; above all, that Protestant England and Catholic Ireland should be reconciled at the existing crisis, and present a combined front against a mighty common enemy. The reply of Pitt, if evasive and weak, was pathetic; he probably felt that his end was near; he declared that he was in favour of the Catholic claims "on principle," but that "an irresistible obstacle stood in the way."

The short-lived ministry of "All the Talents" was not without significance in the affairs of Ireland, but left no permanent mark on them. Fox honestly told the Catholic leaders that it was impossible, at the time, to press their claims; but he intimated that a change would be made in the whole system of Irish government, in the interest of conciliation and peace. This promise was, in the main, fulfilled; the Lord-Lieutenant, the Duke of Bedford, though in no sense a remarkable man, did much to satisfy Irish feelings and hopes; and his departure from the Castle was attended by a loud expression of popular regret. Grattan was restored to the seat at the Privy Council, from which he ought never to have been removed, and was invited by Fox to take high office; a number of Orange magistrates were dismissed from the Bench; more impartial men were put in their places; prosecutions were dropped that should not have been instituted; above all, the severest measures of repression were not renewed by Parliament, and Ireland was governed, for some months, by the ordinary law of the land. Ere long, however, it was found impossible, so questionable still was the state of the country, to avoid having recourse to the coercive system; this, as we have seen, was acknowledged by Grattan; the

Ministry, before it fell, had prepared measures to deal with Irish disaffection and crime almost as harsh and restrictive as those of 1803. At the accession of the Portland and Percival Administration to power, the Duke of Richmond was made Lord-Lieutenant ; he continued to preside at the Castle for rather a long period. His convivial habits and splendid festivities were remembered in Irish society for many years, but as a ruler and statesman he was a mere figurehead ; he simply obeyed the orders he received from Downing Street ; and these were to return, in all respects, to the system of Protestant Ascendency long prevalent, to discourage in every way the Catholic cause, and to govern Ireland, if necessary, by a rod of iron. The Duke, however, had one Chief Secretary whose conduct requires a passing notice. Arthur Wellesley had sat in the Irish Parliament ; he had seconded the Address when the great measure of Catholic relief became law in 1793 ; he was well acquainted with the condition of Ireland ; he had already had a distinguished career in India. He was at the Castle for a few months in 1807–8 ; it might have been supposed that so eminent a man would have had real influence in Irish affairs and government. But Wellesley characteristically kept to the ordinary round of a subordinate's duty ; and though he was too sagacious not to perceive clearly that there was much rotten in the state of Ireland, especially in her administration and landed relations, he did little more than carry out the business placed in his hands, that is the management of elections, the dealing with patronage, and the preparation of coercive measures. With respect to Ireland, indeed, he never exhibited the profound insight and wisdom of which he gave proof in Spain, and in the councils of Europe.

Ireland continued to be under the mode of government to which we have before referred ; it is unnecessary to follow the dreary tale of administration working through severe repression, and of Protestant Ascendency apparently secure. During the years that succeeded the fall of the Fox-Grenville Ministry, the Catholic question was often brought before Parliament; Grattan, as always, was its most powerful champion. But it made no real way in the Houses at Westminster, though the majorities against him rather declined; at the General Election of 1807 England had pronounced against the Irish Catholic cause; many forces, indeed, concurred to defeat it. Canning and Castlereagh, no doubt, were on Grattan's side, but Canning and Castlereagh soon quarrelled, and Percival and the rest of the members of the Liverpool Government were decidedly adverse to the Catholic claims. These, indeed, had little chance of an impartial hearing in the existing state of English and Scottish opinion. A harsh and narrow Toryism ruled the national councils. Things as they were, were to be steadily maintained, whether for good or for evil made no difference. The spirit, too, that prevailed in the Church of England, was very hostile to the Irish Catholics; the Evangelical party, perhaps the strongest, abhorred Popery and all its works; the Erastian party, also very strong, would not hear of a change that might weaken or even shake the Established Church in Ireland. The national sentiment, too, moved in the same direction; Catholic Ireland visibly inclined towards France; was this the time to favour the Irish Catholic, when Napoleon had armed against England more than half of Europe, and was virtually the head of the Catholic Church on the Continent? These opinions were more than once confirmed by unwise utterances of French bishops, and by an imaginary statement of Pius VII. and until the fortunes of the war had begun to change, there was scarcely a hope for the Catholic cause.

Ten years had passed away since the Union; the Irish Catholics had been cruelly deceived; their prospects appeared to be all but hopeless. Fingall, too, and his aristocratic followers, loyal and earnest as they were, had altogether failed; the predictions of the small active party, which had resented the Union, had been fulfilled. Even that party had almost ceased to stir, since Pitt had rejected the Catholic claims; from 1803 to 1807 it was represented on the committee in Dublin by only one public man of ᵣᵢᵣk, John Keogh, a veteran of 1792–3. Meanwhile, however, a real leader was being gradually formed in its ranks, a leader who was to remove the shackles which still kept Catholic Ireland down, and to bring it fully within the Pale of the State, and was long to play a conspicuous part in Irish, British, and even European politics. Daniel O'Connell was born in 1775, a scion of an old family of Kerry Celts, which had suffered much in the civil wars of Ireland, and from the oppression of the Penal Code, but had retained parts of its ancestral lands, had sent distinguished soldiers to the Irish Brigade,[1] and had never lost its place among the landed gentry. O'Connell, although an Irish Catholic, and belonging to a degraded people, had thus associations with the dominant Protestant caste ; we see the twofold influence in his career ; and it had a marked effect on his acts and his conduct. The nature of the man and his training from youth made him admirably fitted to become the champion of Catholic Ireland, and to promote its cause, and at the same time, to avoid the perilous courses, which had led the United Irishmen astray, and even to conciliate much that was best and most enlightened in Irish opinion. O'Connell had the cunning and craft of a conquered race—with the brilliancy and sanguine temper of the Celt, he possessed the hard common sense of the Saxon, his sagacity, his political instinct, and circumstance, in his early years, strongly developed these qualities. As a boy he had been an adept in smuggling—then a common traffic among the Kerry gentry. In his first manhood at the Irish Bar, he became not only a great lawyer but a master of the intricacies of the law, especially in its arts of delay and evasion. He was brought up for a time in France by priests of her old Church ; under this teaching he became a devout Catholic, and acquired deep Conservative sympathies, an attachment to monarchy, property, and the existing

---

[1] The most remarkable of these was Count O'Connell, an uncle of Daniel, most honourably referred to in General Thiébault's Memoirs. Count O'Connell hated the Revolution, and distrusted Napoleon.

order of things ; and he witnessed the excesses of the Revolution, which made so profound an impression on him, that
in his chequered career he always condemned anarchic lawlessness and mere mob violence. These influences had such
an effect on him that, he said, they " made him almost a
Tory," when he went back to Ireland ; but the cruel deeds
of the men in power at the Castle, and the sufferings of his
race in 1798, turned him into the ranks of the discontented
Catholics, who condemned the policy of Camden and Clare,
yet wished to preserve their country's Parliament. O'Connell, however, retained through life what he learned in
France ; and if he became a great popular tribune, and even
directed powerful popular movements, he had the leanings
and tendencies of a real statesman, far-sighted, prudent,
ready to compromise, averse to wild theories and sudden
changes ; there was little in him of the mere demagogue,
extravagant and reckless as often was his language.

O'Connell was still an unknown lawyer when he joined
the small but earnest Catholic body, which vehemently protested against the Union. He spoke with marked ability at
its meetings in Dublin ; he was the author, it is believed, of
its watchword, that it was better to recur to the Penal Code
than for Catholic Ireland to lose the Parliament, in which its
influence was certain to increase. Though kept back by
judges of Orange tendencies, and by restrictions of the Act of
1793, which excluded him from the rank of King's Counsel,
he soon acquired a prominent place at the Bar ; and he
became a leading member of the Association, which, we have
seen, still upheld the Catholic cause in Dublin. The Catholic
petition of 1807—temperate, but firm in its language—was,
it is said, from his hand ; in 1810, when thirty-five years old,
he was elected Chairman of the Committee by a unanimous
vote, and thenceforward became its master spirit.   Fingall
and the other Catholic peers and gentlemen were relegated
to a secondary place ; Keogh was removed from his post
with words of honour ; and the direction of the Irish
Catholic movement passed virtually into O'Connell's hands.
Since 1805 the Committee had done scarcely anything, and

had even recommended a "policy of silent dignity"; but
"agitate, agitate" was the new leader's teaching; he at once
gave a real impulse to the Catholic cause. His ideas, at
first, were, perhaps, rather crude, and borrowed from those
of another day; the Central Committee in Dublin affiliated
itself to local committees throughout the country; an
organisation was thus established in order to promote the
Catholic claims, and for some months it seemed full of
promise. A combination like this, however, was held to be
a violation of the well-known Convention Act, passed after
the Relief Act of 1793, and prohibiting assemblies of a
representative kind. Fingall and other leaders were placed
under arrest; and O'Connell declared the Committee and
its dependent bodies dissolved. Skilled in eluding the law,
but acting within it, he set up in its stead a "Catholic
Board," with "aggregate meetings" in different parts of
Ireland; this arrangement baffled the men of the gown
at the Castle; and the "agitation"—he had made the word
his own—was kept up during the years that followed. The
movement, however, was weak and faint; it was retarded by
a concurrence of causes; Catholic Ireland, in fact, was
divided and had lost heart. The leader, who was to win
its battle, was for a time a commander without an army to
command.

O'Connell, however, never gave up hope; he turned
this interval of time to admirable account. His position
at the Bar had become commanding; he was in the
first rank of Irish advocates, and eminent above all in the
conduct of causes; in the political trials in which he was
always engaged, he employed his powerful, if somewhat
rude eloquence in denouncing the wrongs of Catholic
Ireland, and, indirectly, in pressing its demands. He held
up to execration and contempt Protestant juries packed to
make verdicts safe, and Protestant judges when mere
partisans; he indignantly asked how the Irish Catholic
could obtain justice, even in its highest place, under the
order of things in which he was forced to exist. He also
wrote much in the Irish Catholic Press, and, indeed, had

the chief direction of it ; he was in constant correspondence with leading Irish priests, an order of men he had
begun to court, and whose possible influence in the State he
clearly perceived. By these means he attracted Catholic
Ireland to him ; and he gradually gave a turn to Irish
opinion, which ultimately had important results. In these
years, too, he publicly adopted a course which, he declared,
when dying, was the one next to his heart, if more than
once he seems to have trifled with it. In 1810, and for
some time afterwards, there was a feeble movement in
Dublin against the Union. Grattan gave it a somewhat
qualified support ; but O'Connell boldly pronounced in its
favour, and made more than one remarkable speech on the
subject. He dwelt much, and with pregnant truth, on the
ignorance of British statesmen in Irish affairs, on the
incapacity of the Imperial Parliament to deal wisely with
Irish questions, on the foreign character of its legislation,
and its administrative rule ; and he earnestly adjured
" Irishmen, of every race and faith, to put their evil animosities
aside, and to unite in the interests of a common country,
to acquire again a Parliament taken from them by force and
fraud." O'Connell, indeed, it is scarcely doubtful, had often
Grattan's ideal before his mind, but an ideal not to be
realised by Grattan's methods, and with consequences, in
many respects, of a very different kind.

At this period, however, and for years afterwards,
O'Connell gave his best energies to the Catholic Question.
A remarkable incident divided and even threatened to arrest
a movement already halting and feeble. In 1799, when a
provision for the Irish Catholic clergy was, we have seen,
offered to the heads of their Church, they agreed that
appointments to the Episcopate should be made subject to
a Veto on the part of the Crown, in order to secure the
loyalty of personages of immense authority. This arrangement conformed to the policy of the Holy See, in many
instances, in the eighteenth century ; it was afterwards illustrated in a signal way, by the celebrated Concordat made by
Napoleon ; but after the Union the subject was let drop, like

others of Pitt's unfulfilled projects. In 1808, however, Dr.
Milner, acting as a Catholic prelate in England, declared that
Pius VII. would accept the Veto ; the statement was repeated
by Quarantotti, one of the Vatican's chief counsellors, when
the Pontiff was a prisoner at Fontainebleau. Fingall, and the
Irish Catholic leaders of the aristocratic type, unanimously
agreed to a settlement of the kind ; the principal English
and Scottish Catholics concurred ; and from 1808 onwards,
during several years, when the Catholic claims were advanced
in Parliament, the Veto was made a part of them. O'Connell,
however, from the beginning denounced the project ; he
never opposed an endowment of the Irish priesthood ; but
he would not hear of making the Bishops of his faith
dependent on the State, and subjecting the Irish Catholic
Church to it. The Veto, he insisted, would bring the "evil
Castle influence" into every diocese, nay, every parish ;
it would make the clergy mere tools of the Government ; it
would be better for the Church to have the kind of freedom
it had even under the Penal Code, than to be in the fetters
of sinister and alien power. He took his stand, indeed, on
the very position which Burke had taken before on this
subject [1] ; whether he was right or wrong, he clearly perceived that the Veto and all that it involved would interfere
with a project he had already in view, the combination of
the Irish priesthood and the mass of the people in a great
movement on behalf of the Catholic cause. The efforts of
O'Connell, urged in impassioned speeches, and in correspondence through all parts of Ireland, were soon attended
with complete success ; the Irish Catholic Bishops, after a
moment of doubt, declared that they would not submit to
the Veto ; the inferior clergy, and the immense majority

[1] The remarks of Burke, "Works," vol. i. p. 537, Edition 1834,
deserve attention. I have only space for a sentence from his " Letter
to a Peer," on a policy analogous to that of the Veto :—" How can a
Lord-Lieutenant . . . discern which of the popish priests is fit to
be a bishop ? . . . No man, no set of men living, are fit to administer
the affairs, or regulate the economy of a church to which they are
enemies. . . . Never were the members of one religious sect fit to
appoint the pastors of another."

of the Irish Catholics pronounced against it. The triumph of O'Connell was beyond dispute, but it led to a schism and discords very injurious to the Catholic cause, in Ireland at least. Fingall and his adherents broke with O'Connell, and ceased to attend the Catholic Board; the English and Scottish Catholics condemned the Irish leader, more especially because he had taken the conduct of the Catholic Question out of the hands of Grattan, a striking proof of his rapidly growing influence. The movement, abandoned by its aristocratic heads, seemed in Ireland left to the direction only of a lawyer without rank, and a body of inferior clergy.

The Catholic cause, however, though kept back in Ireland, began to make its way in the Imperial Parliament, when the events of the war turned against Napoleon. The question had been left an open question by Lord Liverpool; and Grattan, with the powerful support of Canning, in 1813 brought in a Bill conceding most of the Catholic claims, which passed a second reading in the House of Commons. It contained, however, clauses, added by Canning, which expressed the policy of the Veto in an offensive form; these were severely condemned by O'Connell, and the measure ere long was lost in committee. Though its acknowledged champion no more, Grattan continued during the following years to press the claims of Catholic Ireland; his speeches were invariably worthy of him; and he found a great adherent in Plunket, who had lately made his way into Parliament and whose speech on the Catholic Question in 1813 gave presage of the renown of an orator, perhaps, without an equal in the assembly that hung on the lips of Brougham and Canning. The majorities against the Irish Catholics declined by degrees; the mind of England and Scotland became less adverse as the national sentiment against them was not now aroused; and their claims were upheld by the whole Whig party rising once more into credit in the State, and by the best and most enlightened intellect of the day. This preponderance of mental and moral force was significant, but one advocate of the first

order made his influence felt on the opposite side. Peel
had entered the House of Commons in 1809; he was soon
recognised as the most capable and eminent adversary of
the Catholic cause. The speech he made on the subject
in 1817, when he had not completed his thirtieth year,
contains the views he held on the question until he was
compelled to recede from them; it was certainly one of
his ablest efforts, and characteristic of the great coming
statesman. He set theological squabbles aside and attached
no weight to the foolish assertion that a Catholic was
necessarily an enemy of a Protestant State. He rather took
his stand on the ground held by Clare, but avoiding Clare's
arrogance and insulting language; he contended that, in
the existing order of things in Ireland, the institutions of
the country, which, for good or for evil, were framed to
maintain a Protestant minority in power, and to secure
it in the possession of the great mass of the land, would
inevitably, and from the nature of the case, be placed in
danger were a great majority of hostile Catholics admitted
to equal privileges and rights; and he dwelt much on the
sanctity of the Union, as a guarantee of the status of the
Established Church in Ireland, which Catholic Emancipation, he was convinced, would assuredly subvert. The
speech was cautious, dexterous, full of the spirit of
expediency and prudence which distinguished Peel; it
certainly embodied much that was true, but it did not
rise to the full height of the argument.

O'Connell repudiated an advocate of the Veto, though
he has paid a high tribute to Grattan's genius, yet if
Catholic Ireland had almost thrown him off, the great
patriot "clung with desperate fidelity" to its cause. He
did not live to see that cause triumph; but after the last
speech he made, in a debate in 1819, the majority against
him was two only. He died revered and lamented the
next year; his is, perhaps, the noblest figure in Irish history.
Nature gave Grattan a keen and profound intellect, the
passion and force of a true orator, the wisdom and moderation of a real statesman. A patriot from youth he denounced

the wrongs of his country; he was the Washington of the Revolution of 1782, the master-builder of the transformed Irish Parliament. The independence of that assembly was dear to his heart; but the great Irishman was a loyal friend of England; he was always true to the British connection. He sought to reform the Irish Parliament, but within just and constitutional limits; he earnestly laboured, when its leading spirit, to bring Catholic Ireland within the Pale of the State; but he detested the United Irish faith and revolutionary ideas of all kinds; he was a firm supporter of order, and of the rights of property. He properly condemned the evil deeds of the men at the Castle before 1798; he tried to prevent the effects by a healing policy; but no thought of disaffection crossed his mind; his only protest against wrong when he failed, was to leave Parliament. He rightly denounced the means employed to bring about the Union; his predictions of its results have been largely fulfilled; he admirably pointed out its grave defects; but he accepted the compact in his later years. "The marriage has been made," he once said, "let us make it fruitful." In the Imperial Parliament he was, by many degrees, the most brilliant advocate of the Catholic claims; no speeches approach his in genius and splendour. But it was Grattan's chief and distinctive excellence that he conceived, even in early manhood, and endeavoured to realise through his illustrious life, the ideal of a united and contented Ireland, freed from the animosities of race and faith, happy under an equal law and a just social order, an ideal made impossible in Grattan's time, but an ideal to which true-hearted Irishmen should aspire.

While Catholic Ireland was being ruled by coercion, and the success of the Catholic cause was still uncertain, a great change had passed over Presbyterian Ulster. The Irish Presbyterians, we have seen, had broken with the Catholic rebels in 1798; their old antipathies of race and creed had revived, and their hatred and contempt of Catholic Ireland increased as Protestant Ascendency was strengthened after the Union. The hopes, too, which had been held out to them, that their staple linen manufacture would rapidly improve, as a result of that measure, had been fulfilled ; though it is probably doubtful if this was not rather due to the progress of machinery and to the effects of the war, which gave a monopoly to British trade, than to the Union regarded by itself.   But the wealth of Ulster had been multiplied ; Belfast was growing into a large seaport and seat of commerce ; and these various circumstances concurred not only to separate the Presbyterian North from the Catholic South more widely, but to attach it firmly to the British connection.   Within twenty years after the Treaty of Union, the province in which the United Irish doctrines had first been successfully preached, nay, in which rebellion had first been hatched, became in its Presbyterian and Protestant parts—and these controlled the entire community—devotedly friendly and loyal to England, a sentiment which has grown stronger and stronger in the progress of time.   Another influence, too, of a very potent kind co-operated in the same direction. The Presbyterian Church had, since the reigns of Charles II. and William III., received a small annual sum from the State ; and a kind of promise had, we have said, been made that an addition would be made to this pittance after the Union.   This was carried into effect by Castlereagh in 1803 ; the Regium Donum, as it was called, was increased many fold, and since then has been largely increased ; and the grant was so arranged as to make the Presbyterian clergy much more dependent on the State than they had been before.   This policy savoured, no doubt, of statecraft ; [1] but it strengthened the ties that bound Ulster to Great Britain.[2]   It is significant of what the results would have been had a similar provision been made for the Irish

---

[1] For the policy which caused the increase of the **Regium Donum**, see Castlereagh, " Memoirs," vol. iv. p. 224.

[2] The effects of the increase of the **Regium Donum** are well described in a remarkable letter in the Castlereagh " Memoirs," vol. iv. p. 289.   How completely separated the Presbyterian North was from the Catholic South in 1812 is noticed by Wakefield, vol. ii. p. 370.

Catholic priesthood, if made generously and without an afterthought.

As for the Government of Ireland, from 1800 to about 1820, its most marked feature was the development of Protestant Ascendency, under repressive laws. This system, no doubt, was prevalent before; it was in the fullest force in the Irish Parliament from 1795 to 1798; but in the years previously it had been somewhat softened; it was certainly strengthened after the Union. Much allowance, indeed, must be made for this; the Irish Parliament had set the example, the Empire was placed in danger by France, Catholic Ireland inclined to our enemy's side, the spirit of the time was harsh and oppressive. But the pernicious results were not the less manifest; Protestant Ascendency acquired augmented power; the subjection of Catholic Ireland became more than ever complete; and this at the time when an armed despot had established religious equality in France. The administration of Ireland became strictly sectarian; the Act of 1793 was set at nought; from the High Sheriff to the lowest county officer every place was filled by the Protestant caste; Protestants only were found in the jury box, and alone decided the course of justice; Catholics, already subject by law to galling restrictions, were excluded from the magistracy, from the army in its higher grades, and from the functions of local government. Yet even these were not the worst results; the system of ascendency and the temper of the time gave a remarkable impulse to Orange tendencies, and made Orangeism spread over all parts of the country. This was promoted by the calling out of the Orange Yeomanry after the unhappy outbreak of 1803; by the direct influence of two Royal Dukes, one, the Duke of York, being the head of the army, and, both notoriously with Orange sympathies; by more than one of the leading men at the Castle; and by a small minority of the landed gentry, who had not forgotten the events of 1798, though certainly not by a large part of the order. A central Orange Association had been formed; Orange Lodges, as they were called, sprung up in every

7

county, and in many found sinister, but active support. The consequences were, in a high degree, unfortunate; lawless societies, setting themselves above law, were banded together, sometimes in formidable strength, to oppress and injure the Irish Catholic ; their work was often exhibited in atrocious deeds ; but it was most manifest, perhaps, in the perversion of justice when administered by purely Orange juries. The Catholics tried of course to retaliate ; the old feud of the Defenders and Peep of Day Boys revived ; Ribbon Societies combined to resist Orangemen ; and, praying in aid the Whiteboy system and making use of agrarian wrongs, kept whole districts in confusion and terror. The law was properly directed against these bodies of men, but it was not administered with impartial justice ; Orangeism was seldom punished for criminal acts of which its adherents had been guilty, Ribbonism was pursued with the sternest severity.

Other characteristics of the affairs of Ireland at this time require to be rapidly glanced at. The Union tended greatly to increase English influence and power in Irish Government, and to strengthen the peculiar system of rule at the Castle. The boroughmongering Peers and Commoners of the defunct Parliament had Irish administration largely in their hands ; they gradually were set aside in this province, Englishmen filled nearly all the higher places in the State, the successors of Clare were for years Englishmen. The government at the Castle for the same reason became more bureaucratic, foreign, and harsh ; it had been tempered by influences which, if those of a caste, were, nevertheless, in a sense, Irish ; and the change was promoted by the weakening of the landed gentry, caused by the rising of 1798, and by what had gone before it. Another feature of the period was a marked depression and want of energy and force in Irish opinion. This, no doubt, had never been strong or really national, but Grattan's observation was not devoid of truth ; the Irish Parliament did represent and embody Irish opinion in a certain measure, and this instrument of thought and discussion had been destroyed. Again,

Castlereagh had been quite wrong in calculating that he could " buy up the fee-simple of Irish corruption" by the Union, the domain of that evil plague of states had, pro- bably, been more or less extended after that measure. Unquestionably corruption ran riot before the Union, but it was encouraged by the means employed to bring the Union about ; it seems to have increased in the years that followed, and to have spread more deeply and been more shameless. No pages in Irish history before the Union contain such evidence of bribery, of peculation, of universal jobbery, of profuse, and even grotesque buying and selling dishonestly in the State as are to be found in the letters of Arthur Wellesley.

A very important change was made in the financial system of Ireland in 1816–17. The calculations of Pitt and Castle- reagh made before the Union proved false as Grattan, Foster, and the twenty peers foretold ; her taxation was doubled, and sometimes trebled ; yet she was unable to contribute the two-seventeenths, that is, the payment of about 12 per cent., to the expenditure of the State arranged by the Treaty. She was therefore compelled to borrow immensely ; her Debt, which at the Union was £28,000,000, had risen to the huge sum of £112,000,000 at the close of the war. It had been agreed, we have seen, by the Treaty, that should the Debts of Great Britain and Ireland and their contributions become in the same ratio, the ideal of Pitt might be realised, and Ireland might be "assimilated to Great Britain in finance," with a special provision, how- ever, in her favour ; this contingency had more than happened before 1815, for the contribution of Ireland, com- pared with the Debt, was less in proportion than that of Great Britain compared with her own. The subject was investigated in the House of Commons, and Resolutions were voted in 1816 to the effect that the time had come when the Three Kingdoms might be placed under the same fiscal system, when the Debts of both islands might be made one, and when their taxation might become identical, as far as was consistent with the Treaty of Union. An Act was

passed, accordingly, which provided for the abolition of the
separate Irish Exchequer, and for the amalgamation of the
twofold Debt; but the Resolutions expressly declared that,
under the new financial system, the taxation of Ireland was
to be "subject to the exemptions and abatements" secured
to her by the Union; that is, that she was not to be taxed
unduly beyond her means. This arrangement, no doubt,
relieved Ireland from a load of debt, but it was no generous
concession, as had been said; it removed only a part of a
burden which never should have been imposed on her; it
was only a small instalment of justice. It was open to the
objection, besides, that it made Ireland subject—if the
liability was indeed remote—to a gigantic National Debt
which she had not incurred, and that in "assimilating her
finances to those of Great Britain" her security for equitable
taxation might be impaired. For many years, however, as
we shall see, the Treaty was respected in this matter; the
taxation of Ireland was not made the same as that of England
and Scotland; Ireland had the benefit of "the exemptions
and the abatements" to which she had a right, and that too
interpreted in the true sense.[1]

Notwithstanding unjust taxation, however, Ireland made
considerable material progress, after the Union, until the
Peace of 1815. The condition of the poorer classes, indeed,
declined by degrees, but imports and exports increased at
least one-third, the rental of the country was augmented;
if some petty manufactures perished, the linen manufacture, we have seen, made a great advance. These signs
of prosperity were most marked in Ulster, but they were
apparent in many parts of Ireland, and if the shallow
optimism of officials made too much of them, for they
were chiefly due to the events of the war, and to the
economic consequences of these, they were, nevertheless,
distinct and real.[2] But a great and disastrous change passed

[1] For the financial arrangements of Ireland made at the Union, and in
1816–17, see the Report of the Childers Commission. The evidence of
Sir E. Hamilton, a Treasury witness hostile to Ireland, is significant.

[2] See the tables and statistics in "Wakefield," vol. i. pp. 680–762; vol.
ii. pp. 1–70. The results are fairly summed up in Mitchell's "History
of Ireland," vol. ii. p. 118, the unwilling testimony of an Irish rebel.

over the country, especially throughout its landed relations, by many degrees the most important, in the years that followed the close of the contest with France, a change due to causes for a long time in progress, but brought to a crisis by social conditions suddenly affected for the worse. The organic structure of the land system of Ireland had not been altered to a very great extent, that is, absentees were numerous, and after the Union had, certainly in some degree, increased; middleman tenures, with their mischiefs, had diminished, but were still common in many counties, shackling property in a kind of pernicious mortmain, and especially oppressive to the tillers of the soil ; and the land, with large exceptions, was in the hands of a peasantry of small farmers, divided in the South and in Ulster, to a considerable extent, from owners different in race and faith. But a concurrence of causes, partly due to the Corn Laws of the Irish Parliament, partly to the effects of the long war which had promoted agriculture in an extraordinary way, partly to the operation of the Relief Act of 1793, which had induced landlords to multiply voters on their estates, in order to gain political influence, and to create thousands of petty tenants, known by the name of forty-shilling freeholders, and not least to the early marriages of a half-servile race, had given an intense stimulus to population. Ireland, which, before the Union, had from four to five million of souls, had at the Peace about six millions and a half. A process, therefore, previously going on, had been accelerated in a remarkable degree; pasturage all over Ireland was replaced more and more by tillage ; the land was split up over immense and evergrowing areas, into little patches, often of the minutest extent, the abodes of dense, teeming, and poor multitudes.

The consequences of this state of things became, by degrees, more and more manifest. Rents rose, not so much owing to the advance of wealth, as from a fierce competition for the possession of the soil, and, in many instances, became extravagant. The owners of the land also lived at greater expense, and especially increased the charges

on their estates, for the value of these seemed ever growing; this was notably the case with absentees and middlemen, and the tendency to exaction, visible before, became
more apparent. At the same time the wages of labour gradually fell, until it reached a point of the lowest depression;
it was, perhaps, from eightpence to a shilling a-day, at a
time of a depreciated currency and extremely high prices.
Wages, too, were generally paid not in money, but kind. The
labourer, a peasant of the lowest degree, occupied a plot of
land and a cabin at a rack rent, his miserable wages being
set against this; he was thus enabled barely to maintain
life on the potato, which formed almost his only food. This
cottar system, as it was called, had existed of old, but it had
been extended to a great and dangerous degree. Masses of
this wretched class, spread densely on the soil, a perishable
root creating, so to speak, a bad truck system, and reducing
them to the depths of poverty; and the condition of the
labouring peasant of Ireland had undergone a distinctly
marked decline.[1] Society, however, was not violently disturbed, though there was much agrarian disorder and crime,
as long as the war maintained high prices, and caused a
large demand for agricultural products, but it was disorganised, nay, shaken to its foundations, when these conditions
were completely changed after the Peace. There was a
sudden and rapid collapse of rents often forced up to an
unnatural rate; a similar collapse of wages, wretched as
these were; hundreds of owners of land suffered immense
losses, and hundreds of thousands of peasants were visited
with severe distress, spreading over almost every part of
Ireland, but especially trying in Connaught and the south
of Munster. It was followed by a series of bad harvests,
which made it terrible in six or seven counties.

In these circumstances the economic and social state of

---

[1] Wakefield, who wrote in 1810–12, before the worst came, repeatedly
asserts (vol. ii. pp. 718, 810 and in other places), that the wages of the
Irish labouring class had greatly diminished from the time of Arthur
Young, and that its position had become worse. See also Newen-
ham's "View of Ireland," 1809, preface, pp. 17, 18.

Ireland was rudely and generally troubled, and here and there was, so to speak, disjointed. The owners of the land acted as was to be expected from the class ; some made themselves conspicuous for deeds of charity, the great majority let things hopelessly drift, a small minority had recourse to harsh measures to remove the impoverished peasantry from the land. The process of ejection rapidly multiplied ; farmers and cottars were driven in hundreds from their homes ; scenes were witnessed like those beheld in England when, after the fall of the religious houses, the rural population was expelled from its seats. These evictions were often in themselves cruel, but they were made ruthlessly unjust in many instances, owing to a circumstance of the first importance to be ever borne in mind with respect to the Irish land system. It is inevitable, under the small farm tenures which prevail in Ireland, that the occupier makes the improvements on his farm, he "creates," as has been said, "its equipment." This still is the case in many countries, and was the case in England in places, even in the seventeenth century.[1] But as a consequence of these additions to the soil the Irish tenant had, even in those days, acquired in thousands of cases a concurrent right in his farm, occasionally ascending to a kind of joint ownership. This had been noticed by Burke many years before ; with the prescience of genius he had foretold that trouble would be the result if this right was not properly supported by law, and he had indicated how it should be protected and fitted into the existing modes of land tenure.[2] Unquestionably, in the great mass of instances, the owners of land in Ireland had respected this right, for otherwise, indeed, it could not have grown up, and in a large part of Ulster it had become established and recognised as the farmer's peculium by long-settled usage. It was nowhere, however, sanctioned by law, and in the southern provinces it was not even

[1] This is alluded to more than once in dramas after the Restoration.
[2] See a most remarkable passage in Burke's "Tracts on the Popery Laws." Works, ed. 1834, vol. i. pp. 445–446.

acknowledged to be an incident of the tenant's possession. When, therefore, evictions were carried out wholesale, and numbers of peasant families were dispossessed, the right was often most unjustly extinguished ; and what really was the property of an entire class was confiscated, in the name of law, without scruple or mercy.

It is evident now what ought to have been the policy of the Legislature and the Government at this grave conjuncture. Famine and distress had been common events in Ireland ; but the Irish Parliament, we have said, had never passed a Poor Law to make property bear the charges of poverty, and to prevent the aggregation of a mass of wretchedness on the soil. The Parliament at Westminster was equally remiss at this time ; but it is fair to remark that not improbably the gross abuses of the English Poor Law, becoming intolerable after the war, may have been the cause that a measure of the kind was not applied to Ireland. The rights of the tenant class, as regards improvements, ought to have been placed under the safeguard of law and made indefeasible by ejectment, but this was not in accord with the ideas of the time ; according to these tenant right would be landlords wrong, a mischievous shibboleth of another day. A different, nay an opposite policy was pursued, unhappily in the highest degree unjust. The law of ejectment was simplified and made very cheap, and local courts were employed to pronounce judgments, by means of which peasants were evicted from their homes in hundreds, and their property in their holdings was torn from them. The system of coercion, too, was employed to carry out these wrongs ; insurrection acts, and the harsh machinery of force, were vigorously plied to vindicate the supposed rights of landlords. The consequences were what was to be expected, agrarian disorder had been rife in Ireland before ; societies of "Threshers," as they were called, had been formed to resist the payment of tithes, a growing burden since the increase of tillage. Agrarian disorder had previously burst out, and continued during a series of years ; it steadily followed the track of eviction as rebellion had followed the track of confiscation of old; Whiteboyism and Ribbonism universally coalesced, and at the bidding of secret societies landlords and their agents were shot, the houses of rich men burned, and atrocities of many kinds done. The law of the land was tainted with evil, it came in conflict with a barbarous social law, which, as O'Connell said, "executed the wild justice of revenge."

The Duke of Richmond had been succeeded by Lord Whitworth, our ambassador to France, after the Peace of Amiens, and by Lord Talbot, a mere noble name; the real governor of Ireland from 1812 to 1818 was Peel. His conduct in office marked, to some extent, if not a change, a turn in Irish affairs. Peel was made Chief Secretary at the age of twenty-four; he had been covered, by Oxford, with her honours; he was looked up to in his family as a rising Pitt; he soon distinguished himself in the House of Commons. He was associated, however, with the narrow Toryism which was the faith of the Liverpool Ministry; he went to Ireland, as to an unknown land, with the prejudices of a Tory of the great commercial class of England. He became a formidable opponent, we have seen, of the Catholic claims; and though he was far too able a man not to discountenance Orangeism and its lawless spirit, he was true to the Protestant Ascendency which he found supreme. He considered Ireland, too, from a purely English point of view, without sympathy with Irish feeling, with no real knowledge of Irish needs or wants; and he carried out a policy in many respects unfortunate. Like his predecessors, he made a free use of repression, and extended it to social mischiefs which it could not remedy; he steadily upheld the rights of landlords, even when these were morally unjust, he gave his sanction to the cheap law of ejectment, the source of manifold and most crying evils. He had no insight at this time into the ills of Ireland, and dealt with them according to a bad system of routine; and he quarrelled with O'Connell and denounced the Catholic Board as a mere nest of sedition. Peel, however, gave proof of his great capacity as an administrator at the Castle in these years. He tried, and not without success, to put a check on the scandalous jobbing of the Irish public service; from this time forward we hear less of Irish corruption. The reform in Ireland, how-ever, then chiefly connected with his name, was the institu-tion, in disturbed districts, of a central police force under paid magistrates, replacing an ineffective local police and the bodies of troops often engaged in this service. This was the origin of the Irish Constabulary and of its present system, one of the most admirable instruments that could be formed to maintain order and law, and a powerful agency in Irish social progress.[1]

As we look back at the dismal tale of coercion, of wrong, of mistakes, of failures which marked Irish administration long after the Union, we are tempted to ask what efforts were made by Grattan and his followers to redress these grievances. But we must recollect the tendencies of the day and the precedents set by the Irish Parliament; English Toryism, too, prevailed in the Imperial Houses, and many Englishmen found seats from Ireland in the House of Commons, the nominees of families still possessing Irish borough influence, which they carried to the market of British politics. The Irish representation, in a word, was filled with a half-foreign element, as O'Connell often pointed out and condemned; yet the House of Commons was not without a small, but very able body of distinguished Irish-men, the supporters of their illustrious leader. The names of Ponsonby, of Parnell, of Tighe, of Hutchinson, and especially of Sir John Newport, a master of Irish finance and commerce, are still remembered as chiefs of this party; they repeatedly made a determined stand against Irish mis-government and the coercive system. They were, however, a handful only, and their voices were overborne by large majorities, and too often by the voices of their own country-men, champions of Protestant Ascendency, and all that this implied. It deserves notice that, at this period, the wrongs of Ireland were more than once set forth and denounced from

[1] The Irish Correspondence of Peel, edited by Mr. Parker, should be studied.

the Irish judicial bench. The fearless independence of Judges Fox and Fletcher, in this matter, should be placed on record, and if another judge, Johnson, was far from discreet, his "Letters of Juverna" contain much truth. These eminent men incurred the wrath of the Castle, and two were persecuted unjustly with shameless severity.

George IV. visited Ireland in 1821 ; he was the only King of England since Richard II. who had appeared in the island save as an enemy, but he received an enthusiastic welcome in the capital ; if the first gentleman of Europe, he shed no honour on the Crown, and the trial of Queen Caroline had but lately ended. The Mayor and Aldermen of Dublin, before denounced as "a beggarly Corporation" by the great Irish tribune, joined with O'Connell and his followers in a tumultuous greeting ; the streets were dense with exulting crowds, and decked out as for a national holiday, the festivities of an overflowing Court were splendid. The spectacle aroused the indignant wrath of Byron, but it had not the less a significance of its own. Too much has often been made of pageants of this kind ; but attachment to persons rather than to institutions has always been a characteristic of the Celtic races, and chiefs and kings are objects of their peculiar sympathy. How little, however, an effusion of sentiment like this had, spite of the predictions of hired writers, to do with the alleviation of the ills of Ireland, or with reaching the sources of Irish feeling was made but too manifest in a few months. The harvest of 1822 very generally failed, and the distress of Ireland, which had been acute, became a destructive famine in several large districts. Hundreds of victims perished in the absence of a Poor Law, thousands were brought to the awful verge of starvation, as the natural result agrarian crime became more than ever widespread and atrocious. The Government made no attempt to remove the causes of these deep-seated and most grave evils, coercion was administered with extreme harshness, evictions multiplied to a portentous extent. But Parliament voted a sum of half-a-million sterling, in aid of wretchedness where it was most trying, and British charity

flowed in freely, as it was to flow in far more largely on a
still worse occasion. And what was infinitely more important, the mind of England was awakened to the condition
of Ireland for the first time, it may be said, since the Union.
A Parliamentary Committee sat in 1824–5 and collected
valuable and most striking evidence, on what may be called
the Irish Question, in its different parts, and especially on
the state of the destitute peasantry.[1] This forms, by many
degrees, the best account of the social and economic
position of Ireland during the first quarter of the present
century.

The Irish Catholic Question had, meanwhile, been making
way by degrees in English opinion. The mantle of Grattan
had fallen on Plunket ; that great lawyer and orator brought
the subject forward in the early part of the Session of 1821.
His speech was, in the main, a reply to the great speech
of Peel made in 1817 ; it was marked by his close logic and
severe eloquence, it was one of the finest displays ever made
in Parliament. Plunket urged most of the topics dwelt on
by Grattan, but the best passages perhaps in this noble effort
were those in which he showed that Catholics had laid the
foundations of our ancient and free monarchy, and that it
was monstrous to charge Catholicism, as such, with hatred
of England and of English liberty. Peel acknowledged that
his opponent "had torn to pieces" the web of his argument of four years before, and that Plunket was "worthy to
wield the arms of the dead Achilles" ; in the House of
Commons the Resolutions moved by Plunket had a small
majority of votes. Bills, however, of like tenor, were
rejected in the House of Lords, the first of several defeats of
the kind ; and as they contained provisions savouring of
the Veto ; they were repudiated by O'Connell and the Irish

[1] I quote a few words from O'Connell's description of the Irish poor
(Evidence, p 10.) : "They have no clothes to change ; they have none
but what they wear at the moment. . . . Their food consists of potatoes
and water during the greater part of the year ; potatoes and sour milk
during another portion ; they use some salt with their potatoes when they
have nothing but water." No formal report was made, but the evidence
should be carefully perused.

priesthood. Yet the decision of the House of Commons was not fruitless ; a change passed over the Liverpool Ministry, Lord Wellesley, a staunch advocate of the Catholic claims, was sent to Ireland as Lord-Lieutenant ; Plunket was made one of his chief law officers ; the system of Protestant Ascendency received a shock ; Orangeism, especially, was discountenanced at the Castle. Up to this time, nevertheless, the Catholic cause had lost strength, apparently, from year to year, in Ireland. O'Connell, indeed, had toiled to keep agitation up, but the Veto had, we have seen, divided the Irish Catholics ; the period of distress from 1815 to 1822 had depressed the country and proved a palsying spell ; the "Catholic Board" had been dissolved, the "aggregate meetings" had almost ceased. The Hour, however, had come, and it was to find the Man who was to become, as he was rightly called, the "Liberator" of Catholic Ireland, and to win for it the freedom too long withheld. In 1823 O'Connell and a few adherents—the principal of these was Richard Lalor Sheil, a young lawyer of extraordinary rhetorical power —founded the last of the organisations formed to uphold the still unsuccessful Catholic cause, the Catholic Association, ere long destined to gain for that cause a wonderful triumph, nay, to become a portent in the political world.[1]

The object of O'Connell was to concentrate an irresistible force of Irish opinion—like that of the Volunteers of 1782 —which would wring from a still reluctant Parliament the concession of the Catholic claims, free from the condition to which he had always objected. The most obvious way to effect this was to establish a Committee in Dublin with local committees throughout the country ; but the Convention Act stood, we have seen, in the way ; it was necessary to give this expedient up. The skilled lawyer, a past master of the devices of his craft, set up in the capital a kind of club, composed of members paying an annual sum, and formed to "discuss the Catholic claims," to

[1] Wyse's "History of the Catholic Association" is rather a good book. Wyse, however, inclined to the policy of the Veto, and was not enthusiastic for O'Connell.

"present petitions" in their behalf to Parliament, and to
"procure subscriptions" in aid of the cause. This, however,
could not accomplish much; to carry out his purpose
O'Connell turned to the Irish priesthood, his loyal allies,
and relied on their influence over their devoted flocks.
This great body of men had completely changed from what
they had been before the Union, submissive children of the
old Church of France, or of Spain, ready to bow the knee
to established power; they were chiefly composed of sons
of the large Irish farmers; Maynooth had filled them with
Irish sympathies; they had no cause to reverence British
rule; they had been irritated by a system of proselytising,
which had found support at the Castle.   Their Church, too,
had acquired increased influence; and while they remained
devoted to their faith, they had imbibed the liberal philosophy of the eighteenth century, and as one of their most
eminent prelates wrote, had "read Locke and Paley as
well as Bellarmine," and cared "more for the principles of
freedom," than for the "Divine Right of Kings."   They
were fitting instruments for a great popular movement;
O'Connell adjured them, in impassioned language, to combine in an effort to promote the Catholic cause, and to
exert their immense spiritual power in its behalf.   Catholic
Emancipation was to be a religious faith preached at the
altars of a thousand parishes; it was to be demanded in the
name of God, to be the object of a general crusade; and,
at the same time, a "Catholic Rent" was to be collected by
the emissaries of the priesthood, far and near, and to create
funds for the temporal purposes, which O'Connell foresaw
might have momentous results.   The chief of these were
to contest elections, to multiply petitions in favour of the
Catholic claims, to subsidise a local Catholic Press, and,
above all, to protect the downtrodden peasantry from the
wrongs to which they were day by day subject.   Harsh
landlords were to be exposed and denounced; Orange
magistrates were to be bearded on the Bench; especially all
that legal ingenuity could do was to be employed to baffle
and defeat evictions.

The movement, inaugurated in this way, showed but faint signs of existence for a time. By degrees, however, it acquired speed and force ; in two years it had gained immense volume. Lord Killeen, a son of the Fingall of the days of Pitt, became one of O'Connell's adherents; most of the leading Catholic gentry concurred ; if the Catholic Association was not openly joined by Liberal Protestants of the school of Grattan—an order of men O'Connell had always tried to win [1]—they cordially supported the Catholic claims. The policy of the Veto was cast to the winds ; the Catholic Association became a really great power, spreading its authority over all parts of the country; O'Connell went on progresses through Ireland, haranguing, agitating, addressing huge multitudes, often pleading the cause of the Catholic peasant, without reward, in the courts of justice. The chief work, however, was done by the priesthood ; they assumed the attitude of the Confederates of 1643 ; in the name of the faith pledged their dependent flocks to make the demands of the Catholic Association their own ; united them, in a word, to a great, almost an universal, movement by appeals to feelings that stir the Catholic heart. Meanwhile their trusty agents got in the Catholic Rent ; the pence given by the millions of a people in distress, rose to hundreds, nay, thousands of pounds a week ; and these sums were applied to the uses marked out by O'Connell. Of these none had such a potent effect as the war waged on unjust landlords and magistrates, and against evictions. The peasantry felt, at last, they had a chance of protection, iniquitous acts and decisions from the Bench were held up to execration and often frustrated ; the plague of depopulation, in the local courts, was stayed in hundreds of instances by skilful lawyers. Owing to this fortunate change, and also because O'Connell earnestly denounced crime, and the priesthood

[1] O'Connell thus referred to the Liberal Protestants of his time, before the Committee of 1824-5 :—"A Liberal Protestant is an object of great affection and regard from the entire Catholic population" (p. 70).

faithfully echoed his words, " avoid outrages, they only help your enemies," agrarian disorder almost ceased in Ireland, in fact the energies and passions of the Irish Catholic were absorbed in furthering a cause sacred to him and patriotic alike.   The movement, we should add, gained increasing strength, as the country, though very slowly, began to revive after the severe trials it had lately gone through.

The power of the Catholic Association had become formidable in the extreme by the Session of 1825.   The Club had grown into a mighty League ; its mandates were obeyed throughout Ireland ; it collected what may be called a revenue ; it maintained order and law by its local agents ; it formed an irregular Government supplanting the rule of the Castle, through a wide circle of social relations.   " Self-elected," said Canning, in the House of Commons, " self-constructed, self-assembled, self-adjourned, acknowledging no superior, tolerating no equal, interfering at all stages with the administration of justice, denouncing publicly before trial individuals against whom it institutes prosecutions, rejudging and condemning those whom the law has acquitted, menacing the free press with punishment, and openly declaring its intention to corrupt that part which it could not intimidate, and, lastly, levying a contribution on the people of Ireland—was this an association which the House could tolerate ? "   The Association, however, had not violated any existing law ; a special statute, called by O'Connell, " the Algerine Act," passed rapidly through Parliament, in order to put it down.   But the great agitator easily broke through this legal net ; as he boasted, " he drove a coach and six " through the Act of Parliament ; the Association reappeared in a somewhat altered form ; it never lost for a moment its hold on the people.   The Liberal party at Westminster at least felt that the movement could not be stopped by these means ; Sir Francis Burdett brought forward Resolutions, translated into a Bill, dealing with the main parts of the Catholic Question ; and this, in spite of an earnest protest of Peel, was carried in the House of Commons by a small majority. A remarkable proof was soon afforded of O'Connell's moderation and statesmanlike views. The triumph of the Catholic cause, he felt, could not be long deferred; yet he gave his assent to what were called, "the wings of this measure"—one of emancipation in no doubtful sense—that is, to a provision for the Catholic clergy to be made by the State, an object he had always had at heart, and to the disfranchisement of the peasant masses, known by the name of the forty-shilling freeholders, and in no sense independent voters. The course of Irish History, in after years, might have been very different had the Bill of 1825 become law; Parliament would have conceded the Catholic claims of its own authority, and with proper safeguards; "a secret of state," in the words of the Roman historian, would not "have been divulged that supreme power could be superseded in its own seat."[1] The measure, however, was rejected by the House of Lords after an intemperate speech made by the Duke of York, the heir to the throne.

This irritating, but indecisive defeat, only moved O'Connell to make redoubled efforts. The influence of the Association became stronger than ever; its chief made appeals to Catholic France, some eminent Frenchmen responding to his call; he sent messages to the Irish in the United States, becoming already a growing power; he advocated the Repeal of the Test Act, and endeavoured to win the English Dissenters to his side. The authority of the Association was made even more manifest at the General Election of 1826. The Catholic Rent was, in part, employed in providing for a series of contests; in the counties of Waterford, of Louth, of Westmeath, of Monaghan, seats were wrested from great Ascendency Houses, and Liberal Protestants returned in their stead; the priests became zealous electioneering agents; symptoms appeared of the defection of Catholic voters from their lords. This success, however, was but the prelude to a more signal,

[1] Tacitus, " Hist." I. 4, " Evulgato Imperii arcano posse Principem alibi quam Romæ fieri."

8

and as it was to prove, a final triumph. Canning, always
the advocate of the Irish Catholic cause, passed away
deserted by his late colleagues ; the Wellington administration came into power ; and Wellington and Peel, the
leader of the Government in the House of Commons, were
steadfast opponents of the Catholic claims, Peel especially
being O'Connell's avowed enemy.   In the summer of 1828,
Mr. Vesey Fitzgerald accepted office ; he vacated his seat
for his native county, Clare ; but his re-election was considered certain at Downing Street, and by the men at the
Castle.   Fitzgerald's father had been a distinguished lawyer,
who had opposed the Union, and been a friend of Grattan ;
he was himself a supporter of the Catholic cause ; he was
one of the foremost of the Liberal Irish Protestants.   But
the juncture was critical, and O'Connell had resolved to
prove what the Catholic Association could do ; even against
the entreaties of Lord John Russell, a rising leader of the
English Whigs, he, though reluctantly, made up his mind
to contest the seat, in person, with the nominee of the
Government.   The events that followed are still remembered ; they decided the issue of the Catholic Question.
The landed gentry of Clare flung themselves into Fitzgerald's cause ; they resented the intrusion of a strange
lawyer, thrust upon them by an alien and threatening
power ; they demanded, as a matter of course, their votes
from the tenants on their estates ; they were convinced
that their forty-shilling freeholders would be submissive as
of old.   But the Association had sent its orders out ; the
priests of Clare called on their flocks, in every parish, to go
to the poll for O'Connell, in the name of God ; the altar, it
was said, was arrayed against the landlord's hall.   The forty-
shilling freeholders threw off the yoke ; they defied their
superiors, and declared for "the Liberator" to a man ;
O'Connell was returned by a large majority, though, as a
Catholic, he could not take his seat in Parliament.   It
was thought an ominous sign that he was enthusiastically
cheered by a detachment of Irish soldiers on the spot.
    The revolt of the forty-shilling freeholders became at

once general; the ties that had bound the peasant to his lord snapped; Protestant Ascendency had received a notable defeat; the power of the Castle was greatly weakened; O'Connell was the virtual master of Catholic Ireland. Protestant Ireland, too, had undergone a change, especially among the higher landed gentry; the fury of Orangeism indeed blazed out, partly in crime, partly in fanatical wrath; but there had been a growing sympathy with the Catholic cause; an overwhelming majority of Irish Protestants, of the better classes, pronounced in its favour. A great meeting was held in Dublin, compared by the Catholic historian of the movement to those of the Volunteers in 1782–3;[1] the Duke of Leinster and the leading men of the Irish peerage was at its head; it declared that the time for Catholic Emancipation had come. The significance of events was not lost on Peel; anti-Catholic as ever, he wrote that concessions must be made; Wellington concurred confessedly against his will; he was "alarmed about an attack on Irish rents"; "the position," he felt, "was no longer tenable." It soon transpired that a great measure of Catholic relief was being prepared, and that by a Government before most adverse; the indignation of the ruling classes of England was intense, and, indeed, spread through the whole nation. George IV. tried to find another Addington in vain; the Tory party protested, not without reason, that it was unconstitutional, in the highest degree, for a Tory Ministry to adopt this policy; Oxford rejected her favourite son, Peel, who had sought her suffrages as a test of opinion; the middle classes were puzzled and vexed; even the Dissenters threw over their great Irish advocate. The large majority of Englishmen, in fact, resented the defeat of the Legislature and the Government by what they deemed to be a subject and inferior race. The sentiment, too, was in the main true; Catholic Emancipation, no doubt, would, in the long run, have become law; but the immediate victory was due to

---

[1] Wyse, "History of the Catholic Association," vol. ii. pp. 41, 44.

O'Connell, to the Catholic Association, and to the Clare Election.[1]

The measure designed to settle the Irish Catholic Question was brought forward in the Session of 1829. The speeches of the heads of the Government were unfortunate ; Wellington avowed that he was yielding, and yielding only because he was afraid of civil war in Ireland ; his attitude was peremptory, harsh, unbending. Peel, more versed in Parliamentary arts, was plausible, dexterous, but unsympathetic ; he dwelt on the progress of the Catholic cause in England from 1800 to 1825 ; he pointed out that the time had passed for half liberty for the Irish Catholics ; " we have removed with our own hands the seal from the vessel in which a mighty spirit was enclosed ; but like the genius in the fable it will not return to its narrow confines, and enable us to cast it forth to the obscurity from which we evoked it " ; there was really no alternative between Catholic Emancipation and a return to the Penal Code. He was, doubtless, in a very trying position ; he had to recant professions he had made for years in the presence of angry and deceived followers ; but he might have spoken of Ireland in a kindly spirit, and concealed his evident antipathy to the Catholic cause. The policy of the Ministry was, however, carried out, spite of vehement opposition in both Houses, largely through the aid of the English Whigs ; the restrictions maintained in 1793 were removed with scarcely a single exception ; the Irish Catholic was at last admitted fully within the Pale of the State, and was placed on all but the same level of rights as the Protestant. Catholic Emancipation, however, itself many years too late, was not accompanied by its proper supplements ; no provision was made for the Irish Catholic clergy,

---

[1] Greville, an admirable observer, and moving in the highest society of the day, describes graphically ("Memoirs," vol. i. chap. v.) the indignation of the King and the English aristocracy. Of the effects of O'Connell's agitation he significantly says (p. 172), "If the Irish Catholics had not brought matters to this pass by agitation and association, things might have remained as they were for ever."

Peel especially insisting on this; above all there was no commutation of the tithe, a reform advocated by Grattan and Pitt forty years before, and the necessity of which had been long apparent. The Catholic Association was at the same time proscribed, and the forty-shilling free-holders deprived of their votes, measures advisable no doubt, but hardly expedient as parts of a great scheme of remedial policy. The worst feature, however, of the Act was this : O'Connell was not permitted to retain his seat for Clare, a mischievous prohibition savouring of petty spite.

Catholic Emancipation had been thus accomplished; no one will now deny that the Irish Catholic was entitled to an equality of rights in the State; nor was the measure itself without good results; it raised a subject people to a higher position; it may have saved Ireland from grave social disasters. But Catholic Emancipation had been retarded for a whole generation of man; it had been achieved under the worst conditions; it was a trophy of agitation, not the free gift of justice; it was a half measure marked with distrust and aversion. That it has had bene-ficent fruits may be admitted; in any case it could not have been long delayed; but it has been attended, at least, with a train of evils. It shook, in England, con-fidence in her leading men; precipitated the Reform of 1832, with its revolutionary and wild excesses; gave the Constitution a heavy blow; made mere agitation an immense force in politics; above all, brought into the Legislature an alien, and often a hostile element which has powerfully affected, and often for the worse, the conduct of Parliament and the administration of the State. Conservative and Protestant England has, during the last seventy years, been compelled over and over again to bow to the will of Democratic and Catholic Ireland; her legislation, her government, nay, her very fortunes have, on many occasions, been shaped by an influence assuredly not for her true interests. Catholic Emancipation has been attended in Ireland with consequences in many

respects unfortunate, and has been productive of grave
and permanent mischiefs. Carried as it was by a violent
popular movement, the champions of which were O'Connell
and an ambitious priesthood, it so weakened the power of
the Irish landed gentry that this has, subsequently, been
all but destroyed ; it placed in their stead a body of men,
devoted to their Church, but disliking England, her rule in
Ireland, and the existing order of things, and it invested
them with far too great an authority. It, in a word, shook
property and the whole upper class in Ireland, and has
ultimately undermined the foundations of the State ; and
though this certainly was not O'Connell's purpose, the
agitation he promoted has had these results. But Catholic
Emancipation has done more ; it has lowered the Irish representation in a remarkable degree ; it has almost banished
Irishmen of independence and parts from Parliament ; it
has introduced into it a large number of men, largely the
instruments of an alien Church and power, with no capacity
for legislation of a rational kind, but hostile to England
and the Protestant name, and chiefly intent on turning
things upside down in Ireland, in order to effect the
Revolution which is their ultimate object. How different
would the results have been had Catholic Emancipation
been accomplished in time, under happy auspices, and with
the required supplements !

The first thirty years of the present century form a
chequered passage in Irish history. The severest repression
was sometimes unwisely exercised ; Protestant Ascendency
acquired increased power for a time ; Orangeism was
more developed, with its many evils ; the Catholic cause
was, unhappily, long put back ; Emancipation, if an act of
justice, was obtained by methods that must be regretted,
and without securities the State should have had, and
effected as it was, was followed by ills that have had
their influence on Great Britain and Ireland alike. There
was much misgovernment and maladministration besides ;
many of the social evils of Ireland were disregarded and
even made worse by law ; and in the absence of a

Parliament on the spot, Irish opinion was weakened, and Irish faction increased. Yet the circumstances of the time must be kept in sight; Ireland was a thorn in the side of England during many of these years; she remained a scene of disorder and source of constant trouble. On the other hand, Protestant Ulster in this period became attached to England, a sentiment that has ever since deepened; notwithstanding a season of dire distress, Ireland, on the whole, made material progress; and as the harsh and selfish spirit of the time declined, England turned to Ireland with kindness and even sympathy especially in the trial of 1822-3. Tory Government was now passing away in Great Britain; the country was eager for large reforms; in Ireland Protestant Ascendency had been hardly stricken; Catholic Emancipation had produced a new order of things; a great change had passed over the whole community; and Ireland, too, was in need of large reforms, political and social, under these conditions. How she was to fare in the era about to open; with a representation in Parliament largely transformed, with some statesmen indifferent or hostile to her, with many anxious to rule her well, but not familiar with her social condition, or with the requirements this needed, dealing too with a community very dissimilar to their own; and what her fortunes were to be in the shock of parties, and when a great and dominant nation was in a state of change —the coming years were ere long to show.

CHAPTER IV

FROM 1829 TO THE FAILURE OF THE REPEAL MOVEMENT

Catholic Emancipation not carried out in Ireland—O'Connell agitates against the Union—Failure of the agitation—Peel's great speech on the Union—The Irish Reform Act—The system of National Education in Ireland—The Tithe War—Severe measure of repression—Reform of the Established Church in Ireland—Proposal of O'Connell—Ten Sees extinguished—The Tithe Question—The Appropriation Clause—Resignation of Stanley and three of his colleagues—The episode of Littleton and O'Connell—Fall of the Grey Government—Retrospect of its Irish policy—The first Melbourne Government—A Tithe Commutation Bill rejected by the House of Lords—The first government of Peel—Another Commutation Bill—Peel defeated on a Resolution for appropriation—Alliance between the Whigs and O'Connell—Emancipation made a reality—Improvement of the Irish Constabulary force and other reforms—Protestant Ascendency and Orangeism discountenanced—Good results—Thomas Drummond —The Tithe commuted but without appropriation—The Irish Poor law—Reform of the Irish Corporations—The Melbourne Government unpopular in England—O'Connell's conduct contributes to this—Fall of the Melbourne Government—The second Administration of Peel—O'Connell revives the movement against the Union—His efforts for a time fail—The movement gradually acquires strength—The Young Ireland party—The monster meetings—Attitude of O'Connell—The movement attracts great attention abroad—Policy of Peel—The Clontarf meeting stopped—Arrest and trial of O'Connell—The sentence reversed in the House of Lords—Vacillation of O'Connell—Decline of his power—The movement collapses.

CATHOLIC EMANCIPATION broke up the Tory party, and was a chief cause of the fall of the Wellington Ministry. During the three years that followed, England was in the throes of the great movement for the Reform of Parliament; the dynasty of the Bourbons was driven from the throne; a destructive plague swept over these islands. The affairs of Ireland could not engross attention, and yet they had become of no small importance. Catholic Emancipation was obviously an incomplete measure; it was above all essential that it should be carried out in a liberal and sympathetic spirit. The Irish Catholic had been made eligible to all offices in the State, except that of the Lord-Lieutenant and the Lord Chancellor. Protestant Ascendency had, in theory, been replaced by religious equality. But the change, marked as it was, could not quickly remove that ascendency from the positions in which it had long been entrenched in Irish government and administration, or give the Catholic the privileges, in fact, enjoyed by the Protestant; the liberation of Catholic Ireland, therefore, should, as far as possible, have been made effective and manifest. An opposite policy was adopted; the consequences were, in no doubtful sense, unfortunate. The Wellington Government made no attempt to provide for the Irish Catholic clergy, or to bring about a commutation of the tithe, measures more than ever necessary at this time; the Government of Lord Grey were equally remiss. It was even less excusable that no effort was made to give Catholic Emancipation a real existence. The Wellington Administration unwisely refused to raise O'Connell to the rank of King's Counsel; the Emancipation Act remained all but a dead letter. Nor was the Grey Government of Ireland formed to attract or conciliate Irish Catholic policy. O'Connell was treated with marked neglect; scarcely an Irish Catholic received an official place; the class was excluded from the magistracy and local affairs, almost as rigidly as had been the case before. Lord Wellesley had been replaced by Lord Anglesey, whose successor had been the Duke of Northumberland; Grey had made Lord Anglesey Lord-Lieutenant again, and the brilliant soldier was a friend of Catholic Ireland. But the real governor of Ireland was the Chief Secretary, Stanley, the celebrated Lord Derby of another day, still remembered as the " Rupert of debate." Stanley had great parts and a gallant spirit ; but he was dictatorial, imprudent, sometimes reckless ; he was ill fitted for a very difficult and delicate post. Like Peel, he was soon at daggers drawn with O'Connell, who gave him the nickname of "Scorpion Stanley," an epithet not wholly undeserved.

In this position of affairs O'Connell recurred to the policy of his early manhood, which, apparently, he had abandoned for years ; he endeavoured to rally Ireland in a movement against the Union. It is idle to say that personal slights were his only motive, though probably these were not without effect ; it is difficult to deny his sincerity, ambiguous as was his subsequent conduct. He may well have argued from recent events that justice for Ireland could not be obtained from a Parliament at Westminster and men in power in Downing Street ; the great triumph he had won had been nearly fruitless ; its practical results had been next to nothing. Nor were his prospects of success apparently hopeless ; the Tories, the heirs of Pitt, had been reduced to impotence ; Grey and the Whigs had strenuously opposed the Union ; men still living remembered the Revolution of 1782 ; the Union was a comparatively new settlement ; Catholic Belgium had just been detached from Protestant Holland. O'Connell again appealed to the priesthood and to his followers in the agitation of late years ; he held public meetings and addressed large multitudes ; he tried to put in force once more the powerful machinery which had wrought wonders from 1825 to 1829. But even in Ireland his efforts did not accomplish much ; the energies of the great mass of the Irish Catholics were devoted, at this time, to a different cause ; the Catholics of England angrily held aloof, and the leading men of Catholic Ireland ; the Liberal Irish Protestants, who had declared for Emancipation to a man, fell away from him and pronounced for the Union. In England and Scotland opinion did not hesitate ; Grey and the Whig and Radical party were quite as determined to maintain the Union and to oppose its repeal as the Tory adherents of Peel and Wellington. Parliament was all but unanimous on the subject. Meanwhile the great tribune had for once failed in his cunning attempts to baffle the law. He had had recourse to his earlier methods ; as soon as one of the Associations he had formed was assailed, he reproduced it in another shape and name ; but the device proved in one instance vain—he was meshed, besides, in the net of the law of conspiracy. He pleaded guilty to part of the charges against him, and though he was never called up to receive sentence, his immense influence for a moment declined ; he was no longer invincible in the eyes of a credulous, ignorant, and easily led people, abounding in the weakness of the Celtic nature.

In spite, however, of this rebuff, and though the agitation against the Union was swallowed up, so to speak, in other movements which kept Ireland in a state of disorder, O'Connell did not abandon the cause of <u>Repeal</u> for a time. He brought the question before the <u>House of Commons</u>, in the <u>Session of 1834</u>, on a motion for an inquiry into the means by which the Union had been accomplished, and as to its past and probable future effects. He must have felt that his labour would be thrown away ; but he was assured of the support of faithful followers, returned for Irish seats at his bidding, and that of the priesthood ; his "Tail," as it was now called, would certainly move with its Head. The speech he made was not one of his best, if a fair specimen of his research and his masculine eloquence. He dwelt on the doctrine that the Irish Parliament had no power to extinguish itself ; enlarged on the corrupt methods employed to destroy it ; insisted that its provisions were utterly unjust, and had done Ireland infinite wrong ; and while he emphatically, and evidently from his heart, declared that he had no thought of separating his country from Great Britain, he demanded that its ancient Parliament should be restored. He was ably answered by Spring Rice, another distinguished Irishman, especially as regards financial and commercial details. Spring Rice conclusively proved that Ireland had made much material and even social progress since 1800.

The most striking incident of the debate, however, was the really magnificent speech of Peel, to this day the ablest defence ever made of the Union. Peel, no doubt, showed no sympathy with Irish sentiment, as already had been the case with him ; he refused to dwell on the history of the Union; he considered the subject with reference to Imperial interests.   But now he ascended to the high ground of principle, and threw plausibilities and after-thoughts away ; he emphatically declared that the Union must be maintained, if England was not to sink into a third-rate Power. Absolute separation, he contended, was to be preferred to the half independence of Ireland under a Parliament of her own, constituted as this would be since the measure of 1829.   The passages in which he described the results of two legislatures in angry and repeated conflict, as, unlike what had happened from 1782 to 1800, would inevitably and unhappily be now the case, are really in a high strain of eloquence ; they are admirable alike in thought and expression.   O'Connell's motion, it is scarcely necessary to say, was rejected by an immense majority ; it obtained the support of one English member only.

The Grey Government had, long before this time, been engaged in projects of reform for Ireland.   It was for a time doubtful—such was the state of the country—whether Ireland was to have Parliamentary Reform at all ; [1] the Bill that was ultimately introduced and carried had not much in common with the great Reform Act of 1832. The Irish representation was but little changed as regards the places that returned members ;   the electoral franchise was placed at a high level ; and O'Connell endeavoured in vain to restore the forty-shilling freeholders to the position they had held before 1829.   The measure, in a word, was Conservative and restrictive, though Ireland obtained five additional seats ; but it had the real merit that it did not attempt to treat a country, with a small, weak middle-class, and still extremely backward

[1] Lord Campbell ("Life," vol. ii. p. 7) wrote, " The common notion prevailing among Liberals in England is that Ireland is wholly incapable of laws and liberty and must be governed by the sword."

in every sense, on the principles that were applied to England; and political mischief was in some degree avoided. Landed property in Ireland was left with some influence for a time; though the followers of O'Connell were becoming numerous, they were not dominant in the representation as yet; and several were able, moderate, and disguished men, such as Sheil, Wyse, the O'Conor Don, More O'Farrell, and others. Another and very important measure of the Grey Ministry was the establishment of Primary Education for the Irish community, on a system which had not been hitherto tried. In the period before the Union, we have said, Primary Education hardly existed in Ireland, as far at least as the State was concerned; the Charter Schools had disgracefully failed; the children of the Catholic millions, the great mass of the people, were left to acquire the rudiments in the "hedge schools," where they were miserably taught, and often learned what they should never have known.[1] A Board of Education was formed in 1806-7; Peel, when Chief Secretary, had turned his mind to Irish Education in its different branches; but nothing really effective was done; the times were not, in fact, propitious. Meanwhile the Evangelical movement of the day had, so to speak, invaded Catholic Ireland, and endeavoured to make a settlement in it; several Societies, extremely Protestant in type, had been formed for the education of the Catholic poor; and these, as may be supposed, laboured to make proselytes, to the intense indignation of the Irish priesthood, one of the reasons, we have said, that they joined O'Connell. These societies had only a short existence; but they were followed by another society composed largely of distinguished Irishmen; and this made a real and earnest effort to bring instruction home to the young of Catholic Ireland. The Kildare Place Society, as it was called, received considerable donations from the State, and was even countenanced by O'Connell; but it required the Protestant Bible to be read in its schools; and

[1] Among the school books were stories of celebrated highwaymen and the Memoirs of Faublas!

ultimately it became proselytising in its tendencies at least.
It fell under the ban of the Irish Catholic clergy ; and as its
schools had never been very numerous, the children of the
humble classes of Catholic Ireland were abandoned, for the
most part, to the " hedge schools." The primary schools of
Protestant, and even of Presbyterian Ireland, were also, with
rare exceptions, bad.

Primary Education in Ireland therefore, when the Grey
Government took up the question, was in a truly pitiable
state, even more pitiable by far than was the case in England.
The mass of the population still grew up in ignorance ;
more than one half certainly could not read or write. A
comprehensive system was inaugurated in 1831 ; its principal
author was Chief Secretary Stanley ; it has had a chequered
history, but very important results. The objects of the
Government were threefold : to provide a good education
for the children of the poorer classes of every form of
religion, at the charge of the State ; to guard against the
proselytism which had been employed against the young of
Catholic Ireland ; and ultimately to make education a means
of reconciling the warring races and faiths of Ireland. The
principles of the "National" system, as it was named, were
these : Schools were to be established in every part of
Ireland to which the children of the poor might resort
without subjecting the parents to any expense ; the instruction to be imparted was to be secular and religious
also ; "secular" instruction was to be given to the pupils
together, by masters and mistresses appointed by the State ;
but "religious" instruction was to be given in the schools,
by the pastors of their respective communions, to the pupils
carefully to be kept apart, according to their different modes
of faith. We shall consider the working of the system afterwards, and when it became developed in large proportions ;
enough to remark here, that, whatever may be alleged
against it, and in whatever degree it has not attained its
objects, it certainly was a great boon to Ireland, a change
for the better in almost every respect, and that, from the
first moment, it had some happy results. The National

Schools spread quickly throughout the country, spite of opposition on many different grounds; they have multiplied in an extraordinary way; they have brought within their scope an immense majority of the children of the humble classes of Ireland; and, defective as they may be in many respects, they have unquestionably done incalculable good. The light of knowledge has dawned at last on a people sunk in the deep night of ignorance a century ago.

Ireland, during these years, had been violently disturbed by a social movement, certainly the worst which had been witnessed since the Rebellion of 1798. The Established Church still continued to exact the tithe; feeble efforts at a composition of the charge had proved vain; and as the small tillage farms of the peasantry had enormously increased, the burden of the impost had become more grievous and hateful. Many of the clergy, too, of the Evangelical school, earnest proselytisers, had pressed their claims harshly; two Prelates, at least, of the Irish Catholic Church denounced tithe in emphatic language; and O'Connell and the great body of the Irish priesthood —they were indignant that no provision had been made for them—echoed the sentiment in a series of public meetings. The peasantry suddenly rose up in the Southern Provinces, and to a considerable extent in the North, in a wild movement against a tax they abhorred; what is still remembered as the Tithe War raged for several years in a number of counties, and brought out all that is worst in the character of the Celt. The methods usually employed to resist the payment of the tithe were to allow a defaulter's goods to be seized, and to prevent a sale by intimidation of every kind; this became a regular system in most parts of Ireland; and the efforts of the law were wholly frustrated, the collection, it is said, of £12,000, costing the State nearly double that sum. But things often assumed a worse aspect; there were frequent collisions between the police and half-armed peasants; blood was shed freely at Newtown Barry, Carrickshook, Rathcormac, and several other places. By degrees Whiteboyism, as it were, made the movement its own; secret societies backed the opposition to tithe, by assassination and horrible crimes; a wave of general disorder swept over the country, more destructive than had been witnessed for years. Not less than nine thousand offences of the Whiteboy type were committed in the space of a few months; and the well-known symptoms of conspiracies of this class appeared in the terrorising of juries, attacks on magistrates, and attempts to paralyse the administration of the law. Runs on banks, and what has since been known as the base crime of "boycotting" were also common; whole districts, in a word, became scenes of appalling disorder. O'Connell and the priesthood, it should be observed, had, unlike what had happened a few years before, been unable to control or direct the movement, or to keep its barbarous excesses under.

It is to be regretted, no doubt, that in too many instances, the law of the land, and that for ages, was the enemy of the Irish Catholic, and that he has too often been driven, in self defence, to resort to a cruel law of his own, and to vindicate it by detestable sanctions. It is unfortunate, too, that over and over again justice to Ireland has been unwisely retarded, and that redress for wrongs has been obtained only through violent agitation and similar methods. But when such a state of things existed as was seen in Ireland from 1831 to 1834, it is idle to say that it is not to be put down by force; what is called coercion, in fact, is the only immediate remedy; it is worse than folly to speculate on its remote causes, and still worse to hesitate in restoring order. The sentimentalist who refuses to see things as they are is really an abettor of anarchy and crime; he may be quite right in deploring misgovernment in the past, and in denying that repression does permanent good; but he is gravely to blame for false and often interested sympathy with sheer moral evil. The Grey Government properly applied to Parliament to cope with and quell the Reign of social Terror, of which Lord Wellesley wrote, about this time, in these words: "In Ireland there is a complete system of legislation, with the most prompt, vigorous, and savage executive power, sworn, equipped, and armed for all purposes of savage punishment, and that in almost every district . . . Lord Oxmantown truly observes that the combination surpasses the law in vigour, promptitude, and efficiency, and that it is more safe to violate the law than to obey it."[1] A very severe measure of coercion was proposed, the severest perhaps ever applied to Ireland ; it prohibited even public meetings of almost every kind, and set up martial law and its courts in disturbed districts, at the will of the Executive Government ; but there can be no doubt that had Grattan been alive, he would have given it unequivocal support. The Bill was opposed by O'Connell with extraordinary skill and power ; he boldly confronted an assembly incensed at his active obstruction and his licence of speech ; he proved himself to be a Titan of Debate, a match for Peel and Stanley under conditions most adverse to him. Lord Althorp, always averse to coercion, defended the scheme but with a faint heart ;[2] the occasion was remarkable for a masterly speech of Stanley, perhaps the most effective he ever made ; the Bill at last became law, but not without difficulty. It is unnecessary to dilate on the results ; they are such as have repeatedly been seen in Ireland. It is not pretended that a radical cure of deep-seated social ills was effected ; but the rule of Whiteboyism was happily put down ; crime and disorder quickly diminished ; in a few months all that was worst was over.

The Tithe War, however, attracted attention to what ought to have been considered many years before, the position of the Established Church in Ireland, and its relations with a Catholic people. The institution had been

---

[1] See also a striking passage, too long for quotation, in Sir G. Lewis on " Irish Disturbances," a work published in 1836, pp. 306-7.

[2] The feelings of even Liberal Englishmen to Ireland about this time may be gathered from these words of Lord Althorp, the mildest of men : " I have no patience with these Irishmen, and am almost inclined to say that no Government has really done justice to Ireland since Oliver Cromwell."

in some respects improved since we have glanced at what
it was before the Union. Its enormous endowments had
no doubt increased, and were more invidious and odious
than before ; its organisation was defective and worked
badly ; it was still conspicuous for its pluralities, its
empty and wretchedly attended churches, and the iniquitous
distinction between its dignitaries and its inferior clergy.
But it had had several eminent divines at its head ; the
activity of its ministers had certainly increased ; its worst
social abuses had been partly removed ; it was no longer
open, in its moral aspect, to reproach and scandal. Still
it remained, as regards the mass of the people, what it had
been since the days of Elizabeth, an outward and visible
sign of conquest, a rallying point for a dominant caste, a
badge of oppression for a subject race, the outwork of
a garrison, not the Good Shepherd's fold ; it was an
object of the inveterate dislike of the Catholic priesthood,
and of the execration of nine-tenths of the Catholic
peasantry by reason of the hated impost of the tithe. Its
position, therefore, was false and not to be justified ; all that
was good in it bore little fruit ; the very virtues of its
ministers only brought its vices and evils into fuller relief ;
its tendencies, we have seen, had became proselytising and
Calvinistic ; and the conduct of its clergy, in the matter of
the tithe, had greatly increased the animosities it provoked.
When the Grey Government took up the question, O'Connell
proposed the Disestablishment of the Church, and a redis-
tribution of its revenues, included the tithe to be commuted ;
a third part of these was to be allotted to the Irish Catholic
Church ; it is to be regretted that this statesmanlike policy,
very different from that of a subsequent time, was not
adopted in 1832–3. But the compact of the Union stood
in the way, and was still respected by public men ; ideas of
Disestablishment were not currrent ; the Ministry had
recourse to a different measure as liberal probably as
Parliament could be induced to adopt. Ten Sees of the
Established Church were extinguished ; the revenues were
applied to the needs of the lesser clergy ; and Catholic

Ireland was relieved from the Church rate, a tax scarcely less unpopular than the tithe.

This reform, superficial and partial as it was, was indignantly denounced by the Tory party, now beginning to raise its head again ; it was condemned as sacrilege in the Church of England ; it was the proximate cause of the Tractarian movement. The tithe, however, of the Established Church of Ireland remained the really important question ; nothing had been accomplished until this was settled. In view of the terrible state of Ireland, the Grey Ministry, no doubt, regretted that commutation had not been carried into effect in the generation that beheld the Union ; and their difficulties were increased by the disagreeable fact, that the sum of £1,000,000 had been lent to the clergy of the Church, as an advance on the security of arrears of tithe, a loan that was evidently a bad debt. The Government, however, brought in a Bill, in the early part of the Session of 1834, in which the principle of commutation was fully recognised ; tithe was to be converted into a rent charge on land, not four-fifths of the original impost ; the measure passed through a second reading ; but ere long it encountered unforeseen obstacles. The Bill for the reform of the Irish Established Church contained an "Appropriation" Clause, as it was called ; that is, part of the surplus revenues of the Church was to be applied by the State to secular uses ; but this was given up at the instance of Stanley, throughout his life a devoted and consistent churchman. But when the Tithe Bill was proposed afterwards, a resolution was moved in the House of Commons, affirming "appropriation" in no doubtful words ; and Lord John Russell, though faintly, expressed his assent. "Johnny has upset the coach," a sagacious politician exclaimed ; within a few days Stanley threw up his office ; he was accompanied by three of his principal colleagues. O'Connell, it is scarcely necessary to add, had advocated "appropriation" and all that this implied, when it had become evident that his plan for dealing with the Church had no chance of success.

The great Reform Administration of 1831–2, supreme in
the House of Commons for a long time, was thus shaken to
its base on an Irish Question ; an Irish Question, too, caused
its final overthrow. The Coercion Act referred to was about
to expire, and Lord Grey, the head of the Government,
wished to renew it. Lord Brougham, however, the Chancellor, disliked this policy, and, without the knowledge of
his chief, he wrote to Lord Wellesley, the successor of Lord
Anglesey, as Lord-Lieutenant, urging him to recommend
a less Draconic measure. Wellesley sent a reply in favour
of this view, but without informing Grey that he had
been inspired by Brougham ; and meanwhile Lord Althorp,
the leader of the House of Commons, had communicated
with Littleton, the Chief Secretary, that O'Connell might be
let know that an extreme measure of repression would not
be applied to Ireland. All this was done behind Grey's
back, and Littleton, having conferred with O'Connell, persuaded the Irish tribune to withdraw a candidate selected by
him to contest a seat with the Government. The Cabinet
met within a few days ; Grey had heard from Wellesley
what his opinion was, but had been kept in the dark about
everything else ; he insisted on bringing forward a measure
much harsher than Littleton had been led to expect ; at the
same time he expressed his resentment at what was little less
than an intrigue against him. The Bill was introduced by
Grey into the House of Lords ; O'Connell at once declared
in the House of Commons that he had been tricked by
a deceitful Ministry ; the exposure was so painful that
Althorp and Littleton placed their resignations in Grey's
hands. Littleton's resignation was not accepted ; but the
Grey Government was already tottering ; and the veteran
minister, eager before to retire from his post, took the
opportunity to resign himself, indignant at what he thought
the treachery of more than one colleague, and what was one
of those " blunders that are worse than crimes." [1]

[1] For further information respecting an incident now forgotten, but of
extraordinary interest at the time, for it precipitated the fall of the
Grey Government, see Hansard *in loco*, the " Memoirs of Littleton,

The Grey Government had passed useful Irish measures, but these hardly fell in with Irish opinion; they did not deal with the worst ills of Ireland; the great question of the Tithe remained unsettled. It had been necessary, too, to " coerce" Ireland ; O'Connell, who had ably supported the Whigs in 1831, had long been their avowed enemy—his phrase "base, bloody, and brutal" is still remembered— above all, Catholic Emancipation had not been really carried out. From an Irish point of view there were grounds of complaint ; in England and Scotland, on the other hand, the movement against the Union and the Tithe War had caused widespread indignation on the increase ; Irish questions, too, it was thought, stopped British reforms ; Ireland, it was evident, could unmake Ministries ; English and Irish opinion, accordingly, had widely diverged. The first Melbourne Ministry succeeded that of Lord Grey ; Althorp was induced to return to his post ; another attempt was made to deal with the tithe in Ireland. A Commutation Bill was, however, rejected by the House of Lords, and the Ministry was soon afterwards dismissed by William IV. Peel became Premier, almost against his will ; at the General Election of 1835 he obtained a majority of English members ; but the following of O'Connell increased in Ireland, and this, though slightly, inclined the scale against him. He had adopted the policy of commuting the tithe ; but he was still opposed to a diversion of the revenues of the Church to secular uses of any kind; a Bill to this effect was proposed by his Chief Secretary, "appropriation" being, of course, left out. The late Ministers were incensed at having been dismissed ; they were eager to have their revenge on Peel ; but how were they to combine the discordant elements of their majority, divided in many ways, and chiefly dependent upon O'Connell, against a Government of great weight in English opinion ? The leader of the Opposition, Lord John Russell, a Parliamentary tactician of the first order, saw his opportunity in the Irish Tithe Bill ; he moved

Lord Hatherton," and the Greville Memoirs, vol. iii. pp. 105–10. Greville is in error on some points.

a Resolution in the House of Commons in which the principle of " appropriation " was distinctly affirmed.[1] Peel was defeated and his Ministry was broken up; as in the cases of Wellington and Grey, an Irish Question had destroyed a Government, in this instance of remarkable strength in England.

The second Melbourne Government followed the first Administration of Peel.   Its Lord-Lieutenant was Lord Mulgrave, Lord Normanby in later years, an accomplished diplomatist and an able man, who succeeded to the office of Lord Haddington ; the Chief Secretary was Lord Morpeth, afterwards Lord Carlisle, a brilliant scholar, who may rank as a statesman. The position of the Government and the state of parties was remarkable, and the course of events that followed. The Whig Ministry was powerless in the House of Lords, where it was confronted by Wellington, Lyndhurst, and, not least, Brougham, indignant that the Great Seal had been taken from him ; it could expect no mercy from adversaries like these, and it was in a minority on all, and especially on Irish Questions. In the House of Commons it was opposed by a distinct, even a large majority, of English members, led by Peel, Stanley, Sir James Graham, and other men of mark ; and the small majority it had, taking the House as a whole, was chiefly composed of O'Connell's " Tail," every year growing into ampler size, and of Irish Liberals and Whigs who usually voted with him. O'Connell had, therefore, the fate of the Ministry in his hands ; those who know English politics may anticipate the result. The Government and the Irish tribune practically made a compact previously denounced at the time as treason to the State, but assuredly not deserving special blame ; they agreed to work together on well understood conditions, and O'Connell on these terms was to support the Ministry. O'Connell consented to abandon the movement against the Union ; to suspend a demand for Parliamentary Reform in Ireland ; and not to press the policy of Disestab-

[1] For a full account of this transaction see "Speeches and Despatches of Earl Russell," vol. i. p. 102.

lishing the Church, which indeed was obviously not feasible. But he stipulated that Catholic Emancipation in Ireland should be made a reality ; that the Tithe should be commuted with "appropriation," as part of the measure ; and that municipal bodies in Ireland should be reformed, on the principle of the analogous reform in England. The conditions were moderate, even statesmanlike ; as far as was possible they were honourably fulfilled. [1]

O'Connell, accordingly, issued addresses, declaring that, while he kept the Question in reserve, he would not for the present agitate for Repeal; the Government, which he highly praised, were to have "a fair trial." The Ministry, on their side, proceeded to carry out the policy to which they were virtually pledged. The first step was to give real effect to Catholic Emancipation, still almost a name ; they were remarkably successful in this effort. The patronage of Ireland, and especially of the Irish Bar, was placed almost wholly in O'Connell's hands ; he was consulted at least on many appointments ; the trust was executed with singular fairness and prudence. Liberal Protestants received a full share of offices in the State ; but Catholics were freely admitted to the magistracy and similar posts ; and eminent Catholics became Law officers of the Crown, and were raised to the Bench in the Superior Courts of Justice, the first instance of right being done in this province for ages. The effect in conciliating Catholic Ireland, as regards its upper and even middle classes, was great ; and simultaneously O'Connell employed his immense influence in promoting order and obedience to law, and in facilitating the difficult task of the Ministry. At the same time earnest and well-conceived attempts were made to place Protestant and

[1] Lord John Russell, afterwards Earl Russell, remarks (" Speeches and Despatches," vol. i. p. 412) : " An alliance on honourable terms of mutual co-operation undoubtedly existed. The Whigs remained, as before, the firm defenders of the Union ; Mr. O'Connell remained, as before, the ardent advocate of Repeal; but upon intermediate measures, on which the two parties could agree consistently with their principles, there was no want of cordiality, nor did I ever see any cause to complain of Mr. O'Connell's conduct."

Catholic Ireland on a true level of equality before the State and the law, and to secure the pure administration of impartial justice. The odious practice of shutting Catholics out of the jury box, and packing it with Protestants only, was happily brought to an end for years; the fountain of Right was no longer poisoned at its source; the practice, indeed, has scarcely ever reappeared in its worst features. The administration, too, of the law, and its procedure in the inferior Courts was recast and improved; partisan magistrates were removed from the Bench; conspicuous members of the dominant caste, who had done wrong, were dismissed from office; the results were in every respect excellent, especially in gaining the good will of the people, and giving it confidence in the law and its ministers. The most notable, however, of these reforms, and that which, perhaps, was most far-reaching, was the reorganisation of the Constabulary force of Ireland, and of its supplement, the paid magistrates, an institution, we have seen, originally due to Peel. The force had hitherto been mainly composed of Protestants, and had been established only in parts of Ireland. It was now fully thrown open to Catholics; its numbers were very largely increased; it was placed in different stations throughout every county. The paid magistrates were, also, doubled and trebled; the system, under these conditions, has had the best results, in supporting order and law, and in promoting the influences on the side of civilisation and peace.

Protestant Ascendency was thus for the first time brought under the wholesome restraint of law in Ireland; the Irish Catholic felt for the first time that he was a free citizen in the State; and the course of justice was improved and purified. A weighty, and as it proved, almost a crushing blow was also struck at Orangeism and all that is implied in the name. The Orange societies had been continually on the increase; they had their lodges in most Irish counties; they were numerous in London, even in the Colonies; they had made their way into the ranks of the army, under the auspices of the late Duke of York;

they had at their head the notorious Duke of Cumberland, far from an honourable scion of the Royal Family. They had given less scope to excesses of crime and violence than had been the case thirty years before, and they comprised more of the "respectable" classes; but they formed a huge association, spreading far and wide, and with ramifications in many lands, of which the object was to injure the Irish Catholic; they were bound together by secret oaths and passwords; they were, in fact, a vast Freemasonry with a sinister purpose; and the conduct of Orangemen on juries and in the processions they regularly held to commemorate battles and sieges especially offensive to Catholic Ireland, annoyed the Government and even all right-minded men. The Orange Societies were charged with a deliberate plot to change the succession of the Crown of England and to give it to Cumberland, their "Grand Master"; the charge, if not above suspicion, was without rea. proof, but the attention of Parliament was directed to it; and, after a prolonged and careful inquiry, the condemnation of Orangeism was striking and complete. The Association was, to a great extent, broken up; the Orange lodges were in many places dissolved; the organisation divested itself of what was most lawless in its character; the sphere of its influence was greatly narrowed. Orangeism, indeed, has not disappeared in Ireland, but it has long practically been confined to a nook in Ulster; it is now a mere survival of an evil past.

The Irish administration of the Melbourne Government deserves the almost unqualified praise of history. Little was done, indeed, to improve the material state of Ireland, which presented dark and alarming features; in this respect we perceive a marked and grievous omission. Much, too, of the good that certainly followed was caused by O'Connell's persistent efforts to discountenance crime and to maintain order; this interference of a popular tribune was not altogether in the interests of the State, or formed a real security for just government. But Catholic Emancipation was made a great fact; Protestant Ascendency was not allowed to run riot; the administration of the law became impartial and pure, and was greatly strengthened in every respect; the evil reign of Orangeism came to an end. These were great and important moral victories, the consequences of which are felt to this day; things in Ireland were placed on a level of right from which they have not since been displaced, at least for any long space of time; it may be said that Government in Ireland acquired new power; that the Union was based on more stable foundations; and that while Protestant Ireland remained as loyal as of old, the whole upper orders of Catholic Ireland became sincerely attached to the British connection, a sentiment which has ever since increased. It deserves special notice that at this conjuncture it was found possible to govern Ireland by the ordinary law of the land without having recourse to coercive measures; and though this state of things was not to be permanent, it was ominous at least of a better future. The change was not without certain drawbacks; but it justified, in the main, the eloquent words of Macaulay: "The State, long the stepmother of the many, and the mother only of the few, became for the first time the common parent of all the great family. The body of the people began to look on their rulers as friends. Battalion after battalion, squadron after squadron, were withdrawn from districts which, as it had till then been thought, could be governed by the sword alone. Yet the security of property and the authority of law became every day more apparent. Symptoms of amendment, symptoms such as cannot be either concealed or counterfeited, began to appear." [1]

A remarkable man, though in a subordinate office, contributed largely to the success of the Melbourne Administration in Irish affairs. Thomas Drummond was Under-Secretary at the Castle in those years; it is exaggeration to say, as some have said, that he was the master spirit of the Irish Government, and the chief author of the change

[1] Speeches, pp. 596–7. Ed. 1882.

for the better in Ireland. This, indeed, was probably due to O'Connell's influence more than to that of any one personage; and Lord Mulgrave and Lord Morpeth and their able law officers are also entitled to an ample share of praise. But Drummond was a man of real mark, strong in purpose, upright, above all, well acquainted with the real state of Ireland; his superiors certainly owed a great deal to him. He was the real designer of the admirable scheme for enlarging and improving the Constabulary force; his office enabled him to effect much in securing a just administration of the law and in holding the scales even between the warring faiths of Ireland. He dealt an equal measure to Protestant and Catholic alike; punished Ribbonism and Orangeism with an impartial hand when societies of either kind had been guilty of crime; and was, in a real sense, not a respecter of persons—a quality hitherto rare among Irish officials. He distinguished himself also in an inquiry into the conduct of the Irish Executive; he showed that it was prudent, moderate, above all just; he baffled angry zealots of the Protestant caste, who had denounced what was being done at the Castle. Drummond, too, gave proof of remarkable insight in a matter involving large Irish interests; he saw that principles that might be rightly applied to England might be inapplicable to a poor and very backward country; and he recommended, in a masterly report, that railways in Ireland should be the work of the State, at least to a considerable extent, and that their construction should not be abandoned to mere private enterprise. Yet Drummond had faults as a public man; he laboured hard, and with marked effect, to strengthen the bureaucratic rule of the Castle; this was one of his objects in increasing the Constabulary force; and the consequences have been not without mischief. Like other men at the Castle, he also showed undeserved dislike to the Irish landed gentry, and was inclined to lay to their charge what really were the effects of a long term of misrule in the past. When he told them, in dictatorial language, that " Property has its duties as well as its rights," they might have retorted that, in Ireland, Government had not fulfilled its duties, severely as it had enforced its rights, and that too in times by no means remote.

The Melbourne Ministry had meanwhile been endeavouring to effect the other reforms in Ireland, with regard to which it had given a pledge to O'Connell. The great question of the tithe, the source of a frightful social war, still remained open, and had been made a mere stalking-horse for the strife of party, as has too often been the case in Ireland; the Government made repeated attempts at a settlement. It insisted, however, on "an Appropriation Clause" for a time—it could not, indeed, decently act otherwise—but Bills to this effect were rejected by the House of Lords, with the evident approval of English opinion. Even a Bill giving "appropriation" up and substituting a tax on the Irish Protestant clergy, was dropped, perhaps with the consent of O'Connell; the House of Lords would not accept the compromise; the House of Commons did not care for the measure. A settlement was at last brought about, after a ruinous struggle of nearly seven years, which had been productive of the gravest mischief. The principle of "appropriation" was abandoned; the Tithe was converted into a Land Tax, three-fourths in amount of the gross impost, and to be charged to the owner, not to the occupier of land—that is, in the great mass of cases, to the Protestant landlord, not to the Catholic peasant. A wise reform was thus accomplished, tardy as it was; the "shepherds" of the Established Church in Ireland ceased, in Grattan's expressive phrase: "to thrust their crooks into the bodies of the sheep"; the Catholic tiller of the soil and the Presbyterian likewise were relieved from an unjust burden; and in the immense majority of instances they never paid the tithe in the shape of increased rent, as economists predicted would certainly happen. The Established Church, too, obtained a new lease of life; opposition to it was in a great measure disarmed; it was not seriously attacked again for nearly thirty years. The reform, however, had another side; it may have been, in a sense, the means of preventing a more statesmanlike and a larger policy. It retarded for a long time the Disestablishment of the Church; it threw into the background the important question of making a provision for the Irish Catholic clergy. It may be remarked that about this time O'Connell pronounced against an endowment of the kind, in contradiction to professions he had often made before; he declared that his Church would not accept it; but the offer, unfortunately, was never really made, and it is more than doubtful if O'Connell spoke what he felt.

The attention of the Government had been directed also to the condition of the poor in Ireland in these years; it introduced and carried into effect an Irish Poor Law, analogous in some respects to that which had recently passed in England. Ireland, we have seen, had not had a Poor Law before; the principle that Property should bear a charge for the support of Poverty had been eschewed in the Irish Parliament; it had not been vindicated even after the Union. The consequences had been disastrous in the extreme; a Report, published in 1837-8, placed on record the appalling fact that, in a population of more than seven millions of souls, nearly two millions and a half were in abject wretchedness, indeed for months of the year on the verge of starvation. This terrible disclosure was, of course, only a passage in the history of a much larger subject, the state of the Irish land system and landed relations; the misery of these multitudes was but the diseased point where a huge social ulcer came to a head, and the Government did not attempt to reach the source of the malady. But it did insist on passing an Irish Poor Law. Ireland was divided into about a hundred and twenty unions, fashioned, in the main, on the English model. The English system of relieving the poor was adopted with stringent precautions, however, against relief out of doors. It deserves notice that the measure was proposed and carried against the advice of an able Commission, and O'Connell went out of his way to condemn it. In this, however, he was clearly in the wrong; his Catholic sympathies with private charity and his strong attachment to the rights of property unquestionably led him astray in this matter. The Irish Poor Law, nevertheless, was a century too late; it proved unequal, we shall see, to meet an emergency of an awful kind that was ere long to occur. But it rightly asserted a true principle, and though its administration has been far from perfect, it has certainly done real and permanent good.

The question of Municipal Reform for Ireland remained; the Government made efforts to cope with it. Municipal life in Ireland, it is unnecessary to say, was very different from what it had been in England. The municipalities of Ireland, with a few exceptions, were petty towns, hardly more than villages, wholly unlike the great corporate towns of the larger country. Corruption and maladministration, no doubt, existed in the governing bodies of many of the English corporate towns, but these evils were checked by a strong public opinion, and to a great extent by the requirements of considerable and increasing places. Such restraints could not exist in Ireland; her Corporations were, for the most part, little nests of peculation, jobbery, and misrule, wretched oligarchies, narrow, mischievous, bad; and they were strongholds of Protestant Ascendency of the worst type, Catholics having been carefully shut out from their governing bodies, though made eligible by the Relief Act of 1793. There were more than fifty municipalities in Ireland in all. The Government, acting on a very able report, proposed to reform them from top to bottom, throwing the governing bodies open to the townsmen, but making the municipal franchise high, no doubt from fear of possible attacks on property. The opposition, however, led by Peel, resisted the measure in the House of Commons; it would make the Catholic masses supreme in the towns of Ireland; it would create a Catholic Ascendency worse than the Protestant; it would promote agitation, sedition, and trouble. Peel put forward a project of his own instead; he gave up the governing bodies as hopelessly bad, but he proposed to place nearly all the corporate towns of Ireland under the control of Commissioners appointed by the Crown, that is, to deprive them of municipal rights. The House of Commons rejected the scheme, but the Bill of the Government was more than once rejected or mutilated by the House of Lords, as always strongly opposed to the Ministry, especially with respect to its Irish policy.

A compromise was arrived at, but not until 1840; it really was a triumph for Peel and his followers. The great majority of the towns of Ireland lost their corporate powers, but the governing bodies of ten, the largest, of course, were reformed, and the·principle of popular election was applied to these. But the municipal franchise was made very high, and the Corporations were deprived of important rights which they had possessed in their unreformed state.[1] Municipal life in Ireland has never had much energy; the conditions, in fact, have been adverse; but this feeble and inadequate measure required before long, we shall see, a supplement. The Irish administration and legislation of the Melbourne Government presented, indeed, a striking contrast: the first was moderate and just, but thorough and bold; the second, transformed or baffled in Parliament, was maimed, halting, and very imperfect. The Ministry was now approaching its end; it was becoming every year more and more unpopular; its decline had been largely due to its Irish policy. Englishmen thought that Irish interests had been preferred to their own; they had become disgusted with Irish questions; their alienation from Catholic Ireland had increased. They disliked O'Connell, too, and especially his "Tail," his satellites, and those of a Romish priesthood; they felt indignant that their Government was controlled by

---

[1] The speeches of Sheil on Irish Municipal Reform are among the best specimens of his oratory. His attack on Lyndhurst, who had described the Irish as "aliens," is a fine burst of eloquence; but he had mastered the whole subject, and he reasoned it out with great ability and skill. Sheil had not the capacity, the depth, or the wisdom of Grattan, but he could rise to the height of a great argument, and Lord Beaconsfield has described him as the most brilliant rhetorician of his day.

his will. And the conduct of O'Connell had added to the force of this sentiment; he had become an object, in England, of contempt and aversion. He had tried to stir up agitation in England and Scotland, and had made an alliance with a school of Radicals; but though he spoke with characteristic power at several public meetings, the movement he inaugurated completely failed. There was little in common, in fact, between British democrats and a great Catholic Irishman devoted to the Throne, and with a sincere respect for the rights of property; and O'Connell was never in favour with the middle class in England, supreme in directing Parliament at this time, and now rallying around Peel and the Conservative party. But O'Connell suffered most, perhaps, in public opinion owing to the attitude he repeatedly assumed in the House of Commons. He did not, indeed, receive fair play; he was over and over again shouted down in debate, and he was exasperated by the abuse lavished on him, especially by the taunts of the newspaper press, which held him up to odium as the "Big Beggerman," forgetting that, if he was the paid champion of Catholic Ireland, he had abandoned a lucrative profession for its sake, and had refused one of the highest judicial offices honourably pressed on him by the Melbourne Government. But O'Connell often descended to the worst depths of Billingsgate; his language in the House of Commons on many occasions was so scurrilous, coarse, and intemperate that he almost put himself outside the social pale.[1]

The Melbourne Administration disappeared after the General Election of 1841; as an Opposition it was for a long time powerless. Peel returned to office at the head of a large majority; many important questions required attention; but "Ireland," he remarked, "was his great difficulty." His position was, in fact, delicate in Irish affairs; he had been identified for nearly thirty years with Pro-

---

[1] It is scarcely necessary to remind the reader that advocates of great causes have repeatedly been rewarded for their Parliamentary services. Edmund Burke, Grattan, and Cobden are instances.

testant Ascendency, in a party sense ; he had resisted
Catholic Emancipation to the last ; he had opposed nearly
every measure of reform for Ireland introduced by the
Grey and the Melbourne Governments. He appeared to be
the able and bitter foe of Catholic Ireland ; with his great
lieutenant, Stanley, he had long been at odds with
O'Connell ; and Stanley had lately proposed a very restrictive measure which would have disfranchised voters in
Ireland by tens of thousands, and that in constituencies
already small. Even before the fall of the Melbourne
Government O'Connell had set Associations on foot which,
he said, were to be " Precursors of Repeal," should the Whigs
fail in "their fair trial ; " he was now released from the
bargain he had made ; he took his course without hesitation
or delay. He announced that the advent of Peel to office
meant the revival of Protestant Ascendency in its worst
forms, the restoration of Orangeism and its sinister power,
the subjection of Catholic Ireland again, the abrogation of the
Liberal policy of late years ; and once more he preached a
crusade against the Union. It is impossible to say whether
this step was, in the main, a party move against Peel, or the
result of a deep-seated conviction ; it is difficult to suppose
that a man like O'Connell, impulsive and sanguine like most
Celts, but capable, sagacious, and with a strong intelligence,
could, after the experience of 1831–4, have seriously believed beforehand, and in his calm moments, that he could
bring Repeal to a successful issue ; that is, dismember the
Empire against the will of an immense majority of the
people of the Three Kingdoms. It seems probable, however, that as the movement progressed, and attained proportions larger and more formidable than he ever dreamed
of, he really thought he could dissolve the Union, though
his subsequent conduct, after a single rebuff, makes even
this conclusion open to question.

O'Connell directed the new movement on the lines of the
great movement of 1825–9. An Association to agitate for
Repeal was formed ; the Catholic priesthood were again adjured to spread its ramifications throughout the country ;

a Repeal Rent was to be collected ; all Irishmen were invited to condemn the Union. And a social movement was to support the political ; as the Irish peasant, fifteen years before, was to be protected from eviction and acts of wrong, so he was now to obtain an improved tenure of land ; for O'Connell knew well, as experience has shown, that a mere outcry against the Union would have little effect on the mass of the people, if it did not directly appeal to their material interests.[1] The agitation on behalf of Repeal, however, was for many months feeble, and even abortive. O'Connell's influence in Ireland had declined, since the Melbourne Government had well-nigh failed on the Tithe and the Corporation Questions ; at the General Election of 1841 his "Tail" had been largely reduced in size ; his ablest supporters in the great Catholic movement of a better day had fallen away from him ; his conduct in the House of Commons had shocked Liberal Irish Protestants. For a long time the Repeal Association seemed to be a mere phrase ; the Repeal treasury was almost empty ; even the priesthood were not enthusiastic in the cause. At this conjuncture a new and unexpected impulse was given to the languishing movement ; this proved to be of remarkable force. A new generation had sprung up since 1829 ; a knot of young, but very able men, had adopted the creed of the United Irishmen, and had recurred to the conception of a free and independent Ireland, forming a real nation in its combined classes ; and as Repeal in their view would further this end, they eagerly cast in their lot with O'Connell. They founded the *Nation*, a remarkable print, which gradually became a great power in the country, as powerful perhaps as the " Drapier Letters ; " they advocated Irish nationality in prose and verse, often of no ordinary vigour and beauty. Thomas Davis, the leader of " Young Ireland," as it was called, and several of his colleagues were, it may be observed, Protestants ; as events were to show, they differed completely from

---

[1] There was a great deal of excessive renting in Ireland at this time ; but it deserves notice that O'Connell refused to countenance a cry against rack-rents, such was his regard for the rights of property.

O'Connell on points of supreme importance; but for the present they were his devoted followers, and quickened the movement almost into a new existence.

One of the first signs of the growing strength of Repeal was seen in a great debate on the subject in the reformed Corporation of the Irish capital, of which O'Connell had been Lord Mayor in 1842. The speech he made on this occasion was his masterpiece; it is the ablest attack on the Union that has been delivered, at least since the attacks in the Irish Parliament, as Peel's speech of 1834 was the ablest defence. It is remarkable that a reply was attempted by Butt, then a rising lawyer of brilliant parts, in after years, as he has been called, the "Father of Home Rule." The Repeal movement now rapidly swelled in its volume; the priesthood at last flung themselves into the cause; the organisation of 1825-9 was formed again; the Repeal Association had its branches affiliated in five-sixths of the country; the Repeal Rent was collected by "wardens" in large sums from thousands of parishes. O'Connell proclaimed that "1843 would be the Repeal year"; he made progresses through many parts of Ireland attended with extraordinary results. From the first moment, indeed, he completely failed to combine Ireland as a whole against the Union; Presbyterian and Protestant Ireland stood angrily aloof, if a few deserters were found from their ranks; so did nearly all the Catholic gentry, and the great body of traders and professional men; the Property and Intelligence of Ireland, in a word, abhorred Repeal. O'Connell was compelled to fall back on Catholic Ireland, and on the priesthood its real masters; in this field his success was immense and imposing, if its true significance remained apparent. Enormous gatherings of peasants were drawn together to places hallowed in the traditions of the Celt, or notable in Irish Catholic annals; and O'Connell addressed "these monster meetings" in the popular oratory of which he was a perfect master, assuring his hearers that Repeal was at hand, and would bring comfort and well-being to all poor men's homes. The most admirable order prevailed through huge masses, sometimes composed of hundreds of thousands of men ; the spectacle they presented was truly wonderful ; O'Connell was not in error in his boast that they were un-exampled displays of " moral force " ; and though he some-times made use of dangerous language, he repudiated "physical force " in any event, insisted upon obedience to the law, and announced that he would accomplish Repeal without "the shedding of a drop of blood," as he had accomplished Emancipation before.   Nevertheless, as History looks back at these scenes, it perceives that, striking and even grand as they were, a great State was never even shaken by such means.

The Repeal movement was looked upon in foreign lands as the uprising of a nation against its rulers.   France and America at this time were not well disposed towards Eng-land ; in both countries thousands were found to hail " the Irish Revolution " with joyous acclaim ; O'Connell was raised to a pinnacle of fame on which he had never stood before, and was deemed by many enthusiasts the leading man of Europe.   Yet the movement was wanting in essential strength ; it was but the swaying to and fro of chaotic masses under a great agitator and priestly demagogues ; and England indignantly pronounced against it.   English-men, in fact, severely condemned the Government because Repeal was not put down by force at once ; the national sentiment was not for a moment doubtful.[1]   Peel confronted O'Connell with calm sternness ; declared that he would up-hold the Union at any risk and cost ; and made preparations to quell the movement should it unhappily lead to an open outbreak.   A measure to restrict the possession of arms was passed ; the number of troops in Ireland was increased ; the

---

[1] The Greville Memoirs abound in expressions reflecting on the Government for its alleged supineness. As to the opinion entertained of O'Connell in foreign countries, see a striking passage in Macaulay's speeches, p. 652. I have room for one sentence only :—" Go where you will on the Continent . . . the first question asked by your com-panions, be they what they may, is certain to be, ' What will be done with Mr. O'Connell ? ' Look over any file of French journals and you will see what a space he occupies in the eyes of the French people."

" monster meetings " were watched by bodies of police ; a few
Justices of the Peace, who had declared for Repeal, were
—a questionable act of power—removed from the Bench.
O'Connell, meanwhile, had gone on with his work ; his
language to the multitudes he addressed became more de-
fiant ; he entangled himself at last in the net of the law.
The " monster meetings " were possibly not illegal in themselves, though they had a tendency to alarm law-abiding
citizens.   But O'Connell had invited the dismissed magistrates to act as "arbitrators" generally, and so to administer
the law ; he proposed to assemble a " Council of Three
Hundred," in order practically to represent Ireland, a
violation of the Convention Act ; and the dangerous law of
conspiracy had him also in its folds.   The Government saw
and seized the occasion ; a "monster meeting" to be
held at Clontarf—the scene of a great Celtic victory—was
stopped ; and O'Connell and his principal adherents were
placed under arrest.

The State trial that followed, save in its final result,
was an unfortunate specimen of British justice.   The
display of advocacy, indeed, in the Four Courts in Dublin,
was worthy of the best traditions of the Bar of Ireland ;
an aged judge remarked that he "remembered the days
of Ireland's forensic eminence, even of Flood and the men
of his time, but that he had never seen such ability before." [1]
But the proceedings at the trial were marked by incidents
that bore the stamp of iniquity, nay, were scandalous.   The
indictment was of inordinate length, and contained charges
ambiguous, perplexing, even untenable ; but compared to
other things this was only a trifle.   O'Connell was the
foremost man of Catholic Ireland ; in a country torn by a
strife of creeds, he was put on his trial before a Bench composed wholly of Protestant judges, the chief of these
being a notorious partisan, as to whose charge Macaulay
remarked, " to him right, however, I will say that his
charge was not, as it has been called, unprecedented ; for it
bears a very close resemblance to some charges which may

---

[1] Greville's Memoirs, vol. v. p. 233.

be found in the State trials of the reign of Charles the Second." [1] Nevertheless this was by no means the worst; the jury were, to a man, Protestants, some dependents and tradesmen of the Castle; and a mistake, if it was a mistake, was made which damned, so to speak, the whole tribunal. The Recorder of Dublin, an honourable judge, had made up the Jurors' Book in the ordinary way; but no less than sixty names were left out of the list afterwards; and many of them, it was proved, were Catholics.[2] This single fact made the trial unjust. O'Connell and his colleagues were placed in the hands of a jury, not only hostile and packed, but arrayed, by sinister means, for a purpose; Macaulay rightly observed: "The only wise, the only honourable course open to you was to say, 'A mistake has been committed, the mistake has given us an unfair advantage, and of that advantage we will not make use.'"[3] The proceedings, of course, were a foregone conclusion; after a prolonged inquiry, in which Justice was mocked in her seat, O'Connell and his fellows were condemned and sentenced; but the verdict carried no moral weight. Yet "Right was done" at last, in the noble words of our law; and that by the House of Lords, O'Connell's declared enemy. The judgment was reversed, partly on technical grounds, which, however, were in the main substantial; some of the charges were indisputably bad, yet a general verdict had been pronounced on all, and this was, in no sense, an imaginary wrong. The decision of the Lords, however, proceeded chiefly on the falsification of the jury panel, owing to the significant omissions from the list. Lord Denman properly remarked that trial by jury would be made "a mockery, a delusion and a snare" if a contrivance such as this was permitted to succeed.   —

[1] Speeches, p. 654.

[2] It was in reference to this that Sheil made use of these happy expressions, in an address to Peel (Speeches, p. 323): "Does not your own heart inform you that history, in whose tribunal juries are not packed—history, the recorder whose lists are not lost—stern, inflexible, impartial history, upon this series of calamitous proceedings, will pronounce her condemnation?"   [3] Speeches, p. 654.

Catholic Ireland was rightly incensed at O'Connell's trial; the Repeal Rent enormously increased; the Repeal Association appeared to have acquired new strength. A few Protestant gentlemen, indeed, joined it; the principal of these was William Smith O'Brien, an honourable but wrong-headed man, not without fine parts, but spoiled by extreme self-conceit; to whom we shall recur afterwards. O'Connell was liberated from an imprisonment little more than nominal; his followers confidently hoped that the Repeal movement would go on with accelerated force, nay, might be brought to a successful end. They were, however, doomed to a disappointment, striking and complete; the agitation, so imposing a few months before, ere long collapsed and literally died out; it was like the gourd that suddenly springs up and as quickly perishes. The weight of years, and the exertions he had made in 1843, had told heavily on the great tribune; the speech he had made at his trial, in self-defence, was wholly wanting in energy and resource; he was already stricken by a disease which was to prove mortal. After petty demonstrations made to cover a retreat, he retired to take rest in the country for a time; he then pretended to adopt, instead of Repeal, a fantastic scheme of a Federal Irish Parliament, which had found a certain amount of support in Ulster; but before long he abandoned the project; he evidently had not given it serious attention. He vacillated and hesitated as to what he was next to do; it soon became apparent that he had no distinct policy; it was whispered that he had made a second alliance with the Whigs; his followers began to fall away; the Repeal Association became a phantom. A breach, too, every month widening, took place between O'Connell and the Young Ireland party. These men were hardly men of action like Tone; but they were true, in some respects, to Tone's ideal; and they had long resented much in their leader's conduct. They aimed at creating a really United Ireland; they were angry that O'Connell had put his trust only in Catholic Ireland, in the Repeal movement, and had made Irish divisions only more manifest. They rejected, too, the shibboleth of "moral force"; declared that Ireland ought to appeal to the sword, should a favourable opportunity arise; and scorned an agitation that had no results, but shouting multitudes and words that came to nothing. Nor did they admire the presence of the priest in politics, or O'Connell's dictatorial and imperious temper; from this time forward they ceased to have confidence in him.

The period, of which we have traced the leading events, so far as these relate to Irish affairs, falls naturally into two parts. The first part includes nearly all the reforms of importance obtained by Ireland during many years; indeed, in the existing generation of public men. Some of these reforms were of great value, and have done permanent and unquestionable good. Catholic Emancipation was made a reality; Protestant Ascendency and Orangeism were kept down; the administration of justice was immensely improved; the system of National Education has borne ample fruits; the great grievance of the Tithe was removed; the Irish Poor Law was a judicious measure. But the great and important subject of the Land—on which the welfare of Ireland chiefly depended—was not even approached by statesmen; and many of the reforms that were accomplished were too late, or were inadequate and injured as they passed through Parliament; taken as a whole, they fell far short of corresponding reforms in England and Scotland, and they were sometimes opposed to Irish opinion. Ireland in these years played a very important part in determining the politics, nay, the fortunes of the State; Irish questions, if delayed, and often badly handled, more than once made and unmade Ministers. The great body of Englishmen resented this; they felt that Irishmen, so to speak, stood in their way; they perceived that the House of Commons had been invaded by an element indifferent or hostile to British interests, since the measure of 1829 had become law; they were incensed that O'Connell and his "Tail" could rule a British Ministry. All this, added to the aversion which Whiteboy crimes and incessant agitation provoked in

England, caused England and even Scotland to turn aside from Ireland; and this sentiment by degrees increased. England and Scotland, indeed, came to the aid of Ireland at a terrible crisis soon to be noticed; but from this time forward, for nearly thirty years, reforms for Ireland were few and found little favour. For the rest it may be observed that, in this period, the bureaucratic rule of the Castle was strengthened, and the Irish landed gentry were still further weakened; the consequences were to prove, in some respects, unfortunate.

The second part of this period ends with the failure of the great Repeal movement of 1843. That movement attained gigantic proportions, and drew to it the attention of the civilised world. But it was without elements of essential strength; if caused by accidents in some degree, its collapse was ignominious and absolute; it has never appeared in the same form again. The real moral it pointed was that Ireland had completely changed since 1800-1. At that time Protestant Ireland, in the main, disliked the Union; it had now become, with scarcely an exception, attached to it; the intelligence and the wealth of Ireland was on the same side; and Repeal was at bottom the cry of Catholic masses, the instruments of O'Connell and an anti-English priesthood, a cry, too, that would have found little support, had not Repeal been associated in the minds of credulous peasants, with ulterior benefits artfully held out to them. The movement aroused again the anger of England, and strengthened the antipathy Ireland had begun to inspire. To suppose that these Realms were to be rent asunder; that an alien and hostile Legislature was to be set up that might paralyse and baffle the Imperial Parliament; and that a Revolution was to take place in Ireland, necessarily attended with calamitous results—this shocked the conscience and common sense of the nation. Macaulay expressed the mind of England when, amidst the plaudits of a crowded House of Commons, he gave utterance to these significant words: "The Repeal of the Union we regard as fatal to the Empire, and we will never consent to it—

never, though the country should be surrounded by
dangers as great as those which threatened her when her
American Colonies and France and Spain and Holland
were leagued against her, or when the armed neutrality of the
Baltic disputed her maritime rights ; never, though another
Bonaparte should pitch his camp in sight of Dover Castle ;
never, till all had been staked and lost ; never, till the four
quarters of the world have been convulsed by the last
struggle of the great English people for their place among
the nations."

CHAPTER V

Peel inaugurates a new policy for Ireland—Its principles—Charitable bequests—Maynooth—The increased grant to the College—Furious opposition to the measure—Its results not important—The Queen's Colleges—Principles of this scheme of education—Opposition of the Catholic Irish hierarchy—The Colleges a comparative failure—The Devon Commission—State of the Irish land system—The Report of the Commission—The failure of the potato in 1845—Widespread distress—The policy of Peel—Destruction of the potato in 1846—Famine in parts of Ireland—Policy of Lord John Russell and his Government—The Labour Rate Act—Useless Public Works—Relief in food—The Poor Law enlarged—Magnificent private charity—Thousands perished, but millions were saved—Emigration on an enormous scale—Death of O'Connell—His character—Final breach between O'Connell's party and Young Ireland—Smith O'Brien—An Irish Revolutionary party—Mitchell, Meagher, John Finton Lalor—Arrest and transportation of Mitchell—A rising planned—The Government forces it to a head—Arrest and sentence of Smith O'Brien and his principal adherents—Collapse of the movement of 1848.

THE mind of Peel usually moved very slowly, but formed rapid decisions when once made up. We see this quality in many passages of his career—when the currency was reformed in 1819, in the long contest on the Catholic claims, in the movement against the Corn Laws in 1841-6; it was one of his marked defects as a statesman, a chief cause of the party hatreds he provoked. Having been since he was Chief Secretary—that is for a period of thirty years—a champion of the Irish Protestant interest, he suddenly resolved, after the experience of 1843, to

become the author of a new and a different Irish policy.
He had arrived at the conviction that it was now impossible to maintain Protestant Ascendency in Irish affairs,
and that the system was an anachronism and effete; he
had been profoundly impressed by the supreme influence
of O'Connell over the Irish Catholic masses, and by the
evident, if ill-defined aversion of Catholic Ireland, in the
main, to the British connection. His purpose was formed,
it would appear, without taking his party into his confidence; it was certainly strengthened, he declared himself,
by the difficulties in which the State was involved, owing to
the attitude of France, in the affair of Pritchard, and of
the United States on the Oregon Question. The main
principles of his policy were these: he firmly took his
stand on the Union, and refused to listen to schemes to
shake that settlement; and he resolved to maintain
Protestant institutions in Ireland as they were, especially
the institution of the Established Church, placed, he
thought, beyond attack, by an international Treaty. But
his aim was to set, side by side of these, other institutions
of a supplementary kind, which he hoped would be well
received by Catholic Ireland, and would gradually lessen
its avowed disloyalty; "You cannot break up," he said,
"this confederacy by force, but you can do much by acting in a spirit of kindness, forbearance, and generosity."
Peel, also, directed his attention to the state of the Irish
land system and of its social relations, and to the condition
of the millions of the Irish poor, questions which he had
neglected in his early years, and which, though of supreme
importance, more important than any other Irish questions,
had hitherto been hardly touched by our statesmen. At
the instance of one of the Ulster members, a staunch supporter of the claims of Irish tenants, and especially of the
Tenant Right of the North, he had appointed an important
Commission in 1843, to investigate and report on those
subjects; to the labours of this body we shall refer afterwards. It is scarcely necessary to say that, in this respect,
the Minister was consistent with his well-known view that,

before all things, the State should endeavour to promote the material welfare of the mass of the people.

Indications of the change in Peel's mind became ere long apparent in Irish affairs. Lord Mulgrave had been replaced by Lord Ebrington ; his successor as Lord-Lieutenant, in the fall of the Melbourne Administration, was Lord De Grey; and Lord De Grey was supposed to have Orange sympathies. He was followed by Lord Heytesbury, a man after Peel's heart ; at the same time appointments were made, which seemed to forebode a return to the days when O'Connell controlled Irish Whig patronage. The first legislative measure in the same direction was seen in the establishment of a Board empowered to receive bequests for Irish Catholic charities—these had hitherto been thwarted by half penal laws—and to administer them in a just system ; this, if not a very important, was a wise concession, which, on the whole, has had excellent results. A second measure was larger and more far-reaching ; it was notable for the furious passions it aroused, if not attended by the consequences its author hoped for, or indeed by consequences of great moment. The College of Maynooth had, we have seen, been founded in 1793-4, for the education of the Irish priesthood ; and the Irish priesthood, as Tone had, indeed, foretold, had become animated with the sentiments of their race, and had given perhaps its most powerful impulse to the great Catholic movement of 1824-9, and to the Repeal movement of 1842-4. But the College was poor and miserably endowed—it was called a Dotheboys Hall in the House of Commons ;—and the Irish Catholic clergy had, for many years, been drawn from the ranks of the lower middle class in Ireland, especially from those of the large Irish farmers, divided generally in race and faith from their landlords. Peel hoped to raise the status of this order of men, to bring into it sons of the Irish Catholic gentry, friends of the Union, and of British rule in Ireland, and so to lessen its power for agitation and trouble, by adding largely to the resources of Maynooth ; he proposed accordingly nearly to treble the fund which the College had

annually received from Parliament, to make it an absolutely
secure gift, and to devote a considerable sum to the erection
of new buildings.   The Bill became law, but not until it
had raised a storm of indignation in England and Scotland
already estranged from Catholic Ireland ; and it exasperated
a number of Peel's followers on whom it had, so to speak,
been sprung.   It was predicted, at the time, that the measure
was a prelude to the much greater measure of endowing
the Irish Catholic clergy, the salutary, but unaccomplished
policy of another day ; and Peel possibly may have had
this end in view.   But the fierce opposition to the increased
grant to Maynooth must have convinced him that the project was hopeless at this time, though it occurred to more
than one of his successors afterwards ; and it was not
brought before Parliament, on the one occasion, when it
might have prevailed.

The College of Maynooth remained on this footing for a
period of about twenty-five years.   The objects of Peel,
however, were not accomplished ; the quality of the Irish
priesthood was not improved ; they continued to be re-
cruited from the same classes ; they were compelled, indeed,
by ultramontane influence to desist, afterwards, from open
agitation for a time, but their sympathies and character have
not changed.   The third of Peel's measures was an attempt
to advance higher education to some extent, in Ireland,
regard being especially given to the Irish Catholic.   Apart
from the English Universities where the sons of the Irish
aristocracy were still generally sent, Trinity College educated,
with the best results, the youth of a great majority of the
Protestant gentry, and of the Protestant professional and
often mercantile classes ; and, as we have seen, it had made
the Irish Catholics eligible to its degrees more than half a
century before.   Many Catholics had been well trained
within its walls ; but Trinity College still confined its
honours and emoluments to the Protestant caste ; it was
a Protestant institution, from top to bottom ; much of its
teaching was opposed to Catholic dogma.   It was not a
seminary for the education of Catholic youths, as a class ;

and yet Catholic Ireland had not a single foundation of anything like the same kind, which the State recognised. True to the principle he had laid down for himself, Peel did not interfere with Trinity College; but he sought to establish, apart from it, a system of education for Irishmen of the better classes, and, above all, for those of Catholic Ireland. The system he adopted was essentially like that of the "National" system of Stanley; but it had differences and peculiarities of its own. Three Colleges, to be named after the Queen, were to be founded in Galway, Cork, and Belfast; they were to be affiliated to a University empowered to grant degrees; they were to be endowed by the State with sufficient funds; and they were to afford an education of what may be called the University type. But the instruction to be given, so far as respects the State, was to be purely "secular," and in no sense "religious;" and as in the case of the National Schools, the youth in the Colleges were to be taught together. But no real provision was made, though facilities were no doubt afforded, for giving "religious" instruction to the pupils apart; and residence in the Colleges was not required.

A system such as this was, for obvious reasons, more difficult to establish and to render flourishing, than the corresponding National system; and it was more open to grave objections. For example, to refer to a single particular, instruction might be in a real sense "secular," were it limited to the first rudiments, as it professedly was in the National Schools, and the children in them might be well taught together; but could education in such subjects as moral philosophy, history, and several others, involving deep theological questions, and religious controversies of many kinds, be deemed "secular" in a rational acceptation of the word; and could the youth of the warring creeds of Ireland be expected to meet and to learn these subjects in common? Quite conceivably, too, "religious" instruction might not be afforded in the Colleges at all; and the dispensation with residence, if in some respects expedient, was to those who know what University life is, a real and solid ground for

complaint.   The plan was at once denounced as " godless "
by the High Church party in the House of Commons ; and
when submitted to the Irish Catholic bishops, who, in this
matter, claimed to direct their flocks, it was met by an unequivocal protest.[1]   A certain number of the body, indeed,
proposed changes, and even hesitated for a short time afterwards, for the want of high education was sorely felt in
Ireland ; but the Government, though ready to make concessions, refused to depart from the principles of the scheme,
and then the opinion of the hierarchy was again clearly
expressed.   As in the case of the National system, we shall
return to the subject of the Queen's Colleges, to which
Parliament gave its assent, when the system attained a
fuller development ; it must suffice here to say that they
have had a certain measure of success in Presbyterian
Ireland ; but they have completely failed as to Catholic
Ireland, for whose benefit they were mainly designed.[2]

The policy of Peel in setting up in Ireland institutions
mainly for the benefit of the Irish Catholic, and in leaving
Protestant institutions intact, was, perhaps, all that Parliament
would have sanctioned at the time ; but it was a superficial
and imperfect policy ; its results were insignificant and of
little value.   We turn to examine the Irish land system of
this day, and the condition of Irish landed relations, to
which the Minister, we have said, had directed his mind.
The main lines of that system had been little changed since
we considered what they had been thirty years before ; they
exist, though almost transformed, to the present hour.
Absenteeism had continued to increase since steam naviga-
tion had bridged the Channel ; but absentee estates were
much better managed than they had been in the generation
that beheld the Union.   Middleman tenures had very much
diminished, a process going on year after year ; but they

---

[1] See the *ipsissima verba* in Duffy's " Young Ireland," pp. 713–14.
There has been much misapprehension on this subject.

[2] For the position of the Queen's Colleges in Catholic Ireland see
Archbishop Walsh on " The Irish University Question," pp. 31, 33, and
the references.

were still numerous in many counties, especially in those
which were most backward; the resulting mischiefs were
grave and apparent. There had been a considerable en-
largement and consolidation of farms, attended, it should be
said, with much social trouble; but the land of the country
in Leinster, Munster, and Connaught, and in by far the
greatest part of Ulster, remained generally in the occupation
of a humble peasantry, separated from their superiors in
blood and religion. The broad features of the land system
were thus essentially as they had been; but they had been
altered in some important respects, and the alteration had
not been in all points for the better. Ireland had made unquestionable material progress; the distress and dearth which
had followed the war had not culminated in famine since
1822–3; the results were seen in the increase of large holdings, in a marked improvement in many rural industries,
in a rise of rent, legitimate in many instances. But the
population, on the other hand, had gone on multiplying
since 1814–20, having been, at that period, some six millions
and a half of souls, it had become about eight millions three
hundred thousand; and the social consequences may be
easily guessed at. The area of extensive farms had been
enlarged; but the land, taken as a whole, had been more
and more divided into petty and much too minute holdings;
and dense and growing millions swarmed upon these, clinging to the soil as a destructive burden. The Poor Law, it
should be added, a new enactment, had drawn a mere
fraction of these masses from the land; it did not fall in
with Irish tastes and habits; to this day it is disliked by the
people.

This state of things necessarily caused the phenomena to
which we have adverted before. Rents continued to be
forced up by the competition for land, and reached the
highest point they have attained in Ireland [1]; in thousands
of cases they were, no doubt, excessive. The owners of the
land went on living fast, and multiplied the charges on their

[1] The rent of land in Ireland has almost certainly fallen considerably
since 1843–4.

11

estates ; as a class they were more exacting than their forefathers ; and this tendency had increased since their social
influence and political power had been greatly weakened by
O'Connell and the bureaucratic rule of the Castle, and since
they had become alienated more and more from their
tenants. The wages of labour had only slightly advanced,
notwithstanding the progress of the country in wealth, owing
to the growth of the dense population ; the cottar
system was more and more extended with its many and
perilous social mischiefs. Enormous tracts of land were
occupied under these conditions ; in these millions of human
beings lived in misery on a perishable root ; society, in fact,
as was truly said, was " based largely" in Ireland, "on the
potato " ; it was the staff of life, the currency, the main
support of these masses ; What would be the results should
it suddenly fail in a country still not well opened, in parts,
by roads, where there was comparatively little retail trade,
where a commercial middle-class was largely wanting, where
the towns were few, and often far off from each other ?
Turning from these strata of society, of which the evils and
dangers were already too manifest, to the condition of the
large occupiers of the soil, of the class really deserving the
name of farmers, we see also a series of increasing mischiefs.
The rate of rent, we have said, was unduly rising ; but this
was only a part of the manifold ills which affected Irish
landed relations. As the wealth of the country had gone on
increasing the tenants of Ireland had more and more made
additions to the value of their farms, had, in a word, made
more and more improvements ; and in thousands of instances, especially in the North, and largely, also, in the
Southern Provinces, incoming tenants had paid considerable sums to outgoing on the transfer of farms : in fact, had
become, in a sense, their owners by purchase. The concurrent rights, therefore, of the tenant class in the land, had
been made infinitely greater than they had been ; and in
tens of thousands of cases, as Burke had foreseen, they
amounted, morally at least, to a real joint ownership. And
yet, save where it was protected by the Ulster custom, this

huge mass of all but proprietary rights remained outside the pale of the law; it depended for its existence on the will of the owners of the soil.

It is unnecessary to repeat that this Tenant Right, as it may be described, in a single word, could never have established itself in Ireland, had it not had the sanction and the support of the landlords as a class. But rights of this kind, especially as they were inconsistent with the strict modes of tenure, ought assuredly to have been made law-worthy; nor can we forget that Irish landlords were divided from their dependents, in race and faith, in by far the greatest part of the country, and of late years had become more divided from them. And while the rights of the occupiers of the soil had immensely increased, their hold on the land had, within this period, been, to a very considerable extent, diminished. The consolidation of farms had naturally caused the dispossession of thousands of small tenants. The forty-shilling freeholders had all had leases for lives; but the forty-shilling freehold franchise had been abolished; they had generally sunk into the position of tenants-at-will. Add to this that landlords had become more exacting; and we see at once how in many parts of Ireland the position of the farmer had become more and more insecure; and how, in this state of things, Law and Fact had begun to come in sharp conflict in the land system. Evictions, no doubt, were much less frequent than they had been during the years that followed the war; but they had been not uncommon ever since; the odious word "clearing estates" had come into general use. The inevitable and unhappy results ensued: the law of the peasant sought to protect rights unprotected by the law of the land; Whiteboyism, Ribbonism, and their fell organisation of crime had never ceased to make their presence felt. The year 1844 was comparatively a quiet year; but it was marked by a thousand cases of agrarian outrage.

The Commission appointed by Peel was composed of landlords; its President was the head of the great House of Courtenay, an owner of large estates in Ireland. It investigated the state of the Irish land system, in a laborious inquiry of many months; it threw a flood of instructive light on the subject. The historical part of the Report is excellent; it showed how existing Irish landed relations grew out of the conquests and confiscations of the past; it set forth very clearly, and in an immense mass of evidence, the salient facts of the Irish land system, dwelling especially on the dangers of a population much too redundant. Some of the recommendations, too, were judicious and good, particularly as to the enclosure of waste lands, and on emigration, to be conducted on an extensive scale, in order to relieve the land from a destructive incubus. But on the principal passage of the inquiry, the true character of the tenure of land in Ireland, and how the land system was to be improved, the Devon Commission went wholly astray; the conclusions it formed were either false or feeble. Looking at the subject from an English point of view only, the Commissioners saw a complication and confusion of rights, in the modes of occupying land in Ireland, where these were dissimilar to English tenures; they warned Irish landlords that the concurrent rights their tenants might have acquired, through additions to their farms, or because money had been paid on their transfer, were the gradual creation of "embryo copyholds," which ultimately would eat the freehold away; they described Irish Tenant Right as an encroachment on the just rights of property. Instead, therefore, of vindicating and proposing to give the sanction of law to the joint ownership, which the Irish tenant often morally possessed, or, at least, advising that he ought to obtain an absolute title to the improvements he had made, and that going back for a long space of time, they practically ignored, or nearly so, his concurrent rights; his position, they thought, ought, as far as possible, to be assimilated to that of the tenant in England, whose superior supplies permanent improvements to his farm. Complete justice, they conceived, would be done to the Irishman, were he to be compensated, under stringent conditions, for improvements he might make in the future; all that he had done in the past was not to be taken into account, might be confiscated, in a word, should the landlord please. They thus attacked the Tenant Right of Ulster, and analogous rights in the other three provinces; and their Report caused widespread discontent and alarm.[1]

Valuable as the work of the Devon Commission was, it proved itself to be in the suggestions it made, as regards the reform of the Irish land system, "a physician," in the pregnant language of Swift, "ignorant of the constitution of the patient, and the nature of his disease," no uncommon defect of Englishmen in Irish affairs. Stanley had by this time gone to the House of Lords; he brought in a Bill founded on the proposals of the Report; but it encountered opposition, and was allowed to drop. Peel's Irish measures had, therefore, nearly all failed; and on the great subject of the Irish Land, the legislation he intended was a mere abortion, though it is to his credit that he was the first British minister who really touched the Question. Ireland was ere long doomed to pass through a terrible ordeal, one of the most appalling of which a record exists, an agony protracted through more than two years, which has left a permanent mark on its history. The potato, which fed the millions of the Irish poor, had always been a precarious root; it had shown symptoms of decay over and over again; in the autumn of 1845, it was suddenly stricken by a mysterious blight; it failed wholly, or partially, in many districts. The aspect of the withered spaces or patches of tillage, which a spectator beheld in whole counties, was more than sufficient to cause alarm; but if we recollect that this perishing root was the food of fully a third part of the Irish people, and was, indeed, almost their only means of subsistence, we can understand the immediate and universal panic that followed. A wail mournful, pathetic, and yet awful, went out, so to speak, from the heart of Ireland; the land seemed smitten by one of the vials of wrath which

[1] This I can attest myself from boyish recollections. The Irish Land Question was also very intelligently considered, at this time, by Mr. Campbell Foster, the Commissioner of the *Times*.

we read of as instruments of Divine Vengeance ; and in a few weeks more than one county was brought, in many places, to the verge of famine, while all suffered from grave distress. The visitation was most severe in Connaught, and in the more backward parts of Munster, especially along the line of the coast, where the roads were few and bad, and the scattered villages could hardly supply the necessaries of life ; and unquestionably, even in 1845, an unknown number of victims died of starvation. But though the calamity was felt everywhere, it had not such fearful results in the more prosperous and thinly-peopled counties ; in these the crops of cereals were extremely good ; there was a remnant of the potatoes of the year before ; and nearly half the potato crop of 1845 was saved. But even at this juncture, Ireland might be compared to a ship stranded on rocks, amidst devouring waves, already sweeping away a part of the crew, while the remaining part looked out aghast for the morrow.[1]

The failure of the potato, strange as it may now seem, was altogether unexpected in the Three Kingdoms. In the presence of what threatened to be a dire catastrophe, the Government, as usually happens in grave crises, was beset by projectors of heroic remedies. The Parliament of that day would have scoffed at plans for preventing the export of corn from Ireland, or for prohibiting the use of grain in distilleries ; ideas such as these would have been deemed insanity. O'Connell, now with one foot in the grave, babbled about Repeal, almost for the last time, and declared for levying a crushing tax from Irish landlords, schemes—the last especially in conflict with the principles of a life—that were but the signs of senile decay. There was, also, a general demand, at least in Ireland, for the employment of the poor on Public Works, which ultimately would repay their cost ; much was to be said for a measure like this, nor was this policy wholly neglected ; but it may be observed that it would have been impossible to organise

[1] For an account of the great Irish famine of 1845-7, see Hansard, Disraeli's "Life of Lord George Bentinck," and the "Irish Crisis," by Sir C. Trevelyan.

such a system, to any great extent, within the short time
that was alone available. History will hardly deny that
Peel did all that a wise and right-minded statesman could
do in an emergency with which it was difficult in the
extreme to cope. He properly rejected mere nostrums;
he properly trusted to the energies of private enterprise to
make provision, in the main, for the needs of Ireland. But
he knew what the social life of Ireland was; he understood
that what has been called "the commercial principle" could
not supply the wants of millions in distress, in a country
with imperfect communications and little retail trade; he
sagaciously refused to apply to Ireland economic rules that
might have worked well in England and Scotland. Interfering as little as possible with the free play of commerce,
he caused considerable importations of maize to be secretly
bought on the account of the Government; these were sent
out to the most distressed districts; unquestionably they
rescued many lives from death. A much greater problem,
however, remained: How were the Irish masses to procure
the means of eking existence out where the potato had
failed? Peel set a system of Public Works on foot, for
the most part of an unproductive kind—speculators were
to be left to attempt reproductive works; and thousands
of peasants, in different parts of the country, were employed
to labour in this way, at wages paid to them by the State.
These works were to be voted by local bodies, and half the
charge was to be imposed on the district; the other half
was to be borne by the nation as a whole. A small sum,
too, was applied to the drainage of estates, and to other
works of a reproductive nature.

Owing to the preservation of much of the Irish harvest,
and to the judicious precautions taken by Peel, the distress
of 1845, cruel as it was, did not, except in a few districts,
become a real famine. The failure of the potato, as is
well known, was the immediate cause of the Repeal of the
Corn Laws. This great event belongs to English rather·
than to Irish history; but Ireland in this, as in so many
other instances, had a most important influence on British

affairs. An Irish Question, too, precipitated the fall of Peel's celebrated Administration of 1841–6, one of the most power-ful this century has beheld. Partly through the distress which prevailed in Ireland, but also owing to the passions aroused by the collapse of the Repeal movement, there had been an outbreak of agrarian crime in the winter of 1845 ; and Peel, having returned to office, when Lord John Russell had refused to form a Government, submitted a measure of Irish Coercion to Parliament. The Whig Opposition and the mass of the Tories, now led by Disraeli and Lord George Bentinck, accepted the principles of the Bill at least ; but they seized an opportunity to overthrow Peel, and voted against the Bill on a frivolous pretext, which led to the resignation of the great Minister. Lord John Russell and the Whig party came into power ; and in a few months they were forced to confront a disaster in Ireland compared to which the distress of 1845 was well-nigh a trifle. The potato was blighted in every part of Ireland in July and August, 1846 ; it did not yield a twentieth part of its usual increase ; the crop of cereals, too, was excessively short ; the harvest, in a word, almost completely failed. The loss in money was estimated at sixteen millions sterling ; this may afford some idea of what the results were in a country already impoverished, and always very poor. Even in the best and most prosperous districts, society was disorganised in a short time ; there was a general calling in of debts and demands ; the landed gentry received but a fraction of rent ; hundreds of farmers of the better class became bankrupt ; thousands of peasants fled from their homes in despair. In less fortunate counties the consequences were, of course, more grave ; but in the districts which had suffered the year before, and in all those which were more or less backward, the condition of affairs became soon appalling. Famine advancing slowly from the coast line, from Donegal south-wards to Kerry and Cork, and gradually making its way inland, threw its dark shadow over a third part of Ireland ; starving multitudes were lifted up from the land and tossed to and fro to seek the means of prolonging life ; and thousands sank into unknown graves.

Lord John Russell and his colleagues adopted, in the main, the Irish policy of Peel in this tremendous crisis. They rejected extravagant and wild projects ; they refused to set reproductive works on foot, at least for a considerable time ; they chiefly relied on private enterprise to find supplies of food for the masses of poverty. Unlike Peel, however, they did not introduce stores of food into the famished districts bought for the purpose at the expense of the Government ; they established depôts of food at certain places ; but they trusted to the energies of commerce to keep these replenished. For this they have been severely condemned ; but it would have been difficult in the extreme to follow a precedent, which must have been carried out on an immense scale, if really effective relief was to be given ; and the error, if error it was, was venial. But how were they to face the terrible question of supporting millions stricken with want and fourfold in numbers those who had been supported in 1845 ? Here again the example set by Peel was before them ; they followed it, but with a marked difference. The local bodies which had voted unproductive works the year before, had been, it was said, wasteful ; the Government, therefore, obtained an Act—known as the famous Labour Rate Act—which enabled local bodies to vote the works, but imposed on the district the whole and not half the charge ; economy, it was thought, would thus be ensured. These considerations, however, were scattered to the winds as the stress of the dire visitation increased ; the local bodies voted unproductive works wholesale, without regard to what the burden might be, in order to save a people from famine. In the autumn and winter of 1846, whole counties of Ireland presented scenes never witnessed before in a civilised land. Thousands, nay, tens of thousands of peasants, marshalled in gangs, were set to make roads, as a rule useless, and, to this day, for the most part unfinished ; for this worthless labour they received the wages which were to keep their wives and children from death. The numbers thus employed, by the spring of 1847, were considerably more than seven hundred thousand men, representing about three

millions of souls ; the expense was not far from a million
sterling a month. Eleven thousand functionaries were, so
to speak, the officers of these multitudinous arrays of poverty
which resembled "the invasion of some barbaric host appalling the trembling senators of Rome."[1]

This system of relief had saved lives by thousands ; but it
was eating up the resources of a half-ruined land ; it even
weighed heavily on the finances of the State ; it was necessarily demoralising and wasteful in the highest degree.
Parliament met in the first months of 1847 ; other remedies
had to be found to deal with the Famine. The Labour Rate
Act was allowed to drop ; the masses of pauper labour were
gradually drawn from the roads ; but relief was afforded in
the shape of cooked food, to be distributed in all parts of
the country, through the agency of relief committees supported by funds advanced by the State. Millions of human
beings were rescued from starvation in this way, and a considerable saving in money was effected ; but the mortality
among the old was very great, owing to the change from a
root to a cereal diet. The Government turned their attention,
also, to reproductive works, and endeavoured to promote
these to some extent at least. They resisted, indeed, a great
scheme of Lord George Bentinck, for constructing railways
in Ireland, with public monies, in some respects analogous
to that of Drummond ; but the state of the national finances
made this all but hopeless ; and the project has been since
generally condemned as unwise. The Government, however, did sanction important measures for the improvement
of estates by loans for drainage, and by advances to the Board
of Irish Public Works ; but for a mere accident they would
have approved of a considerable loan to Irish railways ;[2]
it is untrue to assert that they made no effort to encourage
reproductive works at this juncture. The great measure of
Lord John Russell's Ministry, that on which they mainly
relied to cope successfully, in the long run, with Irish dis-

---

[1] Disraeli's "Life of Lord George Bentinck," p. 367.

[2] A sum of £620,000 was, in fact, voted by Parliament in a subsequent
year.

tress, was a large extension of the Irish Poor Law, under conditions of a very peculiar kind. Long before this time the Poor Houses had been crammed with inmates flying from their homes to escape from death ; but relief out of doors was not permitted by the law ; and the Poor Law system had completely failed to deal with an emergency never foreseen. Relief out of doors was now made lawful ; and a considerable addition to the liability for rates was imposed on the impoverished owners of the soil. Poor law relief, however, was, with rare exceptions, made subject to an extremely severe condition ; no one occupying more than a quarter of an acre of land could make a claim to receive support from the State. The policy of this enactment was plain ; it established a stringent test of poverty, and checked numberless undue applications for relief ; but it was considered too harsh by Lord Bessborough, the Lord-Lieutenant, an able man, who understood Ireland, and the owner himself of large Irish estates. The results of the making of " the quarter-acre clause," as it was called, soon became manifest in many parts of Ireland. Peasants were compelled in thousands to give up their little holdings, in order to qualify for relief ; emigration, already large, set in on an enormous scale, and became ere long that Exodus of the Irish people which has so powerfully affected the state of the country. The petty occupiers of the soil, in fact, were practically dispossessed by the State in multitudes ; for one victim at the hands of landlords there were probably fifty through the operation of the law.

The harvest of 1847 was good ; but Ireland hardly began to revive until, at least, twelve or fourteen months afterwards. How many victims succumbed to famine, and to disease and fever following in its train, it is impossible to learn from any known evidence ; but they must have numbered thousands, nay, tens of thousands. Enclosed spaces at Skibbereen, and near other towns, mark the sepulchres of hundreds who perished ; more significant still were the sad solitudes where the population literally melted away. The protracted agony presented the various

spectacles repeatedly seen in terrible crises, when human
nature escapes from the trammels of routine, and under
the stress of a cruel trial, exhibits itself in its genuine
aspects. Sublime resignation appeared and inhuman selfishness, charity zealous of good works and the basest greed,
the Christian and the shopkeeping spirit ; but the better
qualities of our race were far the most conspicuous. The
attitude of the great mass of the people was one of patience
and submission to the Divine Will ; the domestic virtues
which mark the Irish character, were never, perhaps, made
more manifest. The division of classes, too, which keep
Irishmen apart, were, to a considerable extent, effaced ;
landlords and tenants pulled together in many districts to
minister to the wants of the poor ; the clergy of the Established Church and the Catholic priesthood co-operated
earnestly in the work of relief. Most remarkable of all,
perhaps, was the world-wide assistance given to Ireland in
her distress, by many nations and lands. England and
Scotland contributed enormous sums ; but what was less
to be expected, help came from all parts of Europe, nay,
from the Turkish Empire ; and the United States were
prominent in lavish kindness. As for the Irish landed
gentry their conduct deserves notice, for it was misrepresented at the time, and has been so ever since. A small
minority, terrified by what they beheld, and yielding to an
idea widely prevalent, that the small farmer must be removed
from the land, his means of subsistence having failed, did
resort to eviction in too many instances ; but in this they
only imitated what was really being done by the State.
But the immense majority abstained from eviction, and
often remitted afterwards the rents they did not press for ;
and the beneficence of the great Irish landlords was, in
many cases, princely.[1] A bitter enemy of the order wrote
thus of its acts, during the ordeal of 1846–7 : " The resident
landlords and their families did, in many cases, devote
themselves to the task of saving their poor people alive.

[1] See as to the conduct of Lord Waterford, "The Two Noble Lives,"
of Mr. Hare.

Many remitted their rents, or half their rents; and ladies kept their servants busy, and their kitchens smoking with continual preparation of food for the poor." [1]

Lord John Russell's Government were fiercely assailed by agitators and sciolists for what they did in this Famine; but History pronounces a different verdict. They certainly committed several mistakes; they might, perhaps, have purchased food after the fashion of Peel; they squandered money on utterly useless works, and relied too long on the Labour Rate Act; they may have considered the subject of reproductive works with too strict a regard to economic doctrines. But they were in the right on relying mainly on the action of commerce and of private enterprise for bringing the necessaries of life to the Irish poor; those who condemn them for this only disclose their ignorance. The policy of the Ministry, with respect to the quarter-acre clause of the Poor Law, was just in principle, but, in existing circumstances, was, no doubt, too harsh; and this and their neglect in not directing and regulating the immense emigration that ensued—a subject on which we shall comment afterwards—were probably the only parts of their conduct which appear to be open to serious question. They manfully resolved, on the other hand, to save Ireland from the fell grasp of Famine; and in this gigantic task they, on the whole, succeeded; thousands perished, but the millions were saved. Their acts and those of the Imperial Parliament stand in marked contrast with those of the Irish Parliament in the Famine, perhaps as disastrous, of 1739–41. The Imperial Parliament voted immense sums for the support of the destitute Irish masses, and a considerable part of these were a free gift; the Irish Parliament, not only did nothing in the shape of public and general relief, but passed a law for the better enforcement of rent!

O'Connell had died while the country he loved had been lying, as it were, in the shadow of death. He had reached the summit of renown, in the eyes of Europe, when he

[1] Mitchell's " History of Ireland," vol. ii. p. 213.

conducted the Repeal movement of 1843; within three
years he was a broken old man, who had seen the cause
he upheld fail, and Ireland in the extreme of misfortune.
His closing days were saddened by the wretched divisions
which destroyed the once formidable party he led; by the
annihilation of his towering hopes; he had almost ceased
to exist before the end came. He appeared in the House
of Commons, for the last time, in the beginning of 1847;
but he was but the phantom of the tribune of the past;
the words he faintly uttered were an appeal to save Ireland
from famine.[1]   He passed away in the spring of that year,
mourned by thousands of still faithful followers; he
bequeathed his ashes to his countrymen, his heart to Rome,
true to the faith to which he had been devoted in life.   It
is difficult to form a just estimate of his career; for
Englishmen have never been just to him; Ireland has
seldom been grateful to her few great men; and he was a
star that rose but to sink in dismal eclipse.   But O'Connell
was the foremost man of Catholic Ireland; his gifts were
of the highest order, if marred by many flaws and defects;
and Catholic Ireland owes an incalculable debt to him.
Not the least important and valuable passage in his life
was his alliance with the Whigs, from 1835 to 1840; he
powerfully contributed to good government in Irish affairs;
he reconciled Irishmen, at least for a time, to their rulers.
His conduct in the Repeal movement is less easy to judge;
but it is absolutely certain that he never aimed at separating
Ireland from Great Britain; his ideal was the restoration of
the old Irish Parliament, an ideal that may have appeared
attainable to a spectator of the events of 1782.   For the
rest the recklessness of O'Connell's language, and the
attitude he often assumed in the House of Commons,
whatever the provocation, deserve censure; and a more
high-minded and sensitive man would not have surrounded
himself with a "Tail" of obsequious satellites.   But O'Connell

---

[1] This pathetic scene is well described in Disraeli's "Life of Lord G.
Bentinck," pp. 159–60.   But the date should be 1847, not, as in that work,
1846.

was a truly religious man ; he was a Conservative in his
essential nature ; he hated revolutionary and socialistic
ideas ; he might play the demagogue, but was not a demagogue at heart. Had he lived in these days, he would have
summarily put down the mannikin traders in the worst
kind of faction, who pretend that they tread in a giant's
footsteps.[1]

The smouldering feud between O'Connell and Young
Ireland had become an envenomed quarrel before his death.
The first open rupture took place on the subject of the
" Queen's Colleges " ; O'Connell echoed the phrase of " godless" ; Davis and his colleagues, willing to try the experiment of education on the " United" principle and hostile to
the pretensions of the Catholic Bishops, supported the
scheme under certain conditions. O'Connell and the priesthood roundly denounced them ; and other causes of dispute

---

[1] Greville, a hostile, but discriminating witness, wrote thus of
O'Connell (" Memoirs," vol. vi. p. 88) : " History will speak of him as one
of the most remarkable men who ever existed ; he will fill a great space in
its pages, his position was unique ; there never was before, and there
never will be again, anything at all resembling it. To rise from the
humblest extraction to the height of Empire, like Napoleon, is no
uncommon destiny ; there have been innumerable successful adventurers and usurpers ; but there never was a man who, without altering
his social position in the slightest, without obtaining any office or
station whatever, raised himself to a height of political power which
gave him an enormous capacity for good or evil, and made him the
most important and conspicuous man of his time and country. It
would not be a very easy matter to do him perfect justice. A careful
examination of his career, and an accurate knowledge of his character,
would be necessary for the purpose. It is impossible to question the
greatness of his abilities, or the sincerity of his patriotism. His
dependence on his country's bounty, in the rent that was levied for so
many years, was alike honourable to the contributors and the recipient ;
it was an income nobly given and nobly earned. Up to the conquest
of Catholic Emancipation his was a great and glorious career. What
he might have done, and what he ought to have done after that, it is
not easy to say, but undoubtedly he did far more mischief than good,
and exhibited anything but a wise, generous, and patriotic spirit. In
Peel's Administration he did nothing but mischief, and it is difficult
to comprehend with what object and what hope he threw Ireland into
confusion."

arose, especially as to the application of the Repeal Rent,
which O'Connell had kept in his hands and disbursed.
Smith O'Brien tried to prevent these squalid discords ; and,
indeed, played a conspicuous part in Irish affairs at this
time.   He was a landed gentleman of good family and
estate ; he had begun life as a Whig, of the school of
Grattan ; but as we have seen, he had joined the Repeal
movement perhaps through indignation at O'Connell's trial.
He was received by the great agitator with open arms, and
welcomed as a leader of the Irish cause ; and during the
months of O'Connell's detention the Repeal Association
acknowledged him as its nominal head.   In the period of
the Famine he distinguished himself very honourably in good
works of charity ; but his nature was impulsive and ill-
balanced ; and he made himself remarkable by proposing
schemes of relief to which Parliament and the Government
could not, in justice, listen.   He became extravagant in his
demands, and offensive ; and though his speeches were
treated with good-natured contempt, his wounded vanity
often found vent in treasonable words.   His efforts to
reconcile O'Connell and Young Ireland failed ; and ultimately he threw in his lot with Young Ireland, which distinctly
charged O'Connell with having made a compact with the
Whigs on the formation of Lord John Russell's Government.
From this time forward the Rump of the Repeal Party, now
led by one of O'Connell's sons, as the great tribune was
succumbing to disease, and Young Ireland became inveterate foes ; the Repeal Association practically disappeared,
and the Repeal movement came, even in name, to an end,
in a land desolated by distress and famine.   The Catholic
hierarchy and priesthood, however, did not the less
pursue Young Ireland with sacerdotal hate.

A section of the Young Ireland party had begun, meanwhile, to conspire against the State, and to enter on a wild
revolutionary course.   Davis, the real leader, had died before
his time ; Duffy had confined himself to the work of the
Nation ; after the breach with O'Connell, violent men,
indignant at the collapse of the Repeal agitation, and at

what they described as the "murderous policy" of an "alien government," during the Famine, came to the front and acquired very marked influence over a party that from the first had rejected the "moral force" doctrine. The principal of these was John Mitchel, a Presbyterian of Ulster, and a professed rebel ; Thomas Francis Meagher, afterwards a brilliant soldier, and a rhetorician of no ordinary power ; and, last but not least, John Finton Lalor, an obscure newspaper writer, but an able man, who had read and thought much on Irish affairs, and who, true to the faith of the extreme United Irishmen, pronounced for rebellion backed by agrarian plunder, and maintained that, in this combination, lay the only hope of success. One circumstance seemed to favour the new movement, which begun to make itself felt at the close of 1847. The Famine had checked agrarian disorder ; in the struggle for existence troubles of this kind had ceased, though, as was to be expected, there had been a great deal of ordinary crime, robberies, burglaries, and attacks on property, which the Executive, however, had easily dealt with. But as soon as the worst of the distress had passed away, agrarian disturbance began to revive ; the secret societies regained power ; and Whiteboyism and Ribbonism appeared once more, for these movements in Ireland, it has often been observed, are inspired rather by revengeful passion than by want, and are not the usual outbreaks of mere reckless poverty. Mitchell and his followers found this machinery made to their hands ; and a rebellious conspiracy made by degrees some progress in three or four counties. For a time, however, the movement had scarcely any force ; it was steadily condemned by the Catholic priesthood, who detested Young Ireland and all its works, and by O'Connell's remaining adherents, who warned their hearers against " the counsels of 1798."

Two accidents gave a distinct impulse to the conspiracy in the first months of 1848. The Chartists threatened a rising in England ; the French Revolution, soon to convulse the Continent, had subverted the existing order of things in a great country to which disaffected

Ireland had through centuries looked for support and sympathy. In an evil hour Smith O'Brien recklessly joined men whose worst designs he abhorred in his heart; he headed a deputation to the chiefs of the new French Republic; but though Lamartine dropped a few honeyed words, he had no notion of involving France in a war with England, or even of giving countenance to Irish treason. The House of Commons naturally broke out in wrath when Smith O'Brien made his appearance in it; the unfortunate dupe of vanity and pique now became the ostensible leader of the rebellious movement. The conspiracy assumed, in the main, the form of the United Irish conspiracy of 1795-8, itself fashioned on the model of Jacobin France. A central confederation existed in Dublin, and had affiliated societies in several districts which were to provide the "armed plant of rebellion." Bodies of men were enrolled under the name of " National Guards "; firearms were collected and pikes fabricated in large quantities. A regular plan of operations was laid down; clubs were organised in a number of towns and villages; and the peasantry were called on to " hold the harvest," and to resist by force, or otherwise, the process of the law. The rising was postponed until September, when the rebel commissariat could obtain supplies; the Castle was to be attacked as in 1641 and 1798; the capital was to be given up to plunder and anarchy. A savage Press of the Jacobin type, of which Mitchell was the master spirit, excited the worst passions of man by the worst appeals.

The Lord-Lieutenant, at this time, was the late Lord Clarendon, a ruler who had only just come to Ireland, but a statesman and a capable man of action. The army in Ireland was considerably increased; precautions were taken for the defence of Dublin; the Lord-Lieutenant, it has been said, secretly armed Orangemen, a questionable policy, even in an emergency of the kind. As the virulence of the seditious Press became worse, and the objects of the conspiracy were developed, Smith O'Brien, Meagher, and Mitchell were arrested and tried; the prosecutions against the two first failed, but Mitchell was convicted and justly transported. The summer had now come ; it was high time to put down a movement, hopeless indeed, but not the less to be condemned. Parliament strengthened the imperfect law of High Treason, and suspended the Habeas Corpus Act ; this gave the Irish Executive the power it required, and warrants were issued for the capture of Smith O'Brien and his chief followers. The purpose of the Government was to force the conspiracy to a head, before the conspirators could secure the harvest ; it was the policy of Clare, in 1798, but a legitimate policy carried out without a single act of cruelty. Smith O'Brien and other rebel leaders fled ; they roamed hopelessly through different parts of the country urging the people " to rise in the cause of Ireland" ; but the time appointed for the rising had not come ; the clubs, probably affrighted, refused to stir ; the peasantry, adjured by their priests, stood impassively aloof. Smith O'Brien was entreated by his desperate followers to give the signal of a war against landlords and the payment of rent ; but it is to his credit that he turned a deaf ear to them. Finding himself without any real support he attacked, with a handful of half-armed boys, a small constabulary force ; his associates dispersed, and, in a short time, he was arrested with other rebel leaders. He was condemned to death with Meagher and several of his chief adherents ; but the sentences were commuted, and he ultimately received a pardon ; the rising, in fact, was a mere flash in the pan, and did not call for vengeance at the hands of the Government. One of the last acts of a tragic farce was a free fight between a body of O'Connell's followers and adherents of the Young Ireland party, which Thackeray has described with characteristic wit.

The Irish rebellion of 1848 was treated with ridicule and contempt in England ; but an armed rising was no doubt planned ;[1] and the result might have been very different had

[1] Greville "Memoirs" (vol. vi. p. 226), significantly says : " The outbreak was within an ace of taking place, and seems to have been prevented by an accident and by the pusillanimity or prudence of the Clubs. They

the Government held its hand until the autumn, or even had Smith O'Brien let agrarian disorder loose. The rebellion, however, had never a chance of success; the Catholic clergy denounced it from the outset; it had no hold on the great mass of the people. It left few apparent traces behind; Ireland continued at rest for many years afterwards, a rest, however, largely due to her social condition. Yet the rebellion was not without permanent results, which developed themselves in the fulness of time. John Finton Lalor, we have said, had studied Irish History; he had seen how hopeless Irish revolutionary movements had been, unless linked with an agrarian movement; how completely the cause of Repeal had failed, and every effort to assail the Union, because they had not been associated with attacks on the rights of the landed gentry. He left, so to speak, a legacy of advice to those who might succeed him. "The people," he wrote in substance, "do not care to subvert the British Government; you cannot move them by talk against the Union; what they want is the land of Ireland for themselves; if, therefore, you wish to shake British rule in Ireland, you must link a revolutionary with a socialistic movement, and hound on the peasantry against their landlords—the real English garrison." These ideas, at this period, were not noticed; they were ultimately to bear the expected fruit.

We need not recur to Peel's Irish reforms. They did not permanently affect Ireland; they have not fulfilled their author's purpose. The Devon Commission was ultimately

had established a very perfect club organisation, and were in a state of great preparation, but had resolved not to rise until September. When the suspension of the Habeas Corpus was proposed, Smith O'Brien and the other leaders saw that they must proceed to action instantly, or that they would be taken up, and they proceeded to Carrick, addressed the people, and asked them if they were ready; they said they were, but the clubs must be consulted; he sent to the clubs, but a small body of troops having marched to Carrick the same day, the clubs were intimidated and refused their consent to the rising. This put an extinguisher on the whole thing; if the clubs had consented many thousands would have poured down the hills."

of great importance ; it prepared the way for large changes in the Irish land system ; but for the present it had few visible results. The Famine is by far the most memorable event in this period of Irish History ; it transformed, in the long run, the social state of Ireland, with consequences we shall ere long notice. Whatever may be said by factious malice, or by ignorance that disregards facts, the calamity was generously dealt with by the British Government, and, in the main, on correct principles ; mistakes and short-comings may, no doubt, be dwelt on ; but a people was saved that could not have saved itself. The abortive rising of 1848 was an exhibition of folly and wrong ; it was looked upon in England as a manifestation of base ingratitude ; it contributed to increase the estrangement from Ireland, which had been going on for many years.

CHAPTER VI

FROM 1848 TO 1868

The Irish Exodus--Sufferings of the emigrants—Mistake of the Government—Aversion to Ireland felt in England—The Rate in Aid Act—The Encumbered Estates Act—Results of this measure—The Queen's visit to Ireland in 1849—The Tenant Right Movement of 1850–52—Its progress and failure—The National system of Education, and the Queen's Colleges condemned at the Synod of Thurles—The Census of 1851 and subsequent years—Revival of Ireland after the Famine in 1853 and afterwards—Growth of material prosperity—Social progress—Comparative tranquillity and order—State of landed relations—The Irish representation in Parliament—Cardinal Cullen and the Catholic Church in Ireland—The tranquillity of the country largely deceptive—Omens of future evils—Influence of the American-Irish on the people at home—Mischievous results—James Stephens and the Phœnix Society—Changes in the fiscal system of Ireland from 1853 to 1860—The Income Tax imposed—The spirit duties raised—Great increase of taxation—Injustice of this policy—The Irish movement in America—Fenianism—Its characteristics—Secret societies in America and Ireland—Their operations—Arrest of Fenian leaders in 1865—Abortive Fenian risings—Attack on Chester Castle—The Manchester executions and the Clerkenwell explosion.

IRELAND, cruelly scathed, had been saved from famine ; the petty rising of 1848 had failed. Years, however, were to pass before society, shaken to its base, and being largely transformed, was to return to anything resembling a settled state, and was to present even a sign of progress. From 1848 to 1851 the most marked phenomenon in Irish affairs was the emigration of the people in great masses from each of the four Provinces, indeed, but especially from Connaught and the South of Munster, the scenes of the worst calamities of 1845–7. The Irish Exodus, as it was rightly called, was, almost everywhere, a spectacle of many woes. In many places families of peasants of the better classes toiled painfully in troops along the roads, fleeing, with their household stuff, as before an invading army. Crowds of the victims of harsh ejection, or of the more pitiless measures of the State, could be seen huddled in spots where there was a chance of shelter, on their way from their ruined homes to the nearest seaport. The workhouse and the fever-shed in country towns sent out their inmates to join the departing hosts ; there was not a village that did not add to the tale of the exiles. Numbers of these waifs and strays of a dire catastrophe made their way to the great cities of England and Scotland, sinking to the lowest depths of the social life around them ; some, more fortunate, reached the Australian Colonies, or settled beside primeval forests in the wilds of Canada. But the over-whelming majority found a refuge in the United States, for more than a century the land of the Irish emigrant ; they swarmed into the chief towns of the great Republic ; they created the new Ireland in the Far West, which has so powerfully affected our more recent history. The sufferings of these multitudes, in the long voyage across the Atlantic, were simply appalling. The noble steamers of this age did not yet exist ; the passage was usually made in small sailing ships, in hundreds of instances not seaworthy. The emigrants were abandoned to the tender mercies of merchants not subject to control by the State ; as the demands of misery far exceeded the means of transport, the consequences may be easily guessed at. The emigrants were crowded into the worst kind of vessels, without sufficient supplies of even the coarsest food, without regard to health, comfort, or even common decency, and thousands perished in the terrible transit. It was not until a noble-hearted Irishman—history preserves the name of Stephen De Vere [1]—braved in person, over and over again, the

---

[1] This distinguished man is still living.

horrors of worse than any middle passage, and spoke out in tones that went home to thousands of minds, that the Government turned their attention to an awful subject.

It would, no doubt, have been a gigantic task had the State undertaken to direct and arrange the emigration of these huge masses ; it is questionable if it would not have been impossible. But the Government might have controlled the greed of merchants ; they might have insisted on regulations being made to secure life and health for these crowds of emigrants ; these precautions, in fact, have been taken afterwards. Unfortunately the creed of " Laissez faire " prevailed in the National Councils ; it was not properly applicable to a grave emergency ; unquestionably it had disastrous results ; and this was the worst error, we believe, of Lord John Russell's Ministry in the terrible crisis of this period. Nothing, perhaps, contributed so much to the fierce resentment which burned in the hearts of thousands of Irishmen, as the apparent neglect of the State in this matter ; it left the bitterest memories which still survive. But unhappily at this time, and for years afterwards, the mind of England had turned against Ireland ; a growing estrangement had become aversion. Englishmen believed they had done great things for Ireland ; they were incensed at the rising of 1848 ; [1] and the Whig Government, not unmindful of the effects of the alliance with O'Connell in 1836–41, were far from overburdened with Irish sympathies. And Ireland, at this juncture, was not able to make its influence really felt in Parliament, or to resist legislation against its interests. The remnant of O'Connell's " Tail " was a flock without a shepherd, straying to and fro without aim or purpose ; his ablest followers were for

---

[1] Greville " Memoirs " (vol. vi. pp. 212–16), wrote as follows in 1848 : "The Irish will look in vain to England, for no subscriptions or Parliamentary grants will they get ; the sources of charity and benevolence are dried up ; the current which flowed last year has been effectually checked by the brutality of the people and the rancorous fury and hatred with which they have met new exertions to serve them. . . . England will not be softened towards Ireland, but contempt will be added to resentment."

the most part gratified Whigs ; the Liberal Irish Protestant
gentry—the best Irish element in the House of Commons—
had largely disappeared, Orangeism had lifted its head
since the late rising, and had sent many representatives from
the North into Parliament. Ireland was never more divided,
weak, and helpless ; she was prostrate, too, from the effects
of the Famine ; her public opinion, never really strong,
had practically been reduced to impotence. The Irish
representation, besides, was pervaded by an atmosphere of
corruption, place-hunting and jobbing ; this was especially
the case in the small boroughs, which returned far more
than a due proportion of members ; this tendency had
increased because the Electorate had been diminished in an
extraordinary degree. At no time perhaps, were Irish public
men more despised and demoralised.

Legislation was before long to show how English opinion
was setting against Ireland. Nearly half of the Irish
Unions had become bankrupt, their resources exhausted by
the strain laid on them through the Famine and the lately
enacted Poor Law ; a law was made, known as the Rate in
Aid Act, which compelled the solvent Irish Unions to
supply the deficit. If the principle of this scheme was
legitimate, it ought not to have been confined to Ireland, it
should have been extended to England at least ; but, while
Wexford and Kildare were made liable to contribute to the
needs of Mayo and Galway, Surrey and Sussex were not to
bear the burden. This measure was simply grotesque
injustice ; no serious excuse was ever made for it. Undoubtedly a large part of the advances made by the
Treasury in 1846–7 were remitted ; but Lord John Russell
had properly said that the charge for the Famine in these
years was to be an Imperial charge ; and, in any case,
nothing could justify the imposition on Irish Unions alone,
of rates subsequently made by other Irish Unions, which
these found it impossible to pay.[1] The Rate in Aid Act,

---

[1] Greville ("Memoirs," vol. vi. p. 279) informs us that the Government
were divided on the question of the Rate in Aid. Lord Lansdowne, a
great Irish proprietor, protested against it ; and one of the Irish Poor

however, was nothing compared to a huge measure of confiscation of the Irish Land, which became law in 1849–50.
The Irish landed gentry had, as a class, heavily charged
their estates, in some instances owing to wasteful excess, in
the immense majority for the support of their families ;
and as the value of their land had been increasing for years,
these encumbrances often seemed to be not extravagant.
The Famine, however, and all that it brought in its train, had
ruined this order of men in hundreds ; their rentals had half
disappeared, their debts were unchanged ; and, besides that,
it had long lost its old power and influence, the class stood
very ill in English opinion, because a few of its members
had been oppressive, it being conveniently forgotten that
the State had been the cause of the dispossession of the
Irish peasant, in infinitely more cases than the decried landlord.   In these circumstances, the time seemed come for
making a grand experiment on the Irish land system.   The
process of selling encumbered estates in Ireland had always
been tedious and costly in the extreme ; this, indeed, was,
perhaps, one main reason that so many encumbered estates
existed.   At the instigation of Peel, for some time their
mentor, the Government proposed to transfer these lands,
wholesale and quickly, by a summary process ; to throw
them upon the market in a mass ; and to hand them over to
a new race of owners, more fitted, it was assumed, to discharge the duties of property.   The object of this policy,
Lord Clarendon announced, was to " sell these encumbered
estates cheap," and to attract to them " English and
Scotch purchasers," who, it was taken for granted, would do
them justice, and improve the state of the peasantry on
them.   A new plantation, in a word, was to be made in
Ireland, like the Plantations of James I. and Cromwell, but
by the peaceful methods of the nineteenth century.[1]

Law Commissioners resigned his office.   The measure was compared
to the medieval expedients of taxing the Jews for the relief of
Christians.
    [1] Greville (" Memoirs," vol. vi. p. 274) describes the spirit which
prompted this legislation :—" Charles Wood contemplates . . . that

In accordance with these views, Parliament passed a statute, almost without a dissentient voice, but described by a great equity lawyer, Sugden, as "removing from property the wise safeguards which the Habeas Corpus Act had secured for persons." At this time hundreds of encumbered estates had passed into the power of the Court of Chancery; this was the only tribunal through which they could be sold; and the process, we have said, was tardy and costly, for almost any encumbrancer could delay a sale, and the difficulties of making out titles were great. The Encumbered Estates Act changed this whole order of things; it created a Court for the special purpose of selling embarrassed landlords out; it empowered the pettiest creditor to force a sale; and it gave purchasers of estates of this kind an absolutely indefeasible title, discharged from all claims but those recorded in the deed of conveyance. The results were such as were to be expected, when property worth many millions was awaiting sale; when Ireland was impoverished and in extreme distress, and when the avowed policy of the Legislature and the Government was to transfer these estates cheaply at all possible speed. Lands at rentals of hundreds of thousands a year were suddenly brought into a half-closed market; creditors, struck with panic, called in their demands, without hesitation, scruple, or pity; and the Commission appointed to carry out this policy proved perfectly equal to fulfil its mission. Estates valued a few years before at more than twenty years' purchase, sold for half or even a third of that sum; many honourable families of the landed gentry which, but for the law, would have been saved, disappeared from their ancestral homes; thousands of creditors lost debts once perfectly secure. Confiscation, however, did not stop at what was above; it

fresh havoc should be made amongst the landed proprietors, that the price of land will at last fall so low as to tempt capitalists to invest their funds therein, and then that the country will begin to revive, and a new condition of prosperity spring from the ruin of the present possessors. This may, supposing it to answer, prove the ultimate regeneration of Ireland."

made its evil effects felt in what was below.   In the case of most of these estates, as throughout Ireland, the occupying tenants had improved their farms, and had acquired concurrent rights in them ; these rights, sometimes amounting to joint ownership, were ruthlessly destroyed by the provision in the Act which gave purchasers a perfect title exempt from such claims.   The spoliations of the sixteenth and seventeenth centuries did not do such a wrong as this ; they affected only the owners of the soil, they did not reach the classes beneath them.

These proceedings went on for three or four years ; until, as was indignantly said, the land of Ireland had been flung, like a fox, to a pack of ravening hounds.   The march of rapine slackened by degrees, as the supply of estates for the hammer fell short, and Ireland slowly began to revive ; the price of land ultimately rose to its normal standard, and even considerably increased in the course of time. The Encumbered Estates Act was, however, renewed ; and from 1850 to the present day, about one-sixth part of the soil of Ireland has been transferred under the provisions of the law.   What have been the consequences of this great experiment ; how have the previsions of its authors been fulfilled ?[1]   A profoundly immoral policy does not often succeed ; confiscation in Ireland has usually found a Nemesis.   English and Scotch capital has reached the Irish Land ; but it has reached it in the form of huge mortgages, a foreign drain on its resources of the most exhausting kind ; but English and Scotch purchasers have hardly ever appeared to make the wastes of Ireland blossom like a rose, and to diffuse wealth and comfort through a contented peasantry.   Nine-tenths, certainly, of the estates that were sold fell into the hands of needy Irishmen of the mercantile or the shop-keeping class, without the associations peculiar to landed gentry ; and their conduct was natural to such a class.   Many of these purchasers bought cheap to

---

[1] Greville (" Memoirs," vol. vi. p. 321) remarks : " Clarendon told me he expected the Encumbered Estates Act would prove the regeneration of Ireland."

sell again in time, and became jobbers in land of the worst type ; but the immense majority bought to retain their possessions, and proved themselves to be the true successors of the previously almost extinct middleman, the historical oppressor of the Irish peasant. The means by which these speculators made their bargains were characteristic and deserve notice. They usually borrowed half the purchase money, and instantly raised their tenants' rents in order to meet the accruing interest ; and as the tenants had no rights under the law, they were compelled to submit to what was a wrong in almost every instance. Most of the cases of harsh eviction, of rack-renting, and of other misdeeds, which have been laid to the charge of Irish landlords during the last forty years, may be ascribed to this order of men ; they are deeply responsible for the numberless ills that have followed. The Encumbered Estates Act, and all that has flowed from it, ought to be a warning to British statesmen not rashly to meddle with the Irish Land, a subject they have meddled with, nevertheless, from the days of Elizabeth to the present hour, usually with the result of making bad worse.

In the summer of 1849 Queen Victoria visited Ireland for the first time. The troubles of 1848 were but a thing of yesterday ; a rebellious faction still hid its head in Dublin ; the Exodus was in full swing with its woeful scenes ; the country was stricken with poverty and distress ; there was much social and even agrarian disorder. It might have been expected that the Sovereign would not have met a welcome reception ; but apprehensions of the kind proved to be happily baseless. The Queen, it is true, did not see much of Ireland ; she made no progress through the disturbed districts ; her visit was one of a few days only. But her appearance in the Irish capital gave the signal of an enthusiastic greeting ; impoverished as the landed gentry were, they flocked to the Court in large numbers ; shouting multitudes joined in a chorus of applause ; the few tokens of disloyalty that struggled into light only made the universal acclaim more manifest. The visit was repeated

in 1853 and in 1861, on both occasions with the same
rejoicings; it is to be regretted that the Queen has not
presented herself more frequently to her Irish subjects.
It is sheer ignorance or flattery to pretend that royal
pageants can make Ireland forget her history, can minister
to a mind diseased with evil memories, can turn disaffection
into loyal content, can reconcile Ireland to British rule, as
if by enchantment. But from the days of Hannibal to those
of Napoleon, the Celt has been devoted to rulers of men; his
genius attaches itself to persons and not to things; Henry
of Anjou showed his politic wisdom in winning the hearts of
the Irish chiefs at the Conquest; his successors might well
have followed the example he set. Nor can we doubt that
the presence on the spot, in Ireland, of the personifica-
tion of the "divinity" of the Crown would have had a
powerful effect on Irish nature; it would have touched
chords of feeling in the Irish heart; it would have smoothed
away asperities in Irish government, and given it a dignity
and grace it does not possess; above all, it would have done
much to lessen the ignorance of Irish affairs and ideas,
which has always been the reproach of British statesmen.
The Queen, it is well known, has often expressed a wish
to visit her Irish dominions again, but has been unhappily
deterred by advisers of little wisdom.

A new agitation had sprung up in Ireland ere long, which
gave promise, for a time, of important results. The Report
of the Devon Commission had alarmed Ulster : two Bills
for compensation for improvements made by Irish tenants,
had, like the Bill of Stanley, been dropped; the Famine and
the Encumbered Estates Act had wrought havoc in the
Irish land system. In numberless instances the pressure
of distress had destroyed the peculium of the farmer of the
North, for his Tenant Right had been eaten away by arrears
of rent; eviction and the new Poor Law had "cleared"
estates, and driven their occupants from their homes in
thousands; the new purchasers in the Court set up in
Dublin were already beginning to evict, and to impose
rack-rents. From 1850 to 1852 a movement was set on foot

for a reform of the land system, in many parts of Ireland ; it drew into it the Presbyterian and the Catholic peasant ; it gradually acquired great apparent strength. Its leaders were numerous and largely composed of priests ; but its chief directors were Duffy, of "Young Ireland" renown, and Frederick Lucas, an English Catholic, a man of high character, and of no ordinary powers. A Tenant League[1] was formed of vast proportions ;. it was sustained by subordinate Leagues all over the country ; the demands of their spokesmen are still of interest, for they corresponded, in many respects, with the landed reforms of a later era. These demands were expressed in a formula, known as the Three F's—fair rent, fixity of tenure, and free sale, a mode of tenure analogous to that under the Ulster custom, and, to a certain extent, approved by O'Connell ; that is, rent was to be adjusted, not by contract, but by what the State or arbitration should decide to be just; the tenant was to remain secure in his farm as long as the "fair" rent was paid ; and he was to have the right to sell his farm, under certain conditions, and to put the purchase money into his pocket. Provision, too, was to be made for the discharge, in part, of arrears, which had accumulated enormously since the Famine ; the tenant was to be relieved by a just composition from a burden intolerable in many cases. The movement gained much additional force at the General Election of 1852, for by this time the Irish Electorate had been enlarged to a considerable extent, by a measure passed a few months before ; the Tenant League, in fact, carried nearly all before it. Some fifty representatives were sent from Ireland to support the claims of the League in the House of Commons ; they had been subjected, too, to a stringent test, which throws a significant light on the Irish politics of the day. They were pledged to stand aloof from all parties in the State, to assume an attitude of strict independence, and above all to accept no Government places, a tolerably clear proof of the opinion entertained at the time

---

[1] The name "League" was preferred to the "Associations" of O'Connell, owing to the triumph of the Anti-Corn-Law League.

of the integrity of the great body of the Irish members, and
of the corrupting influences that prevailed around them.

At this juncture the feeble Government of the late Lord
Derby were clinging to office ; but the opposition was
divided by the angry jealousies of the followers of Lord
John Russell, of Palmerston, and of Peel, who had suddenly
passed away two years before. Had the representatives
of the Tenant League in Ireland been, therefore, a really
united body, an independent party could have accomplished much ; it could have held the balance between the
great parties in the State; it possibly might have attained,
in part, its objects. But the discords, so often fatal to
Irish movements, lurked in this instance under a show
of concord ; the Parliamentary members of the League
had not a common purpose ; notwithstanding the pledges
imposed on them, they were separated into two distinct
parties which distrusted and disliked each other at heart.
The first party was that led by Duffy and Lucas ; it formed
a majority of the representatives of the League ; it was
earnest, sincere, and of one mind ; its sole aim was to win
a measure of Tenant Right, and to effect a thorough reform
in the Irish land system. The second party was considerably less in number ; it was composed partly of survivors of
O'Connell's " Tail " and partly of new adventurers in the
field of politics ; and though it had accepted the kind of
self-denying ordinance to which we have already referred,
it was willing to sacrifice the cause of the Irish farmer for
selfish and purely personal objects. The chiefs of this
faction were John Sadleir, an Irish banker and a dabbler in
finance, utterly without scruple but daring and able, and
William Keogh, a young lawyer of great parts, but, at this
time, of desperate fortunes ; and like their adherents these
two men were ready to throw Tenant Right to the winds, if
it stood in the way of their ambitious hopes. Sadleir and
Keogh had been in the House of Commons before ; they
had fiercely opposed the Ecclesiastical Titles Bill of 1851,
Keogh especially making very able speeches ; and in this
way they had become allies of the small but distinguished

Peelite party which, as is well known, had denounced that measure. In Ireland, too, they had found a powerful supporter in Cullen, then the Catholic Archbishop of Armagh, a prelate of great authority and strength of character, who, of course, sympathised with assailants of the Bill of 1851 ; and many of the Irish Catholic bishops concurred. The party, therefore, of Sadleir and Keogh was sustained by a force of immense weight in Ireland ; and while it made loud professions regarding Tenant Right, it was still more vehement in its exhibition of zeal for the Church, in both instances masking its real purposes.

The Tenant Right League, however, presented a bold and combined front in the short winter Session of 1852. A Bill embodying the Three F's was brought in by an able Catholic lawyer ; the prospect for it seemed for a time not hopeless. Lord Derby's Government had, meanwhile, proposed a measure for the compensation of Irish tenants; and as this included improvements made in the past, as well as improvements made in the future, it would have vindicated, to a considerable extent, the joint ownership existing in many instances, and would have gone a long way to settle the question. The League members promised to support the Government, at this moment in a critical state, if their Bill and that of the Ministry were referred together to a Select Committee. Disraeli was willing to accept the offer. But the Irish followers of Lord Derby would not hear of this. Lord Derby and most of his colleagues agreed with them ; the result was that, when the Government staked their existence on Disraeli's Budget, the League members voted to a man against them, and, in fact, were the force that turned them out of office.[1] The Aberdeen Coalition succeeded to power, another striking instance of the great part Ireland has played in controlling Imperial affairs ; and had the League members continued, as a body, to be faithful to their trust, they might have compelled the incoming Government to support a substantial Tenant Right measure.

[1] For an account of these intrigues see Greville's " Memoirs," vol. vii., p. 33.

But the Whig aristocracy were powerful in the Aberdeen Ministry ; they had, many of them, large estates in Ireland ; they thought the Three F's a project of rapine ; and, probably through the Peelites, they had recourse to the negotiations which, even in O'Connell's time, had detached from him some of his best followers. Sadleir, Keogh, and others of their party received places ; the divisions in the League broke suddenly out ; and the Confederacy, which was to win for the Irish farmer his rights, became a dissolving rope of sand. Duffy, Lucas, and their followers, justly indignant at the cynical violation of a solemn pledge, opposed the successful placemen when they sought re-election ; but Cullen, remembering what Young Ireland had been, and without sympathy with any popular movement, some of the Catholic bishops and many priests supported Sadleir and Keogh at the polls, and this finally broke the Tenant League up. The tenants of Ireland abandoned their cause in despair ; they made no effort to advance it for years ; and the reform of the Irish land system, as had been the case with Catholic Emancipation and other Irish reforms, was most unfortunately postponed for a long space of time, and, when the occasion came, was taken in hand under inauspicious conditions, and, above all, very late. It only remains to add that Lucas died, after having made a fruitless appeal to Rome. Duffy, despairing of his country, went to Australia, where he had an honourable and distinguished career. The fate of Sadleir is still remembered ; he killed himself after committing atrocious frauds. Keogh largely redeemed the errors of his youth after he had become a very able Irish judge.

Cullen and his brethren had played a remarkable part in this important episode in Irish affairs ; they had already become conspicuous in another sphere of conduct. The National system of education—we described it before—had been in existence for many years. Though much opposition had been made to it, it had, on the whole, made decided progress. In 1852 the Primary schools had not less than half a million of pupils, and this after the events of the

Famine. The system, however, had been very generally condemned by the clergy of the Established Church and by a large part of the Protestant gentry. These objections were due in many instances to the spirit of the old Ascendency that could not endure equality, but they rested also on a distinct and a solid principle. Education, they insisted, ought not to be cut in two ; secular instruction ought not to be divorced from religious ; a system, established on this basis, postpones what is divine to what is human, and almost sets spiritual things at nought. A few of the Irish Catholic bishops took this view also, and set themselves against the National system ; but a large majority, and probably five-sixths of the priests, availed themselves of the National schools, even if they did not like them at heart. This attitude was approved for a time at Rome ; and, as we have said, the National system had had a considerable measure of success. By degrees, however, it became an object of the suspicion of the heads of Catholic Ireland ; it must be acknowledged not without sufficient reason. The Catholic Commissioners on the Board which directed the system were only two ; the Protestant and Presbyterian were no less than five. This disproportion was evidently unjust, especially if we bear in mind that three-fourths at least of the children in the Primary schools were Catholics. Other and weightier objections besides remained ; the "secular" instruction, which was to be "united," became by degrees not purely secular ; extracts from the Bible and from religious works of a Protestant complexion were let into the schools ; a change was thus effected in the main principle on which the system was established from the first. Space was thus afforded for proselytising of an insidious kind, the evil most dreaded by the Catholic priesthood, and from which they had been promised protection. Nor was this apprehension without solid grounds if it was probably exaggerated to a great extent.[1] In addi-

[1] See, however, a letter of Archbishop Whateley, the leading man on the Board, in which he avows proselytising objects. Education Department Report, 1896-7, p. 226.

tion to this, the Irish Presbyterians had objected to a day being set apart for the "separate religious" instruction, which had been the rule ; the Board had injudiciously consented to this, and the Catholic bishops had made a protest.

It was at this juncture that Cullen was made the virtual head of the Irish Catholic Prelates. He had been brought up in the traditions of Rome ; he was an extreme ultramontane in faith ; he was a type of the Catholic reaction of 1849–50 ; he disliked the moderation and spirit of compromise which had distinguished some of his episcopal brethren. The system of National education was, of course, opposed to his religious views ; and it is only fair to remark that at this time a proselytising movement had begun in Ireland, directed chiefly by Protestant English zealots, who endeavoured, by very improper means, to win Irish Catholics from allegiance to their Church. At a Synod assembled at Thurles in 1850, the National system was, with other things, condemned by the Irish Catholic bishops ; and a demand, which, however, was not complied with, was made for a separate religious system to be extended to the children of every creed in Ireland. In spite, however, of this ecclesiastical ban, the National system has continued to make progress ; the population of Ireland has largely decreased ; and yet a million of pupils are on the rolls of the schools at a charge to the State of not far from a million and a half sterling. It should be observed, however, that efforts have been made to remove the Catholic objections noticed before ; the Catholic Commissioners on the Board have long been equal in number to the Protestant and the Presbyterian ; secular instruction is in a real sense secular, for books of a sectarian tendency cannot be read in the schools when united education is going on ; and attempts at proselytising have been made impossible. This system has provided for many years a tolerably fair supply of secular knowledge to the children of the humble classes of Ireland ; its success, in this respect, if not brilliant, has, perhaps, been sufficient. But the system has failed as

regards one of its main objects ; separate religious instruction does not flourish in the schools ; and the schools have
not reconciled in the slightest degree the young of the
still divided faiths of Ireland. The system, too, has become,
in the main, sectarian ; the schools are comparatively few in
which Catholics and Protestants are found to meet together,
even for secular instruction of the strictest kind ; the schools,
in fact, are for the most part sectarian, that is, composed
wholly of Catholic or Protestant children. A part, however, of the original principle remains ; the schools are
sectarian, but with a conscience clause ; the Bible cannot
be read in a purely Protestant school ; there can be no
emblem in a purely Catholic school while secular instruction is being given. This system, if accepted, is not liked
in Ireland ; it is not in harmony with the sentiments of a
truly religious people ; and but for the immense subventions
of the State, it would not have had even qualified success.
The chief proof of this is that sectarian schools, in which
religion forms a large part of the teaching, though upheld by
voluntary effort, abound in Ireland, and an Education Rate
in support of the National schools would, beyond question,
be bitterly opposed.

The Queen's Colleges had been established by 1849, and
the Queen's University a few months afterwards. If the
system of National Education was denounced by the Synod
of Thurles, these institutions were naturally denounced also,
and that, too, for a more apparent reason. The system
applied to the National schools could not, in fact, as we
have remarked, be legitimately applied to a University
system. As to this, secular instruction could not be fairly
united, for secular instruction of the higher kind necessarily
involves religious questions and disputes, and we have
already noticed other objections. The Queen's Colleges
and University, we have said, have had some success in
Presbyterian Ireland ; but in Catholic Ireland they have
been almost fruitless, especially since the Catholic bishops
pronounced them to be "godless," echoing the language
of High Churchmen in the House of Commons. The

bishops proved that their anathema was sincere; they founded a Catholic University in 1854; its first head was the illustrious Newman; and this institution, as regards the Irish Catholics, has completely superseded the Queen's Colleges and University, though for many years it could not even lead to a degree, and though it did not receive a shilling from the State, and was kept up by voluntary subscriptions alone, the noble contributions of a very poor people. Meanwhile Trinity College, amply endowed, remained a Protestant institution in the true meaning of the word, as it is essentially Protestant to this day. Years, indeed, were to pass before it made its honours and privileges free to the Irish Catholic or admitted him to its governing body. We shall consider the subject again when an attempt was made to deal generally with Irish University education, as a whole, and when a slight concession was made to the Catholic University at a later date. Enough here to say that Catholic Ireland has, in this matter, substantial grounds for complaint.

The census of 1851 showed that the population of Ireland had decreased by nearly two millions of souls from the highest point it had reached before the Famine. This decline has continued down to the present time; the population is now about the same as it was in 1800–5. The future alone can determine whether this portentous change, which has reduced the number of human beings on the Irish soil from eight millions and a half to four and a half millions, and has scattered the Irish race over many parts of the earth, concentrating it chiefly in the United States, will be to the advantage of the estate of man or in the ultimate interests of the British Empire. Unquestionably, however, and for many years, it conduced to the material welfare of Ireland, and was a condition, in fact, of its social progress. The removal from the land of the wretched multitudes, which preyed on it as a devouring incubus, and disorganised the community almost from top to bottom, not only greatly lessened grave and general dangers, but placed the whole order of things in Ireland on a more secure and an improved basis. Millions of acres were thrown open to real and fruitful husbandry. Whole districts, engrossed by swarms of poverty, were made available for cultivators worthy of the name. Nor was this process harsh after the first few years had passed ; a considerable number of English and Scotch immigrants took possession of tracts of land in a few counties ; but the change was usually effected by the consolidation of farms, petty holdings being absorbed into large holdings, and these were usually possessed by the native peasantry. And while the foundations of the land system were thus strengthened, a series of causes concurred to develop the resources and the general wealth of the country. The railway system, gradually spreading over Ireland, brought her products quickly and cheaply to British markets. This was in itself an important gain. Free trade, not yet ruinous to the large Irish farmer, increased Irish manufactures and Irish commerce. A remarkable impulse, too, was given to agriculture in a variety of ways ; the State, under the Acts lately passed for the purpose, made immense advances to the landed gentry, which were applied to works of enclosure and drainage ; the turnip generally replaced the potato in the case of farms of considerable size ; farming machinery, previously very bad, of the best kind was widely introduced ; the breeds of cattle, horses, and sheep were markedly improved. Ireland, in a word, appeared, in the period, which may be said to have begun about 1854, to make a spring forward in the path of progress.

This increasing prosperity showed itself in many visible signs. The Famine and the Exodus, indeed, left their marks of ruin ; some villages were almost blotted out ; few of the small inland towns made a real advance. But the growing wealth of Dublin created noble suburbs; the streets, the shops, the dwellings, greatly improved ; Belfast, not only doubled in extent, but expanded into a flourishing town, a small Liverpool and Manchester within a single area. One of the most notable evidences of this progress was a grand development of Catholic places of worship ;

the miserable chapels of the days of the Penal Code disappeared; most parishes possessed a suitable church;
stately cathedrals, supreme over the adjoining landscape,
rose often on the sites of the fallen shrines of the past.
The mud hovel, also, throughout whole districts gave way to
habitations of a very different kind ; the increase, indeed, of
houses fit for farmers of substance, and of the lower middle
class in the towns, was a distinctive feature of this period.
The structure of society, too, became sounder and more
stable in some respects; and its relations were better
ordered.   The intense competition for land diminished
for a time; rent, which had been raised to an abnormal
level, was kept down at a more natural rate, especially where
the large farm system prevailed.   Wages, which had sunk to
the lowest point compatible with eking out bare life, were
greatly augmented throughout the country; they rose from
about six or eight shillings a week, to nine, ten, twelve, and
even more ; this increase fortunately has been at least maintained.   Nothing, too, was more remarkable than the auspicious change for the better seen in the mass of the peasantry.
The half-starved cottar was a comparatively rare sight ; the
conveniences, nay, some of the luxuries, of life were brought
to the homes of thousands who had not known them before ;
the dirt and rags of the past were not common ; the Poor
Law, operating properly at last, compelled Property to look
after Poverty, and kept crowds of beggary out of view.
Cheap prices and Free Trade had, of course, their part in
producing a transformation rich with hope for the future.

Comparative tranquillity and order followed in the train
of this material progress.   There were instances, indeed, of
agrarian crime occasionally of a very bad type, largely
to be ascribed to the harsh conduct of purchasers from the
Encumbered Estates Court ; the profound Irish divisions of
race and faith appeared now and then in Orange and kindred riots.   But the surface, at least, of things was not
disturbed ; the community was, as a whole, at peace.   The
agitation and troubles of late years seemed things of the
past ; not a whisper against the Union was heard ; the

atrocious agrarian outbreaks, which had convulsed whole
districts, had ceased to shake the frame of society ; Whiteboyism and Ribbonism scarcely made a sign. The unquestionable improvement of the land system produced an
apparently great improvement in the relations between
the owners and the occupiers of the soil, except in the case
of the new landlords. Absentee estates, as a rule, were well
managed ; scarcely a middleman was to be found save in a
few backward counties ; rents were paid with a punctuality
before unknown ; the peasantry were not only submissive,
but seemed contented. There was no symptom of a Tenant
Right movement ; the enactment of laws which, on the
whole, considerably increased the powers of the landlords,
and modified Irish tenures on the English system, ignoring
the concurrent rights of the tenant in the land, were obeyed
without a breath of general complaint. Political agitation
seemed literally dead ; a feeble attack on the Established
Church of Ireland, greatly strengthened by the commutation
of the tithe, was repeatedly treated with contempt in
Parliament ; Liberal Ministers, once allies of O'Connell,
disregarded the demands of Irish popular members ; the
aversion which England had felt to Ireland, became, what
was far worse, indifference. The representation of Ireland
was at its very lowest ebb ; it had but few men of parts in its
ranks ; it was largely composed of seekers for office and
ambitious lawyers ; the Catholic majority of the members
was reduced to impotence, for some continued to hang on
to the Whigs, while others, after the events of 1859–60,
threw in their lot with the Conservative party, supposed
to have Austrian and even Papal sympathies. The attitude of the Irish Catholic priesthood, in these years, was
not less significant. Cullen had received a Cardinal's hat
from Rome ; he was made all but the absolute ruler of his
Church in Ireland ; and fortified in his natural instincts by
what was going on in Europe, he sternly forbade the
Catholic Irish clergy to take part in popular movements
of any kind, and restricted them to their sacerdotal duties.
Veterans of the Catholic League of O'Connell, and of the

Repeal movement of 1843-4 were prohibited from whispering a word about agrarian reform, or even from condemning the harshest acts of landlords. Cardinal Cullen identified all these things, in his mind, with what was being done by Mazzini, Garibaldi, and other enemies of the Church.

The Irish, like all Celts, and especially the French, have had, in their history, seasons of repose, in which angry passions smouldered beneath the surface of things, to break ultimately out in wild disorders. Such was the period after the Plantation of Ulster, followed by the rising of 1641, and the period of the reign of Charles II. ending in the civil war of 1689-91 ; the period we are surveying was to be of this character. The tranquillity of Ireland from 1854 to about 1865 was in many important respects deceptive ; it was but the " torrent's smoothness before it dashes below." Ireland still remained a comparatively poor country, indisputable as had been its material progress ; it was, relatively to England, now advancing by leaps and bounds under the influence of Free Trade, poorer than it had been thirty years before. Great, too, as the development of its agriculture had been, and notwithstanding the wide consolidation of farms, it was still, in the main, a land of small holdings, with all the consequences that this implies ; the mass of the community was a mere peasantry, not unmindful of the traditions of the past. The wealth of the country had largely increased; but it was dependent, in the main, on two accidents, seasons of good harvests and the high prices of the produce of the soil ; it deserves notice that cries of distress were loudly heard after one or two bad years ; and few of the English and Scotch farmers, who had settled on the land, were, in the long run, prosperous. Elements of social danger, if concealed, were thus not wanting ; meanwhile, in the relations springing from the land, by many degrees the most important, changes were at work ominous of ills in the future. The new landlords, we have said, were, as a rule, exacting, creatures of a confiscation of the most ruthless kind ; they resembled the " planters " of James I. and Cromwell ; the old landlords, if not, as a class, oppressive, had

become more commercial in their dealings, and less kindly
to their dependents than even their fathers had been before
the Famine. By this time they had been very nearly deprived of the last remnants of political power ; they had
never recovered from the effects of the Encumbered Estates
Acts, and under the still growing bureaucratic rule of the
Castle, they had become a mere caste, isolated among the
surrounding people, with the privileges of property but
without its influence, more and more like the old noblesse
of France, to whom we have before compared them. This
state of things was not without advantages of its own ;
it contributed to the supremacy of equal law ; it kept down
the Ascendency of bygone times ; but it was not an
auspicious day for Ireland when it was said that she was
ruled from the Castle by police.

Turning from the owners to the occupiers of the soil the
position of affairs was not without signs of evil. Further
facilities for eviction had been given by law ; the insecurity
of the peasants' tenure, increasing since the extinction of the
forty-shilling freeholds, had year after year become more
apparent. Leasehold interests had very largely diminished ;
the land was being more and more held on tenancies-at-
will ; less protection existed than before 1829–40 against
rack-renting and oppressive eviction. And, at the same time,
as the country grew in wealth, the tenant farmers had added
more and more to the land, and had paid larger and larger
sums on its transfer ; yet as before this joint-ownership was
not supported by law ; and the conflict between Fact and
Law referred to before became more evident if not a source
of much actual trouble. Nor can it be forgotten that Lord
Palmerston, at this period the real head of the State, had
described "Irish Tenant Right, as Irish Landlord Wrong," a
mischievous and utterly false saying ; Lord Clarendon and
one of his successors, Lord Carlisle—the Lord Morpeth of
O'Connell's day—had almost avowed that Ireland could
never prosper until the small occupiers of the soil had been
removed from it. The peasantry did not forget all this, and
understood how unsafe their position was ; we must bear

in mind they had now acquired something like knowledge
in the National schools, and though not much positive
wrong was done, and things went on well in a prosperous
time, they were discontented at heart with their lot, and
elements of disaffection and of ill-will abounded, though
very seldom disclosed. The complete absence of agitation
and the calm that prevailed through the community, was
not without real mischief.   The priesthood, reduced to
silence by Cardinal Cullen, had ceased to be the protectors
of their flocks, or even to urge the just claims of the peasant ;
the Irish representation divided, degraded, feeble, was unable
to assert or to vindicate Irish interests, and left them
unguarded from attack or unfair dealing, and from what
was more dangerous the errors of British statesmen.   And
the fruits of this torpor and stagnation were necessarily
selfishness and baseness in political life, and an absolute
collapse of sound and healthy opinion ; at no time was the
remark of Grattan more true, that Ireland required, above
all things, something like a national organ to express the
will of the people.

These elements of evil, however, would hardly have
acquired strength, and a better order of things might have
been evolved had not pernicious influences come from
abroad into Ireland.   The multitudes of the Exodus, we
have seen, had been scattered over many lands, and a new
Ireland had sprung up across the Atlantic ; the exiles were
animated by a common feeling, hatred of British rule and
of Irish landlords, charged by them with the results of the
Famine. The emigrants naturally found leaders ; these men
endeavoured to combine a movement, especially in the
large American towns, in order to further their avowed
objects ; their emissaries were occasionally despatched to
Ireland ; and as the intercourse between the Irish at home
and the Irish abroad became frequent, rebellious and
socialistic ideas, notably with regard to landed relations,
gradually made their way among the Irish peasantry.   The
first symptom of the new movement appeared as early as
1858 in parts of Munster which the Famine had ravaged ;

James Stephens, one of the rebels of 1848, who, with other associates, had found a home in Paris, and had received a Jacobin welcome, had landed in Ireland and set a secret society on foot; a few hundred men were enrolled in its ranks; and the Phœnix conspiracy, as it was called, made a feeble stir for a time. The local leaders, however, fell into the hands of the Government; their puny efforts seemed of such slight importance that their offences were all but overlooked. Stephens and other kindred spirits fled to the United States; they made efforts to combine their country-men into confederacies which, when an occasion offered, should be able to strike a blow at England, in Canada or at home. Their labours, however, were long fruitless; the Phœnix conspiracy had fallen under the ban of the Catholic Church in Ireland; the peasantry, as in 1848, stood aloof; even the Irish in America seemed not enthusiastic in the cause. The movement, in fact, showed no signs of life in Ireland; and it was crossed and baffled by other move-ments essentially of a different kind. A small remnant of the Young Ireland party now advocated constitutional reforms; Stephens and his followers were fiercely hostile to them; and bold Irish spirits had formed a Papal Legion which fought honourably under Lamoricière, and had no sympathy with anarchic and revolutionary views. Tran-quillity still prevailed in Ireland; no wonder that British statesmen, at all times superficially acquainted with Irish affairs, believed the "Irish difficulty" to be a phantom of the past; their attention, indeed, during this period, was chiefly directed to foreign politics.

The fiscal system of Ireland underwent a memorable change from 1853 to 1860. The House of Commons, we have seen, had passed Resolutions in 1816–17, declaring that, having regard to recent events—to these we have referred before—Ireland might be "assimilated in finance to Great Britain," and that she might be taxed as England and Scot-land were, but subject to the "exemptions and abatements," to which she was entitled under the Treaty of Union, the meaning of these terms, when explained, being that she was

not to be burdened unduly beyond her means. An Act, we
have also seen, was accordingly passed, abolishing the
separate Irish Exchequer and the separate Debts of Great
Britain and Ireland, and fusing them into one National
Debt; the ground, therefore, had, so to speak, been cleared
for realising the ideal of Pitt, but subject always to the
above provision for making British and Irish taxation
uniform. This legislation, however, rather aimed at
relieving Ireland from an iniquitous charge of debt, and
from equally unjust taxation, than at identifying her fiscal
system with that of England and Scotland, and, as a matter
of fact, no attempt was made for years to make British and
Irish taxation the same. The two fiscal systems continued
to be completely different; the duties, indeed, on tea and
tobacco were made equal in the Three Kingdoms,[1] and, in
1842, the duty on stamps; but Ireland long remained free
from a number of taxes to which England and Scotland
had been subject for years. Nor is the reason difficult to
seek : the statesmen of the day of the Union had not all
passed away, they remembered the wrong done to Ireland
from 1800 to 1817; the Irish representation still contained able men, survivors of the great school of Grattan,
and O'Connell at a somewhat later period ; these men would
not have brooked injustice done to their country without at
least an indignant protest, to which they would have contrived to give effect. The most remarkable instance of this
fiscal distinction was seen in the Liberal measures of Peel,
the only one great financier of this century who had any
real knowledge of Irish affairs. Peel inaugurated the policy
of Free Trade ; this required the imposition of direct taxes
in order to get rid of indirect ; and he imposed the income
tax on England and Scotland. But he pointedly exempted
Ireland from the charge, and though he slightly raised the
Irish spirit duties for a time, he soon took this additional
duty off.

From the Union until after the first half of the century,

[1] It deserves notice that eminent Irishmen objected to this attempt
at assimilation, notably Sir John Newport.

the fiscal position of Ireland was not doubtful. She had been treated as a distinct country from the nature of the case, as long as she was liable to the contribution fixed by Pitt; after the abolition of her Exchequer, and the amalgamation of her Debt, Parliament had declared that her taxation must be made identical with that of England and Scotland, subject to her fiscal immunities under the Union. But this uniformity had not taken place, if a few attempts had been made in that direction, as the conduct of Peel had very strikingly shown; she was still fiscally a completely distinct country, as she was in government, administration and other respects. Her fiscal system was to be soon transformed, under conditions that must be described as iniquitous; though far from wholly, she was to be brought nearly under the fiscal system of England and Scotland, as had been the hope of Pitt half a century before. The statesmen who had witnessed the Union and knew its traditions had by this time been removed from the scene; the representation of Ireland was pitiably bad and numbered very few able men; England regarded Ireland with the carelessness of contempt; Ireland was in a state of political apathy. Simultaneously Free Trade was adding enormously to the wealth of Great Britain; the development of this policy was deemed the perfection of wisdom; and one of the first requirements for this, as in the days of Peel, was to supersede indirect taxation by direct. The National finances were under the control of the Minister, who has played so remarkable a part in making or in proposing immense changes in Ireland, in after years, but who, at this time, certainly set her financial interests at nought. Mr. Gladstone, disregarding the wise example of Peel, made Ireland liable to the Income Tax in 1853; and between that year and 1860, had, with his successors, more than trebled her spirit duties. The results may be expressed in one or two figures; the taxation of Ireland, still a very poor country, was increased by a sum of nearly three millions and, compared to that of Great Britain, was largely raised; and her "finances," in the words of Pitt, were "as-

similated" to those of the much more wealthy country, if
not altogether, to a very considerable extent.

A grievous wrong was done to Ireland at this time ; it has
been exposed, from that day to this, by well-informed Irishmen. Any opposition made in Parliament was, nevertheless, feeble ; many Irish members, indeed, protested ; but
their arguments had little influence or weight ; and some
were dragged in the wake of a Ministry of which they were
the obsequious satellites. The Question was investigated
a few years afterwards, by a Committee selected from
the House of Commons ; but the representatives from
Ireland were overborne by specious, but utterly false
sophistry ; they did not thoroughly comprehend the subject ;
and Treasury officials succeeded in mystifying the facts.
We shall comment afterwards on this policy, when its
iniquity was dragged fully into the light by the Report of a
Commission, which has received no answer, though it does
not ·enter into the whole field of inquiry.   Two observations, however, may be made here : though Mr. Gladstone
made Irish taxation identical with that of Great Britain in
most respects, he did not venture to assert that Ireland was
not a distinct country, entitled financially to her special
rights through the Treaty of Union.   On the contrary,
when he imposed the Income Tax on Ireland, he maintained that he gave her an equivalent ; and idle as the
pretence was—he released a questionable debt of £4,000,000
and put on a charge which has amounted to £23,000,000
—still this arrangement kept the principle in view.
Ireland, in fact, even at the present hour, is not fiscally
one with Great Britain ; she preserves some immunities
under the Union ; and the tendencies of statesmen during
the last twenty years has been to acknowledge more and
more her separate financial rights.   The second observation
to be made is this : in 1853–60 the prosperity of England and
Scotland was immense ; Ireland was progressing, no doubt,
but had only emerged from the havoc wrought by the
Famine as it were yesterday ; and Free Trade could not be
as advantageous to an agricultural country, even while

agricultural prices were high, as it was to a country of manufactures and trade. The increase of Irish taxation at this juncture was therefore an act of peculiar harshness; no wonder one of Mr. Gladstone's best colleagues has said, in simple but significant words:—" If the House of Commons, in the period 1853 to 1860, when the great enhancement of taxation took place, had fully considered the circumstances of Ireland, they would not have felt themselves justified in increasing the taxation of that country by means of the Income Tax and the equalisation of the spirit duties." [1]

The Irish movement in America and elsewhere swelled gradually into more ample proportions, especially as the Irish increased in numbers in the Great Republic. Stephens usually had his headquarters in France; O'Mahony, another of the " men of 1848," conducted the agitation in the United States, and Mitchell, who had escaped from confinement, co-operated, if apparently to little purpose. The great Civil War between the North and the South retarded the movement for some time; Irishmen were drawn into the conflict on both sides; as their fathers had crossed bayonets in the Peninsular War, as Celts were in the armies of Hannibal and Rome. Meagher, indeed, became a distinguished soldier; it is unnecessary to refer to other brilliant Irishmen who made themselves conspicuous in a fratricidal strife, the most terrible, perhaps, which History has known. But as the conflict was drawing to a close, the movement was extended and became much stronger; it acquired consistency and an organisation in many lands. The object of the leaders, as it had been from the first, was to form a great league of Irishmen, wherever they could be found, against British rule, and, as a part of it, against Irish landlords; no means were to be omitted, however base or atrocious. A gigantic conspiracy thus came into being; it had its centres in America, in Great Britain, in Ireland, attracting to itself congenial Irish elements, formidable in numbers and appearance at least; it had much in common

[1] Report of the Childers Commission, p. 158.

with the conspiracy of the United Irishmen, when these had resolved to take up arms ; and it presented a strange combination of French Jacobinism, of American skill in uniting bodies of men, on a regular system, for a common object, and of Whiteboyism and Ribbonism, with their sinister methods. Its most destructive feature, however, was this : its main operations were conducted in the dark by irresponsible and concealed leaders ; it was, in fact, a secret society of vast dimensions, making itself felt from the Shannon to the Ohio, and working through the secret societies, depending on it and formed everywhere to carry out its mandates. For England and Ireland, not distant from France, where Stephens was the supreme leader, it had its "Committee of Public Safety" and its minor committees, on the model of the great club of Paris ; it called itself the "Brotherhood of the Irish Republic"; in the United States, where O'Mahony ruled, it was known as the "Fenian Association," an old Gaelic name, with its "Fenian" ramifications extending into almost every State.

The leaders of the organisation formed in this way went energetically on with their work. The secret societies enrolled thousands of Irishmen into their ranks in many parts of the world ; the "Fenians," as they were generally called, were to be found wherever the Irish name was known ; they abounded in the American cities, from the Mississippi to the St. Lawrence ; they were numerous in lands under the Southern Cross ; they swarmed in London, Glasgow, and other centres of British wealth and commerce. These levies of revolution were bound together, as their fathers had been in 1797–8, by passwords, oaths, and mysterious signs ; and numbers were swept into an anarchic movement without knowing what were its ends and its character. At the same time efforts were made in many places to manufacture or to procure fire-arms—the rude pike could not cope with the rifle and bayonet—and bodies of recruits were drilled and received a kind of discipline which gave them the semblance of military force. There were attempts, too, not wholly without success, to introduce

Fenians into the British army and to leaven the Irish
soldiery with disaffection; and ingenious devices were
employed to debauch regiments, to set the men against
their officers, and to threaten mutiny. All this was carried
on stealthily and in the dark; but an incendiary Press,
established in scores of towns, gave free vent to the passions
and the ideas which contributed to the force of the movement. One of these prints was issued under the shadow of
Dublin Castle; the teaching of all was essentially the same.
They described England as a cowardly and hypocritical
Power, and her rulers as brutal and false tyrants; scornfully contrasted British sympathy with the national cause of
Italy and British contempt of the cause of Ireland; and
savagely broke out against the policy of constitutional
reform for Ireland, the policy which had been that of
O'Connell through life, and which, even in this season of
frustrated hopes, had still no inconsiderable support in
the country. But the most striking feature of these publications was this: they proclaimed war to the knife with
Irish landlords, breathed fierce detestation of this whole
order of men, and declared that they were no better than
inhuman pirates or vermin, to be swept from the face of the
earth. The Jacobin Press of 1793–4, was not more vehement against the French seigneurs and emigrés; in fact
these writers felt that Irish landlords were loyal adherents of
British rule in Ireland, the destruction of which was their
first and main object. [1]

Ireland was, of course, to be the Fenian battle-field; her
"liberation from the accursed Saxon yoke and from landlordism," the prize of a Fenian triumph. Great efforts were
made to promote the sacred cause in Ireland; manufac-
tories of arms were set up in Dublin; Fenian envoys

---

[1] Volumes could be filled with extracts from these wicked diatribes.
They are not without interest, for they express the sentiments of a
movement of a later day. I quote a few words taken at random :—
" I recommend my countrymen to shoot the landlord-levellers as we
shoot robbers and rats. . . . I am free to admit that Thuggism has
never produced the death by starvation of two millions of people, and
is therefore, compared to Irish aristocracy, a harmless institution."

crowded the chief Irish seaports ; a considerable number
of recruits, nearly all composed of idlers in the towns and
of desperate men, were added to what was called the " Irish
Republican Army."   Drilling by night, also, took place in
some counties ; a force of imposing size was arrayed upon
paper ; maps were made, as in 1798, of lands to be the spoils
of confiscation, in the event of success ; the lands were to
be allotted to the champions of the rights of Ireland.
Secret appeals, too, were made to the peasantry ; but they
turned, from the first, a deaf ear to them.   The occupiers
of the Irish soil had, no doubt, grievances ; they were
ready, as time was to show, under certain conditions, to
take part in a great agrarian movement ; but they had a
keen eye to their own interests ; they saw a prospect of
loss, nay of ruin, for themselves, in a revolutionary scheme
of plunder ; they were still, as of old, a somewhat inert
mass ; they were not suffering, as in 1798, from cruel
wrongs which would arouse even the timid to fury ; above
all, they lent a willing ear to their priests, who, by the express
orders of Cardinal Cullen, denounced Fenianism as the
worst kind of rebellious wickedness.   With scarcely an
exception, they repudiated Fenian teaching ; in fact, the
Fenian leaders had misunderstood their position, their
sentiments, and the only means through which their sympathies could be reached, and they could be led even to think
of taking a side in the movement.   The close of the Civil
War in America, nevertheless, gave Fenianism a real
impulse outside Ireland ; thousands of Irish soldiers were
set free to bear arms in the cause, and hundreds of Irish-
American officers ; as nearly always happens in similar
cases, the reports of emissaries misrepresented the facts ; and
a plan was certainly formed for an armed Irish rising, to be
assisted by a Fenian contingent from the Far West, as the
rebels of 1798 were assisted from France.   The Irish Government, however, had, all through, as has commonly been
the misfortune of Irish treason, been kept acquainted with
what was going on by spies and informers in the pay of the
Castle ;   Lord Wodehouse, the successor of Lord Carlisle,

struck the first blow by destroying the rebellious journal
which had defied British rule, so to speak, in his presence,
and by sending its chief conductors to prison. Stephens,
who had landed in Ireland, was also arrested ; and though
he contrived to effect his escape through the connivance of
one of the prison officials, Fenianism had already received
a weighty blow in Ireland. The conspiracy evidently was
known to the men in power ; timid hearts quailed and
abandoned the cause. The arrested journalists were tried
and severely punished ; the movement seemed to have
collapsed for a time.

An immense conspiracy, however, sometimes dies hard ;
imperfect as may be its essential strength, its secrecy must
be more or less dangerous. The Fenian leaders did not yet
cease to hope ; from the autumn of 1865 to the spring of
1867 they redoubled the efforts and the devices they had
resorted to to effect an Irish rising, to be accompanied, too,
by diversions to be made in England. But the Government
and Parliament had learned what they had to deal with ;
the Habeas Corpus Act was suspended at once ; suspected
persons were arrested by scores ; the importation, even the
use of arms was prohibited, save under very strict precautions. Ireland, in fact, was placed in a state of siege ; and
the armed force in the towns was largely augmented. Rebellion, therefore, and aid from abroad, on anything like a
large scale, were made simply impossible ; the Irish levies,
which had been nominally enrolled, were left without
weapons completely helpless. Dissensions, too, the usual
curse of Irish movements, had broken out among the Fenian
leaders ; Stephens thought discretion the better part of
valour, and did not reappear on the scene ; O'Mahony was
deposed by his colleagues ; the heads of the conspiracy
became at feud with each other. Nevertheless, a petty outbreak took place ; a few bodies of half-armed men rose in
Kerry, in Limerick, and other counties, but were easily
put down by the Constabulary on the spot, a small
Fenian party, which marched out from Dublin, was
cleverly caught and disarmed by a handful of troops ;

some Irish-American officers, who had landed at Cork, and expected to find a military force to command, were quickly captured and sent to jail ; an Irish-American cruiser was compelled to leave the coast. The rising, in fact, was as complete a failure as that of 1848 ; and after the punishment of the chief ringleaders the "rebellion of 1867" was almost forgotten in Ireland. It was otherwise in England, where events happened which made a profound impression on the national mind. A Fenian raid upon the Castle of Chester was frustrated only by mere accident ; a Fenian rescue which took place near Manchester and led to the murder of a peace officer ; the trials and executions which followed ; the fierce execrations which broke out in Ireland as the victims of the law were sent to the scaffold ; the voice of Irish opinion, among the people, which mourned for these men as patriotic martyrs ; and finally the destruction of a prison wall at Clerkenwell, an act of violence committed to effect the escape of a Fenian prisoner of some note :—all this, after a momentary ebullition of wrath, sank deep into the hearts of Englishmen, and especially told on the English Democracy, now beginning to be a great power in the State. These occurrences, with their ominous symptoms, happening after Ireland had been in repose for years, and after British statesmen had repeatedly declared that Irish troubles had for ever been set to rest, caused thousands to think that there still must be something rotten in the state of Irish affairs ; that Ireland must have real grievances and wrongs ; and that a change in Irish policy was a necessity of the time.

The period from 1848 to 1868 forms a very striking episode in Irish History. The emigration of a great part of the people, in circumstances that must be deeply lamented, scattered the race over many foreign lands, and planted it firmly in the Far West ; the consequences have been already momentous ; we do not know what they may yet bring forth. The foolish and pitiable rising of 1848 turned the mind of England against Ireland : this was seen in legislation which cannot be justified, in the Rate in Aid Act, the

fatal Encumbered Estates Act, ruinous to the landed gentry,
and pregnant with many evils—in the bad fiscal measures of
1853–1860 ; and aversion only grew into indifference, a
dangerous attitude towards a weak and divided people. The
removal, however, of impoverished millions from the Irish
soil unquestionably had beneficial results ; Ireland made
real material and social progress, and this has been to some
extent permanent.ɾ The tranquillity and the season of peace
that followed was certainly deceptive in many respects ;
reforms were neglected that ought to have been made, and
good opportunities unhappily lost ; and the political stagnation that marks those years was attended with mischief in
Irish affairs. Yet the order of things in Ireland might have
been made better had not the Fenian conspiracy, expressing
the hatred of the Irish abroad to British rule in Ireland, and
to the Irish landlords, as a class, interfered to create confusion for a time, and, what was infinitely worse, to sow the
seeds of evil, the full harvest of which has not been, even
yet, gathered in. Fenianism cannot be ascribed, in justice,
as it has been ascribed by a school of critics, to the gross
misgovernment of Ireland at the time : it was a movement
that sprung up outside Ireland, and was directed by Irishmen from distant lands ; it found little support from the
Irish community on the spot. The conspiracy completely
failed in its objects, and was contemptible in a certain
sense ; but it powerfully affected English opinion ; it was to
lead to immense changes in the state of Ireland ; and, in
this sense, it was a most important event. Ireland was now
to enter upon a path of reform and trouble, of which the end
it still out of sight ; and, as had so repeatedly been the case
before, she was to have great influence in shaping the
fortunes of England.

CHAPTER VII

AN ERA OF REFORM FOR IRELAND—THE HOME RULE MOVEMENT.

Change of opinion in England and Scotland, with respect to Ireland, after the Fenian outbreak—Demand for reforms in Ireland—The position of the Irish Established Church—Combination of parties against it—Mr. Gladstone insists on its Disestablishment and Disendowment—He becomes Prime Minister after the General Election of 1868—The Act of 1869 disestablishing and disendowing the Church—Its characteristics and results—The Land System of Ireland in 1870—The Land Act of 1870—Origin of the Irish Home Rule movement—Isaac Butt—His scheme of Home Rule—Mr. Gladstone ridicules this policy—The Irish Education Bill of 1873—Its grave defects—It fails to pass the House of Commons—Other Irish measures—Fall of Mr. Gladstone's Government—A large Home Rule party in Parliament after the General Election of 1874—Policy of Butt and his followers—Home Rule rejected with contempt in the House of Commons—Failure of other measures proposed by Butt—Unfortunate results—Butt's authority, as a leader, declines—Rise of Parnell—His antecedents and character—Policy of obstruction—Ability already shown by Parnell—Still further decline of Butt's influence—Irish measures of Lord Beaconfield's Government—State of Ireland in 1877-8—Deceptive prosperity—Symptoms of danger—Optimism of Mr. Gladstone and other statesmen.

THE Fenian conspiracy had failed in Ireland ; but in Great Britain it had caused disorder and trouble ; and in a general sense it was an Irish movement, if it drew the chief elements of its strength from across the Atlantic. It had given rise, we have said, to a widespread conviction, that, notwithstanding the tranquillity of late years, large and searching reforms were required in Ireland, and that earnest efforts must be made to improve her condition ; and though this sentiment was partly due to alarm, for the secrecy and suddenness of the outbreaks had disturbed many hearts, it should be mainly ascribed to a nobler motive. The mind of England, in a word, turned again towards Ireland ; dislike and indifference were replaced by sympathy ; and the judgment of the nation plainly declared that a thorough change for the better must be effected in all that was peccant in the institutions and laws of Ireland, and, if possible, in the state of the Irish community. Of these institutions the Established Church was the one that appeared the most to be condemned, in the existing mood of English and Scotch opinion. Since the Commutation of the Tithe, many years previously, that Church was hardly a material grievance ; its revenues were derived, in the great mass of instances, from the Protestant landed gentry, not from the peasantry ; it is simply untrue, as we have said, that this class paid the Land Tax in the shape of increased rent, in nine out of ten cases at least. Nor were its clergy, as a rule, unpopular ; the odium that attached to them while they were armed with the power of confiscating the crop of the tiller of the soil, had given place to a kindly feeling ; they were generally looked upon as resident country gentlemen, often notable for their good works of charity. Many of the worst anomalies of the Church had also been removed since the reform accomplished by the Ministry of Lord Grey ; its wealth was more fairly distributed, and it did better work than of old ; it had many remarkable prelates and divines ; in Dublin and in most of the large towns it had acquired great and increasing spiritual power. As an institution, in a word, it had distinctly improved ; and for this, and other reasons, Parliament had refused to interfere with it since the day of the Melbourne Government. But it was not the less a grave moral grievance, if we turn our eyes to Catholic Ireland ; it remained tainted with the vice of its origin ; it was but the establishment of a caste of conquerors planted in the midst of a conquered race ; it had no hold

on the great mass of Irishmen.   It was the Church of a
mere sect, not one-eighth of the people ; it still abounded in
pluralities, and in benefices without flocks ; in many of its
parishes a congregation was a mere shadow.   It was, in
short, " in most of its branches a sterile tree without fruit " ;
and its position was made the more untenable because it
represented the Protestant Ascendency in the religious
sphere, which, in the secular, had become a thing of the
past.   A few of its clergy, too, had made themselves odious
by encouraging a proselytising movement of a most sinister
kind.[1]

For these reasons the abolition of the Established Church
of Ireland became a popular demand in England and
Scotland, and in 1867, and the following year, was sustained
by a great force of opinion.   A concurrence of causes
secured for this policy a powerful combination of parties
in the State.   In Ireland, we have seen, " the Young Ireland "
following had never been completely extinct ; it gained
strength when Fenianism proved abortive ; and, with the
Irish Catholic priesthood, and their nominees in Parliament,
the weak successors of O'Connell's " Tail," it had always
denounced the Irish Established Church.   A " National
Association " was formed in Ireland, with Irish Catholic
bishops at its head ; this called for the destruction of the
Established Church ; and through the intervention of John
Bright—he had been bidding in Ireland for Radical support,
and had made a striking speech on the Irish Land system—
it allied itself with the " Liberation Society " of the English
Dissenters, which had the Disestablishment of all Churches
in view.   A rallying point was thus found for parties, before
discordant, to coalesce in attacking the Established Church
of Ireland ; and the state of affairs in Parliament worked
in the same direction.   A Conservative Government held
office ; Disraeli had lately become Prime Minister ; with
admirable skill and resource, if with little scruple, he had

[1] This was an attempt, chiefly promoted by zealots from England, to
bribe Catholic children to become Protestants, literally to set Mammon
against God.

carried a great Reform Bill through the House of Commons ; and, in the existing state of politics, it was not improbable that the Conservative party might remain in power for a considerable time, for the Opposition, composed of Whigs and Radicals of many kinds, was divided, demoralised, and without apparent strength.   On one subject, however, it was found possible to bring these disunited elements together ; they were ready to join in subverting the Irish Established Church, and in inaugurating in this way a new Irish policy.   Mr. Gladstone, who, since the death of Palmerston, and the retirement of Lord John Russell from the House of Commons—he had gone to the Upper House as Earl Russell—had become the chief of the Liberal party, seized the occasion with characteristic energy and appreciation of the drift of public opinion ; in a debate on the state of Ireland, in the spring of 1868, he emphatically pronounced against the Church, declared that the time for its fall had come, and drew the whole Opposition in his wake.

In this attack on the Established Church of Ireland, Mr. Gladstone was less at odds with his former self than must have been inferred from his public conduct.   Sufficient evidence now exists that he thought the position of the Church indefensible even in 1847 ; and in 1863 he had wished to speak out on the subject.   It was, nevertheless, the strange irony of fate, that it fell to the lot of Mr. Gladstone to overthrow an institution of which, for many years, he had been the avowed and distinguished champion ; and certainly in this, as in other passages of his career, he palpably laid himself open to the charge, that he was making a mere party move, in which he had a special interest.   Higher and better motives, however, were, no doubt, paramount ; yet it will hardly be affirmed that, in this matter, he adopted the course of a great statesman, who had only patriotic objects in view.   Lord Russell had made up his mind by this time that the Established Church of Ireland was doomed ; but like Pitt, and nearly all politicians of a high order, he wished that a provision

should be made for the Irish Catholic priesthood ; and, like
O'Connell, he thought that the Catholic Church of Ireland
should receive part of the revenues of the Protestant Church
should this be disestablished and disendowed.[1]   In the
debate referred to, this very policy was approved by Lord
Mayo, the Chief Secretary, the Governor-General of India
of a later day ; and assuredly it would have obtained the
support of an overwhelming majority of enlightened Irishmen, if it was evident that the Established Church could
no longer exist.   Mr. Gladstone, however, announced, in
vehement language, that projects of this kind were out of
date, and idle, and that " concurrent endowment," as it was
called, was not to be thought of ; and he plainly intimated
that the Irish Established Church was not only to be
disestablished and disendowed, but that grants to other
Irish religious communions were to be withdrawn.   Nor
was this all ; in the Debates of the Session of 1868, and
during the electoral struggle that followed, he condemned
the whole system of British rule in Ireland—he had taken
a conspicuous part in it—as deplorable in the highest
degree ; he described Ireland as being blighted by a deadly
upas tree overshadowing the Church, the Land, and the
Education of men ; he assailed Protestant Ascendency, or
what remained of it, in passionate and indignant phrases ;
and he declared that Government in Ireland must, in the
future, be more and more moulded on " Irish ideas."
Whatever may be thought of their foresight and wisdom,
these utterances were, at least, well devised to drive a
Conservative Ministry from office, in a democratic age.

A decisive effort of the national will placed Mr. Gladstone
in power, with a great majority, after the General Election
of 1868.   He addressed himself at once to his Irish policy ;
and brought forward a Bill, in the Session of 1869, for
the abolition of the Established Church of Ireland, and
incidentally for other purposes.   His speech in the House

[1] Lord Russell would, in 1868, have bestowed a far larger part of the
revenues of the Church on its Catholic rival than O'Connell proposed
thirty-six years before.

of Commons was one of his very best ; it was worthy of an orator, who never rose to the topmost heights of eloquence, but was a rhetorician of remarkable power and skill, and always conspicuous for his mastery of details. There was no trace of partisanship or violence in his words ; his object was to show that he was setting the Church free from an alliance with the State, which had been a curse to her, and that he was helping her to fulfil a Divine mission ; he dwelt on these topics in most noble language. Disraeli's reply was made evidently against the grain ; curiously enough he adopted, on behalf of the Church, the arguments his adversary had employed before, in a well-known, but now obsolete book ; but Disraeli's heart was not in his work ; he had condemned the Irish Establishment even in the days of Peel. The measure was only feebly resisted ; it was partly amended in the House of Lords ; but it was not changed in its main principles ; it passed into law at the close of the Session. The Irish Church Act, as it is commonly called, carried out the policy which its author had shadowed forth a few months before ; its primary purpose was to disestablish and disendow the Church ; but it dealt also with the benefits conferred by the State on the Presbyterian and Catholic Irish Churches. We may glance at the chief features of this celebrated law, which, if a scheme of destruction in some of its aspects, was in others constructive and not ungenerous. Under the provisions of the Act, the Established Church of Ireland ceased to be an institution connected with the State ; it was no longer "to rear its mitred front in Parliament ; " its dignities, its benefices, in short, all its offices were no longer to be at the disposition of the Crown. It was deprived, too, of nearly all its endowments ; these were vested in a Com- mission formed with this object ; it was thus disestablished, and, in the main, disendowed, and was placed on the footing of a voluntary church, analogous to the Episcopalian Church of Scotland. The law, however, went further in its sweep ; the Regium Donum given to the Presbyterian Church, and the grant to Maynooth for the Irish Catholic priesthood, were no longer to be charges defrayed by the State, but compensation was to be found for them out of the property of the Disestablished Church.

So far for the work of simple destruction ; we turn to the constructive parts of the measure. Large facilities were wisely afforded by the law to enable the Church to organise itself again ; it was given the fullest powers of concerted action in Provincial Synods, and a General Synod ; it was invested with the right of almost complete self-government ; a Representative Body was attached to it, charged to administer its funds and to protect its interests. The Church, therefore, as Mr. Gladstone intended, was allowed freedom and fair play ; and while parts of its endowments were not taken away, ample funds were reserved out of its late property to satisfy every vested interest, from the archbishop down to the humblest curate. It retained its cathedrals and parish churches ; it was to have its glebes and parochial houses on easy terms ; and an ingenious scheme was devised in the hope of securing a provision for the support of the Church in the future. As vested interests were to be respected, the ministers of the Disestablished Church were to be entitled to receive their former incomes from the funds of the Church set apart for the purpose ; but as this arrangement would lead to difficulty and delay, a "Commutation Fund" was created by advances made by the State on the revenues of the Church, in order to meet and discharge these claims. This fund would amount to a large capital sum. This accumulation would be a real inducement to the laity of the communion in all parts of Ireland to maintain their Church when it should depend on themselves—that is, when the clergy then living had passed away ; it would be a strong incentive to private endowment ; and in this respect the scheme has been very successful. After the provision made in this way for vested interests, the surplus funds of the Church, still a sum of many millions sterling, were to be employed in making compensation for the Regium Donum and the Maynooth Grant, as before mentioned ; and the residue was to be appropriated, from time to time, to the "relief of unavoidable suffering and calamity"—vague words capable of interpretation in almost any sense. Other parts of the Act do not require special notice. Power was taken to enable clergymen who wished to leave Ireland and to pursue their calling elsewhere to "compound" for their incomes ; and the lands of the Church were, as far as possible, to be sold to the tenants occupying its estates, the purchase moneys being in part secured or advanced by the State in furtherance of a policy recently proposed by John Bright.

This measure redressed a grave wrong, as far as Catholic Ireland was concerned ; it removed all but the last traces of Protestant Ascendency in Irish affairs. On the principles, too, in which it was framed, it was just—even generous—to the Church it cut off from the State ; and it provided skilfully for the preservation of that Church in the future. It was, nevertheless, a scheme of destruction ; it is difficult to maintain that a policy of this kind applied to Protestant, Presbyterian, and Catholic Ireland, and to a poor and distracted country especially requiring the help of the State, was a far-sighted or a judicious policy. The worst fault, however, of this legislation was that, while a vast fund was placed at the disposition of the Government of the day, no provision was made for the Irish Catholic clergy—that is, for carrying out the plan of endowment which Pitt had wished to make a part of the Union, which O'Connell had expressly approved, and which had been advocated by every statesman of mark from 1800 to 1867, and by none more plainly than by Lord Russell. It is true that Lord Russell, at the last moment, at the instance probably of Mr. Gladstone, abandoned that policy with great reluctance ; it is also true that the National Association declared against it in language apparently strong. But Lord Russell was about to leave the stage of politics, and doubtless disliked crossing the Liberal leader ; the National Association was working with the Liberation Society, which, assuredly, would have angrily opposed a measure of the kind ; and, after all, the declaration it made simply implied that the Irish Catholic priest-

hood ought not to be made the salaried servants of the
State, and did not imply that this order of men ought to
refuse an endowment made on just and honourable terms.
Lord Grey, the son of the minister of the great Reform Bill,
the last survivor of the statesmen, who, in this matter,
preserved the traditions of Pitt and Canning, placed it on
record, only a few years ago, that an arrangement of this
kind was feasible in 1868–9 ; [1] and his statement has never
been put in question. A great opportunity was probably
lost to carry into effect a policy which few will deny would
have been of incalculable good to Ireland.

Mr. Gladstone had expressed a confident hope that the
Disestablishment of the Protestant Church would be a
message of peace to Catholic Ireland, and be welcomed
with loyal and heartfelt gratitude. The idea only showed
how, like his predecessor, Pitt, he had not fathomed the
depths of Irish questions or rightly interpreted Irish sentiment. His measure was regarded by Irish Catholics as
Emancipation and the Commutation of the Tithe were
regarded in the days of O'Connell and Peel ; it was a concession to disorder, not a free act of justice ; and, besides,
like Emancipation and the Commutation of the Tithe, Disestablishment was many years too late. It may be an
invidious remark that the violent language of Mr. Gladstone
in 1868 provoked in Ireland dangerous and evil passions ;
it is certain, however, that the first effort of his Irish policy
was followed, not by goodwill and sympathy, but by an
outburst of Whiteboyism and agrarian crime. Disestablishment did not soothe or satisfy Ireland ; yet it was probably
well that a real grievance—the ascendency of the Church of
a small minority—did not exist in Ireland during recent
years of trouble. The good done by the measure, however,
was in the main negative, and some of its results have not
been fortunate. The large surplus funds of the Disestablished Church have been partly misapplied and wasted ;
they have relieved the Exchequer from charges which ought
to have been defrayed, in many instances, from the national

[1] See "Ireland," by Lord Grey, pp. 61–63.

taxes. As for the Church since it has been set free from the State, the anticipations of Mr. Gladstone have been more felicitous. The Church, indeed, has had its seasons of trial and distress; it has not been without internal dissension; its financial position is far from assured, owing to the impoverishment of the landed gentry, the class on which it chiefly must rely for support. But it has emerged successfully, as yet, from troubles like these; the moderate, not the extreme party prevails in its councils; above all, as a Christian society, it is better ordered, more full of the spirit of its Master, more zealous of good works, more a beneficent power, than it was as an Erastian appanage of the corrupting Castle. It has been governed and administered, we should add, with much prudence and skill; the capacity and faculty of organisation which its clergy and laity have exhibited in this sphere has done Protestant Ireland the highest honour.[1]

The first branch of the Upas-tree had fallen; Mr. Gladstone set himself to attack the second branch—the land system of Ireland and the relations it had formed. That system had not much changed since the years of tranquillity —from 1854 to 1865; but any changes in it had been for the worse, if we consider the Irish community as a whole. The work of consolidating farms had gone on; fine specimens of farming on a large scale were often to be seen. Agriculture had continued to improve; the breeds of farming stock were becoming every year better; the face of the country showed signs of ever-quickening progress. Nevertheless Ireland remained, as before, a land, for the most part, of petty holdings; the old cottar system had been largely broken up; but even the immense emigration had left the soil in the possession, in the main, of a race of mere

---

[1] An admirable description of the Disestablishment of the Church of Ireland, of the characteristics of the Irish Church Act, and of the subsequent fortunes of the Disestablished Church will be found in Ball's "Reformed Church of Ireland," pp. 258–305. The author, a late Lord Chancellor of Ireland, was one of the ablest opponents of Mr. Gladstone's measure; his speech in the House of Commons on "concurrent endowment" is a masterly performance.

peasantry. As for the real landed gentry, they were what they had always been, divided from their inferiors in race and faith, often kindly and good, seldom harsh or oppressive, but with a turn to strict dealing that had been increasing ; and the new race of landlords, with their evil tendencies, had been multiplying under the operation of the Encumbered Estates Acts. The whole order was probably, at this time, more separated from its dependents than it had been ; and partly through fear of a renewal of the movement of 1850-52, and partly from the assurances of British statesmen that their position was perfectly secure, some landlords had become more and more exacting. As for the occupiers of the soil, the rate of rent had been rising ; and though it was not as high as it had been thirty years before, it was becoming excessive in not a few instances, owing to the growing competition for land following the augmented wealth of the country. The great grievance, however, of the Irish tenant farmer was that to which we have adverted before—insecurity of tenure and the circumstance that, in numberless cases, he had gained, through improvement or from sums paid on the sale of farms, rights often amounting to joint-ownership, and yet that these rights were not protected by law if, in the Northern Province, upheld by custom. This grave and palpable wrong had become worse ; five-sixths probably of the occupiers of the soil in Ireland had sunk into the class of mere tenants-at-will ; even the Tenant Right of Ulster had, in some instances, been "nibbled away" by a certain class of landlords ; and at the same time the joint-ownership, often morally a fact, but legally ignored in the courts of justice, had gradually been more and more developed. Harsh evictions, also, had become more frequent ; and these had been attended with their ordinary result—not a few frightful cases of agrarian crime.

British sympathy with Ireland was still a living force, though the Liberal party had been vexed and surprised that the Irish Church Act was bearing no fruit, and though a severe measure of repression was found necessary to put down the agrarian disturbances which, we have seen, had multiplied.[1] In the summer and autumn of 1869 a number of distinguished English and Scotchmen went to Ireland to examine on the spot the conditions and facts of her land system ; the British Press sent more than one contributor ; a flood of instructive light was thrown on the subject. Mr. Gladstone had his measure ready at the opening of the Session of 1870 ; no minister, who had to deal with an Irish question, had received such valuable assistance before. The speech he made in the House of Commons in bringing in his Bill was a good historical review of the Irish land system ; it clearly explained that Irish land tenure, though nominally the same as that which exists in England, was essentially, and in its working, completely different. The speech, however, was tentative and not striking ; the orator did not openly claim for the Irish tenant rights even approaching joint-ownership, though his language pointed in that direction ; he probably did not wish to alarm hearers, of whom some thought English land tenure perfect, others believed Irish Tenant Right to be an infraction of Free Trade, and the majority knew little about the subject. The most remarkable passages in the speech, however, regard being had to events that followed, were those in which Mr. Gladstone held up to contempt the whole theory of the " Three Fs," at this time the extreme demand of the Irish tenant. " Fair Rent " meant the sub-version of contracts, and could not be properly adjusted by the State ; " Fixity of Tenure " would be the expropriation of landlords, as a class, and would confine the possession of the land to a few thousand farmers ; " Free Sale " was open to grave objections ; these claims, in short, were ex-travagant and incompatible with the just rights of property. Mr. Gladstone significantly added that the Bill he had prepared was to be a final settlement of the Irish Land Question, that it would place the Irish land system on foundations not to be disturbed. He little thought that his decisive arguments, and his solemn pledges were, in a few

[1] See the figures in Grey's " Ireland," p. 79.

years, to be set at nought, and scattered to the winds by himself.

The Conservative party, since the days of Peel, had been more liberal and enlightened than the Whigs, as regards reform in the Irish land system ; though Disraeli made sarcastic remarks on the complexity of Mr. Gladstone's Bill—by no means undeserved criticism—the Opposition accepted a great part of the scheme, and it was not largely altered in the House of Lords. The measure, if very far from perfect, nay marked by plain and far-reaching defects, and giving proof of the obscurity, and, so to speak, the reserve characteristic of the introductory speech, was, nevertheless, in some respects, a statesmanlike and effective reform, and was far superior to every preceding measure of the kind. The Tenant Right of Ulster depending on usage before, received, for the first time, the sanction of law ; the same rule was extended to an inchoate Right, beginning to grow up in the Southern Provinces, though the instances of this were very few ; legitimate security was thus afforded to a series of rights of the nature of joint-ownership, which hitherto had been comparatively insecure, and were becoming more so year after year. The Land Act of 1870—this was its name—went, however, much farther in this direction. It engrafted on the immense majority of Irish tenancies, a Tenant Right of a potential kind, in the form of " Compensation for Disturbance " to be made available when dispossession on a notice to quit was at hand ; it added to this a further Right, that of " Compensation for Improvements," past and present, arranged on an extremely liberal scale, and to be realised when a tenant was quitting his farm. No attempt was made generally to fix rent by the State ; but in a few exceptional cases " exorbitant rents " made a landlord subject to severe penalties, and eviction was discouraged in many ways, in order to give stability and support to the interest of the occupier of the soil.

By these means, though indirectly, and by a circuitous process, the concurrent rights of the Irish tenant in the land, and his joint-ownership, where these existed, were vindicated to a considerable extent ; the land system, as respects the tenants' position, was unquestionably very much improved ; Law and Fact, in conflict before in landed relations, were, in the large majority, perhaps, of instances reconciled. The measure, however, was supplemented by alternatives, not in its true spirit, and having a tendency to weaken it, and to make it less effective than it seemed. Mr. Gladstone, naturally affected by English ideas, and not governed, in this province, by Irish, evidently thought that the Irish system of land tenure, though to be maintained and upheld as regards the rights belonging to the tenant, which it had evolved, ought gradually to be replaced by the English system ; and in order to carry into effect this process, he sought for a model in English land tenure. The Land Act, therefore, enabled the rights of the tenant, whatever their extent or value, to be commuted, by agreement, in almost all cases ; they might generally be extinguished, at least in a great degree, by a grant to the tenant of a lease of thirty-one years ; and, what was more important, tenants of farms of the larger class were empowered to "contract themselves out" of the benefits of the law, that is, to consent to divest themselves of the privileges it conferred. In this way an object of the measure was to substitute English for Irish tenure ; as it was remarked at the time, it was to be hoped that the Irish land system would, in the long run, be based on the footing of pure contract throughout the relations of landlord and tenant. The Act, besides creating large powers of leasing, in furtherance of the last-named object, contained provisions for the formation of a class of peasant owners of land in Ireland—this, we have seen, was a favourite policy of John Bright—and, as in the case of the lands of the Church, so in the case of all other lands, tenants were encouraged to acquire their farms by purchase, the State advancing a part of the purchase moneys.

This Land Act was deserving of high praise ; but it had faults that marred its practical value. It was marked with the *nimia subtilitas* of its author's intellect, worse even in legislator than in a judge; it bristled with exceptions and limitations; it was, in many places, extremely obscure; it was not intelligible to ordinary minds. It was, therefore, far beyond the ken of the unlettered peasant, who either regarded it with the distrust of ignorance, or feared that it would bring on him an attorney's costs; it did not appeal to his imagination, or affect his judgment, as a plain and comprehensive scheme of Tenant Right would have done. Besides, though it really did vindicate the concurrent rights of the tenant and his joint-ownership, it accomplished this only on conditions which the ordinary Irish peasant abhorred; save in the cases of the Ulster or similar customs, the compensation given by the law to the tenant was to be given only on his quitting his farm; and as this was what he could not bear to do, the law seemed to him to be of little avail; it did not keep him in the holding to which he fondly clung. A consequence of this sentiment, too, was that he was willing to submit to almost any terms, such as increased and even excessive rent, rather than abandon his beloved home; the rights, therefore, which he had, in fact, acquired, were practically sometimes to little purpose. The alternatives, besides, which the law presented, had a tendency to weaken its best provisions; in thousands of instances tenants accepted the leases that discharged their claims to Tenant Right, or "contracted themselves out" of the benefits of the Act; and in some of them they were under the influence of undue pressure. For all these reasons the law was not felt to be the great and generous boon it really was; in some respects it did not work well; above all, it afforded the means of being evaded and practically annulled. Able Irishmen predicted its comparative failure at the time: two proposed solutions of the problem that deserved attention. Butt, the opponent of O'Connell in 1842, to whom we shall soon have occasion to refer, recommended that tenancies-at-will in Ireland should be converted into leaseholds for sixty-three years,[1] at rents to be settled by a tribunal of the

[1] "The Irish People and the Irish Land," by Butt.

State; Longfield, a Judge of the Encumbered Estates Court, and, like Butt, a master of the Irish land question, suggested that a Tenant Right, at a fixed value, should be annexed generally to Irish farms, and should be declared to be the tenants *peculium;*[1] a bold and generous extension of the famous Ulster custom. These plans were less ambitious than that of Mr. Gladstone; but they were simple, and might have proved successful; regard being had to subsequent events, it is perhaps unfortunate that the Minister turned a deaf ear to them.

Nevertheless, despite shortcomings and faults, the Land Act of 1870 was well received in Ireland. It made no impression, indeed, on agrarian crime, which continued undiminished for some months, and was only kept under by the coercion, which ultimately, as always, proved an effective check. But Mr. Gladstone's Government in Ireland was, for a time, popular; this, no doubt, was due, in a great degree, to the character and conduct of his Lord-Lieutenant, Lord Spencer, the successor of Lord Wodehouse and the Duke of Abercorn, a singularly upright and sympathetic ruler. A movement, meanwhile, at first trivial, but destined to lead to an era of trouble, which at that moment would have been thought impossible, had begun to make a kind of languid stir; it proceeded from an wholly unexpected source. Macaulay had predicted that Ireland would draw near England if the wrong of the Established Church were removed; Plunket, more profound and knowing Ireland much better, declared that it would arouse Protestant Ireland against the Union, for the Church had been solemnly secured by the Treaty. The words of the great orator proved, to some extent, true; since the failures of 1843 and 1848, scarcely a voice against the Union had been raised in Ireland, as indeed, had usually been the case since the day of Pitt; an agitation against it was now set on foot by a small but active party of discontented Protestants, who pronounced a great international compact broken; and these found adherents among the men of " Young Ireland," who,

[1] " Systems of Land Tenure." Essay by Longfield.

we have seen, had been stirring of late, among the Rump
of the old Repeal following, by tradition faithful to
O'Connell's creed, and among others who had Fenian
sympathies and views, but who thought it prudent to conceal
them at the present moment.

The leader of the new movement was Isaac Butt, to whom
we have cursorily referred before; he was a remarkable
man, who will live in Irish History, though, owing to a
variety of causes, he never rose to the political eminence
he might have attained.　Butt was the son of a Protestant
clergyman of the North of Ireland ; he inherited the ideas of
the dominant caste ; but his understanding was profound,
and his heart generous ; he soon adopted the faith of Burke
and of Grattan, and became a Liberal Irishman, if not in
a party sense, still according to the proper meaning of the
word.　He had great University renown ; quickly rose to a
leading position at the Irish Bar ; and certainly would have
won its highest honours, for he was an excellent lawyer and
a consummate advocate, had he followed his profession
with anything like care and diligence.　He turned his mind,
however, in early life to politics; he had an erratic and
questionable career in Parliament ; and for some years
was almost in eclipse, so desperate and broken were his
fortunes.　Butt, nevertheless, was a man of commanding
intellect, deeply versed in History and Constitutional
Law, an economist of a high order, though not a believer
in the gospel of Cobden, Conservative in his instincts, as
O'Connell was, and though associated with a movement
which had a revolutionary side, and always jealous of the
liberties and rights of Ireland, a reverent supporter of order
and law, and with a strong sympathy with the just claims of
property, interpreted in a reasonable sense.　Such a man
ought to have gained real distinction in the State ; but Butt
was unstable as water, and not made to excel ; with some
of Sheridan's qualities, he had Sheridan's foibles ; he was
improvident, reckless, of a weak character ; though kindly
and good-natured, unable to win confidence ; in a word,
unfit to be a leader of men, or to bow a political party to his

will. Though he advocated their views in most instances, he was distrusted by the Irish Catholic priesthood, and never had a hold on the Irish Catholic masses, a marked contrast in this respect to O'Connell ; nor was this only because he was a Protestant ; Protestants have repeatedly been a great power in Catholic Ireland ; we need only refer to Swift, Grattan, Tone, and Lord Edward Fitzgerald.

In the Debate on the Repeal of the Union, in the Corporation of Dublin referred to before, Butt, the real spokesman of the Conservative party, had rested his defence of the Treaty mainly on the fact that time was still required to prove what its full results would be ; O'Connell, in replying to his young antagonist, predicted that he would "yet become a Repealer." The series of events between 1842 and 1868–70 may have shaken the faith of Butt in a measure he had not defended with his whole heart ; but it was the Fenian movement and its ominous symptoms that caused him to change his mind as regards the Union. He had ably defended the Fenian prisoners ; he had necessarily become acquainted with their designs ; he seems to have thought the conspiracy would have led to a bloody rising, had it been associated with Lalor's agrarian movement ; it was mainly on this account that he put forward his scheme for a great reform of the Irish land system. Be this as it may, Ireland, in his judgment, was in a critical and disaffected state ; the only way to remedy this evil was, he believed, to adopt boldly the policy of what he called Home Rule, that is to secure for Ireland a Legislature of her own, and an Administration dependent on it. Butt, however, perceived that the restoration of the Irish Parliament was all but impossible, in an order of things in Ireland that had been completely changed ; and partly on this ground, and partly because a small party in Ulster had, we have seen, given ear to what was known as " Federalism " in Irish affairs, he proposed a plan founded on a principle of this kind.[1] His views are to be found in a tract, now almost forgotten, but still deserving

---

[1] Butt hinted that, in 1843-4, the Whig party rather favoured Federalism. He gave no authority for a statement certainly unfounded.

attentive study, as being the case made by a very able man for practically doing away with the Union, and giving Ireland a ·domestic Parliament and a Government on the spot.   The work is written in a Conservative spirit, with an avowed purpose to reconcile the scheme of the author with the Constitution as it at present exists, and with a marked aversion to unnecessary change.   Yet Butt's plan was impracticable, and could only appear plausible by keeping out of sight the facts that would make it hopeless ; and, besides, it was essentially unjust, and what he did not, or would not see, it would have subverted the Constitution in a vital part. In his " Irish Federalism " he proposed that a Parliament and an Administration should be set up in Dublin charged with the direction of " Irish affairs " only ; but he did not attempt to define what Irish affairs might mean, a definition which experience and prolonged discussions have since proved to be simply impossible.   Yet this was not the most fatal objection ; Butt proposed, further, that the members of the Irish Parliament should repair to, and vote in the Imperial Parliament, that is that Ireland was to have a direct influence on Imperial, perhaps on British, policy, and very probably to shape and control it, and yet that the Imperial Parliament, as to Ireland, was to be powerless !   The present generation has, at least, learned that such a scheme would be rank injustice, and would annihilate the very foundations of the State.

A Home Rule Association was, nevertheless, formed ; and Home Rule began to be a popular cry in Ireland.   The movement was sustained by a few Irish bye-elections ; but for many months it continued to be weak ; in England and Scotland it was looked upon as mere Celtic foolishness.   Mr. Gladstone, still in the plenitude of his power, convinced of the excellence of his Irish policy, and still believing in the wisdom of the Imperial Parliament, treated the demand for Home Rule with scornful contempt : " Can any sensible man, can any rational man "—he exclaimed with passionate earnestness, and, doubtless, with real conviction at the time—" suppose that at this time of day, in this condition of the world, we are going to disintegrate the great capital institutions of the country for the purpose of making ourselves ridiculous in the sight of all mankind, and crippling any power we possess for bestowing benefits, through legislation, on the country to which we belong ? " [1] At this juncture, indeed, he was devoting himself to the third and last branch of the famous Upas-tree, and was forming a scheme for education of the higher kind in Ireland, which he rightly thought was in need of a large and searching reform. High education in Ireland had undergone no change since Peel had attempted to reform the system, with results that had, for the most part, been failures, and since the Catholic University had been founded, that is for a period of nearly twenty years ; and the system continued to be one-sided and unjust, especially with respect to the Irish Catholic. Attempts had, indeed, been made to throw open the prizes and the government of Trinity College to all Irishmen without regard to distinctions of creed, to enable the Catholic University to become, so to speak, a preparatory school leading to degrees, nay, even to give it some help from the State ; but all these had, for different reasons, proved abortive, and nothing had been really accomplished in the way of reform. Trinity College, with its large estates and endowments, was still a Protestant foundation in no doubtful sense ; its governing body was wholly Protestant ; nearly all its rewards were confined to the favoured creed ; Catholics, indeed, were often admitted within its pale, and had the advantage of the excellent education it gave ; but its teaching was Protestant, nay, anti-Catholic in part. The Queen's Colleges and University remained fashioned on the model originally formed for them ; they were secular places of learning in which religion was not recognised by the State, and was only taught by accident ; they had proved a boon to Presbyterian Ireland, but Catholic Ireland had stood aloof from them, especially since the declaration of the Synod of Thurles. And the Catholic University was still kept outside these favoured seminaries of the State, supported by

[1] Speech on receiving the freedom of Aberdeen, September 26, 1871.

the contributions of a poor communion, and yet a mere school unable to confer a degree.

Mr. Gladstone brought forward his measure of reform in the first weeks of the Session of 1873. The difficulties in his way were very great ; he had to reconstruct an anomalous and unjust system ; he had to deal with powerful and conflicting interests ; he had, if possible, to conciliate Irish sentiment, divided on this and other subjects ; he had to gain the consent of the Liberal party obviously not at one in this matter. He made a singularly dexterous and ingenious speech, and the scheme he proposed was vast and far-reaching ; but it was the worst conceived of his Irish reforms of this time ; and it ended in complete and disastrous failure. We need not examine this abortive project in detail ; it is sufficient to glance at its main features. With the historical and Conservative views, of which his legislation has sometimes borne the mark, Mr. Gladstone proposed to create a University for Ireland, as a whole, which Elizabeth and the Stuarts had wished to create, but which had been swallowed up, as it were, by Trinity College, and, after the enactment of the Penal Code, could not have embraced Catholic Ireland within its sphere. This University was to have a general control over Irish education of the higher order ; its governing body was to be composed in part of nominees of the Castle, in part of the heads of the institutions to be connected with it ; and Trinity College and two of the Queen's Colleges—the third was to be suppressed as useless—the Catholic University and some other Colleges were to be affiliated to it, as subordinate members. The Queen's University, of course, was to be extinguished, for one University only was to exist in Ireland ; but the groups of Colleges dependent on it were to be in very different but unequal positions. Trinity College was to be thrown open, to the fullest extent ; its prizes and honours might be obtained by all who entered its walls, without regard to creed ; but with the exception of a small annual sum, which the new University was to acquire, it was to retain its great endowments intact. The two Queen's Colleges, too, were to be subsidised, as before, by the State ; but the Catholic University was not to receive a shilling ; and this was to be the case also of the other dependent Colleges, if these were of a sectarian character. The scheme, therefore, as regards support by the State, was, on the face of it, in the highest degree, partial ; but this was far from the worst of its curious provisions. ' The new University alone [1] was to confer degrees ; and Mr. Gladstone actually applied with respect to education of the highest type, the principles which had with difficulty been applied to Primary Education in the National Schools, and which as regards the Queen's Colleges and the Queen's University, were not only vicious, but had been denounced as " godless " by the Conservative party, and by the Irish Catholic bishops. The education to be afforded under the proposed system was to be united, but strictly secular ; religious education might be apart, but was not to receive any countenance from the State ; it was, in fact, left to shift for itself ; and that secular education might be purely secular, Modern History, and Mental and Moral Philosophy were to be excluded from University teaching ! [2]

The ignorance of Irish affairs and Irish opinion, so repeatedly seen in British statesmen, was more that ordinarily conspicuous in this scheme ; it is surprising, indeed, that an illustrious son of Oxford should have been the author of such an ill-planned measure. The Bill was literally torn to shreds in admirable debates in Trinity College ; its leading men expressed just and generous views with respect to the claims of Catholic Ireland ; [3] but they were indignant that a famous and ancient place of learning should be made subject to a mere Board of the Government ; above all, that the noblest intellectual studies were to have no place, as far as the State was concerned, in the

---

[1] This has been denied but seems to be the true meaning of the Bill.

[2] For a masterly analysis of Mr. Gladstone's Irish Education Bill of 1873, see a pamphlet by Butt called " The Problem of Irish Education."

[3] I had the privilege of hearing these remarkable debates.

Alma Mater of Ussher, of Burke, and of Berkeley. The Irish Catholic Bishops were even more hostile ; they condemned the project as simply " godless " ; they rightly complained that it was essentially unjust, for while Trinity College, and two Queen's Colleges were to be still amply endowed by the State, the Catholic University was to be left penniless. Every educated Irishman, too, resented that Divinity, Modern History, and Mental and Moral Philosophy were not to be a part of the University course of study ; the measure in this respect was compared to the "monstrum cui lumen ademptum" of the Song of Virgil. These ideas passed quickly into the House of Commons, which became more and more averse to the Bill. Disraeli described the scheme as atheistic, and certainly said what he really felt, for, like Burke, he was a religious man at heart ; he ridiculed and severely censured the exclusion of the best parts of human knowledge, from what was grotesquely called a University's domain ; the whole Conservative party followed their leader.[1] Mr. Gladstone's adherents were divided in mind ; the representatives of the English Dissenters, indeed, grateful that he had pulled down an Established Church, and scarcely knowing what University life is, voted for the measure almost to a man ; but the best and most thoughtful Liberals pronounced against it ; and only eleven out of more than a hundred Irish members gave their assent. The Bill was rejected by a small majority ; though Mr. Gladstone remained in office, his powerful administration was practically broken up, another of the many instances of the great influence Ireland has over and over again exercised on British and Imperial affairs.

The subordinate Irish measures of this Ministry require a few words. The Convention Act of 1793–4 was repealed ; wider latitude was given to organised popular movements. The borough franchise had been enlarged in 1868 ; the Ballot Act, passed in 1872, increased sacerdotal influence greatly in Catholic Ireland. One of the few restrictions of the

[1] The speech of Ball, then member for Trinity College, was also very able and brilliant.

Emancipation Act was removed; a Catholic was made Lord Chancellor of Ireland, for the first time since the Revolution of 1688 ; the Lord-Lieutenancy is now the only Irish office which a Catholic is not eligible to fill. The great Irish reforms of Mr. Gladstone are those which alone deserve much attention. The Disestablishment and Disendowment of the Church unquestionably removed a grave wrong ; but it was hardly a statesmanlike, and was not a successful measure ; it was not accompanied, as it ought have been, with an essential, but neglected, supplement of the Union, a provision for the Irish Catholic clergy. The Land Act of 1870 was a really great measure of reform ; it could have been made the basis of a scheme of almost perfect justice ; but, as it was enacted, it had serious defects, nor could it permanently settle a question difficult in the extreme. The Education Bill was vicious and unfair ; it revealed extraordinary ignorance of Irish opinion ; it was properly rejected by the House of Commons ; and this branch of the Upas-tree has not yet been wholly cut down. This Administration may be fitly compared, as regards Ireland and her affairs, with that of Lord Melbourne. Its legislation was much more thorough and bold, and was attended, on the whole, with more success ; its administration was liberal and just, but had not such striking and beneficent results, no doubt because an O'Connell was not on the stage of politics to represent and to manage Catholic Ireland. It must be added that, under Mr. Gladstone's Government, as under the Melbourne Government of more than thirty years before, British sympathy with Ireland was beginning to cool, though not so markedly, and that from the same causes. There was no O'Connell to exasperate public opinion ; but the nation was becoming tired of Irish questions, and thought Ireland ungrateful for what had been done for her.

Mr. Gladstone's Ministry was replaced by that of Disraeli in the first months of 1874; the change then effected in the direction of the State was felt from the Euphrates to the Andes, and Ireland had a considerable part in producing

the result.   After the General Election of that year, sixty
representatives were returned from Ireland to support the
new found policy of Home Rule ; but they were not backed
by a great force of Irish opinion, though, for the first time
since the days of Pitt and Grattan, they formed a majority
of Irish members against the Union.   The party, as a whole,
was a motley assemblage without coherence or essential
strength ; it was composed of Protestants dissatisfied with
the Church Act, of Catholics with O'Connell's traditions, of
men of Young Ireland earnest in the Home Rule cause, and
of a few who had separation from England at heart, and
were ready to join any movement in that direction.   As in
the case of the Tenant Right League, they were bound
together by pledges to act in concert, to refuse places,
and generally to obey their leader ; but these obligations
sat lightly on them, and they were widely divided in
thought and sympathy.   Butt was, of course, at the
head of the band ; but he was not, we have seen, a ruler of
men ; his previous Parliamentary career was against him ;
he had passed his sixtieth year and was old for his age ; his
adherents were a mere discordant faction, as weak as any
that Ireland had sent into the House of Commons.   The
cause of Home Rule, therefore, had no moral weight ; Butt,
nevertheless, brought it forward in debate for three or four
Sessions.   His speeches were able, dexterous, and well-
informed ; they were temperate and Conservative in tone ;
but the speaker had too much of the forensic manner ; his
accent and demeanour were not in his favour ; he hardly
caught the ear of the House of Commons ; he never grappled
thoroughly with the difficulties in his way.   He was
challenged over and over again, to unfold his plan of Home
Rule in a definite shape, to explain the powers and the
limitations of the proposed Irish Parliament, to show how
a partition could be made between the Irish affairs to
which it was to be confined, and the British and Imperial
affairs it was not to deal with ; above all, to reconcile with
common sense and justice the project that Irish representatives were to sit at Westminster, and to take part in the

government of the State, while the Imperial Parliament was to have nothing to do with Ireland. He was fairly beaten in argument and completely outvoted; of all his opponents none were more convincing and outspoken than Mr. Gladstone,[1] who at once fastened on the anomalies and unfairness of the scheme, ignorant as yet that Nemesis was to commend the poisoned chalice to his lips.

Butt, however, was not a visionary ; he knew that Home Rule was a policy that could only make its way slowly ; he had resolved to supplement it by plans for Irish reforms, which might have a chance of success in a not distant future. The defects of the Land Act were becoming apparent ; he had written a very able tract on the subject ; he laid before Parliament a new scheme of his own, founded on the principle of the " Three F.'s," but keeping its application within bounds and at least easy to understand. He also prepared a plan, analogous to that of Drummond, for the purchase by the State of the Irish railways ; these had mainly depended on private enterprise, and, as might have been expected, had not been very successful, in a poor country, without a great middle-class, and to which the " commercial principle" often is not applicable ; his arguments certainly had real weight. The chief, however, of these, his minor efforts, were projects to change the basis of Irish County Government—conducted for the most part by Grand Juries, bodies of the landed gentry, practically chosen from the Castle—and to make its foundations broad and popular ; and especially to improve the system of Irish Municipal Government, which, we have seen, was contracted and narrow, since it had been dealt with by the Melbourne Ministry. The Corporate towns of Ireland had been so reduced in number, since they had been affected by the

---

[1] Mr. Gladstone's words should be quoted, " Hansard," March 20, 1874 :—" The plan is this—that exclusively Irish affairs are to be judged in Ireland, and that then the Irish members are to come to the Imperial Parliament and to judge as they may think fit of the general affairs of the Empire, *and also of affairs exclusively English and Scotch.*" This last power was possibly not intended to be given by Butt.

Act of 1840, that it had been necessary to give municipal rights, in 1854, to many towns of comparatively small size; these were placed under the management of Town Commissioners, elected in a popular way by the townsmen. But the powers of all the Corporate or quasi-Corporate towns of Ireland remained very restricted, and the franchise was high ; and undoubtedly this made their municipal life feeble, and checked their development and aptitude for self-government, though, as we have said, it is idle to suppose that municipal life in Ireland can resemble what it is in England, a country not of petty towns, but of great and expanding cities. Butt's proposals on these subjects were not without merit ; but these, and all his projects of the kind, were summarily rejected by the House of Commons, indeed, seldom received a patient hearing. This was a mistake to be greatly regretted ; and yet, in the circumstances of the time, it can hardly cause surprise. Mr. Gladstone was taking little part in politics, except with regard to the Eastern Question, as to which he was to be the leader of a mighty movement ; he had been incensed at the fate of his Irish Education Bill ; he had vehemently asserted that every debt due to Ireland by Parliament had been fully discharged.[1] Disraeli, soon to become Lord Beaconsfield, was becoming engaged in the troubles in the East ; his Ministry had little time for Irish affairs ; and, above all, opinion in England and Scotland was rapidly turning again against Ireland, and disliked the idea of further Irish experiments. It had resented that Mitchell, the rebel of 1848, and a fanatic of the old Phœnix conspiracy, had been returned by Irish constituencies to the House of Commons ;

---

[1] Mr. Gladstone's words must again be quoted, "The Vatican Decrees," p. 59 :—" When Parliament had passed the Church Act of 1869, and the Land Act of 1870, there remained only, under the great head of Imperial equity, one serious question to be dealt with, that of the higher education. I consider that the Liberal majority of the House of Commons, and the Government to which I had the honour and gratification to belong, formally tendered payment in full of this portion of the debt by the Irish University Bill of 1873. Some, indeed, think that it was overpaid.

and it was indignant that a movement against the Union should have been the answer made by Ireland to Mr. Gladstone's great measures of reform.

The ignominious failure of the policy of Butt had its natural effect on his ill-united followers. The Protestants, beginning, perhaps, to be alarmed about Home Rule, drifted into the ranks of the Tory party; the Catholics inclined towards the Whig Opposition; the rest of the party was left all but powerless. Butt was a beaten general, with the wreck of an army; but, meantime, two or three of his adherents had had recourse to conduct which they may have thought would compel the attention of Parliament to Irish questions, but which was probably, at first, the expedient of mere despair. One of this obscure group which persisted in obstructive tactics, never witnessed before to such an extent, was a man, still quite young, who had just entered the House of Commons, and was destined to play a conspicuous part on the stage of events, but who, at this moment, was as insignificant as Robespierre, with whom he had certain points in common, seemed to be in the National Assembly at Versailles. Charles Stewart Parnell's figure is still too near us to be viewed in the sober light of History, and passages in his career remain unexplained; but we may glance at his antecedents, and some at least of the features of his character stand out in full relief. He was a scion, on his father's side, of a family which had had distinguished representatives in the Irish Parliament—one, a friend of Grattan, who fiercely denounced the Union—and had also an eminent member of the Imperial Parliament, remarkable for his extreme Radical views; on his mother's side he was an American by blood, and was a grandson of an American of great ability, who had won a name in the war of 1812, and had made himself notable for his hatred of England. Though one of the "English in Ireland" and possessing some English qualities, he thus inherited feelings hostile to England; and educated, though he had been, in England he had learned to sympathise with Irish rebellion in youth, and with what is known as the Irish cause. He had been filled,

in his teens, with tales of the rising of 1798, for his home
was among the valleys of Wicklow ; his surviving parent had
given refuge to Fenian enthusiasts, after the abortive outbreak of 1867; one of his sisters had written for the Fenian
Press ; he had spoken of the executions at Manchester as
of inhuman murders.   He had, however, begun life as a
simple country gentleman, intelligent, indeed, and with
active pursuits, but not, apparently, differing from his fellows
of the class ; and it is not probable, when he entered
Parliament, that he had extreme political views, though he
had taken the ordinary Home Rule pledge.   But Parnell,
though not a well-informed man, and without the wisdom
and genius of a real statesman, was not the less a born party
leader ; he was ambitious, but calculating, calm, stern, and
resolute; inscrutable, but endowed with the greatest strength
of character ; and if absolutely without scruple, and
capable of audacious deception, admirably fitted for
Parliamentary arts and intrigues, and able to direct constitutional and revolutionary movements alike.   He was to
be the Achitophel of the House of Commons of his time,
far superior "in close designs and crooked counsels " to the
ministers and politicians he hoodwinked and outwitted.

Parnell quickly became the leader of the knot of Irishmen
who had betaken themselves to stopping the work of
Parliament.   The devices of some of these men were
clumsy and stupid, for example, one protested against the
presence of the Prince of Wales, in a place reserved for
"strangers" in the House of Commons, and wrangled on
the subject at indecorous length ; others wasted hours on
reading Blue Books and making speeches with the obvious
purpose of causing mere delay.   But Parnell chose his
ground well, and gave proof of real dexterity ; he carried
a few Radical members with him, although he would speak
at interminable length on flogging in the Army and prison
discipline ; in a word he selected popular topics when he
resolved to make waste of the public time ; and more
than once he tripped up the Leader of the House of
Commons, owing to the knowledge he had acquired of the

practice and laws of Parliament. He effectually baffled the Government on several occasions ; and though, with his followers, he was sometimes overcome by the unseemly expedient of prolonged night sittings, his pertinacity, his adroitness, his skill in saying things of the most offensive kind, in cool and measured language, made him a prominent personage in an assembly which has always recognised ability and real power. He gradually supplanted his nominal leader, who had protested against his conduct in the House of Commons ; he became the acknowledged chief of an Irish party in Parliament, increasing in strength and numbers Session after Session, which aimed at further-ing what it called "an active policy," that is at wringing concessions for Ireland, nay, even Home Rule, from a Legislature wearied out by obstruction.[1] Parnell, while thus already placed at the head of what seemed to be a constitutional movement, maintained simultaneously close relations with Fenians and "men of 1867" in Ireland; even then we see signs of the ambidextrous policy he developed afterwards with signal success.[2] He acquired popularity and a kind of renown in Ireland ; by the close of 1878 he had completely thrust aside Butt, whose failure in politics had become manifest, and who was rapidly approaching his end. The fate of the "Father of Home Rule" was presaged by a significant act on the part of the Home Rule League of England, almost wholly composed of disaffected Irishmen ; it deposed Butt as its President, and put Parnell in his stead.

Lord Beaconsfield's Ministry had, meanwhile, carried into effect some Irish measures ; as far as they went these were well designed, though much less ambitious than those of Mr. Gladstone. After the defeat of the Education Bill of 1873, an Act was framed, at the instance of Trinity

[1] Times had changed since Greville wrote thus of Irish obstructions ("Memoirs," vol. vii. p. 165): "The English abhor the Irish and their proceedings, and will never endure that the House of Commons shall be dictated to by Irish Repealers and agitators."

[2] See "The Parnell Movement," by T. P. O'Connor, M.P., p. 169.

College, which made its members eligible to all its honours, without regard to differences of creed, and deprived its governing body of its purely Protestant character; this was highly to the credit of a noble foundation; but the reform, liberal and wise as it was, could not transform the place; Trinity College is still a Protestant seat of learning in teaching and spirit. Not long afterwards another step was taken, if not a bold and decided step, in making the system of high education in Ireland less unfair and one-sided than it had been; the Queen's University was abolished; a Royal University was established, empowered to confer degrees on the students of all Irish Colleges, who passed through the examinations required for the purpose. The Catholic University and other institutions of the kind were thus enabled, though indirectly, to secure degrees for those who were educated within their precincts; but the Royal University is a mere Examining Board, it is not a University in a proper sense; the Catholic University remains unendowed, while Trinity Colleges and the Queen's Colleges possess ample endowments and wealth; Catholic Ireland, we repeat, has here a real grievance. Another measure of the Beaconsfield Government, in the interest of Irish Education, may be also noticed. The secondary schools of Ireland have never ranked high, for Ireland has never had a great middle class; and until this century most of these schools were exclusively confined to the ruling Protestant caste, as many, indeed, are to this day. Since the Union, however, a number of Catholic schools of this description have been founded, another striking instance of the remarkable progress made by Catholic Ireland in social and intellectual life from 1800 to the present time. Few of these schools, nevertheless, of either communion, have flourished as much as was to be desired; a considerable impulse was given to them by an Act, due to the inspiration of Lord Cairns, the Lord Chancellor of England under Lord Beaconsfield, and himself an Irishman of remarkable parts, and a splendid luminary of the English Bar. A system of Intermediate

Education was set up by this law in 1878, in Ireland ; and the students of both sexes in secondary schools have been encouraged to take advantage of it, through the attraction of prizes and other awards. The success of the experiment has been great; but the secondary schools of Ireland, like her public schools, are still comparatively in a backward state.

The surface of things, meanwhile, had become fair in Ireland, since the Fenian conspiracy had collapsed, and agrarian disorder had been put down. The country, on the whole, has never been so prosperous as it was in the years of plenty and high prices from 1871 to 1877. Agriculture and all that pertained to it continued distinctly to improve ; the wealth and the commerce of Ireland increased ; the condition of the peasantry was better than it had ever been ; the value of land preceptibly rose ; tranquillity appeared to be completely restored. Even the Home Rule movement seemed on the decline ; political agitation became very feeble ; Butt and his adherents found few to attend the rare public meetings they now and then addressed. British statesmen began once more to believe that Ireland was in a state of permanent repose ; this was notably a conviction of Mr. Gladstone, who often dwelt on the good effects of his " Irish policy," especially as to the land system, and, with self-satisfaction that appeared justified, announced that the Irish community was " contented and happy." Yet here again, as in the years before the Fenian outbreak, these symptoms of progress and welfare were in part deceptive ; and the optimism of the hour was, in many respects, a delusion. The prosperity and quiet of Ireland depended, as before, on the chances of good harvests and rising prices ; in her social structure and its relations there was still much that was peccant, and this was not improbably on the increase. Rents were being raised, perhaps abnormally fast, though this was the exception, not the rule ; the Land Act had indisputably done good; but it did not satisfy a class that had already acquired socialistic ideas about the land ; it was not felt to be the benefit it really was ; and, as had been foreseen, it had been evaded in not a few instances, and in some through illegitimate conduct on the part of landlords. All this produced irritation and alarm, if as yet not sufficient to cause much attention ; but elements of danger and disturbance were gathering slowly; and well-informed observers of this time predicted that there would yet be a movement against rent in Ireland, especially as the peasantry, in this prosperous season, had lived rather fast and become involved in debt. Meanwhile the Fenian organisation in the United States, though not active, had not been broken up ; though scotched, it was not killed in Great Britain and Ireland ; and its emissaries continued to spread its doctrines against British rule and Irish landlords from Cape Clear to the Giant's Causeway. A young generation, too, of Irish priests had grown up which looked back at the agitation of the past, and was secretly opposed to Cardinal Cullen ; and though it was kept down by the superior clergy, it formed an element that might become perilous. On the whole the face of things in Ireland was serene ; but treacherous mischief and trouble lurked beneath ; and Mr. Gladstone and others were ere long to be undeceived.

The period, of which we have traced the main features, is one of great, nay, of mournful interest, in the affairs of Ireland. It opened with the promise of an auspicious era ; it closed with a condition of things still in appearance hopeful, but really critical, and soon to become unfortunate. The reforms of Mr. Gladstone were great and far-reaching, and certainly were not without good results ; but his Irish Church Act was hardly a wise measure, and was marked by one capital defect at least ; his Land Act was very far from perfect ; his Education Bill was a sorry failure ; and, as too often has been unhappily the case in Ireland, his legislation was too late to produce much effect. The Home Rule movement grew out of the shock caused by the violent subversion of the Established Church in Ireland ; it was a Constitutional movement in its author's design ; but it was an ill-planned and injudicious movement ; and though at this period not really strong, it drew into it bad and dangerous forces, destined, in the near future, to cause immense evils. Home Rule, even as it was proposed by Butt, and the agrarian disorder which prevailed in Ireland from 1869 to 1871, changed British sympathy with Irishmen into estrangement ; this change, unhappily often seen before, became very evident at the close of this period ; it has, with some seasons of intermission, continued ever since ; and this probably will always be the case—a fact Irishmen might well lay to heart—when attempts are seriously made to assail the Union, however dexterously these may be masked, or with whatever authority they may be presented. For the rest Ireland appeared prosperous and tranquil in 1876-7 ; but there was much in her condition that portended evil, to those who could read the signs of the time ; the great majority of her rulers, imperfectly, as usual, informed of her affairs, and, at this juncture, giving their whole attention to the difficult and menacing situation in the East, were soon to learn not to boast themselves of the morrow, and to find in the words of the old saying that " a cat in a closet might do more harm than a lion in a plain."

CHAPTER VIII

THE LAND LEAGUE—THE LAND ACT OF 1881—THE NATIONAL LEAGUE

Death of Butt—Michael Davitt—He arranges the "New Departure" with Fenians in America—Essential character of this movement—Davitt founds the Land League—Parnell its head and master-spirit —Nature and objects of the League—Distress in Ireland at the end of 1879—Conduct of Irish landlords—Parnell's visit to America—The General Election of 1880—Progress of the Land League—The Compensation for Disturbance Bill rejected by the House of Lords —Outburst of crime and anarchy in Ireland—This continues for many months, and only increases—An unwise measure of repression —The Land Act of 1881—Its characteristics and vices—Attitude of the Land League leaders—Arrest of Parnell and others—The No Rent manifesto—Increase of disorder—The Kilmainham Treaty—The Phœnix Park murders—Indignation in England—Severe Coercion Act, resisted by Parnell and his followers—Punishment of crime—Disorder put down—The National League founded—The Administration of the Land Act of 1881—Artful policy of Parnell—Connection between the National League and the party of violence in America—Parnell and his party in opposition to Mr. Gladstone —The Reform Act of 1884—Fall of Mr. Gladstone's Government.

AFTER a feeble attempt to regain authority over the party of which he had been the head, Butt passed silently away in the spring of 1879. Like that of O'Connell, his end was mournful ; in some respects it was even more tragic. He lived to hear the first sounds of distress from his country, which had been heard for a considerable time, though very different from the loud wail of 1845-7 ; his policy had been wrecked, his hopes destroyed ; but, unlike O'Connell, he had been completely forsaken ; scarcely a voice was raised to say

"God bless him," in death ; and he never had influence over the Irish masses. Nevertheless Butt was a great Irishman ; had he had strength of character to sustain his intellect, he would have held a high place in Irish History. He was the last of the Irish popular leaders, who, while seeking to change the Union, sincerely wished to maintain the British connection ; had reverence for British order and law ; and only aimed at Constitutional reforms by Constitutional methods. Those who were to follow him—Parnell was easily supreme—were men of whom some certainly sought to separate Ireland from Great Britain, without regard to the inevitable results ; and many of whom laboured to produce a revolution of the very worst kind, political and social alike, by revolutionary and detestable deeds, and by dragging Ireland through a sea of trouble and anarchy. Butt and O'Connell had much in common ; these men resembled the United Irishmen of 1795–8, without their patriotism, or a real excuse for their conduct.

Meanwhile, in a sky as yet comparatively serene, a little cloud had been growing up in the West, which, "no bigger" at first, than "a man's hand," was to spread in a destructive storm over the Irish landscape. Michael Davitt was a son of a Mayo peasant, who had been harshly evicted after the famine, and had found a home in a little town of Lancashire. The boy was brought up in the hatred of Irish landlords, common to the multitudes of the great Exodus ; he had the quick and vehement mind of the Celt ; and having been doomed by an accident to a sedentary life, he picked up in his studies a good deal of revolutionary and socialistic knowledge. He became prominent among the Fenian recruits ; took part in the abortive raid at Chester ; and soon afterwards was convicted of a grave offence against the State. During a long confinement in penal servitude, he brooded continually on his "country's wrongs" ; and true to the faith of Finton Lalor, which possibly he had learned in his teens, he became convinced that the "national cause" must be associated "with the cause of the land," if anything effectual was to be done, that British rule in Ireland could only be shaken by means of an attack on the landed gentry. He was released from Dartmoor in the last days of 1877, and with other Fenian prisoners of the same type, was welcomed by a deputation in Dublin, of which Parnell—as we have seen, he was not unacquainted with "men of 1867"—appears to have been the leading spirit.[1] Davitt was soon in communication with the Fenian Societies, which still continued to exist in the Three Kingdoms, though their organisation had become very weak, and their counsels were more than ever kept in the dark ; he perhaps expounded to these the new plan of operations he had thought out when in prison ; and proposed that an effort should be made to subvert "Irish landlordism," as a prelude to "national liberty." The Fenian Societies, however — they still retained the name of the "Brotherhood of the Irish Republic" given by Stephens— did not generally respond to his overtures ; they were, as usual, divided by the quarrels of the Celt; and the memories of 1867 were, besides, recent.[2] Davitt had ere long set off for the United States, and, after considerable delay and many disappointments, he found on that soil leavened with Irish rebellion the means of preparing the way, at least, for a far-spreading and destructive movement, in its accompaniments and its full development the most formidable against British power in Ireland which has been witnessed since 1798.

The Fenian conspiracy still retained life, when Davitt reached America in 1878 ; it had its organised bodies and was not inactive ; but it was split up into discordant factions, as was the case on the opposite side of the Atlantic. These parties may be divided broadly into two : one generally known as that of the "Clan na Gael," the other bearing a variety of names, of which the "Irish Brotherhood" was the most conspicuous. The leaders of both factions had a common purpose : "the complete

---

[1] Two, perhaps three, members of this deputation were afterwards implicated, more or less, in the Phœnix Park murders. "The Continuity of the Irish Revolutionary Movement," by Brougham Leech, p. 13.

[2] Evidence of Special Commission and Report, vol iii. pp. 557–586 ; vol. iv. p. 188 ; vol. iv. pp. 479–80.

, severance of Ireland from England" was "their main object"[1]; but they were not wholly agreed on the means; and the dissensions between them had been fierce and bitter. The chiefs of the Clan na Gael, like Moloch in the infernal conclave, were for "open war" with the "enemy of their race"; but, taught by the failure of 1865-7, they had confined their efforts to the creation of a "Skirmishing Fund," for assassination and the use of dynamite; and this had hitherto had no results. The heads of the other following were more akin to Beelzebub; they abhorred England, but "were for some easier enterprise"; nor did the promise of this seem altogether hopeless. They had been struck by the power shown by Parnell and the "active party" in obstructing and baffling the House of Commons; they knew that socialistic ideas were abroad in Ireland, especially in all that related to the land; they had heard rumours of Irish distress; in these elements of mischief they believed some combination might be effected that would do the "tyrant Saxon" permanent harm. Davitt attached himself, from the first, to these men; he devoted months to travelling through the United States, delivering lectures and making speeches, in which he unfolded the scheme he had formed; and gradually he made so marked an impression that the leaders of the conspirators in both camps, agreed that his experiment was worth a trial, and that England might be assailed with success, by "dragging," as Finton Lalor had written "Irish independence" after an agrarian revolt, as "you drag" an inert mass after a quickly moving engine. Davitt and the American Fenians of all kinds made what may be called a regular compact; the negotiator was a notable member of the Clan na Gael, deep in the counsels of Stephens many years before, and lately a trustee of "the Skirmishing Fund"; and the new policy was to be carried out in the "New Departure." The independence of Ireland was, as always, to be the grand object; but Irish "landlordism" was to be the first point of attack; "the recovery

[1] Report of the Judges on the Special Commission of 1888, vol. iv. p. 481.

of Ireland's national independence and the severance of all political connection with England" was to be the end ; but one of the means was to be "a radical reform of the land system, . . . a system founded on robbery and fraud and perpetuated by cruelty, injustice, extortion, and hatred of the people." [1]   As the movement, however, unlike other Fenian movements, was necessarily to be conducted in the face of the day, the innocent phrases of "self government" and "peasant proprietary," were to be employed in order to mask the real purpose.   Davitt was to inaugurate the "New Departure"; but it is significant of what was at bottom meant, that the negotiator went to Ireland at the same time to distribute arms among the remains of the old Fenian levies.[2]

The movement thus skilfully set on foot, had, it will be perceived, a double aspect.   It was treasonable in its chief purpose, the separation of Ireland from Great Britain ; it was socialistic in its designs against the land; but it screened itself behind Constitutional forms ; it had a Constitutional motto, as it were, on its flag; and this was to be its essential nature from first to last.   The campaign was opened in Davitt's birthplace, Mayo ; a great meeting assembled at a place called Irishtown, in the early spring of 1879 ; Davitt, owing to an accident, was not present ; but an assault on "Irish landlordism" was made in vehement language, occasionally breaking out in extreme sedition, several of the speakers being well-known Fenians.   Other meetings of the same kind were convened ; but Davitt, though an earnest, nay an able man, was not fit to lead an Irish agrarian crusade ; he had ideas about "the nationalising" of the land, which the Irish occupier of the soil abhorred ; and very probably the movement would have failed in his hands, as the Fenians had failed to arouse the peasantry in 1865–7, had he not sought the aid of a very different personage.   Parnell by

---

[1] Letter of John Devoy to the *Freeman's Journal* cited in "The Continuity of the Irish Revolutionary Movement," pp. 14, 15.

[2] Report of the Judges on the Special Commission, vol. iv. p. 481. He did not go in the same ship as Davitt.

this time was the undisputed head of the "active Irish Party" in the House of Commons, though many of Butt's old followers disliked his methods; he knew that there was already distress in Ireland; he may have had philanthropic views; but he was certainly aware that the time was becoming ripe for making an attack on the land system. What passed between him and Davitt has not transpired; but probably a plan of action was formed; and at a meeting held at Westport in June 1879, Parnell, amidst moderate and even philosophic phrases, called on his hearers "to hold a firm grip on their homesteads and lands,"[1] the creed of Finton Lalor and the extreme "men of 1848." A few months afterwards, a great Central Land League was founded in Dublin with country branches; this was to carry into effect the new movement, and to disseminate its influence throughout Ireland; Parnell was elected its president with general acclaim. The professed objects of the League were reasonable and fair, "to bring about the reduction of rack-rents" and "to facilitate the acquiring of the ownership of the soil"[2] by its occupants; but this was partly because Parnell feared that an organisation of the kind would be perilous, if not avowedly kept within the limits of the law; and partly because it would be good policy to attract to it timid and faint-hearted men.[3] The real objects of the League, Davitt boasted afterwards, was "the complete destruction of Irish landlordism . . . because landlordism was a British garrison, which barred the way to national independence;"[4] and a pregnant confirmation of this view—"of the seven first chosen officers of the League, four were, or had been," notorious Fenians.[5]

Distress, meanwhile, had been making progress in Ireland, and quickening, as the great Greek historian has said, the animosities, which spring from divided classes. The prosperity of Ireland ceased in 1877; the harvest of 1878 was not good; that of 1879 was the worst seen since the Great Famine. The loss to a country always comparatively poor,

[1] Report of the Judges as *ante*, vol. iv. p. 483.   [2] Ibid., vol. iv. p. 484.
[3] Ibid., vol. iv. p. 485.   [4] Ibid., vol. iv. p. 485.   [5] Ibid., vol. iv. p. 485.

was not less than £10,000,000 sterling ; this necessarily
disturbed all social relations, especially those of the land
system.   The peasantry, we have said, were largely in
debt, as a class ; banks and traders had everywhere made
advances on the security given by the Act of 1870 ; and
now when a really hard time had come, there was a
universal calling in of demands of this kind, and many
farmers were suddenly involved in bankruptcy.   It is
certainly to be regretted, though hundreds did, that the
landlords, as a rule, did not make the reductions of rent
the occasion required ; yet it is not easy to find fault
with them.   Rents had, doubtless, been rising in Ireland
of late years ; in not a few instances they had become
excessive ; but Ireland, as a whole, was not an overrented
land, whatever mere faction has since asserted ; this was
conclusively proved by the unimpeachable Report of a
Commission appointed to make the inquiry.[1]   It must be
remembered, too, that, at this very time, the doctrines of
the Land League had been announced ; the annihilation
of " landlordism " had been preached with extravagant
vehemence at county meetings; the landed gentry had been
insulted and bearded ; besides, they had been assured by
Mr. Gladstone that if the Land Act had taken something
from them, it made their position perfectly safe ; and it
must be added that, in five-sixths of Ireland, they were
separated from their dependents in race and faith, a separation, which probably had become more wide.   They
are hardly, therefore, in justice to be condemned ; but
the circumstance that, as a class, they claimed their full
rents, in the actual state of affairs, must be deemed unfortunate.   Their conduct irritated hundreds of tenant farmers ;
strengthened the socialistic ideas, which, we have seen,
were already current about the land, and gave additional
force to the new agrarian movement—though this as yet
was relatively weak, and did not extend beyond two or
three counties—and moreover, to the Land League's real

[1] See the Report of the Bessborough Commission of 1880, vol. i. p. 3.
It is emphatic on the subject.

purpose. Injudicious, however, as many of the landed gentry were, the disorder that before long followed the evictions to which they were driven to assert their rights, is not fairly to be laid to their charge. It was the movement set on foot by Davitt and Parnell that, beyond question, provoked these evictions; not the evictions which, as has been falsely said, called the Land League, so to speak, into the field, as the defender of an oppressed peasantry.[1]

In the last weeks of 1879, the distress in Ireland, though not widespread, became severe in its ordinary seats, Connaught, and the south-western parts of Munster. The Government of Lord Beaconsfield met the crisis by the advance of funds taken from the Church surplus, and to be laid out, through landlords, on reproductive works, an improvement certainly on the Labour Rate Acts of 1845-6; and Relief Committees distributed large sums in charity. The occasion was skilfully seized by Parnell; the agrarian movement, as indeed was always the case, had received hardly any support, in money, in Ireland, and hitherto had been chiefly sustained from "The Skirmishing Fund";[2] but the supplies to the Land League might now be expected to increase, and an appeal on behalf of the cause in America might prove successful. Parnell sailed for the United States, as the year was closing; he was accompanied by two lieutenants of promise, who have since made a name for themselves in Parliament; a singular conversation took place on the voyage, which strikingly illustrates the general course of his policy. He remarked, among other commonplace things, "that a true revolutionary movement in Ireland should partake of a Constitutional and illegal character," should "use the Constitution for its own purposes, but should take advantage of its secret combination";[3] it is impossible not to see how

[1] See particularly, on this point, the Report of the Judges, vol. iv. pp. 524-5.

[2] Report of the Judges, vol. iv. p. 484.

[3] Ibid., vol. iv. p. 486. The Judges declined to accept Parnell's explanation.

this fits in with the "New Departure" arranged with Davitt, and which Parnell was designed, we may say by nature, to promote. The leader of the "active party" in Parliament, and the recognised head of the Irish Land League received a hearty welcome from many sorts and conditions of men, after he had landed on the quays of New York. The election of a President was at hand ; it was necessary to gain the Irish vote ; the name of Stewart and his exploits were not forgotten ; and Parnell was permitted to explain his views on Ireland—this he did with his accustomed moderation of tone—before the House of the Representatives of the United States. He associated also with politicians of mark ; but his relations were most frequent with prominent men of the Fenian parties of every hue and shade. He mixed freely with leaders of the Clan na Gael, though possibly he was unaware of their extreme views ;[1] became acquainted with a writer on the *Irish World,* an incendiary print of the most execrable kind ; made companions of Fenians of many degrees ; attended public meetings at which he now and then let slip plain treason through a veil of calm and measured language ; in a word, impressed the American Irish, wherever he went, with a sense of his capacity to direct a revolutionary cause. At one of these meetings he openly declared that "none of us, whether we are in America, or in Ireland, or wherever we may be, will be satisfied until we have destroyed the last link which keeps Ireland bound to England.[2]

Parnell's mission to the United States was successful ; he gave an additional impulse to the "Irish cause"; he founded a Central "Land League of America," analogous to the Central League of Ireland ; he received considerable sums of money for the purposes of the "New Departure."[3]   The

---

[1] Report of the Judges, vol. iv. p. 487.

[2] Report of the Judges, vol. iv. p. 488.   The Judges declined to believe Parnell's denial of these words. He made several speeches at this time ; we shall note several of these ; this cool and crafty politician never hesitated to use language that might serve his purpose.

[3] One of the contributors to this fund remarked : " Parnell, there are

work of the Irish Land League was, in his absence, carried on by subordinates, in the fashion already set ; violent speeches were made against landlords at public meetings, and significant hints were dropped as regards the use of fire-arms ; but the methods of the League, though being arranged, were not brought to a state of perfection ; and its power, if increasing, was not as yet great. Lord Beaconsfield, indeed, was the only British statesman who clearly perceived, at this time, the ends of the movement ; his name is not associated with any great Irish reform ; but, from his youth upwards, he understood Ireland much better than his eminent rival ; and when he dissolved Parliament, in the first months of 1880, he declared, in an address, which has become historical, that " an attempt scarcely less dangerous than pestilence and famine," was being made to " sever the Constitutional tie " between Great Britain and the lesser island. This manifesto was covered with ridicule when it appeared, by none more boldly than by Mr. Gladstone, who claimed that the Liberal party was the mainstay of the Union ; but the truth has since been made only too evident, and it was unfortunate for England and Ireland alike, that the great Imperialist and Conservative statesman was driven from power at the General Election of 1880. In view of that event Parnell returned to Ireland ;[1] he fought for the leadership of the Home Rule party with great determination, energy, and skill ; and though even then he was not its official head, he won many seats for followers—several of these were men of revolutionary and socialistic views—who clung to him as faithfully as the " Tail " adhered to O'Connell ; and he soon gained the supremacy to which he aspired. By this time Mr. Gladstone had become Prime Minister ; he indulged, for a

twenty-five dollars, five for bread and twenty for lead," an observation enthusiastically cheered at a Land League meeting. Report of the Judges, vol. iv. p. 490.

[1] On Parnell's return, one of his Parliamentary colleagues made the well known " Hartmann Speech " hinting at the occasional expediency of political assassination. Report of the Judges, vol. iv. p. 488.

while, in the optimistic fancies he had cherished respecting Irish affairs ; he had no thought about Irish reforms ; he would not even renew an Act controlling the use of arms in Ireland, notwithstanding the Land League speeches before referred to.　By degrees, however, as the agitation in Ireland increased, and Parnell and his satellites in the House of Commons dwelt on the tale of evictions becoming, no doubt, more frequent, but exaggerated in number to an immense extent,[1] the Minister, as it were, awoke from his deceptive dream ; he introduced a measure for the amendment of the Land Act of 1870, which, seconded by a Commission charged to report on the state of the Irish land system, and landed relations, would, he thought, suffice to set existing troubles at rest.

A word or two must be said on this project, for though in itself of no great importance, it had a marked influence, in the result, on Irish affairs.　The Tenant Right of the occupier of the soil in Ireland was, we have seen, under the existing law, to be realised only when he was being removed from his holding by a hostile act of the landlord.　"Compensation for Disturbance," by the Act of 1870, was only to be paid when he was being dispossessed by a notice to quit. He was not, except in a very few cases, to obtain this compensation and to have his Tenant Right when he was being removed for not paying his rent—that is, presumably, for his own default.　From this it followed that, as in 1847–50 the Tenant Right of Ulster was greatly imperilled by the pressure of arrears of rent on the tenant's peculium, so, at this conjuncture, the potential Tenant Right conferred by the Act of 1870—that is, the compensation when a tenant was disturbed—was being destroyed, in perhaps not a few instances, by the failure of tenants to pay rents, which they could not pay in a season of distress.　The rights, therefore, of the occupiers of the Irish soil were being confiscated,

---

[1] The method of falsification, unscrupulously adopted, was to represent ejectment decrees obtained in the courts as identical with actual evictions.　Mr. Gladstone seems to have accepted this misstatement ; but probably there were twenty decrees to one eviction.

from an equitable point of view, as evictions, even for not paying rent in a hard time, increased. The Bill of Mr. Gladstone proposed a remedy for this state of things. In certain classes of cases, carefully limited, and subject to many precautions and even restrictions, the Irish tenant might retain his Tenant Right, and Compensation for Disturbance might be advanced to him though he had been in default and had not paid his rent ; and though this legislation was, no doubt, startling, was contrary to the spirit of the Act of 1870, and was open to very grave objections, it was, as affairs stood, to be perhaps justified. The measure was vindicated by Lord Hartington[1] with characteristic sound sense and judgment. It passed the House of Commons, though with large amendments, and rather against that assembly's will ; but it was summarily rejected by the House of Lords—a decision that must be pronounced unfortunate in this as in other passages of the affairs of Ireland.

The "Compensation for Disturbance" Bill, as it was called, was treated by Parnell and his party with contempt; they asserted that it was a mere useless sham.[2] Very probably, circumscribed as it was, it would not have applied to many Irish tenants. But the rejection of the measure gave these men a favourable opportunity to go on with their work ; it enabled them to denounce British rule in Ireland and its garrison of landlords, with a show of plausibility, to masses of ignorant peasants.[3] The Land League meetings suddenly multiplied ; the language of the speakers became more treasonable and ferocious than it had ever been. To find anything like it we must turn to the pages of Marat, or to the frenzy of Jacobinism during the Reign of Terror.[4]

---

[1] The present Duke of Devonshire, a great landlord in Ireland. The speeches of the Irish Attorney-General, Law, were also very able.

[2] Evidence of the Special Commission of 1888, vol. iv. p. 272.
    Ibid.

[4] These speeches, and scores of others of the same kind, will be found in the Evidence of the Special Commission. I select two, by no means the worst, extracts. It will be observed how they correspond to the Fenian denunciations of 1865–70. Mr. M. Harris, afterwards, M.P.,

Through these wicked incentives the power of the League increased; its branches spread over six or seven counties, extending gradually into Leinster from the west. The agrarian movement became more intense, though distress had lessened in a marked degree [1] and evictions were fewer than they had been for months. The plan of operations of what simply was a huge conspiracy against the State had been formed before, but deliberation and money had been required to mature it; and as a year had passed since the first meeting in Mayo, and contributions from America had largely flowed in, the preparations were by this time complete. The methods of the League to strike " landlordism " down had a kind of resemblance to those of English Trades Unions, though essentially they were altogether different. This certainly was of set purpose, for Parnell usually endeavoured, as far as was possible, not to come in too rude conflict with English opinion. In districts where the agrarian movement prevailed landlords were to be compelled to accept rents, sometimes on terms dictated by the local League, sometimes at the valuation on which rates were assessed, always at a reduction grossly excessive ; they were to be terrorised and banned if they ventured to refuse. Landlords, however, obviously might resist ; if they had the temerity to appeal to the law, and to dispossess tenants who would only pay the sums fixed by the League's mandates, the evicted lands were to be left derelict, and all persons who should dare to occupy these, as well as tenants who should pay rents higher than those of the League's estimate were to be ostracised by the whole adjoining neighbourhood. " You must put " a wretch of this stamp—so

said : " If the tenant farmers of Ireland shoot down landlords as partridges are shot in the month of September, Mat Harris would never say a word against them." Joe Brennan, a leading official of the League, exclaimed : "The compensation Irish landlords would be entitled to would be a prison or a rope, for having robbed or murdered the Irish people." Multiply sentences like these by hundreds, and the reader can form an idea of what these utterances were. As for treasonable expressions, they were simply passim.

[1] Report of the Judges, vol. iv. pp. 524–5 *ante*.

Parnell laid down the law—"into a kind of moral Coventry, by isolating him from his kind, as if he were a leper of old ; you must show him your detestation of the crime he has committed ;" [1] so that when lands were smitten by this barbarous interdict, the power of the landlord would be wholly paralysed, and his property could be filched away from him. It is difficult to suppose that a man so able as Parnell did not see that what he described as "an unwritten law" like this would inevitably lead to a frightful social war, and to crime and disorder of every kind ; but as to results he never had a scruple, provided he perceived how to accomplish his ends.[2]

The operations of the Land League were in full swing in the last months of 1880 and in the beginning of 1881. The conspiracy disclosed itself in what was aptly called the Land War, which, conducted by the central organisation and its dependent members, had extended over nearly a third part of Ireland. The plan that had been laid down was systematically carried out ; landlords were offered the rents adjudged to be "fair" by the League on the spot, and if they declined they were denounced by name and held up to execration at village or country meetings, or were burned in effigy by howling mobs, or ostracised by the League's commands, while their demesnes were repeatedly ravaged by "Land League hunts"—savage gatherings of the scum of the neighbourhood. The peasantry were at the same time enjoined to pay only what the League ordered. Specious promises were held out to them : they would get their farms for nothing, or at "prairie rents," if they only kept together and were true to Parnell ; but if they disobeyed they knew what they had to expect. In many

---

[1] For an account of the methods of the Land League, see the Report of the Judges, vol. iv. pp. 495–506. I refer only to the ostensible methods avowed and inculcated.

[2] The only observation Parnell made on a frightful murder which had been committed for contravening the dictates of the League was : "Recourse to such measures of procedure is entirely unnecessary, and absolutely prejudicial, when there is a suitable organisation among the tenants themselves."

instances the landed gentry yielded, isolated in the midst
of a population in revolt; in many the occupiers of the
soil, already swayed by socialistic ideas about the land,
succumbed to artful temptations or infamous threats; and
in a few districts the League had a complete triumph. This
submission, however, was not general, or even often seen.
Many landlords insisted on their rights, and enforced the
law; many tenants paid their rents honestly or through fear
of eviction. The efforts of the conspiracy were then combined to take vengeance on the transgressors of its will.
The odious practice of "boycotting," which, we have seen,
had been first heard of in the great Tithe War, was not
made as perfect as it became afterwards; but it was carried
out with ruthless and far-reaching cruelty against those of
all classes who violated the "unwritten law" of the League.
Domestics of the landed gentry were driven from their
masters' houses; ladies were often compelled to seek the
necessaries of life by night, and stealthily, as they could best
procure them; scores of families fled the country in despair.
The penalties of the League, however, fell far more heavily,
and 'in instances, by many degrees more frequent, on those
of the humbler classes who dared to cross its purpose. The
courageous or the terrified tenant who had committed the
offence of paying what he had agreed to pay, the "grabber"
who had put his foot on an evicted farm, the weak trader
who dealt with an "obnoxious" person, were "boycotted,"
literally sometimes to death; they were refused food, shelter,
medicine, even Christian burial; they were proscribed by
a potent and tyrannous Vehmright, which worked not so
much by bloodshed as by social terror. Such a system
persistently and wickedly enforced could have but one
end—a war of classes and an outbreak of crime. "Boy
cotting," however widespread and barbarous, was, after all,
but a passive thing. It was "a law," Mr. Gladstone truly
said, "that required a sanction"; and "the sanction of boy
cotting was the assassination" that lay behind it. During
this period and that which ere long followed Ireland
witnessed the worst outburst of crime which had been

witnessed since the struggle of 1831–34. Victims among
the upper classes were done to death; but these deeds
were as nothing compared to the atrocious cruelties perpetrated on the peasantry condemned by the League to
its ruthless punishments. This was the distinctive feature,
indeed, of the crisis.[1] For one landlord, agent, or bailiff
who was shot or attacked at least a hundred " grabbers "
or " traitors " were brutally treated; their houses were
often entered by bands of ruffians, significantly known as
" Moonlighters " and " Parnell's Police "; they were sometimes murdered, often shot in the legs; the hair of their
women was repeatedly cut off; their cattle were horribly
mutilated in hundreds of cases. The Central Land League
appears to have had no direct relations with the old agrarian
secret and Ribbon societies, but the local Leagues in all
probability had. These, like Aaron's rod, swallowed up
the less powerful bodies, and made use of them in their
saturnalia of crime.

By the spring of 1881 the League had established a kind
of anarchic rule in different parts of Ireland, superseding
the Government as the law of the land, as the Catholic
Association had superseded them sixty years before. Here,
however, the resemblance between the two organisations
ends; the Catholic Association was sustained by a principle,
had the essential power of a just cause, and reprobated
crime with emphatic force; the Land League worked by
terrorism and sheer cruelty; it addressed itself to the
basest motives; as Mr. Gladstone took care to point out,.
" it was dogged by crime," where you traced its footsteps.
It is a mistake to suppose, as has often been said, that the
League spread over the whole of the country, or was even
omnipotent in any one district. The occupiers of the
soil in Protestant Ulster had grievances of their own; but,
with a true instinct, they saw from the outset that a treasonable conspiracy was at work in Ireland; they rejected its
blandishments and its menaces alike; as a class they

[1] This was over and over again noticed and commented on by the
Judges on Assize in Ireland.

denounced it, and kept aloof. The League, in fact, had
real power in not more than ten or eleven counties ; and,
unlike what had been the case in other Irish movements,
its strength was greatest in poor and backward districts, the
seat of a Celtic and servile peasantry, for in these its teaching,
sordid and vile, and without anything like a true ideal,
and its detestable tyranny, were most likely to prevail.
It was, also, wholly a Catholic movement, confined to the
worst parts of Catholic Ireland ; and it was the irony of
fate that its real leader, though surrounded by a band of
Catholic followers, was, like Tone and Lord Edward
Fitzgerald, a Protestant in name. Circumscribed, however,
as the movement was, within limits comparatively small, it
was, we repeat, terrible, where it prevailed, and marked
with terrible crime. In the two years 1880 and 1881, the
agrarian outrages in Ireland, which, in 1879, a bad year,
was little more than eight hundred in number, reached the
appalling total of nearly seven thousand ; and History
holds the League morally responsible for these, for they can
be referred to no other agency. It is almost superfluous to
inquire to what an extent the directors of the conspiracy
should be held accountable. They did not openly urge the
commission of crime ; but the incendiary speeches many
made led by a natural process to crime ; [1] and with the
honourable exception of Davitt, who, in this matter, proved
himself to be sincere, they scarcely ever denounced crime
honestly and from the heart. Parnell especially winked at
crime, because he saw that it served his turn, as Robespierre
winked at the ravings of Marat, for they strengthened the
forces of the Reign of Terror.

The Lord-Lieutenant of Ireland, at this time, was Lord
Cowper, who had been the successor of the Duke of Marl-
borough ; but the real governor was Forster, the Chief

---

[1] Report of the Judges, vol. iv. p. 520 : "The speeches in which land-
grabbers and other offenders against the League were denounced as
traitors and as being as bad as informers . . . had the effect of causing
an excited peasantry to carry out the laws of the Land League, even
by assassination."

Secretary, the author of the Education Act of 1870, a capable, and especially a just-minded statesman. He had confronted the League as far as lay in his power ; but he was hardly well supported by the Government from the first ; it is believed that he wished Parliament to be assembled to strengthen his hands, but that his colleagues would not follow his advice. A prosecution, however, against Parnell and his chief adherents was attempted at the close of 1880 ; but this was an unfortunate proceeding for many reasons ; the jury, through fear or sympathy, refused to convict. The state of Ireland, nevertheless, had become so frightful that no Government could hesitate to act ; when Parliament met in the beginning of 1881, two measures of repression were placed before the House of Commons. One was simply a Bill to regulate the use of arms in Ireland, on the model of the Act injudiciously dropped ; it became law without much opposition. The other was a kind of retrospective suspension of the Habeas Corpus Act ; it became the occasion of the worst obstruction on the part of Parnell and of those who acted with him, which hitherto had been known in Parliament. The progress of the measure was delayed for many weeks ; the decencies of the House of Commons were violated by disgraceful scenes ; a rebellious Irish faction was enabled to make a decisive change in the time-honoured procedure of the great Assembly it baffled and even degraded. The measure, however, was ill-adapted to meet the crisis ; subordinate agents of the Land League were imprisoned by scores ; but the leaders of the conspiracy escaped scatheless; and the League transferred its chief officials and its machinery to the capital of France, whence its operations were carried on with little let or hindrance. Nevertheless, "coercion," as it was called, was beginning to have its effects ; and possibly the law might have proved sufficient, had the Government showed the determined purpose the occasion required. Mr. Gladstone had denounced the League in passionate language ; he clearly saw that, in his happy words, it "aimed at dismemberment through rapine" ; he had dwelt with emphasis on the deeds of blood that attended its course. But Mr. Gladstone, throughout his long career, was never equal to cope with a grave emergency ; he was essentially a great economic Minister for quiet times ; in Irish affairs he had always shown a disposition to make compromises and even to yield, whenever there was a manifestion of popular force, whatever might be its aim or its character.   While Ireland was still in a state of frightful disorder, and before the law had been vindicated and its power felt, he made up his mind to concede some at least of the demands of the Land League, and to effect a revolution in the Irish land system.

The speech in which Mr. Gladstone introduced this measure, in the Session of 1881, was not one of his felicitous efforts.   It exhibited, indeed, his command of details ; but he did not clearly explain the principles of the scheme ; at heart he was probably opposed to them.   He spoke about proceeding "in the Divine Light of Justice," along a slippery and obscure path ; he scoffed at political economy being applied to Ireland, and sent it off, with a wave of the hand, to Saturn ; he pronounced an eulogium on Irish landlords ; he threw on the House of Lords the blame for the partial failure of the existing Land Act ; he tried to reconcile his new project with that of which he had been the author eleven years before.   All this, however, was tentative and not convincing ; and the orator avoided, perhaps prudently, alluding to his pledge that the settlement of 1870 was to be a final settlement, a pledge on the faith of which millions of money had been advanced on Irish land.   The measure was essentially an elaborate but ill-conceived attempt to extend the system of the " Three F's " condemned by Mr. Gladstone in 1870 and to which we have so often referred, to landed relations throughout Ireland, and to make this the mould, so to speak, of Irish tenures ; but it was a faulty, nay, a mischievous half-measure.   There was no definition of a Fair Rent, the very thing that ought to have been thoroughly defined.[1]   Fixity of Tenure was

---

[1] This was the more reprehensible because Law, Mr. Gladstone's Attorney-General for Ireland, who knew Irishmen, proposed an excellent definition of Fair Rent.

limited to a lease of fifteen years, renewable for ever, through litigation, at these intervals of time; Free Sale, though allowed under certain conditions, was checked and made difficult by somewhat harsh restrictions. The right of the landlord to possess his own estate, to deal with it, and to settle his rents by contract, was summarily and almost completely taken away; but the immense privileges given to the tenant were to be realised, as a rule, with much trouble, and through a tedious, costly, and often recurring process. This was, however, but a part of the complications of the scheme; by an amendment dexterously engrafted on the Bill the Fair Rent was to be a sum from which the value of a tenant's improvements was to be deducted; this involved intricate and prolonged inquiries; and it was wittily said "this is putting a landlord first on a rack, and then giving him the tender mercy of hours of the thumbscrew." A Commission was appointed to carry the measure into effect; it was invested with all but absolute power, especially with regard to Fair Rent; its precedure was to be one of continual lawsuits; and it was to be assisted by a body of sub-commissioners, who, though entrusted with high judicial duties, were to be the tenants on sufferance of the Ministry of the day. The measure, it must be added, was charged with the oversubtlety of Mr. Gladstone's creations, and it drew injudicious and false distinctions; it revealed the desire, conspicuous in the Act of 1870, to replace Irish by English tenure, by provisions which only encouraged eviction. For the rest, the Bill offered increased facilities to Irish tenants to become owners of their farms through advances to be made by the State; but they were still required to pay part of the purchase moneys themselves.

Every reasonable allowance ought to be made for the policy of Mr. Gladstone in this grave matter. He knew what the Land League movement was, but he thought it most dangerous on its agrarian side; he probably believed that he would break its force by a great agrarian law for the behoof of the Irish peasant. The Commission, too, which he had appointed, had reported in favour of a reform in Irish land tenure ; and he certainly calculated, not quite wrongly, that his measure would operate as a self-acting force, that would compel landlords and tenants to adjust their relations, and to fix rents by agreements between themselves, and that the litigation caused by his new tribunal would not be great. The juncture, besides, was critical and perplexing ; yet it is scarcely possible to justify legislation of this kind, vicious in itself, and brought forward when parts of Ireland were virtually in a state of social war ; and assuredly the statesman who gave the pledge, given in 1870, might have paused before he broke it in 1881. The Opposition in the House of Commons was weak in numbers ; but it assailed the Bill with a great force of argument. It was shown that the measure could not be reconciled with the Act of 1870 ; one was socialistic, the other remedial ; one confiscated the rights of the landlord in the guise of law, and by a false pretence ; the other protected the equitable rights of the tenant. It was shown that the Act of 1870 might be amended, so as to secure the just claims of the tenant without having recourse to a revolutionary scheme ; it was clearly pointed out that the effect of the Bill would be to make the position of the Irish landlord nearly that of a rent charger on its own estate, and to convert the tenant virtually into the owner, and that this would be, not only sheer iniquity, but would be attended with the worst social mischief. One of the ablest speakers against the Bill was the present Lord Ashbourne ; he truly predicted that it would lead to litigation without end, and would aggravate existing divisions of class ; he caustically remarked that it would be much better openly to deprive Irish landlords of a large part of their rents, than to despoil them wrongfully through the forms of law. The Bill passed through the House of Commons, though not without misgivings ; in the House of Lords it was admirably exposed and criticised by Lord Salisbury and Lord Cairns ; but it was deemed advisable to allow it to become law, for what had happened the year before was not forgotten ; and many Irish peers gave a reluctant assent, alarmed, no doubt, at the power of

the Land League.   The Duke of Argyll, however, and
Lord Lansdowne, resigned office—they disliked the measure
so much ; and it deserves notice that the Government
declared that Irish landlords would not suffer real loss, and
that if they did compensation should be afforded—a statement to be borne in mind when the whole subject, as is
inevitable, shall be again reviewed.   In Ireland the Bill was
severely condemned by a large majority of thinking and
well-informed men ; it was felt how unfortunate it was that
the counsels of Butt and Longfield had been disregarded
in 1869–70.

We shall notice the operation of this agrarian law as its
effects were by degrees developed.   The attitude of Parnell
and of most of his followers to the measure was characteristic in the extreme.   They either treated it with open
contempt or refused to have anything to do with it ; [1]
meanwhile the terrorism of the League in no sense
lessened, or was only checked by the repressive law that
had been just enacted.   As the Land Act was being carried
into effect, Parnell adopted a course in accord with his
double-dealing nature.   With ostentatious moderation he
proposed that the quality of the new tribunal should bé tested
by cases selected by the League ; while he was assuring the
owner of the *Irish World* that this was to prove how worthless the Land Act was,[2] as some months before he had told
a spy of the Government, who, he understood, was a Fenian
messenger, that the "redemption of Ireland" could be
wrought only "by force of arms." [3]   Mr. Gladstone has
always resented attempts to thwart measures of which he
had been the author ; the hostility of the League had
become apparent ; Parnell had declared that if he was
himself "a great, the Minister was a little robber," for that

---

[1] See a startling passage in the " New Ireland" of Mr. A. M. Sullivan,
M.P., a moderate supporter of Home Rule and an able champion of
Young Ireland, p. 458.

[2] Evidence of the Commission, vol. iv. p. 355.

[3] Report of the Judges, vol. iv. pp. 538–36. Parnell's denial was again
disbelieved.

his design was to cut down rents ; and thereupon the chief
of the League, and two or three of his band in Parliament,
were arrested and sent to prison.   The leaders of the
conspiracy struck back by issuing a manifesto against the
payment of rent ; no rent was to be paid until Parnell had
been set free ; for some months desperate efforts were
made to prolong the rule of disorder and outrage.   The
Land League was proclaimed as criminal by the Government ; but it issued its edicts from its central office in Paris,
encouraging the peasantry "to keep up the fight"; and a
flight of viragoes, like the heroines of revolutionary France,
spread over the country preaching the evangel of " no rent."
The movement, however, to a great extent failed ; [1] the
arm of the law, imperfect as this was, was gradually
putting the conspiracy down, when it was suddenly paralysed by an act of the Government which History will
condemn without reserve.   The facts have not yet been
fully disclosed ; but it appears to be certain that some of
the Ministry had become alarmed at the number of "the
suspected persons" imprisoned under the recent Act ; and
it was resolved to try a complete change of policy.   Parnell
had been conveniently released on parole ; negotiations
were begun with him ; and the Chief of the League gave
it to be understood that if concessions were made about
arrears of rent, and perhaps about the state of things at the
Castle, not only would order be restored in Ireland, but
the leaders of the League might "co-operate with the
Liberal party." [2]   The emissary of Parnell, also perhaps
dropped such words as that "the conspiracy or organisation
which had been employed to get up outrage would now be
employed to put outrage down"; [3] that is, the League
would make a change of front, like the Government.
Forster, who had carried out the law at the peril of his
life, and Lord Cowper at once resigned office ; they were

---

[1] Report of the Judges, vol. iv. p. 508.
[2] Evidence of the Special Commission, vol. i. p. 151.
[3] Evidence of the Commission, vol. i. p. 150.   Report of the Judges,
vol. iv. p. 509.

not ready to pay blackmail to the League to secure its triumph in the shape of a hollow and immoral truce.

The "Kilmainham Treaty," as it was expressively called, was severely condemned in the Lords and the Commons ; it did great injury to Mr. Gladstone's Government, as the "Glamorgan Treaty," made with Irish rebels, brought ruin on the cause of Charles I. A surrender to a conspiracy not yet subdued by the law was not, indeed, the usual policy of British statesmen ; it was not thus that Grey had dealt with the Tithe War, or Peel with the comparatively innocuous Repeal Movement. Parnell was probably playing his wonted double game and deceiving the Government in this arrangement ; he was ready to promise anything to get out of prison, for he was not a man of real courage ; but he had not the will, or perhaps the power, to carry into effect the proposed compact. Be this as it may, Lord Spencer was sent to Ireland as Lord-Lieutenant to further the new policy ; Lord Frederick Cavendish was his Chief Secretary ; it was generally understood that, in a phrase which Mr. Gladstone has made classical, "Conciliation was to replace coercion," and that the League was to be pacified by Irish concessions about the land. These anticipations, however, were not fulfilled ; a frightful deed of blood brought them suddenly to an end. A band of assassins of Fenian origin had been formed in Dublin for some time ; they had over and over again laid in wait to murder Forster ; on the 6th of May, 1882, they slew Lord Frederick Cavendish in the Phœnix Park, and with him the Under-Secretary, Thomas Burke, an able man, who had done much to exasperate the League. Parnell and his followers, we may rest assured, had nothing to do with this execrable deed ; they have been fully acquitted by a legal tribunal ; the crime, too, was against their interest at the time, for their chief, it was believed, was to receive high office ; and we may rightly think they were incapable of even consenting to it. It is more probable that the murder was due to the disappointed fury of a few extreme Fenians ; they had heard that Parnell and some of his party were to be made "instruments of the rule of the Saxon"; the "cause of Ireland" had again been betrayed; warning must be given that no one could escape their vengeance.   But one or two prominent officials of the League had perhaps a guilty knowledge of what was being planned; and, in after years, part of the Press of the League showed a kind of odious sympathy with the criminals when they had been overtaken by the arm of justice.

Before the "Kilmainham Treaty" was made, a measure of repression for Ireland had been talked of, for English opinion had declared against the Land League and its works.   But the appalling tragedy of the Phœnix Park provoked a universal cry for "coercion;" the sorrow publicly, nay, sincerely expressed by Parnell and his followers was treated with scorn; Mr. Gladstone, always swayed by the popular voice, brought in a Bill to carry out its mandate.   The measure was the most severe known since the famous "coercion" of the Tithe War; Trial by jury was suspended in the case of even the worst crimes; the summary powers of magistrates were extended to many offences; whole districts were placed under the rule of the curfew; the Lord-Lieutenant received authority to suppress seditious prints and even public meetings; severe provisions were directed against foreigners, that is, against Fenians from the United States; inquiries to detect crime by inquisitorial means were permitted; districts where crime was perpetrated were made subject to heavy money penalties. Parnell and his lieutenants, abandoning their late attitude, resisted the Bill with the usual obstructive tactics; but England was in earnest, and the Bill became law.   A short but fierce struggle raged for some months between the forces of lawlessness and the law; the League, shattered as it was, was still alive, and put forth its expiring strength; "boycotting," difficult to discover and to repress, was still continued widely in a few counties; and there were several instances of fresh deeds of blood.   But the peculiar feature of the conflict was that the means were adopted which had been tried in 1796–7, to paralyse justice on her own seat;

juries were intimidated by atrocious threats ; several officials of the Courts were maimed or half beaten to death ; judges and magistrates were exposed to the gravest dangers, and were kept in daily fear for their lives. The law, neverthe-less, was boldly and ably carried out ; Lord Spencer and his Chancellor, Sir Edward Sullivan, in force of character not unlike Clare, distinguished themselves for cool courage and judgment ; the murderers of the Phœnix Park were convicted, through the secret inquiries the recent act sanctioned ; the conspiracy, and all that belonged to it, were confronted and quelled. There was a sudden and immense diminution of agrarian crime ; these offences fell from nearly three thousand five hundred in 1882, to eight hundred and seventy in 1883, and to seven hundred and sixty-two in the following year,[1] that is almost to their normal level. It is deplorable, we have before remarked, that violent agitation has, over and over again, been the means through which Ireland has obtained reforms, and not the power of strong and well-informed opinion. But when crime, and that indeed with scarcely any excuse, ran riot, as it did from 1880 to 1882, "coercion," as it is called, is a necessity of State ; and this has never failed when judiciously applied in Ireland. That "force is no remedy" is mere sentimental drivel.

The Land League had, we have said, been suppressed ; when order in Ireland had been partly restored, it reappeared under another name. The skill of Parnell in masking a conspiracy was seldom more conspicuously seen than when he established the Irish National League. Like the "New Departure" arranged with Davitt, like the Land League itself in its first professions, this Association had a Constitutional aspect ; it was to promote Home Rule, Land reform, and local self-government ; its cause was to be sustained in Parliament. It was, however, the old Land League in a seemingly harmless guise ; its organisation, its functionaries, its branches were the same ; at bottom its leaders had the same aim, the subversion of British rule in

[1] Report of the Judges, vol. iv. p. 522.

Ireland, and of Irish landlords.[1]　Its operations, however, in view of "coercion," were for a long time weak and tentative only ; its astute designer probably deceived Mr. Gladstone, though not Lord Spencer on the spot,[2] or intelligent Irishmen, who stood apart from the strife or faction.　The formation, however, of this apparently law-abiding body, had the results, which Parnell, no doubt, expected.　A considerable number of the "respectable" classes, which hitherto had feared or disliked the Land League, fell into the ranks of its successor ; this was especially the case with the Irish Catholic clergy, always a mighty influence in Irish affairs, whom Parnell had tried to gain from the outset.[3]　The attitude, indeed, of the Catholic Church in Ireland, as regards the movement, had been most significant.　An aged prelate, once an ardent Repealer, had denounced the agitation as "Fenian," when it began in Mayo ; this, too, was the view of Dr. McCabe, the successor of Cullen ; and the great majority of the elder and parish priests repudiated the Land League and con-demned its teaching.　But some of the bishops believed the movement to be, in the main, one on behalf of the peasantry ; and many of the younger clergy, who, we have seen, had resented the interdict of Cardinal Cullen, took part in it, and became members of the League.　This tendency increased, as the agitation grew in strength, and spread over a large part of Ireland ; the priests, rulers of their flocks, but also dependent on them, were carried away by a powerful impulse, and in numerous instances joined the League, though often against their real will ; a striking proof how different would have been the result, had they been in the position they ought long to have held, and been honourably endowed by the State.　The order now entered the National League largely ; many were made presidents of its local branches, and directed the manage-

[1] Report of the Judges, vol. iv. p. 532.　The Judges dwell on this point.

[2] See "Continuity of the Irish Revolutionary Movement," pp. 22–23.

[3] Report of the Judges, vol. iv. p. 489.

ment of its local affairs; for the organisation was, apparently, within the limits of the law. It is only right to add that no Catholic clergyman was convicted of crime during the reign of the Land League.

The Commission, meanwhile, chosen to carry out the new Land Act, had been actively engaged in its principal work, the arrangement of "fair," or, as they were called, "judicial" rents. It was all but impossible *but* that, as things stood in Ireland, a tribunal of this kind would do common justice. The tendency was irresistible to bid against the Land League, and to reduce rents as a sop to the peasantry; the Commission was appointed to give effect to a policy, like the Encumbered Estates Commission

260

CORRIGENDUM.

———

Page 261, line 8. For " all but impossible *but* that " *read* " all but impossible that."

determined by the price of the market, but on a calculation usually from a third to a fourth less. The provisions, too, as to exempting "improvements" from rent, just in the abstract as they might seem to be, but not just in existing facts, were made a potent means to cut rents down : " deterioration " done by the tenant as a counter claim to " improvement " was seldom regarded ; and the inquiries on the subject, as had been foreseen, were not only an abuse of the rights of property, but caused frightful demoralisation through unscrupulous swearing. The sub-commissioners, not directed by positive rules, and scarcely controlled by

Ireland, and of Irish landlords.[1]   Its operations, however, in view of "coercion," were for a long time weak and tentative only; its astute designer probably deceived Mr. Gladstone, though not Lord Spencer on the spot,[2] or intelligent Irishmen, who stood apart from the strife or faction.   The formation, however, of this apparently law-abiding body, had the results, which Parnell, no doubt, expected.   A considerable number of the "respectable" classes, which hitherto had feared or disliked the Land League, fell into the ranks of its successor; this was especially the case with the Irish Catholic clergy, always a mighty influence in Irish affairs, whom Parnell had tried to gain from the outset.[3]   The attitude, indeed, of the

by a powerful impulse, and in numerous instances joined the League, though often against their real will ; a striking proof how different would have been the result, had they been in the position they ought long to have held, and been honourably endowed by the State.   The order now entered the National League largely; many were made presidents of its local branches, and directed the manage-

[1] Report of the Judges, vol. iv. p. 532.   The Judges dwell on this point.
[2] See "Continuity of the Irish Revolutionary Movement," pp. 22–23.
[3] Report of the Judges, vol. iv. p. 489.

ment of its local affairs; for the organisation was, apparently, within the limits of the law. It is only right to add that no Catholic clergyman was convicted of crime during the reign of the Land League.

The Commission, meanwhile, chosen to carry out the new Land Act, had been actively engaged in its principal work, the arrangement of "fair," or, as they were called, "judicial" rents. It was all but impossible ~~but~~ that, as things stood in Ireland, a tribunal of this kind would do common justice. The tendency was irresistible to bid against the Land League, and to reduce rents as a sop to the peasantry; the Commission was appointed to give effect to a policy, like the Encumbered Estates Commission of thirty years before; History records what such bodies have done in Ireland from the days of Cromwell to those of Victoria. No attempt was made by the Court to perform its first duty, to determine the principles on which "Fair Rent" was to be fixed; on the contrary it ran into socialism from the first moment. The presiding judge is reported to have announced that the object of the statute was to make "tenants live and thrive;" in other words, the standard of rent was to be not what the land was worth, but what could be paid for it by a peasant, however lazy or worthless; rent was to gravitate to the level of the worst kind of husbandry. At the same time, a complete misconception of the law, the principle of competition was excluded, in considering what a "fair" rent might be; this was not to be determined by the price of the market, but on a calculation usually from a third to a fourth less. The provisions, too, as to exempting "improvements" from rent, just in the abstract as they might seem to be, but not just in existing facts, were made a potent means to cut rents down : "deterioration" done by the tenant as a counter claim to "improvement" was seldom regarded; and the inquiries on the subject, as had been foreseen, were not only an abuse of the rights of property, but caused frightful demoralisation through unscrupulous swearing. The sub-commissioners, not directed by positive rules, and scarcely controlled by the Superior Court, were, at the same time, in the words of one of their members, "let loose upon the estates of the gentry;" the results were what was to be expected, when officials dependent on a Government for bread, do what they know a Government seeks to be done. In the teeth of the Report of the Commission, which had just declared that overrenting in Ireland was not frequent, rents were cut down from twenty to thirty per cent.; rents paid for a century without a murmur were treated like rents raised a year before; the rents of the old noblesse and the new landlords were dealt with alike; nay, the owners of excessive rents fared better than the owners of those which were just. Confiscation, in a word, proceeded in the form of law, as it had proceeded under the Encumbered Estates Act; and it should be added that the Sub-Commissioners were over and over again at odds with each other; agreed only in pulling down rents; and had a direct interest to despoil landlords, for their members held office on the tenure of having continuous work. No doubt some of the County Court Judges made also reductions of rent at this time; and certainly some of these cases were hard; but public opinion would not have endured such a spectacle for six months had it been seen in England.[1]

An Act abolishing arrears of rent, the State contributing part of these to the landlords—the Church surplus was again drawn on—was a complement to the Land Act of 1881. This measure was another concession to the League; it was the *novæ tabulæ* of the demagogues of Rome; it increased the demoralisation of the tenant class in Ireland, but it facilitated the adjustment of Fair Rent; and on the principles of the late legislation something was to be said for it. Parnell, by this time, had become the Dictator of the Home Rule party, and of his satellites in the House of Commons; he bowed this assemblage of Celts to his imperious will; he had the ascendency Robespierre had over the cowering Mountain. He had attained the end

---

[1] Lord Salisbury especially condemned the proceedings of the Land Commission at this time.

aimed at by Lucas and Duffy in 1850-52 ; he was at the head of sixty submissive adherents ; he threw this great weight into the scale of British parties indifferently, as it might suit his purpose. He was usually in opposition to Mr. Gladstone, for he scented the fall of a greatly weakened Ministry ; but he always turned to account for his own ends the alien and really hostile element which, ever since the days of O'Connell, had made its way from Ireland, more or less, into Parliament. At the same time he gave remark-able proof how admirably he could conduct, in his own phrase, "a constitutional and an illegal" movement. His speeches in the House of Commons were nearly all moderate ; if not eloquent or even profound, they showed real knowledge of Irish affairs ; but now and then, when an occasion arose and a suitable audience was found in Ireland or elsewhere, he did not hesitate to use seditious language and to appeal to revolutionary and other evil passions.[1] The National League, meanwhile, had been throwing off its constitutional mask, and revealing itself in its true aspect. Disorder and open violence were repressed by "coercion" ; few deeds of blood or even of outrage were done at this time ; but the conspiracy smouldered beneath the surface ; its real purpose was in no sense changed ; and Parnell and his followers gave it large, if secret, support. The detestable system of "boycotting" perhaps increased ; the heads of the local branches of the League held courts to punish transgressors of the "unwritten law" ; there was no positive resistance to the payment of rent ; but "land grabbers," who took evicted farms, and "traitors to the cause" of all kinds, were subjected in not a few districts to

[1] I take two quotations at random :—"We cannot under the British Constitution ask for more than the restitution of Grattan's Parliament. But no man has a right to fix a boundary to the march of a 'nation.' . . . The day is dawning when we shall have taken the first great step to strike down British misrule and the noble dreams of Grattan, Emmet, Lord Edward Fitzgerald, and every Irish patriot ought at all times be brought to a triumph and realisation." Report of the Judges vol. iv. p. 448. "The Truth about the Land League," by Arnold Forster, p. 26.

what simply was barbarous social torture. In three or four counties thousands of acres were left desolate through this wicked process; the will of the National League prevailed in parts of the country all the more dangerously because the face of things was orderly; landlords were deprived of their rights in this way in many instances; but, as before, the humbler classes suffered the worst. The movement was encouraged from America by the *Irish World,* an advocate of assassination and the use of dynamite, with which Parnell, we have seen, had had relations; and by a vile Press at home, subsidised and even owned by chiefs of the League.[1]

While the conspiracy in Ireland, though alive, was still half dormant, it had become active in the extreme in the United States, the real base of its operations from first to last. Parnell, when he had visited America in 1879 had, we have seen, been welcomed by Fenians of all kinds, including leaders of the Clan na Gael; he had founded the Land League of America corresponding to the Central League in the Irish capital. The relations between the associates thus brought together strengthened as the aggressive movement went on; the Land War in Ireland was, in fact, sustained by contributions from across the Atlantic; for nothing is more certain—and it is most significant—than that if the Irish peasantry, in many counties, were not unwilling to profit by it, they gave it hardly any support in

[1] Extracts, a few only, from these publications, will be found in the Report of the Judges, vol. iv. pp. 510-19. They extend from 1880 to 1885. I select two only. Patrick Ford wrote thus in the *Irish World* in December, 1883 : "England ought to be plagued with all the plagues of Egypt, she ought to be scourged by day and terrorised by night. . . . This is my idea of making war on England." So again, *United Ireland,* December, 1883 : "Surely six hundred Irish gentlemen could not eat their dinner without pouring out libations to the admiration of an old lady who is only known in Ireland by her scarcely decently disguised hatred of this country, and by the inordinate amount of her salary." Thousands of pages of this pestilent and wicked stuff were scattered broadcast through Ireland : the Special Commission (vol. iv. p. 519) found that Parnell and many of his adherents "did disseminate newspapers tending to incite to sedition and the commission of crime."

money, very different from the case of the old Catholic
" Rent," and the subscriptions to Repeal in O'Connell's
time. These funds were largely collected by Patrick Ford,
the editor of the *Irish World*, an ally of Parnell probably
since 1879 ; and it has been conclusively proved that the
Irish leader, and most of his adherents in the House of
Commons, "invited the assistance of," and received ample
subsidies from, the conductor of this abominable print,
which, we have said, had found its way into many parts of
Ireland.[1] Meanwhile the conspirators of the Clan na Gael
had laid hold of the Land League of America, and gradually
had become its masters ; this was completely effected in
1883 when the League, after the Irish model, was changed
into the American National League ; and these desperadoes,
no doubt encouraged by the success of the Irish agrarian
movement, proceeded to carry out the threats against
England, which had for years been their avowed policy,
threats illustrated by the murderous crimes and the explo-
sions of dynamite which ere long followed. Parnell and
his party in Parliament, beyond question, had nothing to do
with these atrocious deeds, no more than with the murders
in the Phoenix Park ; it has not even been proved that they
were cognisant of the ascendency acquired by the Clan na
Gael over the organisations which owed their origin to
them.[2] But Parliamentary followers of Parnell were sent
by him to America in 1882, and during the next few years
to promote the cause of the Irish National League ; some
were present at "Conventions," at which heads of the Clan
na Gael were the master spirits ; and no doubt can exist
that at this period they "invited and obtained the assistance
and co-operation of the physical force party in America,
including the Clan na Gael, and, in order to obtain that
assistance abstained from repudiating or condemning the
action of that party."[3] History will at least pronounce that

---

[1] Report of the Judges, vol. iv. p. 544.　　[2] Ibid., vol. iv. p. 544.
[3] Ibid., vol. iv. p. 544. The relations between the Clan na Gael,
the American League, and Parnell and his party are admirably traced
out in this Report, vol. iv. pp. 534-544.

in this and other instances, a "constitutional and an illegal movement" were associated with most deplorable results.

During the progress of these events in America, and while the Clan na Gael were intent on their project, exultingly announced in the *Irish World*, of laying "London in ashes in twenty-four hours," the "uncrowned King of Ireland," as he was called in the National League, was coolly carrying on the kind of war he preferred at Westminster. He continued to oppose Mr. Gladstone's Ministry, and with his followers contributed to its fall in 1885 ; these had singled out Lord Spencer for worse than Jacobin abuse, because he had fearlessly carried out the law. The shifty Irish policy of Mr. Gladstone had had its part in bringing the crisis about, for opinion in England had declared against it ; but the result in this instance was mainly due to more general and world-wide causes, especially to a disastrous policy abroad. Parliament had passed a measure the year before which has had an important influence on the affairs of Ireland. The Parliamentary franchise in Ireland, we have seen, since the abolition of the forty-shilling freeholds, had always stood at rather a high level, though the electorate had been increased in 1851 ; even the Borough franchise had not been assimilated to that of England in the Reform period of 1867–8. This was in harmony with plain and existing facts ; for it is unnecessary to remark that, in this province, it is far from wise to extend the same system to countries in very different states of progress ; to place backward, poor and uncivilised Ireland on the same level in this respect with England wealthy, advancing, and, above all, trained for long centuries in self-government. But democracy, under Mr. Gladstone, was to have its way ; in 1884, the Parliamentary franchise in counties and boroughs was indiscriminately bestowed on all persons who possessed a house in Great Britain and Ireland, that is, in the case of Ireland, on an electorate composed, in an overwhelming majority, of petty peasants, wretched cottars, and landless labourers, classes on which Rousseau himself would have hardly liked to recognise his idol, "the Sovereign People."

At the same time no reduction was made in the number of the representatives sent from Ireland, who, since the decline of the population after the Famine, were largely in excess of their true proportion, taking any criterion that can be conceived ; Mr. Gladstone would hear no arguments on the subject. The consequences of this two-fold policy were such as naturally were to be expected. The extension of the franchise to masses of almost pauper peasants, ignorant, superstitious, and easily led, was at first greatly to increase the power of the National League, which promised them an Eldorado if they obeyed its commands, and ultimately to give additional weight to the immense influence of the Irish Catholic priesthood, hardly a salutary element in British and Imperial politics. Even more important, it practically deprived the classes in Ireland possessing property and intelligence of all weight in public affairs ; these have been literally swamped, and, as it were effaced, by the degraded Electorate, which hems them in on all sides. As for the representation of Ireland the immediate effect was to increase largely the band which followed Parnell.[1]

The troubled years we have briefly reviewed have not yet produced their final results ; they may prove to be a turning point in the affairs of Ireland. The distinctive feature of the period, as we now see it, was the development of the Land and the National Leagues, and the evil and tragic incidents that followed in their train. This essentially was not an agrarian movement, though it had its agrarian side, for the time most prominent ; it was not, as has falsely been said, the uprising of a wronged peasantry against an oppressive race of landlords. No doubt thousands who joined the League had not rebellious or dangerous ends in views ; no doubt thousands of the occupiers of the soil in Ireland thought only of the reduction of rent in a season of distress. But the movement was a conspiracy hatched in America, rising out of the Fenianism, which had its source in the Famine, supported almost wholly from American funds, only

---

[1] See on this subject some striking remarks, too long to be quoted, in Mr. Lecky's " Democracy and Liberty," vol. i. pp. 22, 23.

using the Irish peasant for its own ends ; and these were to overthrow British rule in Ireland, and its supposed mainstay, the Irish landed gentry. A series of circumstances gave it enormous power ; and it found a leader in Parnell admirably skilled in drawing together its complex forces, in making them effective in Ireland, and in Parliament, and in concealing its real aims and its character. Whether this remarkable man was a rebel at heart, like Wolfe Tone ; whether he was only seeking to rise to power in Ireland by encouraging the conspiracy, and placing himself at the head of a following who bowed to his tyrannous rule ; how far he controlled, or was controlled by the elements of evil he unscrupulously let loose, will probably never be fully known ; all that is evident is that he showed extraordinary power in directing a movement of which he became the master, in artfully maintaining its double aspect, and in effectually deceiving many British statesmen. Too much, however, is not to be made of Parnell's gifts ; had not Mr. Gladstone, over and over again, succumbed to a conspiracy he understood, but would not boldly face, the result would certainly have been very different ; as it was, Mr. Gladstone threw the Irish landed gentry as a sop to Cerberus, and yet did not appease the ravening monster. For the rest, whatever Parnell's ends may have been, the means he adopted or sanctioned were detestable ; there was nothing whatever in the state of Ireland to justify, even to palliate, the execrable deeds of the Land and the National Leagues in this period. But the conspiracy was still far from its close ; it was to proceed to even greater success ; it was, through the aid of a self-deceived statesman and a recreant party, to shake the order of things in these realms, until it was to encounter the clearly pronounced will of the British nation.

CHAPTER IX

THE SURRENDER TO, AND DEFEAT OF HOME RULE

Home Rule in the Parliament of 1880–5—Lord Salisbury in office—
Attitude of the Conservative· party as regards Irish affairs—The
General Election of 1885—Mr. Gladstone suddenly adopts the
policy of Home Rule—The probable reasons—Increase of disorder
in Ireland—Fall of Lord Salisbury's Government—Mr. Gladstone
forms a Ministry—His principal followers refuse to support Home
Rule—The Home Rule Bill of 1886—The Land Purchase Bill—
Characteristics of Mr. Gladstone's scheme—Defeat of the Home
Rule Bill—The General Election of 1886—Complete defeat of Mr.
Gladstone—Lord Salisbury again in office—The Chicago Con-
vention—Parnell's Land Bill rejected in the House of Commons—
Renewal of agitation in Ireland—Boycotting and the Plan of
Campaign—The Crimes Act of 1887—Mr. Balfour Chief Secretary—
Persistent obstruction in the House of Commons—Conflict with
disorder in Ireland—Conduct of Mr. Gladstone and the Opposition
—The Land Act of 1887—The Special Commission—Report of the
Judges—Parnell's policy—Verdict against him in the Divorce
Court—Schism and break up of his party—His fall and death—
Policy of Land Purchase in Ireland—The Act of 1891—The Local
Government Bill for Ireland—It is dropped—The General Election
of 1892—The Government defeated by a small majority—England
still opposed to Home Rule—Mr. Gladstone again in office—The
Home Rule Bill of 1893—Its glaring defects—Debates in the House
of Commons—Closure by compartments—The Bill rejected in the
House of Lords—Mr. Gladstone retires from public life—Lord
Rosebery Prime Minister—His Irish administration and that of
Mr. Morley—General Election of 1895—Complete defeat of Home
Rule—Lord Salisbury in office—Fusion of Unionist parties in the
Government—The Land Act of 1896—The report of the Childers
Commission—Ireland at the close of 1897.

AT the General Election of 1880 Ireland had sent to the
House of Commons some sixty members—about the same

number as in 1874—pledged generally to the policy of Home
Rule.   Some of these men had been followers of Butt ; but
the majority were of the faith of the " active party," which,
we have seen, had become a power, by degrees, in Ireland,
under Parnell's guidance.   As the Land League movement
developed itself, and the objects of its leaders became manifest, the few Moderates abandoned Parnell—especially the
one or two remaining Protestants, who had first pronounced
in favour of Home Rule ; but Parnell had risen to the head
of the party, as a whole, and had strengthened it with new
adherents from time to time.   He had made himself, as we
have said, the master of this band, formed of many and even
diverse elements—nominees of the Irish Catholic priesthood,
mere agitators of a socialistic type, or Fenians in a Constitutional mask—but Catholics, it may be said, to a man, and
nearly all the chiefs of the Land and National Leagues ; and
he had welded it into a submissive faction, which had held
the balance between the great parties in the State, and had
at least hastened the fall of Mr. Gladstone's Government.
Parnell, however, had not let Home Rule drop ; he had
advocated it at Westminster more than once in reasonable
language, the very opposite of the speeches he had made in
Ireland and elsewhere [1] ; in this instance, as in so many
others, he was unscrupulously playing his usual double game.
The Parliament, nevertheless, of 1880-5 had given little

---

[1] This was Parnell's language in the House of Commons : " I have
been charged several times . . . with desiring to make the land
movement of Ireland a lever for disintegrating the Empire.   These
sentences have been taken from speeches. . . . in which I was unable thoroughly to explain the views which I then assumed and still
hold."   This was Parnell's " second voice " in Ireland : " Let every
tenant farmer, while he keeps a firm grip on his holding, recognise also
the great truth that he is serving his country and the people at large,
and helping to break down British misrule in Ireland. . . . We stand
to-day in the same position that our ancestors stood.   We declare that
it is the duty of every Irishman to free his country if he can. . . .
We will work by constitutional means as long as it suits us. . . . I
thought that each one of them must wish with Sarsfield of old, ' Oh that
I could carry these arms for Ireland ! '   Well it may come to that some
day."

attention to Home Rule; with respect to Ireland it had been occupied with efforts to quell the social disorder that prevailed, or to effect a change in the Irish land system; Home Rule made no apparent progress in it. Mr. Gladstone, indeed, about the time of the "Kilmainham Treaty," had dealt with the subject; but he had referred to it chiefly to show that Home Rule could not even be discussed in Parliament until the problem had been solved how to make a distinction between British, Irish, and Imperial affairs, the definition of which had not been attempted.[1] This utterance, however, was the only one of importance that seemed even to leave the question open; the principal followers of Mr. Gladstone, in fact British statesmen, without exception, condemned Home Rule in emphatic language, and declared for the Union with no uncertain voice[2]; and this, indisputably, was the judgment of an overwhelming majority of the House of Commons. Home Rule appeared to be as hopeless in 1885 as it had appeared to be in 1872–4; recent events in Ireland had satisfied impartial minds that it was a dangerous, nay, an impossible policy; and this, though it was known that the late change in the franchise would increase the number of votes from Ireland in favour of Home Rule in a new Parliament. It deserves special notice that a proposal made by Mr. Chamberlain, already a leading personage in the House of Commons, to give Ireland large powers of local self-government, had not received the sanction of Mr. Gladstone's Ministry.

Lord Salisbury came into office in Mr. Gladstone's place; his followers were in a minority in the House of Commons; but the Conservatives had, with Parnell and his band, been in opposition during the last few years. The results were ere long seen, so often beheld, when, under conditions of

[1] See Mr. Gladstone's "History of an Idea," p. 17, the best apology he could make for his conversion to Home Rule.

[2] Lord Spencer thus expressed the mind of his colleagues in 1884: "The statesmen of the nation . . . will not give up one point or one idea which they consider necessary to maintain the United Parliament of England and the Sovereignty of the Queen" ("Continuity of the Irish Revolutionary Movement," p. 23).

this kind, parties, though essentially and even bitterly hostile accidentally combine on the field of politics. The ties insensibly formed were not at once dissolved ; and though nothing like an alliance was made, there was a tendency at least to co-operate for a time. The repressive measure of 1882 was dropped, which Mr. Gladstone had wished to renew in part ; the Lord-Lieutenant, who was sent to Ireland, charged to convey a message of peace, had an interview with Parnell, perhaps about Home Rule ; and a few Conservatives unjustly condemned passages of Lord Spencer's "coercive" policy. Simultaneously Parnell denounced Mr. Gladstone and the late Government in unmeasured language ; they were all that was tyrannous, vile, and base ; and during the contest at the polls that followed, the weight of the Irish vote in England and Scotland was thrown wholly into the scale against the Liberal party. This was an ominous and unfortunate state of things ; the results, not slow to develop themselves, were probably more grave than has been commonly supposed. Parliament was dissolved within a few months ; and though the condition of Ireland was discussed at the General Election of 1885, English and Scotch questions were much more prominent. Lord Salisbury declared emphatically for the Union, though he had let fall words in a recent speech unfairly twisted into a different meaning ; and so, with remarkable earnestness did Mr. Balfour, even now becoming a statesman of mark. But Lord Salisbury and the Conservative leaders mainly confined themselves to British affairs ; they dwelt much on plans to disestablish the Church of England, and even more on the reform of laws relating to the land, and on local government for England and Scotland only. Mr. Gladstone's attitude was not very different, he employed language, indeed, with respect to Ireland, which, he claimed afterwards, showed that he had Home Rule in his mind ; but this, interpreted by his own speeches, to which he appealed in a short time, was assuredly not the meaning of his words ; [1]

[1] See a very remarkable letter in the *Times* of February 11, 1886, in which Mr. Gladstone's previous utterances and speeches are compared.

and save that he insisted on an immediate reform of the in-
effectual procedure of the House of Commons, he enlarged
on the same topics as those of his rival, and evidently
believed that English and Scotch affairs would engross the
attention of the coming Parliament.   One point, no doubt,
as regards Ireland, he repeatedly pressed, he adjured the
Liberal party to give him a great majority, which would
enable him to dispense with Parnell, for it would be
dangerous otherwise to deal with the case of Ireland ; but
no one could suppose that Home Rule could lurk behind
such appeals.   His principal adherents, without exception,
pronounced in favour of the Union quite as strongly as the
chiefs of the Conservative party.

    This, briefly, was the state of public opinion when the
General Election of 1885 took place.   The boroughs in
England largely fell off from their allegiance to the Liberal
party ; but the counties partly redressed the balance.   The
Liberals in Great Britain had a majority over their adversaries of upwards of eighty votes.   In Ireland the contest
was short but decisive ; Parnell called on the country to
declare for Home Rule, an admirable and convenient cry ;
the Catholic priesthood and the National League sent the
lately enfranchised masses to the polls ; intelligence and
property were overborne [1] ; and Parnell secured for himself
and his satellites a majority almost exactly the same as that
which the Liberals had gained in England and Scotland.
In these circumstances, spite of faint denials, it transpired,
before long, that Mr. Gladstone had suddenly adopted the
policy of Home Rule, of which, in the judgment of nearly
all thinking men, he had been for years the avowed
opponent.   In this case, as in that of the Established
Church of Ireland, this rapid change of conduct, questionable as it was, cannot wholly be ascribed to mere personal
motives.   With his tendency to yield to whatever he deemed
to be a manifestation of the popular will, Mr. Gladstone
certainly believed that Home Rule was passionately sought

----

[1] The majority, however, of votes recorded for Home Rule at the
election was comparatively small. See the *Times*, December 21, 1885.

by five-sixths of Irishmen. This alone may have determined his purpose. He saw clearly, too, that if, as seemed probable, Parnell would support the Conservatives for his own ends, the Liberal majority in the House of Commons would disappear, and Parliament would be reduced to a deadlock, a grave evil for the State, of which the danger may have induced Fox, in 1783, to address himself to North, and to form the disastrous coalition of that day. Mr. Gladstone, moreover, may have persuaded himself—and this is probable in a high degree—that since the Conservative dealings with Parnell "coercion" in Ireland had become impossible ; and it must be added that he sincerely wished to act in concert with Lord Salisbury in an attempt finally to settle the Irish Question. Yet these considerations cannot justify the veteran statesman, we think, at this juncture. He must have known that, since the Act of 1882 had expired, there had been a sudden and great increase of crime in Ireland. Not to speak of Parnell and his men in Parliament, he cannot have been blind to the proceedings of the National League, now rapidly acquiring formidable strength. Was this the time to effect an immense change in Ireland, as great as that effected by Tyrconnell in 1689-91 ? The new Parliament, besides, had been assembled to deal mainly with English and Scotch subjects. Whatever were Mr. Gladstone's views as to Ireland, he had never breathed a word to his late colleagues on behalf of Home Rule ; nay, he had sanctioned their recent condemnation of it. Was he, in these circumstances, to reverse the Liberal policy pursued towards Ireland for a long series of years, and to endeavour to drag his adherents in his wake ? Nor were personal motives by any means absent. Mr. Gladstone calculated, there is no reason to doubt, that he could induce the whole Liberal party to follow his lead, and that Parnell and his band would fall into their ranks. In that event he would necessarily become minister again, and would command an overwhelming majority in the House of Commons.[1] "I have not one word to say," he once wrote,

[1] See the *Times*, December 18, 1885. The National Press Agency.

" for changes systematically timed and tuned to the interest of personal advancement." He seems to have been unconscious how the aphorism might apply to himself.

Meanwhile disorder in Ireland had been growing apace ; the tale of agrarian crime had increased a third ; the odious practice of " boycotting " had quadrupled ; the intimidation of juries and magistrates and the defiance of law had become general in not a few districts ; the branches of the National League had suddenly trebled ; and all this though for at least four years there had been nothing resembling general distress.[1] Whatever had been their faults and shortcomings, the Government rightly abandoned the policy of the last few months ; the Lord-Lieutenant, who had, perhaps, dallied with Parnell, and his Chief Secretary were recalled. At the opening of the Session of 1886, the Queen's Speech described the Union as "a fundamental law," and plainly pointed to renewed " coercion " ; and a trusted leader of the Conservative party, true, though very late, to its natural instincts, was sent to Ireland to carry out the intended measure. The occasion was not lost on Mr. Gladstone ; he could no longer act with Lord Salisbury in Irish affairs ; communications were probably opened with Parnell ; and through his support the Liberal party succeeded, though even now rent asunder, in bringing the existing Government to an end on a secondary issue of small importance. Mr. Gladstone addressed himself to form a new Ministry ; but the best of his followers stood aloof, and refused to accept the policy of Home Rule. His Government, with only two or three exceptions, was composed of comparatively unknown men ; and the great Liberal party, "that noble instrument of human progress," which for fifty

[1] Report of the Judges, vol. iv. p. 524. " The branches of the League trebled in 1885." Crime in 1889, 762 cases ; in 1885, 944 ; in 1886, 1,055. Mr. Gladstone's language was no less significant. " The return to the ordinary law, I am afraid, cannot be said to have succeeded. Almost immediately after the lapse of the Crimes Act, boycotting increased fourfold. . . . In October it had increased fourfold compared to what it was in the month of May " (Speech in the House of Commons, April 8, 1886).

years had been dominant in the State, was completely, nay, perhaps finally, broken up. The mind of England, in the meantime, had pronounced against a revolutionary change in Ireland ; the powerful organs of English opinion, infinitely superior to the partisans of politics, in expressing the real will of the nation, severely condemned Mr. Gladstone's conduct; all but universally took the side of the Union ; and, teemed with reasoning, often of real cogency,[1] pointing out the grave and numerous objections to Home Rule. The English press has seldom played so conspicuous a part ; it is interesting to observe what, about this time, was the view taken by the Clan na Gael, the paymasters of the National League and its chiefs, of the policy it assumed to be that of Mr. Gladstone : "The achievement of a National Parliament gives us a footing on Irish soil ; it gives us the agencies and instrumentalities of a Government *de facto* at the very commencement of the Irish struggle. It places the government of the land in the hands of our friends and brothers. It removes the Castle's rings, and gives us what we may well express as the plant of an armed revolution."[2]

Disregarding, however, the signs of the time, gathering ominously in from many sides, Mr. Gladstone persisted in his daring venture. The Bill for Home Rule was brought into the House of Commons on the 8th of April, 1886. Its author's speech was perspicuous, and, as was his wont, went thoroughly into the details of his subject ; it fully unfolded an elaborate and very complex scheme. But it was pervaded by a doubting, nay, a despondent tone ; it presented a plan that was but "a choice of evils" ; it proposed a revolution, but completely failed to show either that this was a necessity of State, or that it would even accomplish its author's objects. We can only describe the measure in its broad outlines, and our comments must necessarily be

---

[1] The letters of the late Sir James Stephen on the whole Irish Question, on Home Rule, and on the proposed legislation of Mr. Gladstone are perhaps the ablest contributions that have appeared on these subjects. They were published in the *Times*.

[2] Report of the Judges, vol. iv., p. 542.

very brief. A Legislative body was to be set up in Dublin ; and this, more properly called the Irish Parliament, was to be almost the Sovereign power in Ireland. This Assembly was to be divided into two Orders, the First composed of peers for a time and of men of substance elected on rather a high franchise ; the Second composed of members elected on the low household franchise already existing. The First Order was to be of one hundred and three members ; the Second of two hundred and four or two hundred and six. The two Orders, as a rule, were to sit together ; but the First Order was to have, for a short period, a veto on the decisions of the Second Order, this, it will be observed, being in an immense majority. The legislation of the Irish Parliament was to be restricted in a great many ways ; it was not to extend to a number of Imperial, and even domestic, subjects. Especially the Irish Parliament was to have no right to impose the taxes of Customs and Excise, this being reserved to the Imperial Parliament. The legislation, too, of the Irish Parliament was to be subject to the veto of the Lord-Lieutenant, analogous to the old Royal veto, and possibly to the veto of the British Ministry — this, however, being open to grave doubt—and the English Privy Council was to have the power, like that of the Supreme Court of the United States, to declare Acts of the Irish Parliament void if in excess of its constitutional rights. Subject, however, to these great limitations—far-reaching, complicated, and very stringent—the Irish Parliament was to rule Ireland ; it was empowered to enact and to repeal laws ; it was enabled to pass resolutions and to do everything which a real Parliament could do or attempt ; and it could practically appoint the Irish Executive, and direct and control it in all particulars, as the Imperial Parliament does for the British Executive. Ireland was to pay a contribution of nearly a fifteenth, that is, of not far from 7 per cent., to the general expenditure of the Empire. This would be a sum of about three millions and a quarter sterling, with a temporary addition of one million ; and the whole revenue of Ireland was to pass through the hands of a high official of the

Imperial Government, and to be applied to satisfy the claims of the British Treasury before the Irish Treasury could receive a shilling.[1] Finally, Ireland was to send no representatives to the Imperial Parliament, though this Assembly could heavily tax Ireland ; and the Imperial Parliament was probably to retain the nominal supremacy over the Irish Parliament, inseparable from its Imperial character, as it does in the case of the free British Colonies.[2]

The Home Rule Bill, as originally designed, was to be bound up with another measure, for the expropriation of the Irish landed gentry ; but this "Land Purchase Bill" was opposed in the Cabinet ; for reasons that may be readily conceived, it was resolved to separate the two measures. Mr. Gladstone brought in the Land Purchase Bill about a week after that for Home Rule ; his speech does not require special attention, save that it was apologetic and pitched in a not hopeful key, like that which he had already made ; but a word or two must be said on the measure, for it was the complement of the general scheme for the new system of governing Ireland and her affairs. Mr. Gladstone had declared, a few years before, that the land of Ireland was worth £300,000,000 ; by a process of calculation he did not explain, he arrived at the conclusion that the rented Irish land, to be the subject of the Bill, was worth only £113,000,000 ; but he distinctly announced that every Irish landlord should have a reasonable assurance, that if it was his wish to part with his lands, and to be bought out by the State, funds would be available within this limit. A sum, however, of £50,000,000 only, to be raised by the creation of stock, was to be forthcoming in the first instance ; the

---

[1] This was a Receiver-General, to be appointed by the supplemental Land Purchase Bill, but certainly to receive the whole revenue of Ireland, in the first instance. Mr. Gladstone's language was precise : "Through whose hands all rents and all Irish revenues whatsoever must pass before a shilling can be applied to any Irish purpose whatever."

[2] Hansard should be studied for a complete account of the Bill, and for an excellent synopsis of it see Dicey's "England's Case against Home Rule," pp. 223–274. A very remarkable work.

supplying the balance was to be left to future Parliaments, which, nevertheless, Mr. Gladstone had no doubt, would do what was just in this matter, and would honourably make up the £63,000,000, should it become necessary to raise that sum. This was the more to be relied on, because it was "an obligation of duty and honour" not to leave Irish landlords in their existing position, when the Irish Parliament should have been established ; and the only way to do this was to buy them out, to give them a fair price for their lands, and so to secure them a just indemnity. The method of working the arrangement out was simple, and need not be described at length. No landlord was to be compelled to part with an acre ; but if a landlord wished to sell his rented lands to the State, he was to receive from the fund to be provided then and thereafter, that is from the £50,000,000 and the £63,000,000, a sum equal to twenty years' purchase of the net rental, after many deductions and out-goings, and, so far as he was concerned, this closed the transaction. The Irish Parliament was to create a "State Authority" to purchase the lands disposed of in this way, and, in a few cases, to become their owner ; but the lands, in the great mass of instances, were to be transferred to the tenants upon them, according to the policy we have referred to ; and the tenants instead of the former rents, were to pay a terminable annuity only, at a much lower rate. The sums accumulated by these means were to be paid to the official mentioned before ; and these, of course, were to form a security for the advances made by the State to the landlords.[1]

The debates in the House of Commons on Mr. Gladstone's scheme were among the ablest ever heard in Parliament. The Opposition attacked the Home Rule Bill in detail, pointing out the mischiefs and vices inherent in it ; the Ministers were ready to concede anything, if the principle of an Irish Parliament were accepted ; but the distinctive feature of the controversy was, throughout, that no case for

---

[1] See Mr. Gladstone's speech of April 16, 1886, for a complete description of the Bill.

a Revolution in Ireland had been made, and that Home
Rule could not possibly do the good that was expected from
it. We cannot examine the speeches that were made; we
offer a few remarks of our own. Mr. Gladstone did not
nearly solve the problem which he had repeatedly said
must be solved before Parliament could even consider
Home Rule. He prevented, indeed, the Irish Parliament,
by his Bill, from legislating on many British and Imperial
subjects; he excluded Irish representatives from the Imperial Parliament. But he did not, and evidently could not,
wholly distinguish Irish from British and Imperial affairs,
and, as a matter of fact, British and Imperial affairs could,
in numberless instances, have been dealt with by the Irish
Parliament. In truth, Imperial, British, and Irish affairs
are indissolubly intertwined; it is impossible to lay them
out under separate heads, and to place these under the juris-
diction of two different Parliaments; on his own showing,
therefore, Mr. Gladstone failed at the outset. Furthermore,
even from the most favourable point of view, the projected
scheme in no sense satisfied the conditions declared by its
author to be essential.[1] It did not secure the Unity of the
Empire, that is the Unity of the Three Kingdoms, as Mr.
Gladstone certainly meant; for it set up beside the Imperial
Parliament a subordinate Parliament, which greatly weakened
its power, and interfered with it in many ways; the two,
therefore, conceivably could come in conflict; how, therefore, could this arrangement secure unity? Nor did it
provide safeguards for the "minority," which Mr. Gladstone
acknowledged would be placed in danger by the institution
of an Irish Parliament; this was the object of the Land
Purchase Bill; but a sum of £50,000,000 would only buy out
a comparatively small number of the Irish landlords, whose
estates Mr. Gladstone had said were worth sixfold that sum;
it was idle to assume that Parliament would make good the
balance;[2] and the "minority" in danger, besides, was com-

---

[1] Speech of Mr. Gladstone, April 13, 1886.

[2] This was most ably shown by Lord Selborne in the *Times* of May
3, 1886.

posed of many and large classes other than Irish landlords.
As to the remaining conditions, the debates conclusively
proved that the proposed measure was not "founded upon
the political equality of the three nations ; " that it did not
create " an equitable distribution of Imperial burdens ; " and
that it could not be in the " nature of a settlement ; " all
the probabilities and facts contradicted its author's assump-
tions.

Passing by, however, considerations like these, in part
personal, in part abstract, the great and paramount question
was, could Home Rule be a beneficent measure, as affairs
stood in Great Britain and Ireland ?   Mr. Gladstone and
his followers all but assumed that the proposed policy would
make England and Ireland friends, and would bring Irish
social troubles to an end ; but they were unable, even
plausibly, to show this ; in this respect they simply begged
the question.   Taking for granted, however, what was not
the case, that there was no estrangement between the two
countries, and had not been for a long series of years, and
that the Irish were a law-abiding people, not separated by
the divisions of ages, and contented and peaceful, at the
existing time, would the scheme promote international
concord, would it satisfy Ireland and conduce to her welfare, or would it, all but certainly, have an opposite tendency ?
The Imperial Parliament and its executive had since the
Union been absolute in Irish affairs ; they could impose
their will, in a moment, on every part of the island; but now
this control would be practically taken away ; would not
this necessarily provoke the resentment of England and
alienate her from Ireland though not alienated before ? The
Irish Parliament, on the other hand, was forbidden to make
laws on many subjects, Imperial, British, nay, even Irish ;
but it was given the essential power of a Parliament, and
the Irish executive would depend upon it ; it would, therefore, have a Constitutional right to protest from the outset
against these hindrances ; to pass resolutions on the prohibited
questions, which probably would be of immense weight, and
to employ its executive to further these ends ; the temptation

to adopt this course would be great ; would all this make
the relations of Great Britain and Ireland happy ? The
provisions of the scheme, too, were in many respects iniquitous, and would have probably combined all classes in
Ireland against them. The staunchest friends of the British
connection would not have tolerated an arrangement
through which they would have no representatives in the Imperial Parliament, and yet would he heavily taxed by it.
Was it rational that the Irish Parliament should have nothing
to do with Irish Customs and Excise ; and that the whole
revenue of Ireland should be intercepted by a British official ?
Was it just that Ireland should pay a great sum as a contribution to the charge of the Empire, and yet was to be
shut out by law from Imperial affairs ; was not this a severe
and degrading tribute ? For the rest the new Irish Constitution was essentially bad ; the suspensive veto of the
First Order would have been like the suspensive veto of
Louis XVI., in a new and democratic assembly ; and the
legislation of this, almost from the nature of the case, would
be improvident, wasteful, and leading to the bankruptcy of
the State.

But what were the actual facts of the case, the facts,
which it needs not a Burke to tells us, determine the qualities of any given policy ? England was the dominant
Power in the Three Kingdoms ; she had interests in Ireland
of supreme importance, which it was essential to her safety
to maintain ; she had millions of her race and faith in
Ireland devotedly attached to the Union and all that the
word implies ; she knew that Catholic Ireland was not her
friend. Ireland was divided by old discords of blood and
religion ; Protestant and Catholic Ireland had stood for
ages apart ; a foreign conspiracy, hostile to British power,
ruled large parts of the Irish ,Catholic masses ; and if the
government of Ireland passed into its hands, as inevitably,
under Home Rule, would be the case, for years it certainly
would be a foe of England, and even more so of Protestant
Ireland. In this position of affairs the intended measure
would do infinite harm to Great Britain and Ireland, and

for Ireland especially, would be a Pandora's box of evils. Take a very few instances of what would take place in events that, reasoning from experience, would probably happen. England declares war against a foreign Power, with which the Irish Parliament, filled with leaders of the National League and with Irish Catholics, would feel active and profound sympathy—Irish History can show many occasions of the kind ; the Irish Parliament and its Executive forbid Irishmen to serve in the British army, and encourage an armed Irish force to assist the enemy ; and, after opposing the war in a hundred ways, stop the contribution to the expense of the Empire. Or suppose again that an Irish Parliament, of the character we have just described, should, as in all probability would be the case, declare for Protection and condemn Free Trade ; or suppose that, as might be well expected, it should deny the right of the Imperial Parliament to raise Irish taxes, to interfere with or regulate Irish commerce, to lay an intrusive hand upon Irish revenue ; nay suppose that, like Tyrconnell's Parliament, it should debase the currency, or issue assignats, of what avail would be the paper safeguards of this scheme of Home Rule against such a course of conduct ? What would be the sentiment of England, in all these cases, what the attitude and policy of foreign Powers, ready to take advantage of a calamitous error ? As to the domestic legislation and administration of a Parliament of this type, they would consist in turning, in Ireland, things upside down ; in placing Protestant under the heel of Catholic Ireland ; in creating a Catholic Ascendency many times worse than Protestant Ascendency ever was ; and if, as is certain, Protestant Ireland would resist, this would either end in open civil war, or in a strife of classes protracted and fierce, followed by misery, desolation, and universal discontent. It may confidently be predicted that, in circumstances like these, England would either reconquer Ireland by force of arms, or possibly cut her off as a separate State ; for, as Peel had shown half a century before, separation was to be infinitely preferred to the kind of half independence, in which Ireland, under the mask of Constitutional forms, had been given the means of thwarting British power, of rebellion, and of the worst kind of misgovernment.

Like all his legislation Mr. Gladstone's scheme was marked with elaborate care and ingenious subtlety. But as a plan for changing the Constitution of these realms, for transforming the relations between Great Britain and Ireland, for setting up in Ireland a new order of things, it may be compared to the work of the Laputan architects, who built a house from the roof downwards ; it would have fallen to pieces in the surrounding element. It could have succeeded on one supposition only, that Englishmen and Irishmen were lifeless puppets, without the passions and wills of human beings ; but Englishmen and Irishmen being what they are, it would, especially in the circumstances of the time, have irritated and exasperated both peoples, and yet let the forces of Revolution loose. To have repealed the Union, and restored the old Irish Parliament, would have been a less dangerous and disastrous policy ; for, in that event, the spheres of the authority of the British and Irish Parliaments would have been defined by ancient and well-known precedents ; there would have been an Irish House of Lords as a restraining influence ; above all, the Irish Parliament would not have been cabined and confined, as it was under the proposed arrangement, nor tempted to break its Constitutional bounds ; and the Irish Executive could, comparatively, have done little mischief. Nor is anything more certain than that Mr. Gladstone had grave apprehensions as to his own policy. His speeches betray misgivings and fears ; his scheme revealed distrust of Ireland from beginning to end. He evidently thought that the Irish Parliament would not work well with the Imperial Parliament, or be loyal to the British connection, for, while he gave it the means of doing infinite wrong, and of defying and thwarting Imperial power, he circumscribed it in every direction, and shackled it in harsh and degrading fetters. He evidently thought that the men in power in Ireland might repudiate her obligations to Great Britain ; else why

did he withhold from the Irish Parliament the right of
imposing the most important taxes, why did he insist that a
Receiver-General was to lay hand on every farthing of Irish
revenue ?   He must have believed that the Irish Parliament
and its Executive would make victims of the Irish landed
gentry, and simply extirpate them root and branch ; for
otherwise he would never have called on the British taxpayer to make himself liable for an enormous charge, which,
if his assurances were to be kept, would have ultimately been
not £50,000,000, or £113,000,000, but from £150,000,000,
to £200,000,000, according to every calculation but his own.
Nor was it the least sign of this profound distrust, that Irish
judges and other officials were, under his Bill, to be permitted to retire from their posts, on their full pensions ; it
was assumed that they could not do their duty, or even
be in safety, under the new Irish Government.

The Home Rule Bill would assuredly have been condemned by every Irishman who had risen to eminence as a
patriot in the preceding century and a half.   It would have
aroused the " sœva indignatio " of Swift, would have
shrivelled up under the fire of Grattan, would have been
treated by O'Connell with contemptuous scorn.   Parnell's
attitude to it was characteristic ; he pointed out clearly its
manifold defects ; this reserve enabled him to disavow it if
he pleased ; he then accepted it, with his obedient followers,
the acceptance giving Mr. Gladstone enthusiastic joy.   It
has long ago been known that this profession was a mere
pretence, and that the measure was regarded as but "a
Parliamentary hit," by the Irish leader, and those who went
in his train ; but what was more significant were the undis-
guised sentiments of the American Fenians of almost all
kinds, on whom the movement in Ireland depended for
support.   At a meeting, at which Davitt was present, held
in the second week of August, 1886, and soon followed by
a great Convention called by the Clan na Gael and their
principal chiefs, to which Parnell sent envoys, chosen from
allies in Parliament, the Chairman of the Assembly described
the Home Rule scheme as wholly insufficient to meet the

demands of Ireland, or to satisfy her aspirations or hopes ; [1] and Parnell never repudiated this plain language ; the National League, indeed, otherwise would soon have come to an end. Meanwhile Mr. Gladstone had strained every nerve to carry into effect his Home Rule scheme ; but notwithstanding his immense authority, and the strong and sometimes perilous ties of party, his efforts and those of his lieutenants, failed. The Second Reading of the Home Rule Bill was rejected by a majority of thirty votes, in a House of Commons crowded beyond example ; but these figures did not represent the real state of opinion ; John Bright declared that not twenty English members were in favour of a measure almost universally condemned. The Land Purchase Bill was necessarily dropped ; but this discomfiture did not lessen Mr. Gladstone's zeal on behalf of the cause he had lately found to be that of "sacred justice." The Parliament, convened but a few months before, was dissolved in order to test the judgment of the Electorate on the new Irish policy ; and Mr. Gladstone exerted himself to the utmost to further the measure on which he had staked his fortunes. But the mind of England pronounced against him ; especially that strong, moderate and well-informed opinion, superior to partisan politics, which has always proved irresistible at grave conjunctures ; this resented tergiversation almost without a parallel ; was indignant that British interests had been set at naught, in a Parliament assembled to deal with them, and fully appreciated the

[1] Speech of John F. Finerty reported in "The Queen's Enemies in America," a tract well worth reading. "We have no desire to force the hand of Parnell or to drive the Irish people into war unprepared ; all that we demand is that no leader of the Irish people who is supposed to speak for them shall commit himself or them to accepting as a final settlement bills of relief unworthy of the dignity of Ireland's national demand. We are perfectly willing to see them accept such bills as that of Gladstone as a settlement on account, but that must not be accepted as closing the transaction. . . . We admit that it may be good policy on the part of Mr. Davitt and of Mr. Parnell to be what is called moderate in tone, but for us, who represent the National idea of the Irish people, it would be worse than folly to conceal our sentiments. We recognise that Ireland is incapable of fighting at present."

dangers and evils of Home Rule for Ireland. At the General Election that followed, England and Scotland returned about three hundred and seventy-five members, composed of Convervatives and old Liberals, against about a hundred and ninety advocates of Home Rule ; no such national verdict had been found since the rejection of the India Bill of Fox, and the rout of the Coalition in 1784. Ireland sent to Westminster eighty-four members, elected through the influences before referred to, to follow in the wake of Parnell ; the Irish representatives who supported the Union were not more than nineteen in number ; but this was no criterion of the strength of the two parties, still less of their true position in the State.

After this crushing defeat Mr. Gladstone resigned ; Lord Salisbury became Prime Minister again. The late crisis had developed a state of things resembling the Whig Secession of 1793 ; the leaders of the old Liberals were urged to take office ; but the time for a complete fusion of parties had not yet come ; the Government was a purely Conservative Government. It had been predicted that the rejection of the Home Rule Bill would cause Catholic Ireland to rise in the frenzy of despair ; but though the National League was daily becoming more powerful, scarcely a sign of discontent on this ground appeared ; as had been seen, over and over again, there was no general or violent movement against the Union, the only real movement in Ireland, indeed, of a political kind, was the opposite way ; Protestant Ulster, to a man, had declared for the Union, and unhappy scenes of riot and trouble followed, to be condemned, no doubt, but not the less significant of the sentiments of a noble Province, half rebellious in the past, but, for many long years in its best and most energetic elements, attached heart and soul to the British connection. The conspiracy, meanwhile, that since 1879 had been the paramount cause of Irish disorder, had been actively at work in the United States, and found aliments in Ireland that gave it new life. The Convention, to which we have before referred, was held at Chicago in the third week of August ; it was a huge gathering of Irish Fenians of every type; its proceedings were very characteristic of the movement, of which Parnell had long been the Parliamentary head. The extreme party and the leaders of the Clan na Gael consented, though reluctantly, that Resolutions should pass in favour of the Home Rule policy, and offering thanks to Mr. Gladstone and Parnell; but the speeches of several of these men were of the most incendiary kind; and two of Parnell's envoys, whose object was to collect funds, expressed themselves in hardly less meaning language, one remarking that it was "our duty to make the government of Ireland by England an impossibility."[1] At the same time an accident had strengthened the National League in Ireland, and had increased the social troubles springing from the land. The Land Commission had reduced rents wholesale, and so had the great majority of the Irish landlords; but there had been a sudden and great fall of agricultural prices; and though there was nothing like the distress of 1879, Ireland was suffering, if in a less degree, from the depression of rural industry which prevailed in England, Scotland, and indeed in other countries. The payment of rent, in a word, had become difficult; and this, in the existing state of Ireland, was an incentive to a fresh agrarian movement.

The new Parliament had met towards the end of August; the Conservatives and old Liberals, nearly combined, were known by the name of the Unionist party. The Irish vote, by the direction of Parnell, reversing the policy he had adopted the year before, had been given to Mr. Gladstone at the late Election; Mr. Gladstone had become more ardent for Home Rule than ever; Parnell with his band, and Mr. Gladstone's followers, may be fitly described as Anti-Unionists. Parnell, holding the threads of the conspiracy abroad and at home, took advantage of the partial distress in Ireland to renew the attack on the Irish landlords, which, indeed, had never completely ceased; he brought in a Bill, which would have annulled the settlement, such as it was, made by the Land Act of 1881, and would have

[1] See "The Queen's Enemies in America," *ante*, pp. 31, 63.

practically reduced rents by one half; and Mr. Gladstone, the author of the Act in question, gave this monstrous proposal a qualified assent. The Bill, however, was peremptorily rejected by the House of Commons; and, just as in the case of the Compensation for Disturbance Bill, the rejection gave Parnell the opportunity he was, doubtless, seeking, that is, as one of his satellites had announced at Chicago, to make "an impossibility" of British rule in Ireland. The National League, we have seen, had, for many months, especially since "coercion" had come to an end, been making in Ireland alarming progress; it had gradually spread over and taken possession of nearly the same area as the parent League; it had long ago lost its constitutional aspect; it had become the director, like the Land League, of a rebellious and a socialistic movement. Nor did its methods differ widely from those of its prototype; its local leaders, indeed, were often of the middle class, and had been largely composed of the Irish Catholic clergy; it was less stained than the Land League with crime, and with open and atrocious outrage; but it was an organisation of the same kind; and it enforced its authority, like the Land League, by boycotting, intimidation, and widespread oppression, especially of the humbler classes. The concentrated force of the National League was now turned against the landed gentry, and through them, as had been the case before, against the whole system of Irish Government. Once more the peasantry, in some counties, were commanded to strike against the payment of rent; and once more the behests of the League were to have the terrible sanction of the well-known penalties. The mode of operations adopted at this time was, however, more ingenious, and perhaps more potent than those which had been tried before; tenants were ordered to demand huge reductions of rent; and if the landlords refused compliance, the rents were to be paid into what was called the "war chest," and to be held by agents selected by the League in order to prevent compromise or backsliding. This "Plan of Campaign" was to have the support of the old methods,

20

an interdict placed on evicted farms, the terrorism of "land grabbers," and "traitors" to the cause, intimidation of all kinds, and above all "boycotting," which had been perfected after a long experience. By these means evictions would necessarily be increased; whole districts would be violently disturbed; a war of classes would be the result; the arm of the law would be largely paralysed; and Government, in many places, would be reduced to impotence.[1]

Parnell certainly sanctioned these proceedings, but he did not directly take part in them; he had put on his constitutional garb, and become an ally of Mr. Gladstone; the Plan of Campaign, indeed, was not of his invention. By the first months of 1887, the conspiracy, working through the National League, had become dominant in many districts, within the limits in which the Land League had prevailed. Its evil influences were, no doubt, seconded, as had happened in 1879–80, by the depression of agriculture, only too general; but they did not owe their origin to this cause; they were, in no sense, to be excused by it. The Land war of 1880–82 was renewed; the incidents that followed were in some respects the same; but there were marked differences that may be briefly noticed. The Plan of Campaign was not applied in its completeness to many estates, for the peasantry could not be induced to pay over their rents, in numerous instances, to servants of the League, in spite of the intimidation brought to bear on them—a

---

[1] The strike against rent in Ireland, of which the Plan of Campaign was the most elaborate specimen, has been compared by apologists to Trades Union strikes, and "boycotting" to "picketing." There is, as Parnell no doubt intended, a superficial resemblance; but the difference is plain and conspicuous. The artisan strikes, so to speak, with his own labour; he pledges this and fights his employer at his own risk; the Irish peasant strikes with his landlord's rent, stakes nothing of his own, and acts as a robber. "Boycotting," too, is essentially different from "picketing," and was carried out in Ireland through a system of crime and terrorism, of which "picketing" in England was never guilty. No wonder that John Bright indignantly remarked, that the comparison "insulted the great mass of the working men of England, who had no direct purpose of dishonesty or fraud, or any of the odious crimes," which had been committed in Ireland.

circumstance of no small significance ; but wherever it was applied there was a bitter struggle occasionally breaking out in crime and outrage, occasionally marked with grotesque features. In hundreds of cases, however, there was a strike against rent, conducted by the local leaders of the League, and more or less backed by the occupiers of the soil ; [1] and the results were like those which had been seen before. Some of the gentry yielded ; many resisted ; evictions, as a matter of course, multiplied ; and lawlessness, culminating in social anarchy, extended rapidly over an increasing area. There was a considerable outburst of savage disorder ; but the distinctive feature of this effort of the League was the extraordinary, and too often the successful spread of "boycotting" and its cruel and base work. This system of organised terror was carried out with an effective force and a dexterity before unknown ; it was aptly compared to a pestilence walking in darkness, bringing misery and even death to numbers of homes, and blighting industry and order in hundreds of places. Officials of the Government of all kinds, juries, traders, and landlords were placed under the ban ; but, as had occurred before, the evil power of this interdict was exercised more widely, and with far greater severity upon the poorer classes. By this time there had been a thousand instances of agrarian crime ; five thousand unhappy beings had been "boycotted" ; and nearly a thousand had been placed under the protection of the police. Protestant Ulster as before held angrily aloof ; but parts of Ireland had fallen into a state resembling that of the Provinces of France, where the rule of Jacobinism had supplanted the regular Government. Many of the Irish Catholic clergy, it must be said with regret, had made themselves morally responsible for this position of affairs, having directly joined in the operations of the League.

History will probably say that Lord Salisbury's Government ought to have sought powers when Parliament met, to cope effectually with the anarchic disorder already mani-

---

[1] Attempts have been made to show that the strike was aimed at bad landlords only. Such statements are absolutely false.

fest in many parts of Ireland. It adopted, however, a
different course; and, indeed, endeavoured for some months
to temporise with the National League, and even to mitigate
the increasing land war by attempts to stop or to retard
evictions, conduct reprobated by a most distinguished Irish
judge. Nevertheless, it quickly abandoned a hopeless policy
when the critical state of Ireland had become apparent;
and at the opening of the Session of 1887, the office of
Chief Secretary fortunately devolved on a capable and
resolute man of action. Mr. Balfour had not yet risen to
a very high place in politics, though his ability was already
known; but his government of Ireland was marked by
qualities which soon placed him in the foremost rank of
our statesmen. He at once brought in a Bill of so-called
"coercion," which, compared to the formidable Act of five
years before, was infinitely less severe and drastic; but
which, he rightly judged, would prove sufficient if steadily
enforced. This measure contained scarcely a single provision which could be deemed unconstitutional in a proper
sense;[1] its principal features were that it transferred to
magistrates the cognisance over the classes of crime through
which the National League maintained its power, from
juries which, as affairs stood, had almost ceased to perform
their functions, owing to the intimidation widely prevailing;
and that it enabled the Irish Executive to put down
Associations it had proclaimed as "dangerous," and as had
been enacted in 1882, to institute secret inquiries for the
discovery of crime. But it certainly created no new offences
as the Act of 1882 had done; it had not an arbitrary or a
vindictive character, and though it was not limited in point
of time, it was little more, save in a few particulars, than an
extension of the summary powers of magistrates, in circumstances that justified, nay, called for it. It might have been
expected that Mr. Gladstone and the statesmen who had
designed "coercion" tenfold more harsh, would not have

---

[1] A clause for transferring the trial of grave crimes from Ireland to
England, that might fairly be considered unconstitutional and unjust,
was dropped.

opposed a measure of this kind, especially as the responsible Government had declared that law and order in Ireland could not exist without it. But the conversion to Home Rule had brought strange things with it ; Mr. Gladstone and his followers threw in their lot with Parnell ; and the spectacle was seen for the first time in the century of a Constitutional Opposition acting in concert with a revolutionary and socialistic faction, which had shown itself to be an enemy of the State, and to have promoted a conspiracy against its power. The Bill was resisted for nearly three months by methods of obstruction before unparalleled ; and it became necessary to put in force the closure—a change in the procedure of the House of Commons, in itself pernicious, but found to be needed, owing to the conduct of Parnell and his band on previous occasions— with a severity hitherto without a precedent. The House, however, had made up its mind that the measure should pass ; it became law by large majorities of votes

A conflict between the powers of Government and of lawless anarchy ere long followed. Parnell kept studiously away ; but some of his Parliamentary band flung themselves into the ranks of the National League, and endeavoured to maintain an unequal fight, here and there by violent, here and there by ridiculous methods. English Radicalism, shattered in 1886, pretended to join in a reckless crusade ; flights of sympathisers landed on the Irish shores to denounce " Balfour's atrocious tyranny " ; ponderous speeches were made in Parliament and elsewhere, condemning the administration of the law that had just been enacted. Mr. Gladstone, of course, was easily supreme ; he laboured to change the plain meaning of words ; the " boycotting " he had described as a base crime was now merely " exclusive dealing " ; the National League now the same as the Land League of old, was an innocent combination to protect the peasantry, not an organisation formed to overthrow the State ; and the orator thundered against the men in power at the Castle ; held up to execration ministers of law and justice, singling out more than one by name for invective ; and especially attacked the Constabulary force, the mainstay of order and law in Ireland. At this grave conjuncture, in short, he acted as no Englishman has ventured to act since Fox had taken the side of Revolutionary France in its struggle with England in 1793–8, and since he had found excuses for Jacobin crime and wickedness ; and this conduct, no doubt to be largely ascribed to impetuosity carried beyond all bounds, and to the inexperience of Irish affairs apparent throughout Mr. Gladstone's career, was strongly censured by the best of the old Liberals, and made reconciliation for ever hopeless. [1] Yet notwithstanding these efforts of faction and party, as to which it was pointedly said that Mr. Gladstone had tried, like his Irish allies, to make the government of Ireland, in its existing form, " impossible," the law was successfully carried out and prevailed ; the National League was suppressed as the Land League had been ; and the conspiracy, though it continued to receive ample funds from America as before, was baffled in the space of about eighteen months, as in had been baffled in 1882–4. Agrarian crime was effectually kept under ; the cases of " boycotting " were soon reduced by a half, and within three years had almost disappeared ; the ascendency of the Government was restored ; the rule of law was again made to triumph ; and all this was done with comparatively little " coercion," because it was felt that the Irish Executive was firm in its purpose. Mr. Balfour, and those who acted with him, deserve high praise ; but they were assisted in their arduous task by a very powerful influence. Rome had condemned the Land League before, but when it had become notorious that the Irish priesthood had largely joined the National League, an envoy from the Vatican was sent to Ireland : and the anathema of the Holy See was pronounced on " boycotting and the Plan of Campaign." The Irish Catholic clergy fell off from the League in scores ; but, unhappily, not before one priest certainly had become implicated in a very grave crime.

[1] See the speeches of Mr. Goschen and of Lord Hartington in 1887 *passim*, not to refer to many others.

The Government, meanwhile, had taken another step on the path of agrarian change in Ireland. In the Land Act of 1881, as in that of 1870, Mr. Gladstone, we have seen, had shown a preference for English compared to Irish tenures; he had excluded leaseholders from a right to the " Three F.'s," and this, though an intelligible, was not a just distinction, in the existing circumstances of the Irish land. An Act, passed in the Session of 1887, allowed leaseholders of all ordinary kinds to obtain the benefits given by the Act of 1881 ; it even enabled a middleman, a strange license, whose rent had been reduced below his own chief rent, to creep out of his contract with a superior landlord. The Act also contained provisions making the process of eviction less odious, and accelerating the time for securing "fair rents"; it would have effected a useful composition for arrears of rent but for the clamour of leaders of the National League, in the interests of local usurers, often clients of the League ; but it partially lessened the hardship of arrears ; and it made temporary reductions of judicial rents in order to meet the undoubted difficulties of these years. The Act was not of very great importance; on the principles of the legislation on which it was based, it may, for the most part, be justified ; but it was another encroachment on the rights of Irish landlords, and it has created another claim for the compensation, which is their due, if Parliamentary assurances are to be of any avail. The Land Commission, of course, cut down the rents of leaseholders as they had cut down all other rents; it has been contended that this proceeding, coupled with the reduction of judicial rents, was the only true cause that Irish disorder was quelled in a comparatively short space of time. This, nevertheless, is a complete delusion ; these measures may have had some influence ; but the number of leaseholders affected by the Act, and who sought for the advantages of the " Three F.'s," was inconsiderable for a long period ; the reductions of the judicial rents were small; these circumstances could not have had a marked effect during the short contest of 1887–89. The leaders of the National

League, besides, treated the new law with the contempt with
which they had treated the great measure of 1881 ; and, as
a matter of fact, the so-called reforms which have wrought
the ruin of hundreds of the Irish gentry, and have evolved
a land system of the very worst type, have had hardly any
real effect on a movement which, it must be borne in mind,
did not spring up in Ireland, but was the offspring of a
conspiracy wholly of foreign origin.

A remarkable train of incidents in these years threw a
striking and lurid light on the affairs of Ireland, since the
movement directed by Parnell had been set on foot.   While
the Crimes Act, as it was called, of 1887, was slowly making
its way through Parliament, the *Times* newspaper published
a series of essays pointing out the relations that had long
existed between the extreme Fenians in the United States,
and the leaders of the Land and National Leagues, and
charging Parnell and his followers with grave misdeeds ;
and this great exponent of English opinion indignantly
demanded if Mr. Gladstone had made a political alliance
with this manner of men.   A short time afterwards the
Times gave to the world copies of letters alleged to have
been in Parnell's hand, and all but approving of the murders
in the Phœnix Park, at least of the murder of Thomas Burke ;
it challenged a judicial inquiry upon the subject.   Parnell
simply declared that the letters were forged, and refused to
accept the challenge of the *Times*, but after the lapse of a
year, an accident caused public opinion to turn to the controversy again, and to insist that a full investigation should
be made. A special Commission, composed of   three
English judges, was appointed by Statute to inquire into
the series of charges made by the *Times*, and to report the
conclusions they found to Parliament ; this tribunal held
its sittings during many months, and probed the matters on
issue to the very bottom ; the voluminous evidence collected
is the best extant commentary on the whole troubled period
of Irish history from 1879 to 1886.   We have already
indicated, in part, the decisions made by the judges—men
of intelligence and character of the highest order ; but, at

the risk of repetition, we bring together the main findings of this notable verdict, premising that the *Times* had not dealt with the political side of the agrarian movement, and did not prefer any charges of treason, that the lesser agents of the Land and the National Leagues were not brought before the Court at all, and that the inquiry, therefore, was in these respects limited.   Notwithstanding this, a more damning sentence was never pronounced on a body of public men. One of the accused persons was wholly acquitted; but all the others were more or less condemned for offences of no ordinary kind.   It was proved that some, when they joined the Land League, sought "to bring about the independence of Ireland as a separate nation"; and that all conspired to prevent "the payment of agricultural rents," in order to drive out of the country the Irish landlords, styled by the conspirators the "English garrison."   It was proved that these men "disseminated the *Irish World*," and newspapers of this kind; that if they did not directly incite to crime they incited to the "intimidation" that produced crime; and that, excepting Davitt and some others, they did not denounce the "intimidation" which had this effect to their undoubted knowledge.   Finally, it was found that these men promoted the defence of "agrarian crime"; that they paid money to compensate criminals of this class; that they received funds through the notorious Patrick Ford, the advocate of dynamite before referred to; and that, as we have said, they "invited and obtained the assistance of the Clan na Gael" and similar bodies of worthies, and, in order to obtain it, kept a judicious silence.[1]

The verdict of the judges on several minor charges was "not proven," or "not guilty"; the accused are entitled, of course, to the benefit.   It is necessary to say a very few words on another charge intrinsically not important, but important in the circumstances of the case, and that has caused much confusion of thought and deception.   The *Times* alleged that Parnell and some of his followers did, indeed, occasionally "denounce" crime, but did so

[1] Report of the Judges, vol. iv. pp. 544-5.

insincerely, and with the intention to "make their supporters" think the "denunciations not sincere"; the principal
proofs of this were the letters which, we have said, condoned
the Phœnix Park tragedy, and were stated to have been in
Parnell's writing. It was proved beyond doubt that the
letters were not in Parnell's hand, and that they were
wickedly forged by a man at one time the owner of a
journal sold to the Land League; this villain killed himself
when the discovery was made; and Parnell obtained a
complete acquittal on this charge. The charge, however, we
repeat, was a minor one in itself; but it involved a personal
accusation of great gravity; and Mr. Gladstone and his
followers made the acquittal an occasion for insisting that
all the charges had either failed or were of no weight, and
that any other findings of the judges might be dismissed as
worthless, though the whole verdict had not yet been pronounced. The House of Commons rang with the shouts
of these partisans—little knowing what time was soon to
bring forth—when Parnell entered it, after it had been
shown that the letters were forged; the unreflecting multi-
tude, always inclined to sympathise with any one it believes
is wronged, and to look superficially at complex questions
requiring attention to be understood, very largely thought
that an adverse verdict on the capital facts of a great inquiry
involving issues of extreme gravity, was of no avail, decisive
as it was, because Parnell had not been consenting to the
Phœnix Park murders! Nothing could be more illogical and
absurd, especially if it is borne in mind that, on the question
of insincerity, there was a great deal in the evidence before
the commission to condemn Parnell. The judges refused
to believe him more than once on his oath; and it was
clearly proved that, on one occasion at least, he deceived
the House of Commons of set purpose.[1] As to the
judgment of thinking and well-informed persons on the
verdict given by the Commission, it has thus been summed
up; the sound opinion of Englishmen fully concurred :—
" The Report unveils Parnellism to the whole world, and

[1] Evidence of the Commission, vol. iv. p. 303.

discovers to us a movement which, under the outward show
of legality, is based on conspiracy, and which seeks to
effect constitutional changes, by weakening the executive,
and defying the law of the nation. The respondents, we
now know, are conspirators ; they are not the advocates of
reform, but the leaders for revolution."[1]

The acquittal of Parnell, however, on a personal charge
improved his position in the House of Commons, always
generously disposed to its own members, and even made
him popular, in a certain sense, in England. By this time
his alliance with Mr. Gladstone was complete ; the new
Liberals and the band of Parnell formed a Parliamentary
Opposition, voting together ; and Parnell turned his advantage to excellent account. He had conferences with Mr.
Gladstone about Home Rule, and possibly agreed to some
general scheme ; he occasionally appeared at public
meetings in England, and, with chosen lieutenants, spoke in
dulcet tones of the international concord, and the " Union
of Hearts," which would follow when Ireland had obtained
" self-government." His attitude, as regards Ireland, was
very much the same ; he condemned " boycotting " and the
" Plan of Campaign," especially when the Crimes Act was
doing its work ; he preached moderation to the National
League ; and though he made no real impression on
Irishmen who could think, by his patriotic appeals, or on
the classes which had property to lose, he attracted a few
Protestants into the ranks of his party, a striking proof of
his political craft. In the autumn of 1890 his prospects
seemed full of promise ; but the Nemesis of duplicity,
almost without a parallel, and of conspiracy veiled behind
a mask was at hand ; he suddenly toppled down in complete
ruin.

Proceedings in the Divorce Court taken against him by
the friend who had negotiated the " Kilmainham Treaty,"
proved that socially, as well as politically, he was a false-

---

[1] "The Verdict,' by A. V. Dicey, 1890. This masterly tract should
be read. See also the " Report of the Special Commission," by Vindex,
Law Review, Nov. 1890.

hearted man ; the decree pronounced against him was a signal rebuke to his conduct. Events followed of curious and dramatic interest, that have ever since had an influence on the affairs of Ireland. For about a week it seemed as if the matter of the divorce would be little more than a nine days' wonder, and that Parnell's position as the leader of a party, and a public man of no ordinary importance, had not been shaken. Mr. Gladstone, his ally, remained silent; the Irish Catholic prelates, the self-named champions "of religion and morals," made no sign ; the Parliamentary and other satellites of Parnell declared enthusiastically in favour of their chief, at a great and representative meeting held in Dublin. At last, however, what is called the "Nonconformist conscience" showed that it had been pricked by the recent scandal ; Parnell was denounced from a hundred English dissenting pulpits; and Mr. Gladstone, always sensitive to popular cries, gave it to be understood that it would be fatal to the cause of Home Rule should Parnell remain at the head of his party "at the present moment." This view was communicated to Parnell's followers assembled at Westminster for the approaching Session ; and the Irish Dictator at once showed of what stuff he was made, and revealed himself in his true character. Disregarding honourable confidences of every kind he announced that Mr. Gladstone's coming project of Home Rule was a mere sham and a delusive measure ; he called on the "Irish People" to stand by "their chief " ; he defied traitors and fools to attempt to depose him. Ere long a majority of Parnell's band, throwing their late pledges and promises to the winds, made up their minds to ask him to resign the leadership ; his only reply was that "if he was to be sold, he was to be sold for value " ; and, with singular adroitness, he induced them to approach Mr. Gladstone and to inquire of him, if he was prepared to bring in a measure of Home Rule, with much larger concessions than that of 1886. The object of this policy is apparent; Mr. Gladstone, of course, refused to treat ; scenes of recrimination and fury ensued ; and ultimately the main body of the adherents of Parnell broke away from the leader they had half worshipped for years, though they did not openly dare to thrust him aside.

In unscrupulously playing this artful game, Parnell believed that he had put his recreant followers in the wrong, and that he would still retain his position as the " uncrowned king." They had been the dupes and instruments of a slippery statesman, who would not give them anything like a pledge ; he alone was the apostle of real Home Rule ; the Ireland of the National League would rally around him. But Parnell had not reckoned with a mighty and organised power, the authority of which has, at all times, been well-nigh supreme in Catholic Ireland. The heads of the Irish Catholic Church had probably never trusted Parnell ; he was a Protestant, and in league with Fenians, with whom they never had the slightest sympathy ; they at last followed in the wake of English Dissenters, and issued a manifesto against the threatened Dictator. This strengthened the majority which had fallen away from him ; and it is now known that many in this servile band had long resented the imperious conduct of their chief, and were bitterly though secretly hostile to him ; and, as in the case of Robespierre and the men of Thermidor, they welcomed the opportunity for a decisive rupture. Parnell, however, retained his haughty self-confidence ; a small body of faithful dependents still clung to him ; he went to Ireland to make a desperate effort on his own behalf, in the name of " Irish Nationality," and phrases of the kind. He succeeded in assembling great gatherings, composed mainly of the mobs of the towns ; he addressed these in impassioned language ; his speeches disclosed his strange and double-dealing nature. The moderate politician who had accepted the Home Rule Bill of 1886, repudiated that measure as mere imposture ; the friend of Mr. Gladstone and of the new Liberals had no scurrilous words bad enough for them ; the prudent leader, who had lately checked the National League, was now ready to let Revolution loose, and declared that Ireland's "independence" had been the object of his life. As for those who had deserted him, they were the scum of the earth, knaves and reprobates of the worst kind ; and here it may be admitted he was not wholly in the wrong ; few leaders have been so suddenly and basely betrayed. The whole power, however, of the Catholic priesthood was concentrated against the defeated chief ; Catholic Ireland fell away from him ; election after election proved adverse to his hopes ; his late followers vied with each other in trampling him down, and in covering him with the foulest abuse. After a fruitless struggle of five or six months, his strength suddenly gave way, and he soon died ; if not undeserved, the end of few public men has been so dismal and dark a tragedy. History has yet to say her last word upon him ; but Parnell essentially was a conspirator ; and no one, perhaps, has been so successful in combining a conspiracy hatched abroad with a Parliamentary, but most dangerous movement at home. Parnell cannot be called, in a true sense, a statesman ; but certainly he had statesman-like views ; some of these on Irish affairs are of no doubtful value. For the rest he was a natural ruler of men ; in sheer force of character he towered, not only over the submissive band which crawled at his feet, but over the English politicians he outwitted and deceived. Unquestionably, however, had he had to deal with a Minister different from Mr. Gladstone, he would never have achieved what he did ; more than one of the English Ministers of this century would probably have cut short his career. That he did his country good may be, perhaps, admitted ; but when we weigh the doubtful good against the enormous evil, it is difficult to give him a word of praise.

In 1890 another attempt was made to effect a great change in the Irish land system. For a long time, we have seen, it had been the policy of John Bright and other statesmen to try to make tenants in Ireland owners of the lands they held. This had been aimed at in the Land Acts of 1878 and 1881 ; but it had never been contemplated in those days that if the State made advances for this purpose the tenants should not pay part of the

purchase moneys. Since Irish tenures had been transformed by the "Three F's" it has been contended by the
Conservative party that this "created" in Ireland a kind of
"dual ownership" in the land, assumed to be an intolerable
thing, and that the only way to escape from this grave
mischief was greatly to encourage the system of tenant
ownership. During the short-lived Ministry of Lord Salisbury in 1885 the Lord Chancellor of Ireland, Lord Ashbourne, carried a Bill through Parliament by which a
fund of £5,000,000 was provided to give effect to this
policy. Ample security was taken to protect the State;
but, instead of paying as hitherto part of the purchase
money, the tenant was to have the whole sum lent him
by the State, repayable by a terminable annuity much lower
than an ordinary rent. The transaction, therefore, was not,
in a real sense, a purchase; it was, properly speaking, a
gift akin to a bribe. Tenants naturally took advantage of
it, at least for a time; and the £5,000,000 were ere long
expended in converting some hundreds of this class into
owners, in cases where their landlords were willing to sell,
for the process was to be voluntary on the landlord's
side. The policy was pronounced successful. Application
was made to Parliament, a few years afterwards, for a
second sum of £5,000,000 for the same purpose; but
though the security provided was the same, it was found
very difficult to obtain a vote for the money. In 1890 a
Bill, which became law in 1891, was introduced to carry
out the system on a much larger scale. A sum of about
£30,000,000 was made available, secured, not only by the
annuities representing the loans and by the guarantees
provided by the previous Acts, but by charges on Imperial
grants to Ireland, and ultimately on the Irish counties; and
it was confidently predicted that so-called Land Purchase
would rapidly proceed under these conditions. For reasons,
however, which we cannot dwell on, those expectations
have not been fulfilled; the whole sums advanced by the
State to turn tenants of farms into owners do not largely
exceed £10,000,000—about a fourth part of the sum set

apart for the purpose. We shall recur to the subject when we review the existing state of the Irish land system : enough to say that this legislation, in our judgment, is vicious in principle and a mistake ; that it has not hitherto done good in any reasonable sense ; and that, at the present rate of progress, it cannot much affect landed relations in Ireland for many years. The Act of 1891 had an excellent supplement : a "Congested Districts Board" was created to improve and develop the poverty-stricken region in the west and south-west of Ireland, even now sometimes the scene of much social distress ; and this has done good and valuable work.

In 1892 Lord Salisbury's Ministry made an effort to place the system of Irish Local Government, for the most part, on a popular basis. This subject, we have seen, had been taken up by Butt ; it was unfortunate that Parliament had not dealt with it in times comparatively free from troubles in Ireland. Local Government had been almost transformed in England by the establishment of County and lesser Councils ; in the interest of the Union it was deemed expedient to extend the new system to Ireland, under just conditions, so that no grounds of real complaint should exist in the matter. County Government in Ireland, we have said, had for many years, in fact since the Revolution of 1688, been mainly in the hands of the grand juries—that is of the leading gentry at the different counties nominated by the sheriffs, 'and practically by the Castle ; it had once abounded in grotesque abuses, as the readers of Maria Edgeworth's novels know ; but the grand juries had long been under strict central control, and they had performed their functions very well for three-quarters of a century at least. The institution, however, was out of date ; it was a survival of the Protestant Ascendency of a bygone age ; and, at the same time, Irish Municipal Government had, we have seen, been placed on a narrow foundation, and municipal life in Ireland was very feeble. A Bill was introduced to remedy this state of things ; but for two decisive reasons it could not correspond with the English original in some of its features. The National League, by Parnell's express direction, had largely laid hold of Irish elective bodies, such as Town Commissioners and Poor Law Guardians ; these were more or less hostile to the Irish landed gentry, and in many instances did them not a little harm, by violent denunciation and the maladministration of funds ; [1] and there was much danger that should they acquire large powers of local government without restraint, they would despoil owners of land of their property in some districts. In Ireland, too, the ratepayers were composed, unlike what is the case in England, in a very great degree of poor and easily led peasants who contributed comparatively little to the rates, while the landed gentry contributed not far from the half ; and in the absence of an intelligent and powerful middle-class, at all times a most unfortunate want in Ireland, it was feared that these indigent masses, if given a voice in local government, would do a great deal of mischief. The measure proposed a large scheme of County, and of what was called Baronial, Councils, analogous in many respects to those of England ; but it provided safeguards against these evils in a series of carefully devised checks ; it made some large towns areas for County Councils ; and certainly it was a statesmanlike project, and would have made an immense change in Irish local government, and, it was to be hoped, a real improvement, if no doubt some of its provisions were somewhat harsh and narrow. It was, however, treated with ridicule and scorn by Mr. Gladstone's following, and by the remains of what once had been the strong band of Parnell, on the plea that it did not conform to the English pattern—an argument hardly worth notice considering the distinction between the two cases—but really because it did not favour Home Rule ; and it was ultimately dropped by the Government with regret. A measure of the same kind has been promised for the present Session, and will, doubtless, see the light before these pages ; but it will almost certainly resemble the Bill of 1892, with this difference, that an opportunity

[1] See the Evidence taken before a recent Committee of the House of Lords on the Administration of the Poor Law in Ireland.

now exists, through a proposed change in the modes of local taxation, to strengthen the safeguards before referred to.

The Local Government Bill of 1892 was the last Irish measure of Lord Salisbury's Ministry. Parliament was dissolved in the summer of the year; the General Election presented many curious features. The Conservative Government had been six years in office; the notion that each side ought to have its turn, so general in democratic England, inclined "the pendulum" as it has been called, against them. The wonderful energy shown by Mr. Gladstone, at an age beyond the ordinary span of life, gave him the support of thousands of voters; and as he had assiduously proclaimed that the "cause of Ireland" was that of the "masses against the classes," Home Rule became identified, in the minds of many, with popular progress and even social liberty. The danger of Home Rule, too, had seemed greatly diminished; the formidable band of Parnell had been broken up; the conspiracy in Ireland had been put down; the appeals made by Irish orators from a hundred platforms, in behalf of "self government," had not been fruitless; all this favoured the policy of 1886. But two paramount causes especially came in aid of Home Rule; it was sedulously announced that the new measure which, in the event of his regaining power, Mr. Gladstone would bring in as to Irish affairs, although it had been carefully kept in the dark, would be free from the evils of its predecessor; and Home Rule had the artificial support of the process known by the name of "logrolling" never so conspicuous hitherto in our national politics. It was associated with projects for Disestablishing Churches, with Temperance, Labour, Suffrage and Taxation questions, in short, with a series of English Radical cries; and the authors of these backed it, with pretended zeal, chiefly in order to propitiate Mr. Gladstone, with whom Home Rule, notoriously, was the first of all subjects; all these influences necessarily told; Mr. Gladstone's followers, it is well known, boasted confidently that they would "sweep the country." These hopes, however, were not realised ; the new Liberals, we may now call them Radicals, were successful, indeed, in Scotland and Wales ; but England declared against Home Rule again, though not so decisively as six years before. The General Election in Ireland was marked by incidents of an ominous and unfortunate kind. The band of Parnell had been split into two factions ; these rushed at each other furiously at the polls ; the miserable divisions of Irishmen, their reproach for ages, were placed in prominent and grotesque relief. The Catholic priesthood exercised its immense influence, with little scruple, against Parnell's adherents ; sacerdotal power, in fact, ruled nine-tenths of Catholic Ireland ; the faction opposed to Parnell gained an easy triumph. More than eighty representatives from Ireland declared for Home Rule ; but they were very different from the compact phalanx which had been so skilfully directed by the "uncrowned king"; they were hostile fractions of an army that had lost its commander.

Taking the Three Kingdoms as a whole after the Election closed, Mr. Gladstone found himself at the head of a small majority of some forty votes in the House of Commons, but a majority held together mainly by the power of his name, and really divided into separate groups, ill-united, and each with objects of its own. The prospect for the aged statesman was not bright ; but his majority was able to place him in office once more ; Lord Salisbury resigned after an adverse vote. Soon after the beginning of the session of 1893 Mr. Gladstone introduced the measure which, for the second time, was to carry into effect the policy of Home Rule. His speech was a marvel for a man of eighty-three, and was, perhaps, more confident than that of 1886, but it was marked by omissions indicating the weakness of old age, and, in one matter of supreme importance, it certainly revealed a want of grasp of the subject. The Bill resembled in many respects the Bill which had been defeated before ; but it was widely different in some others, especially in one of the greatest gravity. An Irish Parliament was to be again created ; but it was to be a

much smaller body than that of 1886 ; there was to be a
Legislative Council analogous to the First Order, but composed only of forty-eight members, the Irish Peerage being
excluded ; and there was to be a Legislative Assembly
corresponding to the Second Order, but consisting of only
a hundred and three members, the number of representatives from Ireland in the House of Commons.[1] The
Legislative Council and Assembly were generally to sit
apart ; but the Legislative Council, like the First Order, was
to have a temporary veto on the acts of the main Assembly ;
this body, it should be noted, like the Second Order, commanding a majority that made it supreme. The new Irish
Parliament, like its defunct original, was to be limited in
its legislation in a whole range of matters, as regards
Imperial and Irish affairs ; it was not to impose the taxes of
Customs and Excise ; and it was to be subject to the same
veto, and to nearly the same control of the English Privy
Council as its predecessor had been. The new Parliament,
however limited in this way, was to be a Parliament in the
proper sense of the word ; it was to govern Ireland like the
Parliament of the previous Bill ; and an Irish Executive
was to be dependent on it with the whole administration of
Ireland in its hands. As respects finance, the unpopular
" tribute " was given up, and there was to be no Receiver-
General over Irish revenue ; Ireland was to make directly no
contribution to the general expenditure of the Empire ;
but her customs were to be appropriated to defray any Imperial charge she ought justly to pay ; and this was calculated
at a sum of about two millions and a half sterling, with a
temporary addition of about a million more—a sum much
less than that proposed in 1886. But infinitely the most
important distinction between the two measures has yet
to be noticed. Mr. Gladstone had excluded, six years
previously, all Irish representatives from the House of
Commons ; on this occasion he proposed to let them in

[1] The number of one hundred and five Irish members, fixed by the
Reform Act of 1832, had been reduced to a hundred and three by
the disfranchisement of two boroughs.

in the considerable number of eighty members. They were to have no power to vote upon British questions, but on Irish and Imperial would possess the right ; it is almost certain that Mr. Gladstone did not appreciate, perhaps at any time, the immense consequences this provision involved ; at least his acts and speeches pointed in that direction. It remains to add that the supremacy of the Imperial Parliament was clearly asserted in the Bill of 1893 ; but it was still a supremacy in name only ; and there was no supplemental measure, as there had been in 1886, for buying out Irish landlords, through the agency of the State. The question of the Irish land, indeed, was postponed for three years, to be left afterwards, probably, to the Irish Parliament ; and it is very remarkable that Mr. Gladstone did not even allude to this capital subject in the speech in which he brought in the Bill.

The debates on the second reading of the Home Rule Bill began on the 6th of April, 1893. They were as able, perhaps, as those on the project of 1886, but, except in the instance of Mr. Gladstone, they were less impassioned and less earnest : the measure, it was soon understood, was fore-doomed to failure. The objections in our judgment con-clusive, apparent in the original Bill, were equally manifest in the present scheme ; and there were other objections perhaps even more weighty. Still less than had been the case in 1886, was there any reason for an immense Constitutional change, for Ireland was quiescent, and made hardly a sign ; still less was there even a prospect that this could be successful. The distinction between British, Imperial, and Irish affairs, always deemed essential, was not drawn more perfectly than it had been drawn before ; indeed Mr. Gladstone admitted that it could not be drawn with anything like an approach to completeness. The conditions declared to be necessary were not nearly satisfied ; the conditions, indeed, in favour of the minority were not satisfied at all ; there was no proposal to expropriate the Irish landlords and to indemnify them at the risk of the State ; they were evidently to be soon thrown as a prey to their enemies ; the obligations of

"duty and honour" were cast to the winds. It was obvious
that the Imperial Parliament and Government would have
hardly any power in Ireland, and yet that the Irish Parliament would be held in bondage in respect of subjects of
great importance ; and that angry conflicts would inevitably
ensue, especially in the existing relations between the two
countries. The fiscal provisions of this scheme were less
unjust to Ireland than those of the measure of 1886 ; for
Ireland would have a powerful voice in the Imperial Parliament and could not be taxed without being represented ;
but the Irish Parliament would have no control over the
largest parts of Irish taxation ; and as the allocation of the
Irish customs to the payment of an Imperial charge would
leave the Irish Parliament, in this matter, free from respon-
sibility of any kind, encouragement would be afforded to
wholesale smuggling, and the British Treasury would
certainly be a heavy loser. For the rest, the Irish
Parliament and its executive, if restricted in many points
of importance, could in others do almost as they pleased;
and as had been predicted in 1886, they would, in all
probability, use their immense authority in doing revolutionary work in Ireland, political, social, and agrarian alike.
The most decisive objection, however, to the Bill, was the
proposed license to eighty Irish members to appear at
Westminster and to have a right to vote on Irish and
Imperial, but not on British questions. Mr. Gladstone
had felt that the exclusion, by the Bill of 1886, of Irish
representatives from the House of Commons, was not to
be defended for many reasons ; he seems not to have
perceived that their inclusion, under the conditions of the
Bill of 1893, indeed under any conditions of a Home Rule
policy, was absolutely incapable of being defended at all.
Assuming, as was not to be assumed, that a real partition
could be made between British, Irish, and Imperial subjects,
this strange proposal would necessarily lead to a complete
and not infrequent paralysis of the State, and would make
Parliamentary Government simply hopeless. For if Irish
members were to be permitted to vote in the same House

of Commons, on certain questions, and were not to be permitted to vote on others—to vote, say, upon peace or war, but not to vote on British trade or taxes—the inevitable result would be, as was clearly shown, that there would not be a stable majority in the ruling House of Parliament ; that no Ministry would be safe for a week ; that, in a word, Parliamentary affairs would be brought to a deadlock. This state of things obviously could not be endured ; but the only escape from it would be from bad to worse ; it would be to make Great Britain and Ireland separate States, united only by a Federal tie; that is to destroy the British Monarchy of the nineteenth century, and to place in its stead a Confederacy that would not act in concert, and that probably would perish at the first real trial—not to speak of the effects on Scotland, and perhaps on Wales.

The Home Rule Bill of 1893, in short, differed in almost every respect for the worse, where it differed from the Bill of 1886; the In and Out plan, as it was contemptuously called, that is, the power of voting bestowed on Irish members—was proved to be impossible by reasoning to which there was no answer. The second reading, nevertheless, passed by a majority in appearance still unbroken ; the English and Scotch Radicals were in need of the support of Mr. Gladstone for their own objects, and also of their National League allies ; and England, it was not inaptly said, was sold for a mess of Radical pottage. But meanwhile, and for weeks afterwards, public opinion in England and in Protestant Ireland, was stirred to its depths ; and loud and angry protests were made against the revolution which it was being tried to force on the country. The powerful Press of England distinguished itself again ; petitions flowed in largely from the English counties ; the Home Rule Bill was publicly burned in the City ; notable deputations waited on Mr. Gladstone and denounced his policy with no uncertain voice. The attitude of the Irish Protestants was even more significant ; an immense gathering assembled in the heart of London, under the presidency of the Duke

of Abercorn, the foremost of the noble settlers of Ulster ; it
was attended by delegates from all parts of Ireland, representing the intelligence and the wealth of nearly the whole
community; the Catholic Ireland of loyalty and of the
landed gentry had at its head the descendant of the Fingall
of the days of Pitt ; and the meeting, one of the most
imposing that was ever seen, condemned Home Rule in
impassioned language, and declared that the only hope of
safety for Ireland lay in the Union. A number of similar
meetings were held, and were addressed by the chief Opposition speakers ; and Lord Salisbury, at one of these in
Belfast, predicted in bold and confident words, that "this
intolerable and imbecile Bill, due to the insane eccen-
tricities of a single statesman," would never "be placed on
the British statute book."   The sentiment of the great
majority of the nation, in fact, made itself felt ; and this
was the more significant because there was scarcely a sign
of a contrary feeling in Great Britain or in Ireland herself.
The petitions in favour of the measure were few in the
extreme ; even the Radical English Press was almost silent,
and there was scarcely a public demonstration on behalf of
Home Rule save a meeting comparatively small in Hyde
Park.

This state of determined hostility, on one side, and of
indifferent apathy on the other, was of bad omen for the
success of the measure. The Bill went into Committee in
the second week of May ; the Opposition encountered it
with a mass of amendments ; and if obstruction was to be
ever justified, it was justified in a case in which an attempt
was being made to subvert the ancient Constitution of these
realms, on the plea of conceding Home Rule to Ireland,
and that against the manifest will of the nation.   The
progress of the measure was extremely slow ; every effort
the Opposition made to secure the supremacy of the Imperial
Parliament, over Irish affairs, in a real sense, and to protect
Ulster and the rest of Protestant Ireland, was defeated,
though with majorities beginning to fail ; the English
Radicals, eager to have their way, and their Irish satellites

dreading British opinion, insisted, it is believed, on a course being taken, which stands out as one of the worst acts to which the House of Commons ever gave its assent. Mr. Gladstone, probably against his will, required that discussion on separate parts of the Bill should come to an end on days named beforehand, and should finally cease on a given day ; this closure by compartments, as it was called, was reluctantly adopted by a small majority ; and a process, fitly compared to that of the guillotine, brought the resistance of the Opposition, at last, to a close. The Bill passed the third reading on the 1st of September, but by a majority of only thirty-four votes ; more than half of it had not been examined ; but the parts of it which had been debated had been so transformed that its author could hardly have recognised his own work. The financial arrangements had been given up ; there had been several other important changes ; but the most notable change was the abandonment, in despair, of the celebrated In and Out project. Eighty Irish members, as before, were to appear at Westminster ; but the restriction placed on them was taken away ; they were now to have a right to vote on all questions Imperial, Irish, and British alike ! This shameful proposal, which might have given representatives of the National League an absolute power over any question which might come before the Imperial Parliament, while that Parliament was practically deprived of effective control over Irish affairs, meant simply that the Constitution was to go to wreck ; it would ultimately, like the In and Out scheme, have substituted a Confederation of the worst type for the Parliamentary Monarchy of these kingdoms ; and it is only right to observe that three or four of Mr. Gladstone's supporters protested against it. It was, in fact, the vicious and obsolete plan of Butt presented in the most offensive shape ; had Mr. Gladstone forgotten how, twenty years before, he had condemned it, with pitiless logic and in scornful language ? [1]

[1] For a very able analysis and review of the Home Rule Bill of 1893, as it was first brought into the House of Commons, see " A Leap in the Dark," by A. V. Dicey.

This ill-starred measure was forced through the House of Commons by " logrolling " and " logrolling " only ; the separated groups supported each other, to gratify Mr. Gladstone, and for their own purposes. It was opposed, too, by an overwhelming force of public opinion ; in fact, it would not have passed the third reading had it not been notorious that a project, all but universally condemned and even ridiculed, could by no possibility become law.[1] In these circumstances the decision of the House of Lords, as had been foreseen, was a foregone conclusion. The Bill was brought before the Peers on the 5th of September ; it was severely censured by a number of speakers, especially by Lord Salisbury in impressive language ; but what must have galled Mr. Gladstone most, were the grave reproaches of old friends and colleagues, notably of the Duke of Argyll and of Lord Selborne, both of whom blamed his policy and conduct alike. The most remarkable speech on the side of the Government was the cynical utterance of Lord Rosebery ; he invited the Opposition to cut the Bill into shreds, and showed an unconcealed distrust of Home Rule. The measure was rejected by a majority tenfold in numbers ; the rejection certainly was in accord with the national judgment considered as a whole. Not even an attempt was made to set up a cry that the House of Lords had set the will of the House of Commons at nought ; in Ireland, as had happened in 1886, scarcely a murmur of dissatisfaction was heard, a striking proof in this, as in many other instances, how fictitious and weak is any Irish move-ment against the Union, as a national settlement, and apart from socialistic and kindred ends. Mr. Gladstone, it is

---

[1] The author of the chapters on English History in the " Annual Register " of 1893, though inclining to Home Rule, admits this, p. 215 : " No greater evidence could be found of the indifference with which the public received this measure than . . . the general acquiescence of all parties in its certain rejection by the Lords. . . . Among the Liberal party there were not a few to admit that the Bill was altogether unworkable, and would not have been allowed to pass from the Commons, in its actual shape, but for the certainty that in any shape it would ultimately be rejected."

said, wished to dissolve Parliament, as he had dissolved it
in 1886, on the desperate chance that the country would
adopt Home Rule ; but he was dissuaded by colleagues who
read better the signs of the time. The veteran ere long
retired from public life ; his last speech characteristically
was an attack on the House of Lords which had ventured
to cross his purpose. In his case, as in that of Parnell,
History has yet to pronounce on what he achieved for
Ireland. We may, however, remark that his Irish policy
is plainly divided into two parts ; in the first he carried
important reforms ; but his Education Bill was a bad
measure, and his Church Act failed to do the good which
he might have, perhaps, accomplished. In the second
phase of his Irish career, he certainly was in difficult straits ;
but he temporised with, and at last surrendered to, a faction
which a bolder Minister would have defied ; his Land Act
of 1881 was a mischievous agrarian law ; his attitude in
Opposition, from 1886 to 1892, was unworthy of an eminent
statesman ; his Home Rule Bills, we are convinced, would
have been fatal to the State.

Lord Rosebery was the successor of Mr. Gladstone ; he
showed from the outset that Home Rule was a political
nostrum not to his taste. It is unnecessary to follow the
course of his shortlived Ministry, the weakest since that of
Lord Goderich ; nor shall we dwell on its final collapse.
A single remark may, however, be made ; a measure affect-
ing the lands of the Three Kingdoms and imposing on them
an enormous charge, was carried by the vote of the National
League members, allied for the most part with British
Radicals ; this was one of the many striking instances how
Irish party has, since the Union, often had a decisive
influence on British interests. A word must be said on
the administration of Irish affairs, since the fall of Lord
Salisbury's Government in 1892. Mr. Gladstone's and Lord
Rosebery's Chief Secretary was Mr. Morley, one of the few
Englishmen who really has a faith in Home Rule ; as far
as in him lay he tried to rule the country in what seemed
to him to be the Home Rule spirit. He entered into a close

alliance with the section of the Home Rule party, which
had broken away from Parnell's followers, and owed its
position chiefly to sacerdotal influence ; and a kind of
compact was made between them that Ireland was to be
kept quiet, if, even apart from the great subject of Home
Rule, Irish administration should be in so-called Irish
interests.   The experiment was not very successful ; the
Executive, as it had the power, suspended the Crimes Act ;
and there was a partial revival of agrarian disorder, but not
one that requires much notice.   For the rest Mr. Morley
probably hoped that, as a Minister in Ireland, he would
prove a second Drummond ; but though an able and well-
meaning statesman, he had no opportunity to show what
was in him.   He raised a number of Catholics to the
magisterial bench, a policy doubtless in principle right ;
but some of his selections were not fortunate, for which,
however, he is hardly to be blamed.   He appointed, besides,
a special commission to investigate the claims of evicted
tenants, but this came to an inglorious end ; and a Bill he
introduced to restore to their farms the sufferers from the
Plan of Campaign—an ill-conceived and unfair measure—
was properly rejected by the House of Lords.   Another
Bill of his which' aimed at extending the operation of the
Land Act of 1881, and at injuring still further the Irish
landed gentry, passed a second reading in the House of
Commons ; it was an emanation from the National League ;
but it only struggled, as it were, into life.   On the whole
the Irish administration of Mr. Morley was not remarkable
either for good or for evil ; its principle feature was,
perhaps, its weakness.

Lord Rosebery's Ministry eked its existence out until the
summer of 1895.   The General Election that followed was,
perhaps, the most remarkable of the many that have taken
place since the Revolution of 1688.   The numerous
interests assailed by logrolling united to keep out the men
lately in office ; public opinion resented their futile attempts
to cling to posts they had held against the will of the
people.   But the influences which determined the result

were more powerful and enduring than these. England and even Scotland were indignant that Irish affairs had engrossed the attention of Parliament, it may be said for years, to the neglect of interests of supreme importance ; England especially was incensed that, under the guise of a bad measure for the supposed good of Ireland, it had been recklessly proposed that she was to be ruled by Irishmen, supporters probably of the National League, while she was not to rule Ireland at all ; and that her ancient Constitution was to be destroyed in the process. Once more the moderate and enlightened opinion of England triumphed ; the Anti-Unionist party suffered the most complete defeat a party has suffered since the accession of the House of Brunswick. Four hundred and eleven Conservatives and old Liberals were returned from Great Britain to the House of Commons against a hundred and seventy-seven followers of the late Government ; and these last were at odds with each other on the Irish Question. In Ireland the Election presented the same features, or nearly so, as that of 1892. The factions that had split in two after the fall of Parnell, flew at each other's throats as savagely as before ; the priesthood again used their commanding influence if not so openly as three years previously ; seventy members of the party they upheld were sent to Westminster in opposition to twelve still true to the memory of their old leader ; intelligence and property were again overwhelmed. Lord Salisbury returned to power once more with a majority of more than a hundred and fifty in the House of Commons ; but the Unionists had become completely fused ; and the most distinguished leaders of the old Liberals took high office under the new Government.

This Ministry has been in office for nearly three years ; it has necessarily been very largely engaged in dealing with English and Scotch questions, left in arrear ; in foreign affairs it has had to battle with a sea of troubles. Time has yet to pronounce on its Irish policy ; but this hitherto has not commended itself to impartial and well-informed Irishmen. The only important measure it has accomplished has been a further extension of the recent Land Acts, and a further encroachment on the rights of Irish landlords, with additional peculiarities of its own ; and the attendant circumstances have been unfortunate. The Land Act of 1896, as it is called, removed some of the few restrictions, in the interest of property, left in 1881 and 1887 ; it admitted certain classes of Irish tenants to the benefits of the " Three F's " ; it placed the law as to the exemption of tenants' improvements from rent, on foundations to a considerable extent untried. It contained also a principle never applied before ; a Court was empowered to hand over estates extremely burdened with debt to their occupiers, by a compulsory process, on the terms of what is erroneously called Land Purchase ; the results, trivial as yet, may be far-reaching. The Bill, dealing practically with the whole land of Ireland, was hustled through the House of Commons with unbecoming haste—an instance of the " lazy contumely," in Grattan's phrase—characteristic of the treatment of Irish affairs ; one of the ablest and most independent of the Irish members walked out of the House of Commons to express his disgust. The measure passed with much difficulty through the House of Lords, despite its loyalty to the men in power ; some of its provisions, indeed, imperil the rights of property, especially the rights of the owners of ground rent in towns, not in Ireland only, but throughout Great Britain ; in fact the nature of this legislation has been at last perceived. A Bill for a reform of Irish Local Government has, we have said, been announced for this Session ; it may be a comprehensive and a well-conceived scheme ; but a great opportunity has been afforded to a Government of extraordinary strength, to deal effectually with the Irish Question as a whole ; it is to be hoped it will take advantage of this, though it has not yet made a sign of this policy. Meanwhile the Land Commission and its dependent agencies, availing themselves of the Act of 1896, and of the excuse the depression of agriculture gives, have proceeded still more ruthlessly to cut down rents, and still further to wrong the Irish landed gentry. They have been a good deal engaged of late in renewing the leases for fifteen years created by the Land Act of 1881 ; the reductions of rent they have made have been beyond measure ; no justification can be found for them. In this process of confiscation they probably think they are doing what the Government wishes to be done ; we shall not decidedly pronounce on this ; but there is a special, and we believe a conclusive, reason why the fixing of "fair rents" should not be committed to this tribunal. The Land Commission is, so to speak, the broker of the State in carrying out the policy of so-styled Land Purchase ; it has a direct interest to cause land to be sold cheap, as the old Encumbered Estates Court had, especially as the available fund is not large ; and it has, therefore, a direct interest to make rents as low as they can be made. This creates a conflict of duty and interest, that ought not to exist ; it is simply a matter of reproach and scandal ; such an abuse England, we repeat, would not brook or tolerate. The late proceedings of this tribunal, indeed, have caused such vehement complaints in Ireland, that a Commission has been appointed to report upon them ; this has been conducted with great ability and care ; but the terms of the inquiry have been so restricted, that it is scarcely possible that right will be done.

An event happened in 1896 of grave importance in the affairs of Ireland. Ever since the fiscal arrangements in 1853–60, a feeling existed in the minds of most thoughtful Irishmen, and had been growing, that serious wrong had been done ; the conscience of Mr. Gladstone had perhaps been stirred ; he appointed a Commission in 1893 charged to inquire into, and to report upon the financial relations of Great Britain and Ireland, in this respect following the example set by the Chancellor of the Exchequer of the preceding Ministry, an authority of the very highest order. The Commission was composed, for the most part, of Englishmen, men of character, parts, and in this province experts; the inquiry continued for many months, with a late Chancellor of the Exchequer of Mr. Gladstone as head; it embraced many details and views of the subject; the Report, published in the autumn of 1896, is a document of the very greatest value, throwing a flood of light on a subject hitherto little explored. The Commission followed the only lines they could follow consistently with the unquestionable facts of History. Proceeding on the principle which no British statesman, not even Mr. Gladstone forty years before, has since the Union ventured to impugn, that however Ireland may be "assimilated in finance" to Great Britain, according to the old ideal of Pitt, she is, nevertheless, to be regarded, financially, as a distinct country, entitled, under a solemn Treaty, to special immunities of her own, the chief of these being that she is not to be unfairly taxed, they applied this criterion to the financial order of things existing in 1893 and for a considerable time; the results of their labours were certainly striking in the extreme.[1] The revenue and taxation of Ireland compared to that of Great Britain has been of late from about £7,300,000 or £7,800,000 against £85,000,000 or £89,000,000, that is from about an eleventh to a twelfth part, in other words from eight to nine per cent. of the whole. But if the resources of Ireland are considered—and this is her true fiscal position—and every conceivable test be applied—Death Duties, Income Tax and indeed all others—her means cannot be reckoned as more than a twentieth at the most of those of England and Scotland, that is, if Ireland is not to be unfairly taxed, her taxation ought to be a twentieth only, that is not from £7,000,000, to £8,000,000, but certainly less than £5,000,000, not eight or nine per cent., but about five per cent. Ireland has, therefore, been overtaxed between two and three million sterling, and that for more than a generation of man; and if the account be taken on a basis perhaps more sound, the excess will be a much larger sum. If taxation ought to be imposed on the surplus remaining over and above the cost of the necessaries of life for the

---

[1] We have already referred to the financial rights and privileges of Ireland, as a distinct country, under the Treaty of Union. See on this subject the Report of the Childers Commission, pp. 38, 150, 166.

community as a whole, then, as this surplus, in the case of
Ireland, would be very much less than in the case of
England and Scotland, due proportion being of course
observed, her taxation ought to be not a twentieth, but a
thirty-sixth part only of that of the other Two Kingdoms,
that is a sum certainly less than £3,000,000.[1]

For educated Irishmen versed in the subject, this Report
contained little that was not known or suspected. But it was
a State paper chiefly the work of Englishmen ; it placed the
whole case in the fullest relief ; it dissipated the sophistry
and the mystification which had concealed the truth. It
was treated in England at first with contempt ; when its
significance was perceived it was angrily censured ; attempts
were then made to deny the facts it brought out, or to refute
the conclusions formed by its authors. No real answer, however, has been forthcoming ; and no answer is possible if
History is not to be ignored, and the Treaty of Union is not
to be trodden underfoot. Meanwhile the Report had a
profound effect in Ireland ; it revived, amidst the dissensions
of class and party, something like a really patriotic feeling ;
it has united Irishmen as they have not been united for years,
in making a steadfast demand for financial justice. This
claim was for some time set at nought ; but the Government
saw that this would not do ; they adopted a course which,
if rightly followed, ought to satisfy impartial and fair-minded
men. The Commission did not traverse the whole field of
inquiry ; it did not consider, at least thoroughly, whether a
counterclaim, more or less large, might not be made against
the excessive taxation of which Ireland legitimately com-
plains ; and a promise has been made that another Commission shall investigate and report on the subject. This
pledge has not been yet redeemed ; but a breach of faith,
doubtless, will not be committed ; and though the terms of
the proposed inquiry are hardly fair to Ireland, the truth
can probably be made manifest. In another grave matter
connected with finance, the Government showed anything

[1] See on this important point the evidence of Sir R. Giffen, the
highest of all authorities on Statistics. Evidence, vol. ii. pp. 17–18.

but fair play to Ireland, and were nearly making a dangerous mistake. Ireland has an unquestionable right to a proportionate share in any sum voted for the relief of agricultural rates ; but this was denied for some time, until the indignation loudly expressed by Irishmen, and the remonstrances of the English Press, compelled the Ministry to change its purpose. Ireland is to obtain this sum, like England and Scotland, but on the condition, it would appear, that the proposed Local Government Bill shall pass ; this limitation is obviously out of place. We shall glance at the whole subject again when we survey the present state of Ireland ; enough here to remark that the question of the relief from rates has nothing to do with the much larger question of the excessive taxation imposed on Ireland ; justice done in this matter by no means implies that justice is to be withheld in the other.

The close of 1897 has left Ireland in such a state of repose as has not been seen since the first Fenian outbreak. The violent movement of 1879–87 has ceased ; the strife of classes and the evil passions caused by the Land and the National Leagues are at rest ; the cry for Home Rule, never really intense, and sustained only by quite different cries, is not heard outside petty party gatherings ; agrarian crime has sunk to the lowest ebb ; the peasantry are nowhere disturbed ; social order prevails, and rents and debts are paid, though agricultural depression still exists. Partisans and sciolists may attribute this happy change to the agrarian revolution which has been wrought by the wholesale reduction of rents and the confiscation of the rights of landlords, and these events have doubtless had some effect, though this will not excuse a false and unjust policy. But the change, remarkable, yet not without example in several passages of Irish History, is essentially due to quite different causes. The foreign conspiracy to which the disorder of late years in Ireland is to be mainly ascribed is, for the present, in complete suspense ; it sends no supplies to the conspiracy at home, and has reduced this to mere impotent despair ; the old chiefs of the Land and National Leagues are for the time unable to do mischief ; Parnell has still a few faithful followers ; but his formidable band is a thing of the past ; even the sacerdotal faction has been rent in twain ; the classes that once upheld these leaders have no faith in them. These are the true reasons that Ireland is now at peace ; yet it would be a mistake to suppose that the fires are not beneath their ashes ; nay, that all in the state of the country is of happy omen. The conspiracy, quiescent as it is, retains life ; this exhibits itself in signs that cannot be mistaken, though it is a feeble and, at present, a harmless spark ; that it will regain its old strength is hardly possible ; but it contains elements that may yet do evil. Our rulers, it is to be hoped, will keep this steadily in mind, and will not be led into the optimistic negligence, with regard to the real needs of Ireland, characteristic of their predecessors from 1854 to 1865. Ireland demands statesmanship of the best order to raise her present condition to a higher level ; large and searching reforms have to be yet accomplished ; she has to be wisely and well governed ; the men now in power will, we trust, seize an occasion to do a noble work, such as perhaps has never presented itself before.

The period, of which we have followed the course, is certainly the most momentous passage in the History of Ireland since the Union. After the lapse of more than three-fourths of a century, a British statesman, suddenly yielding to the menaces of a conspiracy he ought to have crushed, and completely misunderstanding the import of events, attempted to undo that great settlement, and that under conditions which made his conduct, not only an act of the gravest backsliding, but a betrayal of National and Imperial interests. Mr. Gladstone engaged in this bad enterprise apparently without much previous reflection ; he contrived to destroy the Liberal party, but his policy ended in ignominious failure. His two Home Rule Bills remain monuments of disastrous imprudence ; both would have done infinite harm to Great Britain and Ireland ; the last especially would have subverted the State, and our Constitutional and Parliamentary modes of government. Both schemes were annihilated by the sheer force of opinion ; neither, we may be assured, will ever reappear ; if a Home Rule policy, which is not impossible, be reduced again into a definite form, it will certainly be on a very different model. It is improbable, however, that the attempt will be made ; the Radical party, shattered by Mr. Gladstone, is evidently trying to set Home Rule aside, though it can hardly dispense with its Irish allies, or to reproduce it in a shape which must be condemned ; the demand for Home Rule by itself in Ireland is also seen to be false and hollow.   The experience of years, in fact, has conclusively proved that this policy rests on no solid basis ; it was a surrender to a revolutionary and socialistic faction ; it will hardly receive the countenance of another British Minister.   This period, too, beheld the exposure, before a high tribunal, of the character of the foreign conspiracy, which, laying hold of congenial elements at home, and making use of social distress, convulsed Ireland for a series of years, and has reduced the Irish land system to a state of chaos, because an emotional statesman chose to give way to it.   It also beheld the memorable fall of one of the most remarkable men of this age ; the complete disintegration of Parnell's submissive following is a conspicuous proof of his power as a leader of men, and of the influence which he possessed in Parliament, and which enabled him to play a great but unprincipled part.   The conspiracy at home and abroad is now dormant ; but if it has been scotched, it has not been killed ; we have not yet seen its final extinction, though there are many signs that this is not distant.   Meanwhile Ireland is in profound tranquillity ; now is the time to apply to her the amending hand with sound judgment, wisdom, and caution, for she has suffered greatly from the events of the last twenty years politically, economically, and in her social structure.

CHAPTER X

IRELAND IN 1898

Material condition of Ireland in 1898—Ireland still divided into three peoples—Position of Catholic, Presbyterian, and Protestant Ireland in the State—Fall of Protestant Ascendency and the resulting consequences—Landed relations in Ireland—Complete change effected in the interest of the tenant class, and to the injury of the landed gentry—Prevailing tone of sentiment and opinion in Catholic, Presbyterian, and Protestant Ireland—Lingering feeling of disaffection among the lower classes of the Irish Catholics. The Irish Presbyterians devotedly loyal—Feelings of the Irish Protestants and especially of the landed gentry—The present institutions of Ireland—Results of the disappearance of the Irish Parliament—State of the representation of Ireland—The Disestablished Church and the Catholic Church of Ireland—State of Irish literature—Low standard of education in Ireland, except at Trinity College—Results of the Union—The Home Rule policy—The demand for Home Rule largely fictitious—Proposal to hold the Imperial Parliament in Dublin occasionally—The Irish Land system—Imperative necessity of reform—The Financial Relations Question—Local Government and a Catholic University—Other reforms expedient—Reflections—Conclusion.

HAVING sketched the History of Ireland during the last hundred years, I purpose briefly to describe her existing state ; I shall follow, as nearly as possible, with respect to the present time, the arrangement adopted with respect to 1798. The material progress of the country has been decided, if we consider the century as a whole ; but it has not been so rapid or great as once appeared probable ; it has been exceedingly slow since about 1876 ; there has been positive retrogression in one branch of industry of the highest importance. The capital, with its noble public buildings and fine suburbs, has continued to improve ; the

distinction between the dwellings of the rich and the poor
so painfully significant at the time of the Union, has sensibly
diminished in the last thirty years. Some of the country
towns show a corresponding change ; and Belfast has, even
in this generation, prodigiously increased in population and
wealth ; as a centre of commerce it is by many degrees the
most flourishing of Irish cities. The development of Catholic
places of worship, to which we have adverted before, has not
ceased, hard as have been some years of late ; it is a visible
and very striking sign of the growth of Catholic Ireland in
well being and power, and of the devotion of a still deeply
religious people. The most conspicuous proof, however,
perhaps, of this material progress is the astonishing change
which has taken place in the habitations of the community
in the last half century. The miserable hovels of the past
are relatively extremely few ; they were not far from half a
million in 1841 ; they are now little more than twenty thousand in number ; the houses of a better kind have nearly
doubled within the same period. The agriculture of Ireland
is still backward, and has not, especially of late years, made
the improvement made from 1854 to 1877 ; but, compared
to what it was a century ago, it is infinitely better and of a
less rude character. The landscape in whole counties has
been transformed, and no longer wears a look of abject
poverty ; millions of acres have been enclosed and drained ;
in the methods of husbandry, in the quality of the crops,
in the breeds of animals, there has been a most admirable
change. Ireland is still a poor country, as she has always
been ; parts of Ireland are still exceedingly poor ; and Irish
trade and manufactures, with two or three most notable
exceptions, are not prosperous. But in all these respects
there has been a real advance, if we look back over broad
spaces of time ; and the improvement in the condition of
the humbler classes in the last sixty years has been beyond
dispute. The grandsons of the peasants who flocked to
the huge gatherings of the Catholic Association and the
Repeal meetings are very different from what their parents
were ; they would hardly be recognised by O'Connell if

alive ; they are no longer attired in rags ; the potato is no longer their only food ; east of the Shannon, at least, they present an appearance of comfort absolutely unknown in his day. The wages of agricultural and other labour have not declined in Ireland of late years, though industry has been in many ways depressed ; they are more than what they were in the time of the Great War measured by the price of the necessaries and the conveniences of life. Nay, if we take a variety of tests, not, indeed, conclusive but of some value, such as returns of railways and deposits in banks, Ireland seems to have grown somewhat richer within the last twenty years.

The picture, however, has a darker side ; there are considerable drawbacks from this partial welfare. Cork has probably declined in the last half century ; Galway and even Limerick are almost in decay ; many country towns and villages still show the ruinous effects of the Great Famine, or have suffered from the disappearance of small industries. Scores of the seats of the gentry, once happy homes, are desolate; they reveal the disastrous work of the Encumbered Estates Acts, and of the mischievous legislation of 1881 ; it is remarkable how few great demesnes have been made and great mansions built in the last century. Owing chiefly to the operation of Free Trade, which has been, no doubt, of immense advantage to the mere peasant, by cheapening the price of the necessaries of life, but has done grave injury to the substantial farmer, the agricultural products of Ireland have largely diminished in value since 1851 ; the area of husbandry of all kinds, and even of the best pasturage, seems to have probably decreased.[1] Through the effects of

---

[1] See the figures. Report of the Childers Commission, p. 43.

	1851–55.	1866–70.	1884–88.	1889–93.
Crops	£58,537,000	£45,365,000	£35,752,000	£34,643,000
Stock	£39,348,000	£59,630,000	£55,827,000	£54,312,000

causes, besides, to be briefly noticed, when we shall review
the present state of the Irish land system, agriculture, it is
all but certain, has declined, especially as to arterial drainage,
one of the first requirements of a wet country, and even as
to the stocks of animals of the higher classes; the consolidation of farms, a beneficent process, if carried on under just
conditions, has, it may be said, very nearly ceased; and it
is absolutely untrue that the artificial attempts which have
been made to transform Irish land tenures have, in any
real sense, improved the cultivation of the soil; their
principal consequences as yet have been the destruction of
thousands of acres of woodland ruthlessly cut down by so-
called "purchasing" tenants.   Pauperism in Ireland is
distinctly on the increase much as the people dislike the
Poor Law; in the backward districts of Connaught and
Munster a large population is always on the verge of want;
and the taxation of Ireland, local and general, is enormous
compared to what it was from 1782 to 1800, the general
taxation, too, being found to be far too high by the Report
of a Commission as yet not answered.   Nor is anything
more certain than that if Ireland, as a whole, has advanced
in prosperity since the Union, the corresponding advance of
England and Scotland has been many times more decisive
and rapid.   The growth of Great Britain in wealth has been
prodigious, especially in the last half century, that of Ireland
has been comparatively small and feeble.[1]   Nor are the
reasons difficult to seek; the age has been one of material
inventions; and the mineral products of the larger island
have been instruments of supreme importance in developing
the commerce and the vast opulence which have been
evolved under these conditions.   The policy of Free Trade,
too, adopted by England, has doubled and trebled the
resources of a nation depending, perhaps mainly, on its
gigantic trade and manufacturing system;   and Great
Britain has been for a hundred years a well-governed and
peaceable land, in which order has been reconciled with

[1] See on this point the remarkable figures in the Report of the
Childers Commission, p. 43, and the observations of Mr. Childers, p. 185.

freedom. The contrast Ireland presents is striking and mournful ; her mineral products are very small ; her trade and manufactures are not important ; she has, unhappily, been often misruled and injured by agitation and social troubles. These circumstances account for this wide distinction : but the fact remains that Ireland in 1898 is relatively far more behind England than she was a few years before Pitt carried the Union into effect.

The population of Ireland in 1892 is between four and five millions of souls, not very different from what it was at the time of the Union. It has been enormously reduced in the last half century ; this diminution has had many good results, but it stands out in conspicuous and sad contrast with the growth of the millions of England and Scotland. The Irish community, as has been the case for ages, remains separated into three peoples, differing from each other in race and faith ; the distinction is fully at least as marked as it was in the day of Pitt and of Grattan. The position in the State, however, of those divided units has undergone a complete change in the period of which we have followed the course ; a revolution, in fact, has passed over Ireland nearly as thorough as the revolution which has transformed France. The most distinctive feature of this metamorphosis, as it may be called, has been the fall of Protestant Ascendency, and all that this implies ; but there have been other features of extreme importance. Catholic Ireland is a people of about three millions and a half, regarding it as a whole, it may be said that it has completely and long emerged from the thraldom which was its lot through nearly all the eighteenth century. It has been fully brought within the pale of the State ; it is beset by no hindrances in the race of life ; it is under the rule of a law that has ceased to be a respecter of persons. The Catholic aristocracy, noble pariahs a hundred years ago, are the equals of their Protestant fellows, and, indeed, can hardly be distinguished from them ; they have given many eminent men to the public service ; not a few have made a name for them-

selves in Parliament.   Many Catholics have become large
owners of land ; the Catholic trading and professional
classes, if still not numerous and not powerful, have
risen extraordinarily in the social scale.   As for the
mass of the Catholics it is still, to a considerable extent,
a mere peasantry ; but it comprises thousands of men of
substance ; its resources of all kinds have immensely
increased ; if still nominally, for the most part, under
superiors, divided from it in race and faith, it has been
set free from the domination of these, and has acquired
rights and privileges which would have been deemed impossible even thirty years ago.   Presbyterian Ireland has
a population of about half a million of souls ; it is still a
community in the main of traders and farmers, distinct
from the classes above it in many ways ; but it has had
the full advantage of the expansion of the wealth of
Ulster ; and the Presbyterian peasant has the benefits of
the same law in his interest as his Catholic fellow.   As
for Protestant Ireland it is a people about six hundred
thousand in number ; it contains the same classes it contained a century ago ; and its members are scattered over
all parts of the country.   But it has long ceased to be an
exclusive ruling caste ; the revolution which has taken place
in Ireland is especially apparent in the Protestants of nearly
all classes.   They are still a majority in commerce and the
learned professions ; the great trading firms of Ireland are,
for the most part, Protestant, and so have been the leading
men in medicine and at the Bar.   But the Protestants of
the lower orders, who had once the advantages of a dominant class, are now at a disadvantage in many of the walks
of life ; they are a small minority in the midst of a Catholic
people, which certainly has no sympathy with them.   The
most remarkable, however, of all these changes is that which
has occurred in the position of the Protestant landed gentry.
A hundred years ago these men were lords of all that they
surveyed ; they had a monopoly of honours and power in
the State ; they were the masters of a Catholic race little
better than helots.   They have lost and for ever this pride

of place ; the semblance of authority they retain is a mere shadow; they are without political and even much social influence ; they are controlled by the bureaucratic Castle; they are isolated amidst a population often not friendly ; compared to their forefathers they have been reduced to poverty. They have been stripped of the power which made them a ruling class ; if, as we have said, they at one time had much in common with the old noblesse of Monarchic France, they at present resemble in many points that noblesse after the 4th of August, shorn of their dignities and not lords even of their own estates.

This revolution has gravely affected the whole political and social life of Ireland ; but it is most conspicuous in her landed relations especially important in an agricultural country, and also because of her history in the past. The lines of the old Irish land system still exist ; but they are the lineaments of a phantom compared to those of a living being. Absenteeism still very largely prevails ; but, as has been the case for at least sixty years, absentee estates are much better managed than they were in the times before the Union ; for example Wakefield, a very acute observer, described the Devonshire domains in the South of Munster as in a state of misery in 1812 ; they have long been the seat of a flourishing tenantry. The old middleman tenures have all but disappeared with their numerous and complex social mischiefs ; it is to be hoped, at least, that the legislation of late years will not develop a second race of middlemen, and create another system of bad land tenure. In the three Southern Provinces and in half of the North the peasantry still live on the lands of landlords divided from them in religion and blood ; and this is the case to a considerable extent in Presbyterian Ulster. But they are no longer dependents of these men ; the subjection of the past has completely vanished ; the days of precarious tenancies, of unjust evictions, of the confiscation of the tenants' rights, of excessive rents, of other kinds of oppression, have become little more than traditions of evil, which, though unduly magnified, no doubt existed. The Irish tenant has acquired proprietary rights in the soil, which more than vindicate the joint-ownership which, even thirty years ago, was not law-worthy; he has, in many instances, become an owner of land at no charge to himself, by the help of the State; and though the legislation which has had these results is open to the very gravest objections, it has certainly wholly trans-formed his status, and has virtually effaced the old rule of his landlord. He is, in a word, favoured, in an extraordinary way by law; a century ago he was almost a predial serf; he has now advantages which his class in England and Scotland does not possess and might well envy. The status of the Irish landlord, on the other hand, has been utterly degraded to his extreme detriment. He has not only been deprived of the power of doing wrongful acts, which, what-ever may be said, were far from frequent; he has practically had his lands taken from him, in the sense of real and uncontrolled ownership. He is little more now than a pensioner on his former estate; he has scarcely any power over his former tenants; he cannot even contract for his rents; these are determined, for the most part, by a tribunal of the State, which has carried out a policy against his interests, and has confiscated his property by an unjust process. The land system of Ireland, in short, has been almost turned upside down for the benefit of one class and to the harm of another, during the period from 1870 to the present time.

The order of things in Ireland has thus been immensely changed; the change in the sentiments of the community, which has followed, although marked, has been less decisive. The feelings, the opinions, the ideas of Catholic, Presby-terian, and Protestant Ireland still largely run in the grooves of the past, and retain a great deal of their old character. The Catholics of the upper and the higher middle classes have acquired self-reliance and independence; they are less timid and inert than their forefathers were; they are, for the most part, loyally attached to the British connection. If we except the aristocracy of noble birth, many men of these orders were in the ranks of the United Irishmen; very few

took part in the movement led by Parnell ; not one, we
believe, among the landed gentry. As for the humbler
classes and the Catholic peasantry, they have felt the
influence of education and increased knowledge ; they
have shaken the yoke of Protestant Ascendency off, at
least, to a very considerable extent ; they stand, so to
speak, on a higher plane of existence. But they are still
largely a passive and easily-led mass ; they have exchanged
their old masters, in a great measure, for new ; they are, in
too many instances, the dupes of mere demagogues ; and,
as always, they bow to the will of their priests if not so
submissively as a century ago. They have been injured,
too, by contact with the Fenianism of the United States ;
they are not free from socialistic and wild ideas ; they have
been demoralised by the Land and the National Leagues,
wherever these have had real power, and by the agrarian
legislation of 1881–87. Essentially Celts, they show the
Celtic tendencies ; they will often remain quiescent, for a
a long period, and then, at the bidding of leaders they trust,
they will suddenly break out into vehement passion, and do
mischief in movements of extreme violence. They have
shown these characteristics over and over again, and very
decidedly, even of late years ; and these classes, which unhappily form the principal part of Catholic Ireland, are in
no sense loyal to British rule, and are more or less discontented with the state of things around them. They
supply the multitudes which shout sedition at mob gatherings assembled by designing men ; and though nothing
probably could induce them to rise like their ancestors in
1798, for the wrongs of that time are things of the past, and
they have little really to complain of save too common
poverty, still they have no sympathy with existing law and
government, and they are not attached to the institutions
under which they live. The fact is unfortunate ; but if we
look back to the history of Ireland in the remote past, nay,
even in the last hundred years, it is intelligible to fair and
reflecting minds. The immense majority of the Catholic
Irish belong to a race which has cruelly suffered ; even in

the present century they have emerged only slowly and painfully from a state of subjection ; above all, as a general rule, they have only obtained concessions and acquired rights through agitation and by giving trouble. No wonder, then, that they retain traditions of the past ; that they are jealous, suspicious, not reconciled to our rule, that a kind of vague disaffection exists among them, that they are not friendly to England and refuse her a sign of gratitude. To gain the hearts of these masses, and to win their true allegiance, ought to be one of the first objects of British statesmanship ; but this can only be the gradual work of time, and of wise, prudent, and just government ; it will not be accomplished by the use of nostrums of a political or a social kind.

The Presbyterian Irish have changed more in sentiments and feelings than the Irish Catholics. They are still widely divided from the aristocracy who own the land ; they retain the stubborn character of the Teutonic Scotsman ; they are not free from socialistic ideas as regards the land, due largely to the legislation of recent times ; they have been clamouring of late for what is known as "the compulsory purchase" of their landlords' estates, that is, for an act of robbery by the State and for a bribe for themselves. But the people which filled the army of Washington and fought against us in the great American War, and which was at heart rebellious, in 1795–8, have become for long years devoted to our rule ; they are the determined supporters of the Union. While they stand completely apart from the Catholic Irish, they have forgotten the vain dreams of the United Irishmen. They now form the flower of the population of Ulster ; it has been the chief triumph achieved by the Union that they have become fast friends of the British connection. The fall of Protestant Ascendency and its manifold results have not sensibly affected the tone of opinion of the Protestant Irish towards the race from which they have sprung. They also firmly uphold the Union which a century ago they generally disliked ; they have remained true to England and the State, much as they have suffered from the revolution which has destroyed the domination, at one time their birthright. Yet it would be idle to deny that real discontent rankles in the hearts of the large majority of the landed gentry. Undoubtedly they held a position they ought not to have held ; they formed a ruling caste, planted in the land by conquest and confiscation of the worst kind, to lord it over a subject race. Undoubtedly they had excessive power, which, from the nature of the case, they sometimes abused, though for a century and a half they have not been mere oppressive tyrants. But they were placed in this position by England and English Kings and Parliaments, and they bitterly feel that in the last half century they have not only been shorn of their old authority and have suffered from spoliation of the most sinister kind and that effected under the pretence of law, but that over and over again they have been deceived, nay, betrayed by the assurances and pledges of British statesmen. No class in the Three Kingdoms has been so grossly wronged from the days of O'Connell to the present time. We need only refer to the Encumbered Estates Acts, to the dicta of Lord Palmerston against Tenant Right, to the speeches of Lords Clarendon and Carlisle promoting eviction, to the promises of Mr. Gladstone in 1870, to the ruinous legislation of the last few years. They have, in fact, been made scapegoats of a mean and thoroughly selfish policy, repeated on a great many occasions ; and this, though they have been, and still are, the truest champions of British rule in Ireland, and though in her southern provinces, at least, they form the best elements of civilisation and progress. It should not be forgotten that the declared foes of England described them accurately as the "British garrison," the annihilation of which was their first object in their conspiracy against the State in Ireland.

A spirit of lawlessness, widely prevalent, was, we have seen, a marked characteristic of the Ireland of the last century. It would be untrue to assert that this evil spirit has been exorcised from the Ireland of this day, or that the whole Irish community is a law-abiding people. The agrarian movements of 1879–82, and again of 1886–7, accompanied, as they were, by disorder and crime, unhappily form a proof to the contrary; and so is the power acquired by the Land and the National League organisations distinctly opposed to the law. It is unquestionable, too, that, even at this moment, a conspiracy against our rule in Ireland exists ; feeble as it has become, it makes itself manifest in denunciations of England and her rights, in exultation at any reverse that befalls her arms, in avowed sympathy with her enemies in any part of the world, in shriekings against " landlordism " at public meetings, in boasts that the " patriots" at the present day seek the objects of the United Irishmen by other means, in celebrations of the rising of 1798. Yet this lawlessness, if we carefully look back, is much less than it was a century ago, is a mere shadow of what once was a dangerous substance. The agrarian movements of late years were of a foreign origin outside Ireland ; they were at most confined to a few counties ; they never had a hold on Protestant Ulster ; they had no support from the better and wealthy classes. Compare this with the state of things which existed in Ireland in 1795–8, and the difference will be at once apparent. The lawlessness of the last twenty years was as nothing to that which prevailed when a rebel Directory sat in Dublin, when a Geraldine was ready to appear in the field, when even gentlemen of high degree were involved in treasonable plots and designs. Nor was the anarchy caused by the Land and the National Leagues nearly as far spread as the anarchy of the Tithe War ; nor were the crimes of the later period half as numerous as those of the earlier time. It should be remarked, too, and this is important, that the Whiteboyism, the Ribbonism, and the secret societies, which were the curse of Ireland a century ago, and continued until, so to speak, yesterday, seem to have become, in a great degree, extinct. Too much is not to be made of this ; but Ireland has been almost free for a time from these terrible signs of social disorder. On the whole, it may be said with truth that if lawlessness in

Ireland has not disappeared, it is not nearly as formidable as it once was ; it does not exist among the upper classes, and among the middle is seldom seen ; it is confined to a narrowing area, and receives infinitely less support than was the case in another age.   And nothing is more certain than that this bad influence is by many degrees more under the control of the law and subject to the repressive power of the State than it was in 1798, or even at a later period.   The Irish Parliament and its Executive could never cope success-fully with Whiteboyism and its deeds of blood ; and was almost paralysed by the rising of a hundred years ago ; the Land and the National Leagues were promptly suppressed when the Government chose to make use of its power.   It is scarcely necessary to add that the social lawlessness, so general in Ireland three generations ago, especially among the landed gentry, has long ago become a thing of the past.

As we pass from the present state of Ireland to her institu-tions, the disappearance of her Parliament at once strikes us.   That Parliament was the Assembly of an oligarchy of sect ; it was filled with corruption and bad influence ; its legislation was seldom in the interest of the people ; this was at times very unjust and draconic.   It contained, neverthe-less, many remarkable men ; and its administration of Irish affairs, though often marked by jobbing, was not devoid of insight.   It is now useless to inquire whether, as some have thought, it would have fulfilled the noble ideal of Grattan, and expanded into a truly National Parliament, embracing within its sphere Irishmen of every race and faith, recon-ciling the discords and feuds of ages ; it was certainly abolished by evil means, and at a singularly inauspicious time ; but it could hardly have survived the shocks of 1798–9, and its extinction probably was a necessity of the day.   Its disappearance, however, was not without bad results, long manifest to impartial and well-informed Irish-men.   It afforded an arena to able men for the display of their eloquence and fine parts ; this was especially the case with the great Irish gentry, and in a lesser degree with the

Irish Bar ; the successors of Flood, Foster, Newport, and many other worthies have not found a place for themselves in the Imperial Parliament. But a worse result was that foreseen by Grattan ; the Irish Parliament, bad institution as it was, did form an organ of opinion, in a certain sense, national ; this, in a country like Ireland, distracted by old divisions and with a weak middle class, was of great importance ; to the want of such an organ we may partly ascribe much that has been worst in Irish politics since the Union, and even much that has been bad in Irish social life, especially the decay of patriotic and public spirit, and the unquestionable increase of dissensions of class. It is difficult, too, not to connect the fall of the Irish Parliament with the state of the representation of Ireland for many years, though the two phenomena are, to a great extent, distinct. The scornful prediction of Grattan need not be repeated ; but it is notorious how that representation has declined, steadily and continuously, since the Union, and especially since the Emancipation Act of 1829, and how degraded it is in its present condition. Since the distinguished men who went from College Green to Westminster passed gradually away in the course of time, the " Irish Members," as they are rather contemptuously called, have never had many great names in the House of Commons ; but contemporaries of O'Connell, Sheil, and several others were certainly superior to their successors of this day. The great majority of these are now split into angry factions, composed of instruments of the Catholic priesthood, of leaders of the Land and National Leagues, of followers of Parnell and of waiters on fortune ; and they have little capacity, weight, or influence. Some of these men have revolutionary objects at heart, especially the destruction of the Irish landed gentry ; but just now they do not often show their hands ; nearly three-fourths of them seem to be content to be dragged, as was the case thirty years ago, at the tail of the self-styled Liberal party, which cannot do without their votes, but regards them with distrust. Ireland was, perhaps, never so ill-represented before ; her Conservative members are a mere

handful ; it is characteristic of Radical views, that Trinity
College, which at present sends two very able and independent Irishmen to look after its interests in the House of
Commons, and, of course, to play their part in the consideration of Irish affairs, was to be deprived of its members
in a Home Rule Parliament.

We have already referred to the Disestablished Church of
Ireland, separated from the State by the measure of 1869 ;
further comments on the subject would be superfluous.
The organisation and government of that Church attest the
energy and the capacity of the Irish Protestant race and the
moderate religious views of the immense majority ; unquestionably it is far more a spiritual power, more abounding in
the "living water" from a divine source, than it was in the
times when it leaned on the Castle. The only danger which
threatens it is, we have said, the impoverishment of the
landed gentry, the class which, in the main, upholds it ; this
is one of the reasons that the Irish Catholic priesthood
and the National League have had some objects in common.
As for the Irish Catholic Church it has considerably
changed, even since the days of O'Connell and the Repeal
movement. Its material resources have enormously
increased ; they appear in its fine cathedrals and places of
worship, and also in the number and wealth of its religious
houses and schools. Externally, there has been a great
Catholic revival in Ireland in the last half century ; and the
Church still possesses supreme authority over probably five-
sixths of Catholic Ireland. Nevertheless, that influence is
not what it was; the growth of education and socialistic
ideas have weakened it to an appreciable extent ; the
Church has suffered from the alliance with the National
League of too large a number of its less experienced clergy ;
and a party of Catholics exists in Ireland, which refuses to
bow to its rule in politics, and regards its pretensions with
suspicion and dislike. The last twenty years have signally
shown how lamentable it has been that the Catholic Church
of Ireland was not honourably endowed by the State, as
Pitt and his best successors desired, and as was, perhaps,

feasible had Mr. Gladstone chose.   Had this been the case,
the Church would not have been compelled to follow, to
some extent, movements of which its most far-sighted heads
disapproved ; it would certainly have condemned the Land
and National Leagues as these were unequivocally condemned at Rome.   For the rest, the Irish Catholic Church
is no friend of Protestant England, or even of the institutions which exist in Ireland ; if we look back at History
this cannot cause surprise.   It is, nevertheless, a great Conservative power, which it should be an object of a wise policy
to win to the side of law and order in Ireland ; and it
should never be forgotten that England owes a great debt
to it for what it has accomplished in the past.   It is mainly
due to the work of the Catholic Church of Ireland that its
persecuted and proscribed communion did not become a
people of brutalised savages under the Penal Code of the
eighteenth century.

The intellect of Ireland, at the present time, seems to be
less brilliant and less fruitful than it was in the generation
before the Union.   Ireland, indeed, possesses eminent
names in Letters, Science, and the Fine Arts ; but she
has no thinker to be compared with Burke, no dramatist
like the author of the " School for Scandal," no novelist
who approaches Maria Edgeworth.   She can boast of public
speakers of merit, of luminaries of the Bar, of a few able
men in politics ; but she has no orator to be named with
Grattan and with many others in her old Parliament, no
advocate equal to Curran, O'Connell, Plunket, no statesman to stand beside Grattan, Foster, Sir Laurence Parsons,
and others of that time.   Much of her best intellect has
flourished in foreign lands ; it has not found a field for its
power at home ; this is notably the case with the great
landed gentry, few of whom have given, or could give proof
of the capacity and talents of their fathers a century ago.
Education in Ireland has made real progress ; the great
majority of the Irish people are as well instructed, perhaps,
in the rudiments, as the great majority of the English ; and
secondary and high education has, on the whole, improved.

But a fifth part of the community even now cannot read or write ; and, with the exception of Trinity College, which has made a distinct advance in the course of a century, in all that constitutes a great place of learning, the institutions for the education of the middle and higher classes are not all that they ought to be, and are, at best, inadequate. We have explained the causes of this before ; enough to say here that ample and wise reforms, in harmony with Irish aspirations and wants, are certainly required and should be effected ; the standard of education of the better kind in Ireland is still much lower than the same standard in England and Scotland. As to the administration of justice in Ireland, it is scarcely necessary to say that this has been simply transformed with the best results ; undue severity, partiality, corruption on the Bench, whether in its higher or lower spheres, have been absolutely unknown for two genera-tions at least ; and though judges and magistrates have, of late years, unhappily been compelled to come in conflict with agents of the Land and the National Leagues, their acts have never been seriously impugned. Of the results of the Poor Law, I have written before; the system, undoubtedly is not liked in Ireland ; but, on the whole, though not very well administered, it has established the principle that Property must support Poverty, and this has had beneficial effects. It can hardly be said that the tone of public opinion in Ireland has made a real improvement. It still represents the old divisions of race and faith, and the animosities and feuds of class ; it is still passionate, unre-flecting, and deplorably weak ; it is wanting in moderation and breadth of view, in political sagacity and public spirit ; it embodies itself in a Press, not without ability, but characterised by the same defects. And it is unnecessary to repeat that, as I have pointed out, Ireland is far behind Great Britain in civilisation and material wealth, relatively farther, at least in some respects, than she was before the Rebellion of 1798, and that if her middle class has risen in the social scale, it is still comparatively weak, and possesses little influence.

The present condition of Ireland is largely due to
calamitous events in bygone ages, but, in this century, it has
been evolved, under the Union, and all that has been
incidental to it.   That great settlement has not fulfilled the sanguine hopes of Pitt ; in many respects it
has proved to be a failure.   Even as a Protestant Union,
in the phrase of that day, it was a half measure badly
accomplished ; it only extinguished the Irish Parliament,
by evil means and at a disastrous time ; it left Ireland,
to a great extent, a separate State ; we see the results,
as Foster and Grattan predicted, in the Repeal and the
Home Rule movements.   But its operation as to Catholic
Ireland was far worse ; it was dishonoured by a grave breach
of faith ; it left Catholic Ireland deprived of rights, which
an Irish Parliament certainly would have conceded ; it
retarded its liberation for many years ; it was not accompanied by the great measures which Pitt saw were essential
to its success, Catholic Emancipation, the Commutation of
the Tithe, and a provision for the Irish Catholic clergy, this
last of supreme importance, but now become impossible.
It has been, too, if not a consequence, at least a circumstance
connected with the Union, that the organic structure of
society in Ireland has been transformed with results not
beneficial in many respects ; the power of an aristocracy
has been destroyed, and replaced by a bureaucratic system
of rule, not unlike the centralised administration of the later
Bourbons, the vices of which Tocqueville has so vividly
described.   Under the Union England has often been
estranged from Ireland, made hostile, or, what is worse,
neglectful ; if parts of Ireland have become attached to
England, the greater part is not in sympathy with her, nay,
remains sullen and disaffected at heart.   And it would be
idle to deny that a great deal of the Irish legislation of the
Imperial Parliament has, since the Union, been faulty in the
extreme, especially in all that relates to the land.   It has been
marked by the incapacity to understand Ireland, which has
been the common error of so many public men ; it has been
occasionally selfish, unjust, oppressive, as we can clearly

perceive in the province of finance,[1] in which Ireland has been sacrificed to British commerce, as Grattan foresaw would be the case. Even when it has been beneficent and wise, it has, over and over again, been too late, as we see in the instances of Catholic Emancipation and the Commutation of the Tithe, and even then it has been often extorted by agitation and a war of classes, and injured by suspicion, aversion, and distrust. The British administration of Ireland has had the same defects; many Englishmen who have directed Irish affairs have been able and distinguished men, but very few have been, in a real sense, successful; the best Lord-Lieutenant and the best Chief Secretary of the last eighty years have been Irishmen, for "they were racy of the soil," and knew the Irish people. Nor is it less certain that while Ireland has had a most potent influence on the affairs of England, nay, has more than once determined British and Imperial policy, Irish interests have, in the course of the century, been more than once set aside and neglected, under the stress of British and Imperial questions, and, above all, that Ireland and her fortunes have repeatedly been made the prize of the strife of British factions, with results that true Irishmen can only deplore. The Commutation of the Tithe was confessedly a necessary reform; how long was it delayed by party manœuvring and wrangling about the Appropriation Clause! The policy that disestablished the Irish Protestant Church was just, but it was carried out, not for the real good of Ireland—it would otherwise have been a very different measure—but mainly in order to unite the divided British Liberals, and to gratify that "Nonconformist Conscience" which aspires to the pulling down of all established churches. Many similar instances might be referred to; one of the last and most striking is the support given by English and Scotch Radicals to Home Rule; they

---

[1] See the remarkable observations of Mr. Childers, Report p. 160. I have only space for a few words : "Just as Ireland suffered in the last century from the protective and exclusive policy of Great Britain, so she has been at a disadvantage in this century from the adoption of an almost unqualified Free Trade policy for the United Kingdom."

advocate a policy they really dislike, and dangle it before an Irish faction, because they cannot dispense with its votes.

These results, doubtless to be regretted, have not all been caused by the Union; many have only been coincident with it. Let us, however, take the other side of the national account, and consider the good which the Union has brought in its train. It is now left out of sight, but should not be forgotten, that England might never have triumphed in the Great War, had Ireland not been ruled by the Imperial Parliament, from 1800 to 1815; loyal as the Irish Parliament indisputably was, a strong centralised Legislature and Executive was required in our struggle for life and death with Napoleon. This, probably, is the best excuse that can be made for the very questionable conduct of Pitt ; the Union, in the existing state of the world, was a necessity of State to be secured at any hazard and cost. The Union, however, has been attended with good results for Ireland, on the whole, far outweighing the incidental evils. It has been owing to this measure that the transition from Protestant Ascendency, and its numberless ills, has been accomplished in Ireland, with errors, indeed, but without extreme social convulsions and shocks ; it is difficult to suppose that, after the events of 1798, this could have been effected by an Irish Parliament, though it could have been in 1794-5. Ireland has, on the whole, made progress since the Union, if this has been comparatively slow and small ; this would probably have been less under an Irish Parliament, if we bear in mind what the state of the country was in 1800-1, and the insecurity, the ruin, and the furious passions of class which the unhappy rebellion had produced and developed. Under the Union, besides, the great grievances from which Ireland was suffering a century ago, have been removed, often indeed, not wisely, and, in many instances, too late ; but the Tithe is gone ; the dominant Church has fallen ; all that was vicious in Irish "landlordism" is a thing of the past ; education has been widely diffused ; the Irish land system, utterly bad as it is, has been reformed in the interest of the occupiers of the soil. The two principal benefits, however, which have followed the Union—and these have been decisive and far-reaching—are that Presbyterian Ireland, hostile in 1791–8, has become devotedly attached to England, and that the loyalty of Protestant Ireland has grown stronger ; and above all, that the authority of the Imperial Parliament and its Executive have kept down the strife and angry passions of Irish factions, if it has not reconciled animosities of class and faith, and that it has made the law more generally respected and obeyed than was ever the case in the days of the Irish Parliament. This, assuredly, is an enormous gain ; it is, perhaps, the one great advantage that can be set off against the evils caused by the decline of the landed gentry and the ascendency of the bureaucratic rule of the Castle, which has secured for law a more effective sanction than had existed in Ireland at any previous time. And if we calmly reflect what the state of Ireland was after the horrible catastrophe of 1798, we shall probably understand how it has come to pass that the Union has done less good than was expected from it.

The Union has endured for well-nigh a century ; it is one of the cardinal institutions of the State ; it has become, so to speak, a part of the frame of these kingdoms ; it is inseparably connected with the national life. England has been called upon to undo this great settlement, at the bidding of a conspiracy formed in distant lands, and at the instigation of a statesman, in his old age, false to his former and better self, against the will of loyal Protestant and Presbyterian Ireland, and of the large majority of the people of Great Britain, because a part of Catholic Ireland is disaffected to our rule. This plain statement of the case ought to be sufficient to convince impartial and thinking men of the real nature of a thoroughly bad policy, which, as it were but yesterday, would have been treated in the Councils of England with the contempt with which Canning treated it in another age. A very few remarks may, however, be made, for the British Radical party has, in words at least, declared itself to be pledged to Home Rule for Ireland. Mr. Glad-

stone has been rather a great economist than a far-sighted
or profound statesman ; he has never shown, in his long
career, that he really understood·the noble art of government. He has twice attempted practically to break up the
Union ; his most ardent admirers would probably now
admit that his efforts to set up in Ireland a separate Parliament were sorry and most disastrous failures, regarded by
England with well-marked aversion. The irremediable faults
of his Home Rule Bills, their anomalies, their absurdities,
above all, the ruinous mischiefs they would have caused,
have been fully and effectually exposed ; I have touched the
subject in this brief narrative ; it is unnecessary further to
deal in it. It may, however, be affirmed, almost with certainty, that Home Rule for Ireland will never again be
presented to Parliament in these forms ; should this evil
policy be adopted once more by a British Minister, it will,
we know, be under quite other conditions. We are now
told that England, Scotland, Ireland, and perhaps Wales,
are to be treated "to Home·Rule all round" ; in other
words, that three or four local Parliaments are to be formed
for the management of the local affairs of these realms, and
that Imperial affairs are to be directed by an Imperial
Council. It is not easy to believe that this project has been
seriously made ; the Radicals must know that it could not
become law ; and there is reason to think that they put it
forward to please and to dupe their Irish allies. Not a
single community in the Three Kingdoms has shown that it
desires a policy of the kind ; and the objections to it
cannot be overcome. It would mean that a new and written
Constitution would replace the ancient and unwritten Constitution of this Imperial State ; and that a Federation,
essentially a weak Government, and from the days of the
Achæan League to those of the United States, liable to
internal dissension, intrigue, and disruption, would be put
in the stead of the undivided and powerful British
Monarchy. This should be enough to prove the folly of
such a scheme ; but other objections are at least as decisive.
No stable Federation has ever been formed out of the

fragments of a dismembered Monarchy; it requires that
organised states should exist beforehand; and no Federation could long endure if one State greatly preponderates
in strength.   These simple facts absolutely condemn this
policy; England, in truth, under this order of things,
would annihilate such a Federation, at the first real
trial, as easily as Gulliver broke the petty chains of
Lilliput.

Home Rule, whatever the form it may assume, means the
creation in Ireland of a Parliament of her own, and of an
Executive dependent on it.   This policy, I believe, disguise
it as you may by securities, safeguards, and devices on
paper, would be a calamity for Great Britain and Ireland
alike.   From an Imperial point of view it means that a
government, hostile to England, almost from the nature of the
case, could threaten the main avenues of British commerce,
and could give the enemies of England, in the event of
war, a base of operations of supreme importance.   It means,
further, that the Parliament of the United Kingdom is to be
restricted, perhaps paralysed, in the very seat of its power ;
and that England is to abandon populations of her own
race and faith, as decaying Rome abandoned her most loyal
provinces.   It is scarcely necessary to point out what would
be the effect of such a policy in the judgment of foreign
Powers ; it would be a confession of weakness and treachery,
which might well combine a League of States, jealous of
England, against her, and be the successor of a League of
Cambray.   From an Irish point of view it means turning
everything upside down in Ireland, very probably civil war,
certainly a strife of class like that of 1641, of 1691, of 1798,
followed possibly by the establishment of a domination of
sect more odious than any Ireland has yet seen, perhaps by
reconquest, assuredly by general bankruptcy.   It is difficult
to imagine that Englishmen will ever sanction such things,
or could be blind to the evident perils ; they have repudiated
projects of the kind on two occasions ; and the English
democracy possesses the strong political instinct which their
rulers have displayed through a great history.   And this is

the more certain because the demand for Home Rule is un-
real and fictitious in Ireland itself, and is put forward on pre-
tences altogether untrue. The cry against the Union had
never any force in Ireland, unless it was accompanied by
other cries, especially by a cry for agrarian plunder;
"rapine," as Mr. Gladstone rightly exclaimed, was associated
with "dismemberment" in 1880-2, and this has been seen
in other Irish movements; nor can it be forgotten that the
defeat of Home Rule did not evoke a sign of discontent in
Ireland, because, whatever demagogues may say, the Irish
peasantry do not care about it. Home Rule, too, it must be
borne in mind, is justified only on the assumption that
Ireland is a "nation" with "national" ideas and aims; but
this assumption is opposed to the plainest facts of History.
Ireland, no doubt, might have become "a nation," but
the events of centuries have made this impossible; she has
for ages been divided into three peoples, locally united but
morally standing apart; and these have no "national"
aspirations in any rational sense. The basis of the argument for Home Rule fails; and as to the pleas that all that
Ireland seeks is the "management of her own affairs," and
that the "majority of her population" demands this, these
shibboleths can deceive no reflecting mind. Ireland's
"management of her own affairs," involves a revolution in
the polity of the State; and as to the "demand of the
majority" this begs the question, for England must have a
voice in the matter, and ignores the circumstances that
looking at Ireland alone, five-sixths of the property and
intelligence of the country maintain that this demand, if
conceded, will have the direst results, and that, after all, as
Burke once drily observed, "Government is not a mere
affair of arithmetic."

The Union, therefore, must be maintained, for the security
of the State and Three Kingdoms; after the experience of
1886 and 1895, this fundamental law will probably not be
assailed. The degradation of the Irish electorate, and the
excessive representation of Ireland in the House of Commons,
are questions which statesmen will have to consider; but

these, like the reform of the House of Lords, will, doubtless, be postponed until the next Reform Act shall effect another Constitutional change. The Union, however, has brought ills with it ; can nothing be done to remove or diminish these, as our Parliamentary system exists at present ? These ills, and they cannot be denied, run ultimately up to the want of knowledge of Ireland, and to the resulting want of sympathy, which have been the distinctive faults of British public men, and of English and Scotchmen in the Houses at Westminster,[1] and have long been but too obvious to well-informed Irishmen. These faults are partly due to defects in the English national character ; partly to the difficulty which a Teutonic race has in understanding a race; in the main, Celtic, especially when this is poor, backward, and on a low plane of civilisation and social life ; partly to the rapid and frequent changes in the administration of Irish affairs, caused by our mode of Parliamentary government ; but largely, too, it must be allowed, to the extravagance and the vehemence of so-called Irish opinion, from which sober-minded Englishmen and Scotchmen turn away with disgust. This ignorance and indifference, however, are grave evils ; they have been attended with unhappy results ; they should, if possible, in the direction of affairs of Ireland, be replaced by knowledge, experience, and a really kindly state of senti-ment. This object is one of extreme importance ; it would probably be, in a great measure, attained, were Parliament occasionally to assemble in the Irish capital, and to govern Ireland, as it were, on the spot. This is not a new and un-heard-of policy ; it was seriously proposed by distinguished Irishmen, and was entertained by the Whig Opposition, during the Repeal Movement of 1843 ; it was unfortunate that

---

[1] Dozens of passages from the writings of Swift and Burke, and from the speeches of Flood, Grattan, and other eminent Irishmen, might be quoted on this subject. I take a speech from O'Connell after the Union :—" We are governed by foreigners ; foreigners make our laws ; . . . as to Ireland, the Imperial Parliament has the additional disadvantage springing from want of interest and total ignorance. I do not exaggerate ; the ministers are in total ignorance of this country."

it was allowed to drop.[1]   The inconveniences it might produce would be mere trifles compared to the advantages it would
certainly bring with it.   It would be much that the presence
of Parliament in College Green would necessarily add to the
wealth of a poor country, and probably make Ireland an
attractive resort for the traveller.   But it would be infinitely
more that Parliamentary Sessions in Dublin would gradually,
but surely, make our British rulers familiar with Irish ideas
and needs, would lead them to adapt legislation to these,
would place them in contact with Irish feeling, would make
them know Ireland, in a word, and touch their hearts.   One
of the best results, we believe, would be that they would
learn how hollow and false is the cry for "Home Rule."

Meanwhile Ireland requires the amending hand; this
should be applied with judgment and skill; she is in need
of large and searching reforms.   Her land system has
become a chaos of manifold ills; it is impossible that it
can remain in its present state if the community is to make
steady and real progress.   Political economy, despite Mr.
Gladstone, has not fled from this planet to hide in Saturn;
it watches, so to speak, the ruin done in Ireland by the contempt that is shown to its well-known laws.   Owing to the
operation of the recent Land Acts, the rental of the Irish
gentry has been recklessly cut down by tribunals which are
simply a reproach to the State, and that though an impartial
Commission had reported in 1880–1, that Ireland, as a
country, was not overrented, if overrenting existed in not

[1] See a remarkable letter from Lord Waveney in the *Times*, "Home Rule
Reprint," vol. i. p. 303.   Sheil, greatly trusted by the Whigs, referred to
the subject at O'Connell's trial.   Report, pp. 325–6.   I quote a few sentences : "The benefits to Ireland, which would be derived from such a
plan, nobody can doubt.   It would have the advantages without the dangers
of a Repeal of the Union.   There would be no dismemberment of the
Empire ; no Catholic Ascendency to be dreaded ; no predominance of
one party over another.   The intercourse between the two countries
would be augmented to such an extent that their feelings would be
identified ; national prejudices would be reciprocally laid aside. . . .
You would see the country again inhabited by its ancient nobility.
What a magnificent spectacle this city, would then present !"   The
whole of this fine passage deserves study and reflection.

a few instances.[1]   Agricultural depression, no doubt, exists in Ireland ; but it has been much less severe than in England and Scotland ; the market value of Irish land has scarcely really fallen ; and the wholesale and unjust reduction of rents has, with other mischiefs, had this result, that by unduly increasing the price of the tenants' interest, it has subjected incoming tenants, when farms are bought and sold, to what practically are huge rack-rents.   It is an incontestable fact that, of late years, through the proceedings of the Land Commission and its dependents, the value of the fee-simple in Ireland has been lowered fully a third, and the value of Tenant Right has been raised in the same proportion ; and no answer has been made to the plain inference, that this means a confiscation of landlords' property, veiled, indeed, and gradual, but not the less certain.   Those who reflect on what confiscation involves, and especially a vast confiscation of the Irish land, that it destroys enterprise, banishes capital from the soil, and prevents free commerce in a main source of industry and wealth, will deem this an enormous evil, not to speak of the fatal precedents it has made for revolutionary legislation of a socialistic tendency.   Yet this is only a part of the innumerable ills which have flowed from the present system of the tenure of land in Ireland.   The landlord has been divorced from his estate ; he is little more than a recipient of an annual sum, in the arrangement of which he has no voice ; he is, therefore, precluded, as it were by law, from improving what were his lands at one time, and he will not expend a shilling on them.   The consequences have been already grave ; though, unquestionably, in the great mass

---

[1] I quote a significant passage from the Report of this Commission : " Though the amount of the rent was always at the discretion of the landlord, and the tenant had, in reality, no voice in regulating what he had to pay, nevertheless it was unusual to exact what in England would have been considered as a full or fair commercial rent.   Such a rent over many of the larger estates, the owners of which were resident, and took an interest in the welfare of their tenants, it has never been the custom to demand.   The example has been largely followed, and is, to the present day, rather the rule than the exception in Ireland."

of instances, Irish tenants have made the additions to their farms, still, in arterial drainage, and in bettering the breeds of animals, the Irish landlords have done a great deal in the past; in these two particulars, as we have seen, there has been probably a falling off of late, and this is because the landlords, as was to be expected, have, under existing conditions, stopped their outlays. The whole case, nevertheless, is a great deal worse, if we consider it from another and wider point of view. The lands of Ireland have been placed under what may be called leases for ever, renewable every fifteen years, through litigation, by a tribunal of the State, which fixes the rents they are to yield; it is scarcely possible to conceive a more vicious system, one more pregnant with bad results and troubles. In these circumstances the Irish tenant is not only subjected to a vexatious lawsuit, at short intervals of time, not only encouraged to distrust and dislike his old landlord, he is positively tempted and urged to run out and exhaust his farm, in order to effect a reduction of rent when the period of renewing his lease comes round. This process of deterioration has been going on apace; it is but a repetition of what has occurred in Bengal where the ryots, under the Permanent Settlement, have succeeded in lowering greatly the amount of their rents; agriculture in Ireland has, in consequence, suffered, and that to a very appreciable extent, not to refer to the animosities and ill-will which the system provokes.[1]   It should be added, and this is important, that as the "fair" or "judicial" rents fixed by the State are many degrees lower than the true rents, this has necessarily caused subdivision and subletting, marked vices of the old Irish land system; and this is gradually reproducing the almost extinct middleman, the oppressor of serfs holding at rack-rents.

This train of social evils has long made itself manifest; the policy of what is called "Land Purchase" has been inaugurated in the hope of doing away with these, and of placing the Irish land system on a less unstable basis. We

[1] See on this point the mass of irrefutable evidence recorded by the Commission presided over by Sir Edward Fry.

have already seen what that policy is ; landlords, who wish to sell their estates to their tenants, may obtain the price from the State, through the Land Commission ; and the moneys are advanced to the tenants, who have not to lay down a shilling themselves, and redeem the advance by paying an annuity, for a series of years, much lower than the legitimate rent. In the sense that these annuities have been reasonably well paid, and that the State has hitherto not suffered, this process has been, in the main, successful ; but this is only a very small part of the subject. The policy which plants an Irish tenant in his farm, not through a contribution or effort of his own, but by the medium of a gift, akin to a bribe, is, I am convinced, a bad policy ; it will never create a class of peasant owners, conservative, law abiding, hard working ; the experience of human nature teaches the exact contrary ; it is idle to argue from the case of the peasantry of France, who really purchased their lands, and, for that very reason, are a respectable and industrious order of men. It is untrue, I repeat, that these falsely named "purchasers" have, as a rule, improved the lands they have acquired ; the cultivation of them is often very bad ; in fact the best agriculture of Ireland, by many degrees, is that under the system of free contract, in the case of the few large farmers holding leases made anterior to 1881, and who have not had their rents fixed by the Land Commission, and have settled with their landlords in conformity with the state of the times. As we have seen, too, these "purchasers" have, in hundreds of instances, cut down the . timber growing on their lands ; they are often needy and hopelessly sunk in debt ; and as the annuities they pay are far less than a true rent, they sublet, subdivide, and mortgage wholesale, with all the evil consequences of acts of the kind.[1] But whatever opinions exist on this subject, it is evident that "Land Purchase," under these conditions, cannot materially affect the present land system for a very considerable space of time. Out of a sum of about £40,000,000 set apart for this purpose, since 1885–91, little more than £10,000,000

[1] I can attest this from very large personal observation.

24

have, we have said, been expended ; at this rate of progress it would take ages to affect a large transfer of the Irish land. Nor are the reasons difficult to perceive ; Irish tenants will not "purchase," while the Land Commission is whittling away rents progressively year after year ; they will wait for a basis of "purchase" more in their interest. Besides it is a complete mistake to suppose that the Irish peasant, in the Southern provinces at least, has any craving for freehold ownership ; such a tenure is contrary to the genius of a Celtic race ; he will accept it when it is for his clear advantage ; but the idea never entered his head until he took it in through Land League teaching.

The present state of the Irish land system, and the failure of "Land Purchase," on voluntary lines, to effect rapidly a large transfer of the Irish land, have produced a demand, not without support, for what is called the "compulsory purchase," of all the estates of the Irish landlords, and for placing their tenants in their room as owners. It might be enough to say that this policy is not possible, and will be always rejected by the general taxpayer. In whatever degree the Land Commission carries out the object of cutting down rent, the rented land of Ireland has never been valued at less than £150,000,000 by fair judges ; it is still probably worth £200,000,000 ; does any one suppose that Parliament would vote a sum equal, perhaps, to the ransom France paid to Germany, in order to make Irish tenants possessors of their farms ? This policy, nevertheless, could it be accomplished, would be unnatural, disastrous, and, in no doubtful sense, infamous. A volume on this subject might well be written ; I have only space for a very few sentences. Ireland is a land of a low watershed, of great sluggish rivers, of immense marshes and plains, of small towns widely apart from each other ; peasant ownership, on an extensive scale, could never flourish under such conditions. The process of "compulsory purchase" as proposed, means turning the tenant class of Ireland into owners everywhere, through what, I repeat, is morally a bribe ; these men would be, in the words of Burke, in an analogous instance, "rocked and dandled into their possessions" by the State, the "grantees of a confiscation," wholesale and unjust; it is contrary to the very nature of things, that such a body of proprietors could become a loyal population of thrifty freeholders, could, in a reasonable sense, be prosperous. Let it not be forgotten that this is the very scheme put forward by the Land and the National Leagues ; Parnell, who understood Ireland, always insisted that the general transfer of the Irish land to its occupants would only make them more " patriotic " than before, that is better instruments to effect his ends ; and peasant owners thus artificially made would assuredly be wasteful, extravagant, and not industrious. They would, as a corresponding class is already doing, subdivide, sublet, and encumber their lands as a rule ; middleman tenures would grow up over whole counties ; large parts of Ireland would return to the state in which they were before 1845–7. This would be inevitable from the simple circumstance that these peasant owners would pay the State less than a natural rent ; it would be as certain as that water runs down a hill ; it would fall in with, and stimulate inveterate tendencies. What, too, would be the necessary results of the universal and forcible expropriation of the Irish landed gentry ? In the Southern Provinces of Ireland, at least, they form the best elements of civilisation and progress ; are these to be blotted out and to perish ? An Irish Local Government Bill will soon become law ; every one who knows Ireland must be aware— the leaders of the Land and the National Leagues form no . exception—that it cannot be conducted with success, without the Irish landlords, who, as Grand Jurors, are the only class which has had any experience in County Government. " Compulsory Purchase," besides, is simply robbery ; no confiscation of the same kind has been effected in modern Europe, not even in the France of the Reign of Terror ; is Ireland once more to be made the victim of what she suffered in the sixteenth and seventeenth centuries, for the results of wholesale spoliation do not vary ? [1]

[1] It has been assumed by the advocates of "compulsory purchase"

The policy of the "compulsory purchase" of the Irish land would have been laughed at as folly a few years ago ; it would not be listened to at the present time had it not been backed by several powerful interests, and found advocates in ignorant and self-sufficient writers. Lazy politicians, who have no thought of principle, and do not know Ireland, profess to believe it would make Irish Government an easier task, that it would save them a certain amount of trouble. The owners of the mortgages on Irish estates, English and Scotch capitalists, as a general rule, see in this process a probable means of realising securities, now in danger ; a very small minority of Irish landlords, encumbered beyond relief, hope that in this way they may save something for themselves from a shipwreck. The chief absentee landlords are perhaps not disinclined to part with their estates, at the cost of the State, and to invest the proceeds elsewhere ; a set of doctrinaires, who have never seen Ireland, and have never been in contact with a Celtic peasantry, imagine that, by converting them into owners of their farms, without requiring them to pay a shilling, and through an act of palpable and general wrong, they will be transformed into a people of loyal and thriving freeholders. But no statesman has pledged himself to this policy ; an overwhelming majority of Irish landlords regard it as shameful and cruel injustice ; and though a movement in its favour exists, it is to be hoped that it will be not carried out, as was the case of the Encumbered Estates Act, a scheme of confiscation that has proved worse than a failure. The avowed argument for "compulsory purchase" is, in fact, founded on grotesque ignorance. The legislation of 1881–7 has, it is said, "created a dual ownership" in the Irish land ; this is a detestable state of things ; the knot must be cut by selling out the Irish

that the Irish landed gentry, after having been deprived of their rented lands, would live at home on their demesnes, and be available for local duties and County Administration. This is in the highest degree improbable : after a treatment which, in the words of Burke, would have "made them displumed, degraded, metamorphosed, unfeathered, two-legged things," they would almost certainly leave Ireland.

gentry by force. But, in the first place, this legislation no more "created dual ownership" in the Irish land system, than it "created" the mountains and lakes of Ireland; it only developed it under the worst conditions. In the second place, this "dual ownership," properly understood, is the natural mould of Irish land tenure; it is the old joint ownership, which the Irish peasant has possessed, morally, in his farm for ages, at least in a great mass of instances; it is the peculium which he wishes to have secured for him, and which he does not care to exchange for freehold owner-ship. And, in the third place, "dual ownership" is a far more general mode of land tenure than the single ownership which prevails in England, and in England alone; we see it even in the English copyhold; it is quite common all over the Continent, nor has it been incompatible with prosperity and peace. This idea about "dual ownership," in truth, only shows how little the subject has been con-sidered; and, in the case of Ireland, it simply means that it suggests a policy which, from every point of view, would cause an agrarian revolution widespread and disastrous. It is at bottom the old idea of the Tudor lawyers: "Irish usages are bad, make them English by force."

Voluntary "purchase," therefore, having had but little effect, and "compulsory purchase" being quackery and wrong, we are forced, by a kind of exhaustive process, to consider the Irish land system on the side of tenure, and to see how a reform of this is feasible, as affairs now stand. Every thinker from Burke to Stuart Mill, to Butt, and to Longfield, not to refer to other less distinguished names, have looked at the subject from this point of view; it is the only one from which it can be regarded con-sistently with equity and sound policy. All have practically agreed on the main facts; the occupiers of the soil in Ireland, in thousands of cases, have for centuries had a joint ownership in their farms; this ought to be protected by a long or a perpetual tenure, at a reasonable rent that does not encroach on their rights.[1] It ought to be feasible

---

[1] See again Burke's "Tracts on the Popery Laws," vol. ii. p. 446,

to effect a reform of Irish land tenure, that is in the relation of landlord and tenant, in harmony with these reasonable and true principles. With large exceptions in the cases of pastoral farms, of farms rightly the subjects of free contract, and of farms not of an agricultural kind, the rented lands of Ireland ought to be placed under a system of perpetual or long leases, so as to secure the rights of the tenant, reserving to the landlords what may be called their royalties and the power to enforce their claims, not by eviction, but through a sale of the land. After the legislation of the last seventeen years, the rents of these leaseholds must be adjusted by the State; but they ought not to be fixed by the Land Commission and its sub-Commissions, agencies which have an interest to work rent down, and with which Irishmen are not satisfied; they ought not to be fixed at short intervals of time and through costly litigation—all this doing the mischief to which I have already referred; they ought not to be fixed subject to claims for exemption, in respect of improvements—a prolific source of intolerable wrong, and of demoralisation and hard swearing frightful to think of.[1] On the contrary, they should be fixed for the length of the leases; and they should be fixed by a valuation made by the State, a certain allowance for improvements being made on the spot, with a right of appeal, but at the peril of law costs, to a tribunal consisting of a single judge of established reputation, one for each province, the judge being assisted by trained agricultural experts. Such a reform could not do perfect justice; but it would be infinitely to be preferred to the present vicious system; it would get rid of innumerable mischiefs at once; it would enable landlords and tenants to know their rights—a knowledge they

ed. 1834; Mill, on "The Irish Land Question"; Butt, "The Irish People and the Irish Land," *ante*; Longfield's essay in "Systems of Land Tenure," *ante*.

[1] "It has never been known in the memory of man," wrote Swift (Life by Craik, p. 139), "that an Irish tenant ever told the truth to his landlord. . . . If they paid you but a peppercorn a year they would be readier to ask abatement than to offer an advance." This class has left descendants.

practically do not now enjoy; it would quiet possession, and moderate a war of class; it would in all probability quicken agricultural progress. It is remarkable that Parnell, when in his constitutional mood, spoke strongly of a reform on these lines; and Mr. Gladstone, no doubt conscious of the ills caused by his Land Act of 1881, if not very distinctly, expressed his assent.[1] The landlord, in justice, ought to receive an equivalent for the loss of his reversionary rights; this should be in the nature of a small fine payable to the recognised owner of the fee. The whole subject of the compensation of the Irish landed gentry for the losses they have sustained by legislation since 1881 would remain open, and a word or two may be said. That they have been wronged and despoiled cannot be really denied; they have been promised compensation, in that event; this could be best afforded by advances made by the State for paying off the mortgages on their lands, at a low rate of interest, the State issuing debentures, which could float in the market. At the same time mere family charges, by many degrees the largest, ought to be reduced by the State, as it has reduced rents; it is sheer iniquity to leave these charges untouched when the State has diminished the security on which they rest.[2]

The subject of Irish finance must be also treated, and a reform be effected in this province, unless Parliament shall refuse to do Ireland justice. A Commission of the very first authority has, we have seen, reported that Ireland has been

---

[1] On this occasion Mr. Gladstone did me the honour to refer to a tract on the subject written by me in 1888, "The Land System of Ireland," reprinted from the *Law Quarterly Review*. Mr. Gladstone's Home Rule policy I believe to be fatal; his Land Act of 1881 has done infinite mischief; but undoubtedly he has grasped the essential facts of the Irish land system more thoroughly than any other British statesman.

[2] The Report of the Fry Commission has appeared since I wrote these lines. In grave language it confirms nearly all my strictures on the Land Commission; and it suggests a scheme for fixing Irish rents by the State nearly the same as that which I have here indicated, and which I have advocated for many years. This most important document and the evidence attached to it ought to be diligently perused.

overtaxed, and that for a period of more than forty years, by a yearly sum of between two and three millions sterling ; this significant judgment speaks for itself. And this excessive charge is all the more grievous because Ireland is a poor country, compared to Great Britain, poor in the extreme ; and, as every one knows, taxation falls more severely on a backward than on a prosperous people.[1] No real answer has been made to the Report ; the evidence it has brought together has not been refuted ; attempts at an answer have been merely frivolous. I shall glance, however, at two of these, the most plausible that have been put forward. Taxation, it is urged, is imposed on populations, not on lands ; but Englishmen, Scotchmen, and Irishmen are charged alike, Irishmen having, indeed, a slight advantage ; a landlord in Devon, in Perthshire, in Kerry, pays the same income-tax on a rental of £1,000 a year ; so does a merchant in London, in Edinburgh, in Dublin, in Belfast, in respect of the profits he makes in trade ; so commodities are equally taxed in the Three Kingdoms ; the peasant in Surrey, in Inverness, in Kildare, is charged equally for his tea, his tobacco, his porter, his spirits. Equality in this matter is, therefore, equity ; this "Irish cry" is a mere delusion ; the taxation of Ireland cannot possibly be in excess. Yet this so-called argument is a poor sophism, apparent if we examine the question. Suppose that an equal tax had been levied from wines, when Henry V. was master of England and France ; would the charge have fallen equally on a vinegrower in Champagne, and on a farmer of Sussex, who never reared a grape ? Or suppose that coal were equally taxed in England and Ireland, would the people of England, a land of coal, be as little charged as the people of Ireland,

---

[1] Report of the Childers Commission (p. 182), quoting from Pitt : "If one country exceeded another in wealth, population, and established commerce in a proportion of two to one, he was nearly convinced that that country would be able to bear ten times the burthens the other would be equal to." And again (p. 14), quoting from the late Mr. Nassau Senior : "I do not believe that Ireland is a poor country because she is overtaxed, but I think she is overtaxed because she is poor." The whole of this evidence is of real value.

a land of turf ; or that, if coffee were equally burdened in London and Paris, would not the Londóner, who drinks not much coffee, have an advantage over the Parisian, who drinks a great deal ? Examples of this kind might be added in hundreds ; equality, in this matter, may not, therefore, be equity ; on the contrary, it may be gross iniquity. And this, at this moment, is actually the case, if we consider the existing system of taxes ; a grave wrong is done to Ireland, nay to Scotland, in this respect. Beer and whisky are taxed alike in England, in Scotland, in Ireland ; Englishmen, Scotchmen, and Irishmen pay the same impost on a gallon of beer and a gallon of whisky, whether the gallon be consumed in an English, a Scotch, or an Irish household. But Englishmen drink a great deal of beer, and very little whisky ; Scotchmen and Irishmen do the exact contrary ; they drink a great deal of whisky and very little beer ; but the tax on whisky, by an alcoholic standard, is very much higher than that on beer ; it follows that Scotchmen and Irishmen are much more heavily taxed than Englishmen on the beverages they habitually drink.[1] The difference comes to a very large sum indeed ; Ireland, therefore, and Scotland, compared to England, are, in this particular, unjustly charged.

The only reply vouchsafed to this plain conclusion may be unconscious, but is offensive insolence. " Irishmen," it is said,—I put Scotchmen aside—" are a people who have very bad tastes ; let them drink beer not whisky, and their grievance disappears ; at all events whisky is not a necessary of life ; if they choose to consume it, they really tax themselves." Is it possible that sciolists, who write in this strain, do not see that persecution of all kinds may be justified on these very premises ? " How very bad is the taste of these nasty Huguenots," may have exclaimed the Camarilla of Louis XIV. ; " let them become good Catholics, and they will have no cause to complain ; at all

---

[1] Attempts have been made to prove that Englishmen drink as much spirits by the head as Irishmen. But the results obtained are completely misleading, and depend on ludicrous misrepresentation.

events their damnable heresy ruins their spiritual life ; if
they choose to stick to it, they have themselves to thank."
I content myself, however, with a single remark. Let us
suppose that the case between England and Ireland
were reversed, with respect to the taxation of whisky and
beer, and that beer were taxed relatively much more than
whisky ; how long would a Government last which should
venture to make use for Englishmen of an argument that
has been thought good enough for Irishmen : how soon
would it be swept out of existence ? We pass on to the
second position taken by those who have carped at the
tenor of the Report. "It is true," it is admitted, "that
Ireland is a very poor country, equally true that taxation
presses more heavily on an impoverished than on a rich
community ; but Dorset and Wilts are poor districts compared to Lancashire, Yorks, and Middlesex ; yet all these
parts of England are charged alike ; how then can Ireland
have a special grievance ; how can her taxation be, on this
ground, unjust ?" This argument, however, ignores
History ; it puts out of sight the indisputable fact that
Ireland, under the Treaty of Union, is fiscally a distinct
country, entitled to fiscal privileges of her own, the chief of
these being that she is not to be unduly taxed, beyond her
resources, this being the meaning of the technical phrase of
the "exemptions and abatements" secured to her ; it
regards Ireland, in a word, for financial purposes, as simply
a collection of English counties. But no statesman has
ventured to make this assertion ; no statesman has openly
acted on it, from the day of Pitt to that of Mr. Gladstone ;
and it is a dangerous as well as a false assumption, for it
sets a fundamental law of these realms at nought. It is
scarcely necessary to quote from the Report on the subject :
" If it is asked why a distinction should be taken between
Great Britain and Ireland, any more than between Kent
and Yorkshire, the answer is that Ireland entered into
partnership with Great Britain under a formal Treaty of
Union, which did, to a certain extent, by the recognition of
the claim of Ireland to abatements and exemptions, main-

tain the position of Ireland as entitled to separate treatment, as a whole, so far as relates to taxation. It must also be remembered that, as a matter of fact, Ireland has at all times, since the Union, in various degrees, received such separate treatment. Ireland cannot, therefore, be regarded merely as a group of counties of the United Kingdom." [1]

These arguments, therefore, may be dismissed ; comparing her resources with those of Great Britain—and this is certainly the true criterion—Ireland has been largely over-taxed for a long period ; and the overcharge may be larger than appears in the Report. The Commission, however, we have seen, did not exhaust the inquiry in one of its parts ; a grave question arises whether the overcharge may not be subject to a deduction before the account shall be closed. Ireland, we have said, pays from £7,000,000 to £8,000,000 taxes ; but she costs the State, it is alleged, more than £5,000,000 ; she contributes less that £2,000,000 to what is called the charge of the Empire. This proportion, no doubt, has not always held ; but the balance of £2,000,000 or so, it seems probable, will, in the future, rather lessen than increase ; the Treasury, it is contended, has a counterclaim, in respect of the expenditure of £5,000,000 and more, in favour of Great Britain and against Ireland. This counterclaim, as it has been presented, must be largely cut down ; for example, the interest on loans to Ireland which has been paid, and the interest on loans which have been misapplied and wasted, cannot constitute a just set-off ; and many items have been placed against the account of Ireland—for instance, the expense of the Lord-Lieutenancy—which are not Irish but Imperial charges, and cannot form a counterclaim in a reasonable sense. Unquestionably, too, when the Union became law, it was never contemplated that sums expended in Ireland could be deemed a local charge as distinguished from an Imperial charge [2] so as to afford a ground of set-

---

[1] Report of the Childers Commission, p. 166.

[2] See the whole of this part of the subject ably discussed in the Report of the Childers Commission, pp. 22–3.

off ; and all expenditure in Ireland that relates to Government and Administration, in most of their parts, must be deemed, in the main, Imperial ; a counterclaim, in this respect, cannot be very large. A counterclaim, nevertheless, to a certain extent, it is probable, exists ; the cost of Primary Education, and of the Constabulary force in Ireland is between £2,000,000 and £3,000,000 ; this is all but wholly defrayed by the Imperial Treasury ; the corresponding charge in England is defrayed from local sources, at least in a very great measure ; here a considerable set-off should be, perhaps, allowed. A few other items of set-off—one of these seems to be the extravagant cost of the Irish Land Commission—in all probability, too, may be found ; the Commission reported that, under all these heads, a just counterclaim would not exceed £500,000 ; but, we repeat, it did not thoroughly treat the subject ; and £500,000, it is believed, is much too small a sum. The present Government, we have seen, has pledged itself to appoint a new Commission to report on this branch of the case ; the pledge, doubtless, will be redeemed ; but if a balance shall be struck in favour of Ireland, Parliament, it is to be hoped, will provide for it in a proper spirit. Ireland, indeed, has acquiesced many years in a wrong ; she has no right to ask for a change in the British financial system. But if a debt be due to her, she is entitled to insist on, and to obtain justice ; the rather that from 1853 to this year her interests have been sacrificed to those of England and Scotland. Let Parliament, in that event, justify the words of Pitt : "The liberality, the justice, the honour of the people of Great Britain have never yet been found deficient." [1]

A Catholic University for Ireland ought to be established ; this measure would be simple justice too long delayed ; I have dwelt on the subject before in this brief narrative. The question must be postponed to a future Session ; but the present Government ought to settle it on broad and wise principles ; it will be upheld by the enlightened opinion of the United Kingdom ; it ought not to fear Orangeism or "the

[1] "England's Wealth Ireland's Poverty," by T. Lough, M.P., p. 72.

bray of Exeter Hall." A measure of Local Self Government
for Ireland has been promised for this year ; I need not
recur at length to the subject. The Bill ought to break
down, to a very considerable extent, the system of centralised administration, and government by Boards appointed
by the Castle, which prevails in Ireland ; it ought to give
Irish Local Boards, which, no doubt, will resemble the
County and Local Councils of England, large and popular
rights of self-government. It should make some provision
for Private Bill legislation on the spot, for this ought not to
be carried on at Westminster, at least in its initial stages ; it
should enable the Local Bodies to have concurrent powers
to deal with matters in which they have common interests ; it
should, I think, infuse a popular element into the Castle
Boards ; it would, of course, commit County, and in fact
Municipal Government to the County and Local Councils
it would create. But, for the reasons before referred to, it
must be accompanied with strong safeguards to prevent the
Local Bodies from running riot, from doing acts of
extravagance and wrong, and from injuring the property of
the landed gentry ; for otherwise it would prove a deplorable
failure, and would lead to open confiscation and waste.
These safeguards should consist of a strong Local Government Board, with ample powers of superintendence and
restraint, so that the Local Bodies should be under effectual
control ; there should be something like an Upper House in
every County Council, possessing a right of veto, suspensive,
if not absolute ; above all the Superior and the County
Courts of Ireland ought to be enabled to check and set aside
proceedings of the Local Bodies in contravention of law.
Subject to securities of this kind, a wise and generous
measure of Local Self Government for Ireland ought to do
great good ; it ought to expedite the material, even the social
progress of a country which stands much in need of this
reform. Not the least of the advantages it probably would
bring with it would be that it would afford the landed gentry
an opportunity, in some measure at least, to regain their
position and influence among their countrymen ; they would

certainly, from their experience on Grand Juries, take a
natural lead on County and other Councils.   I will add that
I hope this whole question will not, as has been said, be
mixed up with and made dependent on any fiscal question,
whether with regard to taxation or rating ; this would be
a bad and an offensive policy.[1]

A few other remarks may be made on circumstances
relating to Irish affairs.   The Lord-Lieutenancy was all but
abolished nearly fifty years ago ; but it is an institution
which has existed for seven long centuries ; it will probably
survive for a considerable time, numerous as are the objections that may be made to it.   Royalty should certainly
make its presence felt in Ireland ; not, indeed, that, as
silly flatterers have said, this could effect a magical change
in Irish opinion and feeling ; but the residence of members
of the Royal Family on the spot would be a beneficent
influence in a poor country, and for a community loyal in
its true and natural instincts, though, unhappily, these have
been greatly perverted.   The times have fortunately changed
since Ireland sent many of her noblest sons to lead foreign
armies ; an Irishman, Wolseley, an Irishman, Roberts, are
the foremost of living British soldiers ; but there are no
Irish Guards, and few Irishmen in our Artillery ; we see
here a bad tradition of the past, and a want of tact and
sympathy.   So, too, the descendants of the Scotch
Jacobites have, for the most part, regained their lands and
their honours ; the representative of the last of the Celtic
Kings of Ireland has no place on the roll of the Peerage ;
the sons of once princely Milesian Houses yield precedence
at Court to the ennobled offspring of Cromwellian troopers.
These things may seem trifles, but they are nothing of the
kind, if we reflect on the sad memories of Irish History ;
England here might learn a lesson from France, far her

---

[1] The Local Government Bill of this Session has been brought forward
while these pages have been going through the Press.   It appears to
me not to go far enough in extending the principle of Local Government in Ireland, and to be very inadequate as regards the safeguards it
proposes.   I confess I regard it with grave misgivings.

superior in dealing with populations she has made her subjects, as her magnificent unity proves; Lorraine and Alsace remain morally her own. For the rest the essential differences between Great Britain and Ireland have long ago assured well informed persons that it is a capital mistake to apply the principles of mere private enterprise, and of individual effort to a whole range of Irish affairs, which, in Great Britain, have been applied with admirable success. The people of Great Britain are, in the main, Teutonic; the people of Ireland are, in the main, Celtic; England is essentially a very rich and progressive land; Ireland is essentially poor and backward; for these reasons alone the State ought to do for Ireland much which in England and Scotland may be left to be done by the citizen. Ireland is literally crying out for material reforms, which can be accomplished through the Government alone; her resources will never be well developed unless Parliament and the Executive speed the good work. Mr. Balfour did much in this direction by the establishment of the Congested Districts Board, and by the construction of light railways; but this is, at best, a beginning only; an infinity of things has yet to be done. Here again England might look to France, a Celtic land, in which the State has, in this province, taken the initiative, and been supreme for ages; she might even look to the records of the dead Irish Parliament, the Public Works of which have been often of rare excellence. And Ireland requires, before everything, material improvement; she has suffered frightfully from the effects of the troubles and the bad legislation of the last twenty years.

The true student of History cannot hope that the deep-seated and inveterate ills of Ireland will disappear, or even be greatly lessened by any policy for a considerable space of time. In 1844, at O'Connell's trial, Sheil uttered these fine and pathetic words—"Mad men that we are . . . we precipitate ourselves on each other in that fierce encounter, in which our country, bleeding and lacerated, is trodden under foot; convert an island, which ought to be the most fortunate in the sea, into a receptacle of misery and degradation ; counteract the designs of Providence, and become conspirators against the beneficent intents of God." [1] More than half a century has gone, and the old dissensions remain ; the animosities of race and faith survive ; Ireland has but just emerged from a kind of Servile War ; her feuds and passions of class still live, if kept down by the power of the law ; there is much that is sinister and vicious in her social order. Yet can any one feel surprised who has pondered over her annals, over that dreary tale of prolonged misgovernment, of anarchy and rebellion constantly breaking out, of conquest and confiscation of the very worst kind, of the fatal domination of caste and sect, of institutions, not beneficent, but essentially bad. Butler has said with truth that a life of repentance cannot do away with the consequences of sin in the past ; the distempered frame of Irish society may, perhaps, never be restored to perfect health. Impartial History will not determine on which side the balance of wrong inclines, as she looks back at the succession of woes from which Ireland has suffered through long and dark centuries ; if England and her rulers have been gravely to blame, let it not be forgotten what provocation they received, and how Ireland, over and over again, crossed their path at dangerous and great crises, and sealed her own doom by her wretched dissensions. For these things the Englishmen of this day are in no sense responsible, nor the Irishmen if they do not seek to revive evil memories which should be left in oblivion ; but the deep traces of the past cannot be easily removed ; they are engrained in the hearts, the thoughts, the feelings of millions ; they will long cause discontent in Ireland, vague and ill-defined, but not the less real. They will assuredly not be effaced or lessened by destroying the Constitution of these realms, or flying from present to infinitely worse evils or yielding to a false revolutionary cry, and seeking in Home Rule that "Union of Hearts," which is perhaps

[1] Report of O'Connell's trial, p. 304. The Bar and the bystanders rose in tumultuous applause.

the most senseless of all shibboleths ; they will not be affected by creating in the Irish land a succession of new " interests " by means of confiscation, like the Anglo-Norman, the Elizabethan, and the Cromwellian, " interests " of the past, an evil policy which the experience of ages condemns. The statesman, really worthy of the name, must rely on the gradual but sure effects of legislation on sound principles, of administration sympathatic and just, above all, on Time moving with healing on its wings ; the " Arch of Peace," as the poet sang, will be yet formed over the troubled waters which at present flow between two divided peoples.

THE END.

INDEX

UNWIN BROTHERS, THE GRESHAM PRESS, WOKING AND LONDON.

www.ingramcontent.com/pod-product-compliance
Lightning Source LLC
Chambersburg PA
CBHW051519100726
47898CB00005B/1513